HISTORICAL

Your romantic escape to the past.

Uncovering The Governess's Secrets

Marguerite Kaye

Rescuing The Runway Heiress

Sadie King

MILLS & BOON

UNCOVERING THE GOVERNESS'S SECRETS
© 2024 by Marguerite Kaye
Philippine Copyright 2024
Australian Copyright 2024
New Zealand Copyright 2024
First Published 2024
First Australian Paperback Edition 2024
ISBN 978 1 038 91755 3

RESCUING THE RUNAWAY HEIRESS
© 2024 by Sarah Louise King
Philippine Copyright 2024
Australian Copyright 2024
New Zealand Copyright 2024
First Published 2024
First Australian Paperback Edition 2024
ISBN 978 1 038 91755 3

Published by
Harlequin Mills & Boon
An imprint of Harlequin Enterprises (Australia) Pty Limited
(ABN 47 001 180 918), a subsidiary of HarperCollins
Publishers Australia Pty Limited
(ABN 36 009 913 517)
Level 19, 201 Elizabeth Street
SYDNEY NSW 2000 AUSTRALIA

Printed and bound in Australia by McPherson's Printing Group

Uncovering The Governess's Secrets

Marguerite Kaye

MILLS & BOON

Marguerite Kaye has written almost sixty historical romances featuring feisty heroines and a strong sense of place and time. She is also coauthor with Sarah Ferguson, Duchess of York, of two *Sunday Times* bestsellers, *Her Heart for a Compass* and *A Most Intriguing Lady*. Marguerite lives in Argyll on the west coast of Scotland. When not writing, she loves to read, cook, garden, drink martinis and sew, though rarely at the same time.

Visit the Author Profile page
at millsandboon.com.au for more titles.

Chapter One

Marianne

Edinburgh—
Thursday 2nd August 1877

The day began as it always did. I woke with a start, and the first thing I was aware of was the stench. Unmistakable, like nothing else, an acrid mixture of bleach, damp blankets and stale air, mingled with urine and over-boiled cabbage, resonating of fear and dread. There it was as usual, a tang on my tongue and in my nose, making my stomach roil, my breath come fast and shallow.

A cold sweat coated my body, making the thin cotton of my clammy nightshift cling to me. My fingers were like claws, pawing at the bedding, clutching it high up to my neck. And as usual I lay completely still, eyes scrunched shut, ears straining to catch whatever noise it was that woke me. The scratching and scuttling of vermin behind the skirting? Moaning? Howls of pain? Screams of fear and panic? Barked orders demanding silence?

Silence!

I listened intently, struggling to hear over the thudding

of my heart, but there was nothing. I forced myself to take a deep breath. Another. Yet another. All the time straining to hear. Still silence reigned.

It happened slowly as it always had since I arrived in Edinburgh, the fog of terror dispersing in my mind, the dawning awareness of my true surroundings. There were sheets on my bed as well as blankets. My pillow was soft, not scratchy with rough straw filling. I eased my glued-shut eyes open to see a watery grey light filtering in through the window, the curtains open to reveal the lack of bars. My heart slowed. My mouth was dry, but the vile taste was gone.

I breathed deeply again, easing the tension in my shoulders, and sat up in bed. *My* bed. In my own bedroom. I could see the reassuringly familiar outline of the chest of drawers, the stand with my ewer and bowl.

I shivered then, as I always did as the sweat cooled on my skin, and I placed my feet on the floorboards, easing stiffly upright like a woman much older than my thirty-three years, stumbling to the window to push up the sash. Cold air rushed in. There was a light misting of rain, the kind that soaks into your bones without you even noticing. They call it a smir here in Scotland. A soft word for soft rain.

'Smir…' I murmured under my breath. The word, in my English accent, sounded harsh.

The last echoes of the past that haunted me every morning retreated as I leaned out of the window as they did every morning. The memories would be locked away again until my guard was down, when sleep claimed me again. I had another day of freedom to look forward to, I reminded myself, as I did every day without fail. I would never, ever again take for granted the simple pleasure of opening a window, feeling the elements on my face, sucking in the fresh air. Not that the air in Edinburgh was fresh, not by any means. It's smoke-filled, sulphurous, and I knew the rain would leave smut on my skin if I continued to lean out of the window, but I didn't care.

The Old Town tenement that I called home was at the eastern end of the Grassmarket. The more respectable end, or perhaps the least disreputable would be a more accurate description. There was no trouble at night in the close, my neighbours locked their doors at nightfall, and if I met them during the day, they'd nod politely with their gazes averted. The close itself was clean, the roof in good repair, the rent dearer than the lodgings on the farther side of the square near the meat market and the West Bow, made notorious by Burke and Hare, the infamous resurrectionists. All in all, the Grassmarket was not the type of area you'd expect a woman of my upbringing to inhabit—which was, of course, one of the reasons I chose it.

It was a far cry from the large salubrious town houses of the New Town where I earned my living. My various employers would be appalled if they ever discovered where it was I lay my head at night, but when they asked—rarely, and only ever the wives—I would prevaricate. They never persisted, instinct or experience telling them that such questions were rarely rewarded with anything other than unpalatable answers. I could have told them some unpalatable truths myself, had I chosen. Not about my circumstances, but about their own, the injustices and betrayals which they unwittingly endured. I never volunteer my insights, not any more. I have suffered too much to risk the consequences.

Aware of my mind skittering back to the past, I focused

on the view. Across the Grassmarket, rising high above the cobbled square loomed the castle, grey, solid, imposing, perched on a huge crag of volcanic rock. In the shadow of that seemingly impenetrable fortress, the square below me was metamorphosing from night into morning. It was a ritual I loved to watch, for it was full of noise and bustle, a daily affirmation of life in all its various forms.

On the opposite side from my four-storey tenement, the dray carts were rumbling down the steep incline of the Bow, bringing in supplies from the railway and the canal and the docks at Leith for the many taverns and traders whose businesses were in the process of opening up for the day. Wooden casks of ale for the White Hart and the Black Bull, a multitude of goods for the other warehouses and carriers.

That morning there was the distinctive smell of tobacco leaves being delivered to the manufactory. I could smell the roasting beans too, wafting up from the coffee houses, as ever overlaid by the stench coming from the meat market known as the Shambles.

I kept well away from that end of the Grassmarket, even during daylight. The crowded, vermin-infested rooms of the cheap lodging houses down there doubtless continued to harbour other types of vermin, criminals and ne'er-do-wells of all types, but mostly they were home to the poor and displaced, those newest incomers to the city. Vagrants, they were commonly labelled, but they were simply destitute and desperate. They moved on quickly if they could, those people, away from the Grassmarket if not from the Old Town. I preferred to remain here, among the immigrants and refugees, being one of them myself, though I kept myself apart.

On cue, regular as clockwork, the young woman with

her plaid shawl over her head appeared from the Cowgate and crossed the square to the Black Bull. I reminded myself that I was fortunate to be able to support myself doing work that I enjoyed, for I have always loved children. I named the woman Flora, for the plaid she wore made me think of Flora MacDonald. I watched her as she, a woman of habit as I had become, entered the tavern.

In my imagined version of her life, she ordered coffee and bread. It was more likely she drank strong spirits to help her sleep after the night she'd spent earning her living up near the castle. That part of the story I invented for her was unfortunately accurate, for I'd spotted her once, making her way there as I returned late from my own employment. She was not morning-tired as she was now, but evening-bright, her plaid draped to reveal the low cut of her gown, her eyes darting about in search of custom. I called her Flora because I would not call her harpy or slut. People, especially women, must do whatever it takes to keep the wolf from the door. It was dangerous work. Brave Flora.

Her arrival at the Black Bull was my signal each morning that it was time to prepare for the day. I shivered as the rain started to fall more heavily, and closed the window. My robe was faded blue wool. I wrapped it round me, pulling the sash tight. I had purchased it second-hand, like all my clothes, and made it good with my mending. I once loathed having to wield my needle, despite the fact that in that vile place there were times when my neat stitching saved me from more arduous tasks in the laundry or the kitchen. But every stitch I set reminded me, back then, that there would be no end to them. I was being stitched into the very fabric of the place.

The darns in my clothes were different. My stitches

made the garments mine. The smell of vinegar and carbolic soap and lavender water made these two rooms in the old, creaking tenement mine too. My sanctuary. I was safe here. Every morning, that was the final part of my waking ritual, to remind myself of this.

'I am safe here,' I told myself firmly.

As time passed, the odds were more and more in my favour that it was true. Three years had passed, after all. But I knew, that morning, as every morning before, as I dressed, as I made myself my cup of breakfast coffee, as I prepared to go out into the cold morning air, to cross from the Old Town to the New Town, I knew that my resolve would falter as night fell. In my bones, in my heart, I didn't believe I would ever be safe. I would always be waiting for that dreaded hand on my shoulder.

I locked my door and descended the close stairs, and made my usual final check of my surroundings, though after three years I wasn't sure who or what I was checking for. Then I set out for my current place of work. Today was another day like every other, I thought. I had no idea how wrong I would prove to be.

Chapter Two

Rory

Edinburgh—
Thursday 2nd August 1877

Standing in the doorway of the coffee shop, I wrapped my hands around the steaming tin mug of coffee. It was looking set to be another typical August day, with leaden skies and twenty different varieties of rain to look forward to. A pure minger, in other words. I'd forgotten what it could be like, the so-called Scottish summer. Seven years down south in England had clearly softened me up.

To be fair, those seven years had also kept me out of harm's way, and made me—comparatively, mind—a wealthy man. Being back here was the last thing I wanted or needed. The last thing anyone in this city wanted, I was willing to bet.

You can't say you weren't warned, Sutherland. I told you not to poke your nose in, but you didn't listen.

That old familiar voice resonating in my head made my hackles rise, for try as I might—and I'd tried, trust me, over the years—I still couldn't bring myself to believe I'd been wrong. The case stank to high heaven. It wasn't the first time I'd been warned off, nor the first time I'd been told that I was ruffling the wrong feathers. The thing was, I saw that as an essential part of my doing my job properly—without fear or favour. That's what sealed my fate in the end. The powerful person who felt threatened by investigation, whoever they were, knew I couldn't be bought, and they knew I wouldn't rest until I'd got to the bottom of whatever it was reeked.

I was warned, but I didn't see it coming all the same. Insubordination, I was accused of, as well as placing my fellow officers in danger, blackening the good name of the Edinburgh police and taking bribes—that was a belter! Trumped-up charges, all of them, full of innuendo and singularly lacking any evidence, but they were plastered over every newspaper in the city, the very same papers that had been happy to sing my praises over the years. I paid the price for my former success and the unwanted fame that accompanied it.

There's nothing like a dramatic fall from grace story to sell a newspaper. There was no need for the wheels to turn in any formal manner. I was found well and truly guilty by the press for crimes that didn't even exist, while the real crime I'd been trying to solve was swept firmly under the carpet. What's more, it was made very clear to me by my superior that there would be no road back.

You've made some very powerful enemies, Sutherland. So powerful that I can't guarantee your safety. My advice to you is to get out of this city, and if you value your life, you'll never show your face here again.

He reckoned he saved my skin, and he was probably right. He didn't need to either. He was a good man, but unlike me, he knew his place in the Edinburgh hierarchy. It pained him to stick the knife in, and it was bloody agony for me, but that wasn't even the worst of it. The worst part was the look on my da's face when I told him what had happened. He took my side without question, which was a small consolation, until he'd had time to think it over.

'You have to find a way to clear your name, Ruaraidh,' he'd said, in that soft Highland accent of his that decades in Glasgow hadn't rid him of. 'You can't let those vile things they said about you stand.'

'I can't, Da,' I'd told him, though I didn't tell him why.

'M'aither,' he'd corrected me, as he always did when I called him Da. Aside from the curses and the way he pronounced my name, it's the only Gaelic I have. No one pronounces my name the way he did. Ruaraidh. Rory. It's a subtle distinction, too subtle to bother with now that he's gone.

I stuck to my guns and I never promised to do as my da bid me, not even at the end, when he was dying. It's a salve to my conscience, though not much of one, that I never lied to him. I did what I had to do to save my skin, and I kept well away from Edinburgh. Until now.

Not that I was back, risking life and limb, to stir all that up again. No, I'd have to put up and shut up on that one, as I'd been doing for the last seven years. I was here to get the job I'd been employed to do done, and that was all. I planned to keep a very low profile and get the hell out of the city for the second time and for good as soon as I could, with my hide intact. Edinburgh was a big city. I, of all people, should know how to keep myself hidden in its shadows.

It stuck in my craw, I'll admit that, but what choice did I have, save to let sleeping dogs lie? I wasn't going to rake over old ground, and I definitely wasn't going to set about rattling the skeletons in the closet that likely still lurked here. I'd moved on, made a new life for myself, and it was one that I enjoyed, where I was my own man. The fact that it had brought me to Edinburgh, where my old life had begun and ended in disgrace was just a very unfortunate coincidence. That's what I told myself, and it was the truth, though not all of it.

It was the mystery of my current case that piqued my interest at first. Solving mysteries was my bread and butter, I was good at it, and this had smacked of something I could really get my teeth into. Then there was the fact that the outcome would prove life-changing for the woman concerned, if I found her. Life-changing in every way, mind. Some of what I knew was going to come as a hell of a shock to her. Mind you, what I'd learned myself about her in the last few weeks had shocked *me* to the core. She'd been to hell and back. It made my blood boil, every time I thought of it.

All the same, when it became clear that she was most likely here in Edinburgh, well of course I thought twice about it—though no more than twice. Maybe I should have, but I'm not superstitious like my da. *M'aither!* I'm practical, like my ma. A real Weegie, my ma was, a salt of the earth, Glaswegian to her bones. My da never really got over losing her.

Any road! There I was in Edinburgh, finishing my coffee, and there she was, the subject of my current case, right on the stroke of eight, coming out of the tenement close. She was tentative, always so wary. Standing in the open doorway peering out carefully, as nervous as a deer emerging into a forest clearing, her nose tilted in the air as if sniffing for danger. And on cue, there it was again, the minute

I set eyes on her, that odd lurching in my belly. My gut was telling my brain that she needed protecting, and bits of me that I didn't care to acknowledge were sending another message entirely to another part of my body, a part that shouldn't have had any interest in this case whatsoever. I was the hunter, she was the prey, I reminded myself, but that word didn't sit right with me. Quarry? More accurate, but I still wasn't happy with it. Quest? I liked that word better.

She stepped into the street and set off, passing within a couple of feet of me. I didn't need to stay too close though, I knew where she was headed, up the steep incline of Victoria Street, past St Giles and on to the Mound, before crossing down into the New Town past the National Gallery and on to Princes Street.

I scanned the broad cobbled street to make sure the Grassmarket was clear of former acquaintances, though I wasn't really expecting to see any. There had been a good few of them down at the West Bow end of the street, men I'd put away, men who'd helped me put others away, but seven years was a long time. They'd have moved on, one way or another. Then I pulled my hat further down over my brow and set out in pursuit.

I strode out, a man with every right to go about his business, neither furtive nor swaggering, hiding in plain sight. I was good at that, I always had been. I'd changed my appearance too, since those Edinburgh days, my hair cropped much shorter, my face clean shaven, my clothes the sombre, well-cut attire of a gentleman of means. Stay alert, but don't keep looking over your shoulder, that was the key to invisibility, and I needed to remain invisible, because though I might be perceived as the hunter, I was very much aware that I could easily become the hunted if my presence in Edinburgh was discovered. My quest was ahead of me, but if I was discovered, I'd be the quarry, unwittingly being stalked by someone else. And unlike me, their motives would be malign.

It might sound difficult, following one person while keeping an eye out for anyone who may be interested in me, but it was second nature. Only when I got close enough to *her* did I become more focused on what was ahead rather than behind me or off to the side. There was a supple sway to her body, a natural grace that would have drawn more eyes than mine were it not for her pace, which was fast, covering a lot of ground very quickly, though she never gave the impression that she was in a hurry. It was an easy, confident pace, completely at odds with the nervous way she peered out into the street every morning and one of the many contradictions about her that I found intriguing. Mind, if she really was the woman I was looking for, the way she walked was hardly relevant.

'You know fine and well she's the one,' I muttered to myself as I waited for her to cross over Princes Street before continuing, for the traffic this morning was surprisingly light. I was procrastinating, which wasn't like me, delaying concluding the matter because I was drawn to her, and I wanted to know more about her. I told myself I needed tangible proof, but I *knew* it was her. The last photograph I had might be nearly five years old, but the haggard woman with the dark circles under her big eyes staring at the camera in what I had learned was a classic institutional pose, was definitely the same woman in the faded blue cloak who was now walking up Hanover Street.

Then there was the name she'd assumed—too much of a coincidence, that. And there was also the address of her rooms. I knew she was in demand, I knew roughly what she must earn, and I knew she could afford better, a respectable area where everyone knew their neighbours and their business. In the Grassmarket, people didn't ask questions, they made a point of not being curious, and I reckoned that's why she chose to live there.

Marianne Little, who was now Marianne Crawford, was also entitled to yet another name. And to another life too, very different from the one she now led, as an agency nanny or governess, currently employed to look after a prominent businessman's nursery while his wife awaited delivery of their fifth child. She hadn't a clue what fate had in store for her and that was starting to bother me. That she'd endured and survived the last few years and come out of it in her right mind was nothing short of a miracle. I'm not sure I'd have fared as well in her shoes.

And now, just when she must be thinking herself settled, I was going to unsettle her. I would be the bearer of extraordinary good news, true enough, but it was going to turn her world upside down, and it was complicated. I had no clear notion of how I was going to go about telling her and no idea at all how she'd take it. I was a complete stranger, I couldn't exactly go walking up to her without a by your leave and launch straight in. Thankfully, I was under orders to say nothing yet. For once, I was glad to be obeying those orders.

I ducked behind a brewer's cart piled high with wooden beer kegs and set off again on her tail. The New Town was problematic for me. It's where the great and the good of Edinburgh reside, and some of those men were high on my list of people I wanted to avoid. I was prepared to bet that whoever had had me silenced was among them. I couldn't get over how far the area had expanded in the years since I was last here, new crescents and circuses with private gardens, imposing town houses and terraces stretching all the way towards Coates in one direction, and Stockbridge in the other. Who was buying all those grand houses, on land where no one of note would have dreamed of residing only a few years ago? I couldn't be sure any more, of who lived where, so my heart thumped a bit harder every time I went near those big, wide cobbled streets. During the daylight hours, most of them would be at their place of work, but not all of them. I looked different. I acted confident. It was enough, I told myself, trying to put it to the back of my mind.

I got to the corner of Queen Street just as she mounted the steps of the town-house door. She used the front door, not the servants' entrance at the back in the mews, and there was a few moments' delay today, in answering her knock. It gave me a chance to study her. It wasn't a hardship to look at her, not in the slightest. She was tall, likely she'd be able to look me straight in the eye, which wasn't something I was used to, being over six foot in my stockings.

She was too thin, in my humble opinion, lack of appetite rather than lack of funds, I surmised, and she *had* put on some very necessary weight since that last photograph I had in my keeping had been taken. Her hair was a deep chestnut colour with a natural curl. High cheekbones. A nose that wasn't in the least bit pert and that some might even call assertive. A determined chin. Big wide-set eyes. Hazel in some lights, green in others. Cat-like, was how one of her self-styled carers had described them. That particular man had been very insistent about her eyes being her most striking feature other than her height.

'Ordinary otherwise, you'll struggle to pick her out in a crowd,' was what he'd said dismissively to me as he handed the photograph from their official records over, but even in that image, the first I'd seen, with her face set, part-defiant, part-fearful, I was struck by her. In the later images, the defiance was harder to detect. Doubtless, they'd tried to grind it out of her. They hadn't succeeded though. Despite everything she'd been through, despite all they'd inflicted on her and all the cruel names they'd labelled her with, she'd escaped, and here she was, making her own way.

Just like me? I'd been wrongly tagged too. I'd been called names that could have destroyed me, and my ability to make a living, just as she had. We were both survivors. I knew I shouldn't be drawing parallels. It was one thing to admire her, to feel sympathy, even to acknowledge the attraction I felt, but quite another to be finding connections between us.

Detachment, not becoming involved, not taking sides, were the watchwords of my profession. True, I rely on my instincts, that goes without saying, but I back everything up with facts, logic, hard evidence. Generally, I don't allow myself to feel anything save sympathy or pity or most likely suspicion. But this woman—ach, I keep coming back to it, she *drew* me. I felt that we were alike in a profound way, that there was an affinity between us. That was a very dangerous road to go down, for it affects your judgement, so I decided the best thing to do was to ignore it.

The door to the town house was opened by a male servant. She stepped inside without looking over her shoulder. Above me, the grey skies were very reluctantly parting to reveal the odd patch of blue, just about enough to make a pair of sailor's breeches, as the saying went. I'd been keeping her under surveillance for almost a week now, and without fail, she brought the weans into the communal Queen Street Gardens to play, often remaining there for much of the day. I usually stayed outside and out of sight, but on impulse I decided to use the key I'd managed to obtain, at no small cost, to gain entry. I took up position on a bench in the furthest corner, opened my newspaper up, and waited.

Chapter Three

Marianne

Edinburgh—
Thursday 2nd August 1877

I noticed him the moment I entered the gardens with my current charges. Queen Street Gardens are private, for residents only, but they don't belong exclusively to the Oliphants, the family who then employed me. We regularly had them to ourselves however, we children's nurses, nannies and governesses, and when the weather was what they call driech here, I was often the only one to venture out. My four charges had protested the first day I insisted they come outside with rain threatening, but they quickly came to enjoy playing outdoors when they learned they could shout and squeal and run about as much as they liked, without having to keep quiet for fear of disturbing their mamma, who was close to her due date.

It's only a man in search of some peace and quiet to read his newspaper, that's what I told myself, for I sensed no threat from him. Quite the opposite. Oddly, my first instinct was that he was a man to be trusted, and that's what piqued my interest, for it's such a rare feeling—in fact I'd go so far as to say unique in my experience, when it comes to the opposite sex. No, not entirely unique. I trusted once. Never again.

I kept an eye on him as we set about playing our game, myself and the children, and though he was very good at covering it up, I was aware that he was watching me. I have always been sensitive to other people, to their moods, their thoughts. I don't mean in the common way, it goes beyond that, my talent, or gift, or whatever you care to call it. I think of it like the valve on a gas light or an oil lamp. It's always on at a peep, a low glow, just sufficient for me to see by, and provided there's nothing of interest it stays like that.

But if there's something needing more light shed on it, or if a person was suffering an extreme emotion, it's turned up, allowing me to—to sort of focus. Like the microscope in the playroom, that's a better analogy. The microscope was a gift to Mr Oliphant from the famous Dr Simpson who lived next door at Number Fifty-Two. Mr Oliphant, having no interest in matters scientific, gave it to Ronnie, his eldest boy, who wasn't in the least bit interested either, but his sister Lizzie was—it was she who showed me how to peer through it. The object on the glass slide was a blur at first, then you turn the dial and it becomes clearer, and the more you turn the dial, the more detail you see.

Only I don't have any control over my personal dial, it adjusts itself. There have been many times when I have wished that I had the ability to switch the blasted thing off, for it has led me to understand things I didn't wish to understand, provided insights into others that cannot be 'unseen'. I have learned to live with my skill, but I have also learned to keep it to myself. A lesson I will never forget.

Not long after we arrived in the gardens, we were joined by Mrs Aitken, the governess from Number Forty-Two, and I concentrated most of my attention on the children for a while. Mrs Aitken was always more than happy to leave the management of her charges to me while she sits on a bench and imagines herself by a fire in a cottage in the country with a cat on her lap and a companion seated in a chair opposite. She takes such enormous pleasure in it that I don't mind looking after all the children, and in any event they play happily together.

Ronnie it was, who threw the ball far too forcefully over the head of its target, his sister Maureen, making it bounce across the grass towards the man on the bench. Maureen protested loudly, while Lizzie went running after the ball and I followed her. The man caught it before it went into the bushes, clutching it close to his chest.

'I beg your pardon,' I said, 'I'm afraid we interrupted you.'

He blinked at me, staring, and I had the oddest feeling that he didn't want to talk to me, but at the same time, he was most eager to do just that. When he did, his words were mundane enough.

'Here you go, wee one,' he said, handing the ball to Lizzie and smiling down at her. She smiled back, and ran off to re-join the game.

'Thank you,' I said, knowing I should follow her but finding myself reluctant to move.

'No problem. My name is Sutherland. Rory Sutherland.'

My hand reached for his outstretched one of its own accord, though it was my wont to avoid the touch of men. I don't wear gloves when I'm with the children. His were tan, good quality, and obviously custom made, for they fitted very well over his big hands. The contact sent a shiver, of the warm kind, if there was such a thing, through my body. Instead of snatching my hand away, I wanted to curl my fingers around his, which reaction so distracted me I just stood there, my hand in his, looking like goodness knows what.

It was he who broke the contact, and now it was my turn to look confused. I didn't offer my name. I said nothing, yet I could not make my feet turn around to walk away. I tried to make sense of my reaction, for I had to concentrate on breathing, yet I was not afraid.

'It's good to see the wee ones out enjoying the fresh air,' the man said, after what seemed like an age. 'Though it's fresher than it should be, for August, even for here.' It seemed that he too wanted to prolong the conversation.

I clasped my hands together, keeping them safely away from the draw of his. I was belatedly wary, though still I sensed no danger, only—I don't know, curiosity? No, it was stronger than that. 'You're from Edinburgh, then?' I said.

'Glasgow originally, though I'm told I have too much of the Highlander in me to sound like a proper Weegie.'

'Weegie?' I queried, for it was a word I'd never heard before. *'Weegie?'*

'Weegie,' he repeated. 'It's a nickname for Glaswegians. Not always intended as a compliment either.' There was a smile lurking in his eyes, which were brown, fringed with long lashes that were much darker than his fair hair.

I raised my eyebrow, allowing a smidgin of my curiosity to show. 'Would that make a native of Edinburgh a—an Edinburghian?'

He laughed. 'Truth is,' he replied, 'there's no name for a native of Edinburgh. They've not the unique identity of we Weegies, you see. In fact,' Mr Sutherland added, affecting a stage whisper, 'they're an inferior tribe, though they cover it up well with their superior airs and graces.'

His smile was infectious, though I'm usually immune to such things. Combined with the soft brogue of his accent, it had a most unsettling effect on me. Drawing me in, was the only way I can think to describe it, a physical pull or lurch or—oh, it was obvious what I was feeling, even if I didn't recognise it at the time. 'I have not noticed that,' I said to him, inanely. My mind was distracted by my body, which made my voice sound very unlike my own. 'I find everyone very friendly in this city.'

'Aye,' he agreed, his accent and his smile broadening in an extremely appealing way, 'but that's because you've never been to Glasgow, have you? You don't know what you're missing,' he added, when I shook my head. 'How did you end up here, may I ask? Judging from that accent, I'd say you hail from well south of here. Do I detect a trace of Yorkshire, maybe?'

'You are a linguist, Mr Sutherland?'

'So I'm right, then?'

It has become such a habit of mine, to refuse to answer a question or to prevaricate, I had done so automatically. I couldn't see what possible harm it would do, to answer him, yet I still chose to prevaricate. 'To everyone here, I'm a Southerner, they make no distinction.'

'It matters all the same though, doesn't it? A Glaswegian like myself doesn't like to be labelled an East Coaster. A Yorkshire woman such as yourself would take umbrage if I thought you a Brummie?' He waited, but when I volunteered only a shrug, he smiled again. 'Either way, you're a long way from home. What brought you here?'

'I am employed as a governess,' I said, unwilling to end

the conversation, but not willing to volunteer more than necessary. Should I be concerned by his interest or was he simply making conversation? It was odd, but the more I tried to read him, the more opaque he became to me. I was conscious only of the persistent feeling that I could trust him, and the equally persistent tug of attraction.

'Those weans look like a handful,' he said. 'Have you looked after them for long?'

'Only four of them are in my charge, and my position is temporary.'

'It looks to me like they're pretty fond of you.'

'And I of them, most of the time.'

'Then may I ask why…?'

'Their nanny has taken leave for six months to nurse her mother. I am covering for her, but as a matter of fact, I prefer not to stay too long in one household. I like the variety,' I added, before he could ask. 'And I do not like to risk becoming overly fond of my charges.'

'Is it easy to get work in your line? Are the recommendations by word of mouth, or is there an agency? I know nothing of it.'

'Why do you ask? Are you married yourself, Mr Sutherland? Do you have children?'

'No, and no.'

'Then I fail to see why you could possibly be interested in how to acquire a nanny or a governess.'

'Very true, I…' His voice trailed away. While we had been talking, he had been fully engaged in our conversation. Now, he was distracted, looking over to Queen Street, adjusting his stance marginally to put his back to the iron railings. 'I was merely curious, as I said.'

His attention was still on Queen Street. Mr Sutherland

was a rugged, rough-hewn man, broad and solidly built, but his features were handsome. I reckoned he must be about forty. Tanned skin. Clean shaven. Good clothes, but unobtrusive. A man who didn't dress to impress or be noticed. A man who was now most determined not to be noticed by the policeman who had stopped to talk to a manservant on the steps of the house next to my employer's home. Distracted as he was, he relaxed his guard on his feelings, and the wariness in him was unmistakable to me. 'What's the matter?' I asked, before I could stop myself.

He gave himself a shake. 'Nothing at all.'

A lie, and now I could not contain my curiosity, which was odd, for I do not court interest, and simply by remaining with him, continuing the conversation, that was what I was doing. It felt like the right thing to do. I had no idea why, only that it was. 'That policeman you were looking at comes along Queen Street every morning, around this time,' I told him.

'Good to know that some things don't change.'

'I don't know what crimes he thinks will be committed in broad daylight.'

Though he was obviously itching to turn around to get a better view, Mr Sutherland maintained his stance and his pretence of indifference. 'Just as well I didn't steal the children's ball and run away, then.'

'You don't seem the criminal sort.'

He gave a bark of laughter. 'You'd be surprised, they come in many guises.'

The truth of that statement sent a shudder down my spine. So many crimes I had witnessed and experienced, though none of them were against the law of the land.

He sensed my change of mood immediately. 'What is

it? Someone walk over your grave? It's a saying,' he added. 'It means…'

'I know what it means. Your policeman is on his way again.'

He allowed himself a quick glance and on seeing the policeman halfway along the street, I sensed his relief. But his guard was then immediately up again as he turned his attention back to me. 'I've enjoyed talking to you. Do you think—?'

'I must get back to the children.' I interrupted him before he could propose another meeting, because I was worried I'd say yes. I was then contrarily disappointed when he nodded in agreement.

'I've taken up enough of your time, I'll take myself off.'

'The gate is locked.'

'I have a key,' he said, producing the item from his coat pocket. 'How do you think I got in, by vaulting over the railings?'

I meant to bid him good day and walk away, but my feet continued to refuse to co-operate. 'A man your size would find that easy enough to do.'

My quip amused him, though my own tone, light and almost teasing, took me aback. 'Aye well,' he said, with another of those beguiling smiles, 'I'll admit I've vaulted a good few in my time.'

'While on the run from the long arm of the law?'

'Quite the opposite, in fact.'

'Quite the opposite? What do you mean by that?'

He studied me for a moment, his lips pursed, and I had the strangest feeling that beneath his heavy lids, those brown eyes of his could read my thoughts. 'It's a bit of a long story, but I could tell you, if you're interested. Maybe I could walk you home after work?'

'No.' He couldn't possibly read my thoughts, but all the same, I felt—wary. Not threatened, definitely not threatened. It was so very odd. 'No,' I said again, because I wanted very much to say yes. 'I really must get back to my charges.'

I was already backing away. He sketched a bow, and made no attempt to stop me. I joined my happy little band of children, throwing myself into the game. Out of the corner of my eye I watched him fold up his newspaper, unlock the gate, and quit the gardens. I would have willingly bet he walked in the opposite direction of the policeman, though I couldn't see him.

The strange encounter gave me much pause for thought as I resumed my duties, with only half my attention on the children. To say that my encouraging Mr Sutherland's attention was unusual would be an understatement of the greatest order, yet that was what I had done. I couldn't understand why. He was interested in me, which ought to have put me on my guard—and it had to a degree, but I had never at any point felt endangered. I was horribly accustomed to being questioned, interrogated, *investigated.* I once was foolish enough to believe that if I answered questions honestly, earnestly, it would make a difference.

I eventually realised that what was required of me was to echo my inquisitors' opinions, not to offer up my own. I couldn't bring myself do that, despite everything that I suffered as a consequence, so I developed the habit of silence. A habit that I had willingly broken with Mr Sutherland, who had been questioning me but who had been *interested* in what I had to say. Then there was the fact that I found him difficult to read. He was a challenge. And he was also a conundrum, a man who was not a criminal, but who was afraid—no, wary—of the law.

I tried to dismiss Mr Rory Sutherland from my mind, but my inner dial was already turned up too high for me to do that. Ought I to have agreed to another meeting? Funnily enough, and I had no idea why or how, I was sure our paths would cross again regardless. That certainty gave me another of those odd shivers. Not cold but anticipation—excitement.

The children's ball hit me square in the middle, brought me back down to earth. 'It's time for our luncheon,' Lizzie informed me. 'Did you not hear the one o'clock gun?'

'Mrs Crawford was away with the fairies,' Ronnie said gleefully, a phrase that always made me shudder, however innocently intended. 'And Mrs Aitken has been snoring her head off for the last half-hour.'

Hearing her name awoke the governess who, to give her credit, was on her feet and quite herself in an instant. 'Gentlewomen do not snore, Ronald, and even if they did, you ought to know that a young gentleman would never mention such a thing. What's more, if I had been asleep, how is it that I know you took two of the boiled sweets that Maureen offered you instead of one? Now what do you say to that?'

Ronnie's answer was a blush and a muttered apology.

'How did you know…?' I asked Mrs Aitken.

'Since I was asleep?' she asked sheepishly. 'An educated guess. He's a greedy little boy. I must thank you, Mrs Crawford, for keeping an eye on my charges.'

'There's no need. You have been having trouble sleeping.'

'Why yes, I have. How did you—?'

'A guess, that is all,' I interrupted her.

'It is true what is said of you, you are a most perceptive woman, Mrs Crawford. Mrs White at the employment agency considers it a very happy day, when you arrived in Edinburgh and chose to register with her.'

A very happy day it was indeed. The first day of the new life I had almost despaired of living. I will never forget it.

Chapter Four

Marianne

Three years previously

The Trustees of the institution located in the Scottish borders where I had been confined for almost four years were extremely proud of their forward-thinking reputation. In addition to gardening, the inmates here could contribute to the monthly magazine, read in the library, and even on occasion attend theatrical performances. The Physician Superintendent was a pioneer in his field, a revered and respected man in the community with a genuine vocation—or so he believed. He was much admired by the other staff, and held in great awe by many of the other inmates. Though not by me.

In the first institution where I had been held, I defied them and tried to escape. I was moved here after that, and kept confined. I experimented with compliance in the hope of release, but they kept setting the bar higher, so I resumed my former tactics, and returned to my former defiance. I was intent on one thing only, and that was freedom.

The price I paid form my lack of co-operation became

increasingly high, for they don't like to fail in these places. They ensure that all dissenting voices are kept from their precious trustees and benefactors, so I was forbidden access to the privileges of the library, the theatrical performances, the garden. After my first attempt at escape, I was placed in isolation. But they did not break me. The punishments they inflicted fed my burning sense of injustice. I would not give in. I would not even pretend to be the woman they proclaimed me to be. I would be myself.

It was a beautiful spring morning, that momentous day. I could see the cloudless pale blue sky from my tiny window. Those fortunate inmates considered to be low risk were working outside in the fresh air. I was inside, in one of the locked cells at the rear of the building, the wing to which none of the trustees or benefactors were given access. Perhaps they didn't even know it existed. More likely they did not ask, content to tell themselves that carpeted, panelled rooms and corniced ceilings, the wide staircase that swept upwards from the light-filled atrium, reflected the full extent of the building. It did not.

In this particular wing the institution was laid bare to the bones, making no pretence of being other than what it was. We were isolated, but we were never alone, we, the most problematic and troublesome of the inmates. Screams and moans seeped through the walls of the cells. Smells oozed under the doors. Footsteps echoed in the corridors. At night, shadows danced menacingly and ghosts haunted the halls.

When the bell began to sound, I thought I had confused the day, and that it was the call to Sunday service, but the jangling, clanging peels were too frantic and irregular for church bells. The rush of staff outside my door made it clear what was happening. An escape! I closed my eyes, focusing my entire being on that other person fleeing, wishing them well, urging them on, even though I knew that this was well beyond my powers. I can sense things, but I cannot change them. When my cell door was flung open I was deep in my thoughts, so that the hand roughly shaking my shoulder made me cry out, jump up, arms raised in defence.

'Marianne! Marianne! You must hurry.' The woman grabbed at the rough cotton shift that was my only permitted clothing. 'Take this off. Quickly.'

My troubled mind could make no sense of this demand, for the woman was one of my few allies. Was a new form of treatment about to be inflicted on me? Cold water dousing, which they called hydrotherapy, presumably to make it sound less barbaric, was the latest innovation here. I clutched at my shift, retreating from her.

'Marianne! There's been an escape. They are all rushing after him, do you understand? There's a little time, only a little, if you want to risk it.'

'Risk it?' Understanding came fast, and with it I acted, grabbing the bundle she was holding out. Not towels and a robe, but a uniform, like hers. Fumbling, heart thumping, my breathing shallow and rapid, as was hers, between us we got me into the clothes and boots. Outside, the corridor was deserted but not silent, the cries of the others locked behind those doors making an unearthly din.

I turned to bid my saviour farewell, but she grabbed my hand. 'This way.'

'You cannot risk…'

She pulled me forward. 'Keep your head down and follow me. If anyone stops us, let me do the talking.'

Her livelihood was at stake, I knew how much she needed the work that the institution provided her with, but there was already no going back for me, so I did as she asked me, hurrying after her along the corridor, through locked door after locked door, down unfamiliar passageways and staircases smelling of urine and cabbage and bleach and fear, until we emerged suddenly into the bright sunlight at the rear of the building. The alarm bell was still peeling insistently.

'He was in the market garden. He'll have gone over the wall to the east—or tried to,' my saviour said. 'I doubt he'll make it. Come on. Don't run, just walk purposefully, as if you are one of the staff like me, as if you have a right to be here, do you understand?'

Without waiting, she set off. I followed, my heart thumping so hard I thought I was going to be sick. My feet were not used to wearing boots. The heels rubbed, they felt heavy, awkward, as I made my way along the gravel paths, past stables and outhouses, past the macabre carriage we all dreaded seeing, the one they used to cart us on the final journey from the institution to the church crypt, an open coffin on four wheels. I shuddered, thinking of the man who was even now perhaps over the wall, fleeing in a bid for freedom.

On we went, on a seemingly endless, roundabout journey towards another gate in the high stone wall.

Make haste. Freedom. Make haste. Freedom.

I repeated the words like a litany, a prayer, with every painful step, struggling to keep pace, struggling not to break into a run.

At the gate, she fumbled for the key, struggling to turn it, cursing under her breath. Her cheeks were bright red. I felt my own face, pale, damp, with shaking hands. At last the lock turned. She pushed me through. 'Good luck, Marianne.'

I paused for a moment to take her hands. 'What if they find out you helped me?'

'They won't. I'll join the search party as soon as I've locked the gate.'

'Thank you,' I said fervently. 'Truly, I cannot thank you enough.'

'I owe you, Marianne. You literally saved my life. One good turn, and all that.' She pulled a scrap of paper and a bundle of coins from her apron pocket. 'Go there, as quickly as you can.' She pushed me forcefully through the gate. I heard the lock turning. I fled.

I don't recall much of the journey to Scotland's capital city from the Borders, which I made by stealth, not daring to travel to the nearest town and the nearest railway, but walking for days, sleeping in barns, sending heartfelt gratitude to my saviour, though I knew she would not sense it. *I owe you,* she had said. I had saved her life. The one time since my incarceration when I had revealed what my instincts were screaming at me. It had been a huge risk, given her position of authority, but now it seemed it had paid off.

I walked and I walked, until I deemed myself far away enough to risk a train to Edinburgh. There, hungry and bedraggled, I sought out the address my saviour had given me. An employment agency. It took the last reserves of my courage to make myself cross the threshold. I was braced for immediate rejection given my appearance. Mrs White studied me for a long moment before she ushered me into a back room and gave me tea. I had no references, but Mrs White didn't ask for any, nor did she question where I had come from, what or who I was running from, who I was. She asked me what I could do to earn my keep and I answered honestly. My love of children and the pleasure I took in looking after them was genuine.

Mrs White took me at my word. Later, when I was settled in lodgings, and had taken up my first assignment, I asked her why had she taken such a chance on me, a complete stranger.

'Because once, a long time ago, when I was seeking refuge and a fresh start, another woman helped me. We need to stick together, we refugees from the injustice the world heaps upon our sex, Mrs Crawford,' she said, using the name I had taken in tribute to my saviour.

'I promise you,' I told her most earnestly, 'that I will never give you cause to regret it.'

Chapter Five

Rory

Edinburgh—
Friday 3rd August 1877

What an eejit I'd been, sitting there on that bench skulking behind my newspaper without a plan. Back at my digs, once I'd calmed down a bit, I saw that the time had come to stop messing about and act. *Mrs* Crawford, she called herself when she registered with the employment agency here, three years ago. If she *was* married, it made things a hell of a lot simpler in one sense, but if Mrs Crawford was Marianne Little, she couldn't possibly be married. Crawford also happened to be the surname of the woman who had helped her gain her freedom. Having spoken to her now and re-examined the various photographs, I knew I'd found her, and I sent my employer a telegram telling him so.

The conversation that morning had added fuel to the fire of my wanting to know the woman better. It wasn't only the strength of character she must have to survive, I wanted to know what made her tick. She fascinated me. Aye, that was it, fascination, a good word, for it was more than physical attraction. *That* I could have ignored easily enough, until the case was done and dusted, and I could return to London. I'm not a saint, I enjoy the company of women, when I have the time and inclination for it. That sounds callous. It's not. I know my limitations, they were brought home to me by a woman in this very city. I'm a man who enjoys physical intimacy, but I'm not the domestic kind. I made the mistake of thinking I was, once. I make no promises these days, I keep company with women who don't require promises. Was that callous? I prefer to think it's being honest.

Any road, what I was feeling for Mrs Crawford wasn't like that. It was more a—I don't know, something more basic and at the same time, something more—more like a pull. I'm not going to say anything daft, like she was meant for me, because that would be bloody stupid, but I was right taken with her. She wasn't what I'd expected. Her wry sense of humour, for a start. After what she'd been through, I expected—well, someone more bleak, I suppose. Her experiences must have scarred her, but she hid the scars very well.

I knew some of what she'd been through, from the real Mrs Crawford, the woman that Marianne Little took her name from. It had taken me a couple of weeks to get to that point in my search. As usual when you're looking for someone or something, it's about knowing who to ask and what to look for. Was she dead, was she married, the woman I had been tasked with finding? Parish records are a slog to wade through, and back in the day, when I worked here in Edinburgh, it was a task that was always delegated to the newest and most junior member of the team—provided they could read, of course.

I never delegated. You can tell someone to check this

name and see if they're on the burial list, or see if they're married, but that's all they'll do, and in my experience, it's just as often what you find that you're not looking for that's important.

In a way, that's what happened with Marianne Little. I was in the right parish, and I was looking at the right registers, but there wasn't a trace of her, alive or dead. My next call was the parish priest, a new appointment, but he put me on to his predecessor, and there was a man who liked to talk, especially if you had the foresight to bring a bottle of his preferred tipple. Which I did. It was he who remembered the scandal of the woman some branded a witch. It was he who pointed me in the direction of the York institution.

Dealing with the men in charge of those places requires a different approach. You can't come out and tell them what it was you want or they'll start harping on about confidentiality and patient privacy. Places like that, what they're always in need of was money. New inmates or new funding, and if you offer the possibility of both it gets you through the door. I can put on a posh accent. I can play the gentleman if required. And I'm very, very good at leading a conversation down a certain path.

That's the other thing about those professional men. They like the sound of their own voices. They like to expound their theories. And in doing that, they tell you about their cases. Marianne Little was one of their failures, though the man I spoke to didn't put it that way, needless to say. Incurable, he said of her, and not suited to their trusting environment. What he meant was, she'd escaped, and the man who paid to keep her locked up had caused a stooshie. That's when I got the proof I'd been looking for. The signature on the papers of the man who paid her bills was the man I'd suspected from the first. It was no surprise to discover that it was all about the money, but I can't tell you the blind fury that took hold of me, seeing that name.

I nearly gave myself away, but when I'd calmed down and rid myself of the very pleasant image I had of throttling him, I got things back in perspective. He was oblivious of the fact we were on to him, and like to remain so. Once I'd found his victim and got her safe, assuming she was still alive, then I'd find out how he managed to get her locked up. Then I'd have all I needed to get him locked up in return. But for now, that could wait.

Marianne Little had been transferred to somewhere distant and secure. That was my next port of call, and it was there that I discovered she'd managed to free herself. My heart soared at that news. I wanted to cheer. I struggled to keep the smile off my face as I listened to the man in charge of that much larger institution, who clearly bore a grudge against her. He had been hoping to publish a ground-breaking paper. He had been planning on making his name by curing her. She'd let him down badly by escaping. I could tell he knew nothing about how, and it was clear he didn't care what had happened to her either. I had to sit there for another half-hour listening to him going on about his next pet project, and fervently hoped that he or she would blight his ambition by escaping too.

I'd seen enough of the place by then to work out it would take some doing to get out of it, which meant the woman I was looking for must have had help. It was by trawling through the local press that set me on the right track this time. Another escape around about the time I reckoned Marianne Little disappeared.

A man, poor soul, he was once Queen Victoria's piper,

and had convinced himself he was her husband. He was last seen on the banks of the River Nith and it was assumed he had been swallowed up by the quicksands. The search for him had involved nearly every member of staff at the institution, so it would have been the perfect diversion. I tracked down Mrs Crawford easily enough since she was in charge of the most secure female ward, but persuading her to talk was more difficult.

I knew better than to offer *her* money. If she'd risked her position to help an inmate escape, she must have had a very strong motive for doing so. She was prickly when I mentioned Marianne Little, and by that time I was prickly enough myself about what had happened to the poor woman and what she'd been put through. It was gie easy for me to let fall enough sense of the disgust I felt to set her off on the injustices of the case. Mrs Crawford was adamant that Marianne Little had been held unfairly and unnecessarily, and I counted her opinion considerably higher than any of those in charge of the institution, who were happy to bend the truth to fit their desire to keep banking the fees and donations. Besides, I knew what Mrs Crawford did not, the real reason *why* Marianne Little was being locked up.

Knowing when to take a risk with someone, when to trust them, was vital in my job. So I told Mrs Crawford the bare bones of why I wanted to find the woman she'd helped escape, and I let her see enough of the proof to assure her that Marianne Little's fortunes were going to change radically, if only I could find her. Thanks to Mrs Crawford, I then had a city, an employment agency, and a fairly accurate date. It wasn't long before I found the woman herself. Alive and looking very well indeed, to my immense relief and delight.

So there I sat, having my coffee that morning in Edinburgh's Grassmarket, mulling over what to do next. Against the odds, I'd found the woman I had been paid to find. Marianne Little had been judged and condemned without a trial, just like me. I hadn't suffered anything like what she had, but the fact we had that in common added to her appeal—I could see that. It was also a very big part of my determination to see justice done for her, make sure the bastard responsible for what he'd put her through paid the price for what he'd done.

Four years of suffering he'd inflicted on her. Four years of being held unjustly, treated in ways that would make your blood run cold. Once I'd done collecting the evidence against him, he'd be locked up for the rest of his wretched life. Meantime, he was carrying on oblivious of the clock counting down his remaining days of freedom, and what I had been instructed to do was think about what might be the best way of going about informing Marianne Little of her change in circumstances and pending good fortune.

Think about it, but don't do it, thank the stars. I wasn't much more than a complete stranger to her, and it was all going to be a huge shock. Did she know anything of her heritage? Very little, would be my guess, so what she was going to hear would pull the rug from under her. I had the proof of it, it wasn't a case of her not believing me, but would she listen? And if she did, what would it do to her? She seemed strong-willed, but it was clear to me, from the way she hid herself away from the world, from her wariness every time she left the sanctuary of her rooms in the Grassmarket, that she was still looking over her shoulder. She'd escaped, but she wasn't free. She was much more vulnerable and fragile than she appeared.

What's more, if she was going to lay claim to her real heritage, the press would be all over it, for it's not often a lost peeress was rediscovered. The sorry tale of her recent past was bound to come out too, especially if she was to give evidence against the man who had locked her up. I knew what it was like to find your name all over the press. Just thinking about how she might react to that gave me the heebie-jeebies, because all my instincts told me she'd run for the hills, and then I'd be back to where I started from.

It would need to be done sensitively, in a way that didn't make her take fright and bolt. I'd need to get her to talk to me, find out what she knew, what she didn't and fill in some of the gaps. And how was I going to do that, when she'd already turned down my suggestion of meeting up again? Though on reflection it seemed to me, she hadn't done so very convincingly, and that gave me hope. The obvious thing would be to sit in Queen Street Gardens again, but there were several reasons for not doing the obvious thing. I needed to speak to her on her own, without the children to distract her, and without putting her on her guard.

Then there was my most ardent desire to avoid becoming an object of interest to the locale's regular policeman. I doubted very much that any of the constables on their beats would know me, they'd all have retired, moved on or moved up, but if the man was worth his salt, he'd notice me. It was what a good policeman did, took note of strangers, kept an eye out for anything unusual, and the more conscientious among them—which was most, in my experience—took notes. Last, but certainly not least, was my desire to avoid the New Town when possible. Despite the passing years, the risk of sticking my head above the parapet was real, the potential consequences genuinely fatal.

And then there was the woman herself. She seemed to be quite content with the life she had made in this city. Just as I had done myself, she'd forged it from the ashes of another life, out of necessity. It was nothing short of a miracle that she'd done so. If any of the families who had entrusted her with their children's well-being got so much as a sniff of her recent past, there would be hell to pay—and she'd already been to hell and back. Mind you, if any of them discovered that they'd been employing a peeress as their governess, that would be a whole other story in the newspapers.

The more I thought about the situation, the more complicated it seemed to me. She'd escaped, she hadn't been released. Once the full story came to light and the wheels of justice were set in motion, there was no chance that the private institution she'd escaped from would want her back, but she'd be branded as an ex-inmate for ever. The press would have a field day with that one, and she—I swear, when I thought of what she would have to go through in front of a judge and jury, it made me sick to my stomach.

Was I making too much of it? At the end of the day, what she would hear from whoever told her in the end was life-changing—and I mean seriously life-changing. Provided the legalities could be ironed out, that was. I sighed, not for the first time wishing that at least one bit of the situation was simpler. Baby steps, I said to myself. That's what I'd take with her. Edge forward, but slowly. That was the only sensible approach.

I threw some coins down on the table and headed out into the Grassmarket, scanning the crowd first. Better safe than sorry. I'd stretch my legs and clear my head. There were so many parts of the city I'd be wise to avoid, but up on Salisbury Crags, I'd be unlikely to meet anyone I knew. And the view from Arthur's Seat over the city spread out below me in all its glory had always been one that did my heart good.

My walk blew away the cobwebs, and gave me an appetite, but the only plan I came up with was to try to bump into Marianne Crawford on her way home from work. For this, I chose the Lawnmarket. In the years I'd been away from Edinburgh, they'd finished the work on the High Kirk. St Giles certainly had a new majesty, along with a whole new look, though the famous crown steeple that was a landmark of the Old Town had been left untouched. The new stone was already blackening, and the kirk brooded over the square now that all the old buildings had been demolished, like a big black crow.

I positioned myself in the shadows of the main entrance in the early evening, eyeing the carved gargoyles that guarded the portico. Malevolent creatures, with their tongues sticking out, they were presumably intended to prevent evil spirits from entering the sacred edifice. The evil spirits, in my humble opinion, were those flapping about in their legal robes over at Parliament Square, but I'm willing to admit to a bit of bias there.

I was beginning to get concerned that somehow I had missed her, when I spotted her—at precisely the same time as she spotted me, and made her way across the Lawnmarket to join me.

'Mr Sutherland. What a coincidence.' Her tone made it clear that she thought it was nothing of the sort. 'What are you doing here, lurking in the shadow of St Giles?' she asked.

'I like to take a walk before dinner, and this is a good place to watch the world go by.'

'While keeping yourself out of sight?'

'Evidently not, since you spotted me.'

'I had a feeling we'd bump into each other again.'

'And I rather hoped we would,' I admitted, relieved to be able to speak something close to the truth.

'Why?'

She looked me straight in the eye when she asked the question.

'You interest me,' I told her, which was honest enough.

'In what way?'

She quirked her brow again, such an odd thing to find alluring, but there it was, and there I was, despite my previous resolutions not to be distracted, struggling not to be distracted by my body's reaction. 'That's a very personal question, from someone who has not even disclosed her name.'

'I am not one for small talk.'

'Yet you made an effort yesterday, in Queen Street Gardens, when we met,' I retorted.

'I felt obliged to fill the silence while you were watching the policeman.'

'In fact, what you did was interrogate me about my interest in him. That was not small talk.'

'And you did not answer my questions, Mr Sutherland.'

'I've answered more of your questions than you have of mine. You have still not put me in possession of your name.'

She narrowed her eyes at me, and I thought for a moment that I had crossed an invisible line with her, but what she said was not the reprimand I anticipated. 'I have the distinct impression that you know it already.'

What to say to this? The woman was a most astute observer, and I didn't want to lie, never mind have her catch me out. Truth was, I knew all three of her names, which was one more than she did herself. 'Mrs Crawford,' I conceded. 'That's what I heard the other nanny call you, though she did not mention a first name.'

'It is Marianne, and she's a governess, not a nanny.'

'I am never sure of the difference.'

'They have much in common, for both are usually underpaid, over-used and under-valued. Oh, and always of the so-called weaker sex, of course.'

'And which are you, Mrs Crawford, nanny or governess?'

'Either or both, depending upon what is required. I am fortunately in sufficient demand to be able to quit any establishment which under-values, under-pays or over-uses me.'

'You are good at your job?'

She gave me a crooked smile, taking her time, as I was now realising was her wont, before answering. 'The women I work for know that they can trust me.'

'And they can pay you well too. Queen Street is a very prestigious address.'

'Edinburgh has a great many wealthy families, and the New Town is full of prestigious addresses.'

'You must have come to Edinburgh armed with excellent references.'

'Must I? You make a great deal of assumptions about me.'

'And you deny none of them, so I reckon I've been pretty close to the mark.'

For the first time, she looked uncomfortable and failed to meet my eyes. She was difficult to pin down, this conversation was like a game of chess, but she wasn't a liar.

I decided not to push her for the moment. The clouds had finally decided to drop some of their rain, and it fell lightly but persistently. 'You'll catch a cold if you stand here in this,' I said to her. 'May I escort you to wherever you were headed?'

'No,' she replied, immediately on her guard. She had taken a small step back, but she had not turned to leave. 'Why are you here, Mr Sutherland? In Edinburgh, I mean. It's a bit of a long story, you said, yesterday. I'd like to hear it.'

She had surprised me, and I surprised myself at how pleased I was. 'Shall we go inside, out of the rain?'

'Inside?' She glanced around at our surroundings, and then over at the church. 'Do you mean the church?'

'It will give us some shelter from the weather, and though it's Presbyterian now, it was originally built for the faith in which I was raised. I am fairly certain I'll not be smited for crossing the threshold.'

'What about me? I have no faith, will I be safe inside, do you think?'

I glanced about me at the Lawnmarket and the High Street, where those who lived in the shadows of the Old Town were emerging as night fell, and the lights from the taverns in the wynds were beginning to flicker. 'Safer inside than out here.'

'On the lookout for the police again, Mr Sutherland?' She didn't wait for me to reply, but turned towards the church. 'Come then, let us converse inside.'

Chapter Six

Marianne

Edinburgh—
Friday 3rd August 1877

The interior of St Giles brought me up short as I crossed the threshold, for though I had never been inside, it felt familiar. The cathedral was a vast echoing structure, the vaulted ceiling of the nave soaring so high above us that it could barely be made out in the gloom, intimidating, and much bigger than any church I had ever entered. There was so much space, so few places to hide, and the glimmer from the various stained-glass windows I found oppressive rather than impressive.

Aware of Mr Sutherland behind me trying to close the door softly, I forced myself to take a few steps further in. The church had undergone extensive renovations in the last few years, I knew, and my sensitive nose twitched at the smell of newly sculpted stone that mingled with the musty smell and a depressing sense of the urge to repent that I associate with all places of worship. Which explained the feeling I'd had, that I'd been here before. Religion, in the institution from which I had escaped, was deemed to be soothing to troubled souls. I had never found it so, but perhaps that was because it was not my soul that troubled me.

There were a few figures scattered about in the open pews beyond the transept, closer to the altar, but one of the aisles on the left was empty and slightly less exposed. Mr Sutherland followed my lead, his tread light for such a big man.

'I promise that I intend you no harm, Mrs Crawford,' were his first words to me, spoken softly and with a mind to the acoustics of the place.

'I would not be here with you if I thought so,' I replied. And yet, what on earth was I doing here at all, with a man who was always looking over his shoulder, and who looked too closely at me? I should be avoiding him at all costs, yet here I was, conniving with his desire for my company. 'What is it you want from me?' I asked, thinking it might help me to understand what it was I wanted from him.

'I thought it was a case of what *you* want from *me*? Why I'm here in Edinburgh, wasn't that what you wanted to know?'

I took my time answering, concentrating all my attention on him. He baffled me. I was here because I was convinced, though I had no idea why, that I ought to be here with him. What I got from him was the same, a strong sense of his *wanting* to be with me, but nothing more, save that I felt—no, safe isn't the right word, I felt anything but safe. I felt jumpy, as if I was expecting something exciting to happen. Jittery was the word Mrs Oliphant would use. My blood was tingling with anticipation. I wanted more—more of this man's company, I mean, and that was such an unusual feeling—these days, unique.

I had been silent too long. He had been studying me, just as I'd been studying him. It didn't make me uncomfortable, it wasn't as if he was analysing my features for signs of my condition! It made me blush. It made me acutely aware of myself. And of him.

'Would it help,' he asked me, 'if I told you that my intentions are not in the least improper?'

No, I imagined replying, for my own thoughts are extremely improper. As if I would say such a thing, but the idea of it made me smile. Then he raised his brows, wanting to know what had made me smile, and I felt my cheeks getting hotter. 'Not that it is at all relevant, but you have already told me you are not married. And neither, as it happens, am I.'

'Really, *Mrs* Crawford?'

'An employer's wife can confide in a widow, Mr Sutherland. I would not be so popular if I was *Miss* Crawford.'

'Do wives commonly confide in their governesses?'

'The role of wife and mother can be very lonely. I am a very good listener.'

'And wise counsellor?'

'What do you mean?' The question startled me out of the conversation.

He spread his hands, shaking his head. 'I am interested, that's all. I have never been married, but I'd always assumed that a wife would confide in her husband. The idea that she'd be lonely…'

'When a man comes home from whatever business takes him out all day, he wants to see his wife in a pretty gown smiling across the dinner table, listening to his tales of the outside world. He isn't interested in the mundane domestic world she inhabits, the exhausting task of raising his children, and the painful task of bearing them. I listen, Mr Sutherland, but that is all. My days of providing counsel of any sort are over.'

Too late, I realised my mistake. Had he missed the implication? I couldn't understand my outburst. I couldn't understand why I had even answered his questions. I was so intent on trying to find a way to change the subject, his next one caught me off guard once more.

'I'm lost now,' he said, looking anything but. 'Are you saying you have been married, or what?'

'No, I have never been married, and I never want to be!' I had spoken too loudly. I clasped my hands tightly together, taken aback by my own vehemence. I ought to walk away from this conversation and this man, but once again my feet refused to co-operate.

'I didn't mean to upset you,' he said softly. 'I beg your pardon.'

'I am not upset.' I spoke through gritted teeth.

'I'm sorry all the same,' he said.

He was, I could tell that he meant it. I wondered if he'd leave now, but he made no move, looking at that moment just as baffled as I felt. I found that reassuring. I tried to assess his thoughts but with little success, and so instead I tried to understand my own motives. I don't believe in fate, but my instincts were telling me that I was meant to know this man. Why?

Was it a simple case of finding him attractive? I thought myself immune to such feelings, my body numbed for ever by the betrayal and scars that had been the result of my first and only experience of love. What I mistook for love. Was my body finally healed enough to make its own demands, even if my mind was damaged for ever? I did not wish to recall that other man, nor to compare him with Mr Sutherland. This was different. Not love, that I would never risk, but allure? Magnetism? Was it that which made me seek him out, and which kept me in his company even when I knew it was unwise?

It was not Mr Sutherland who made me feel unsafe, it was his effect on me. I liked the way he looked. He was a tall man, and well built, but he was not one of those men who use their size to intimidate. I shivered, the pleasant kind of shiver, recalling the heat of his hand through his gloves, and wondered, what would it have been like had he removed his glove? What would his touch be like? His lips?

Once again, I realised I'd been silent, and that I was being silently studied. Could *he* read *my* thoughts? At that moment, as our eyes met, I felt it, a tug, like a rope tightening between us, the absolute certainty that he too felt this—this compulsion. That we were two haunted, hunted souls destined to meet.

It was a ridiculous and fanciful thing to think, especially in a church, but the conviction took root, and allowed me at last to focus on what mattered—not what I felt for the man, but why I gravitated towards him. 'We have strayed far from the point of this conversation,' I said. 'Which was not for you to question me, but for me to question you. Were you in the gardens yesterday, by accident or design?'

'I didn't arrive with the intention of speaking to you,' he answered, taking his time, choosing his words carefully, which was something of a habit with him. 'If the ball hadn't been thrown in my direction I wouldn't have spoken. But it did and I'll confess I was glad it did, for I wanted to speak to you, and once I had spoken to you, I wanted to speak to you again. I was curious about you and if you don't mind my saying, I got the strong impression you were curious about me. Even if you did turn down my invitation to meet again,' he added with a faint smile, 'here we are, after all.'

I had regained control of myself, and saw no harm in admitting that much. 'A man who is afraid of the law, but who is not a criminal, is interesting.'

'I'm not afraid of the law.'

'You didn't want that policeman to see you.'

'I didn't think he'd recognise me. I just didn't want to stand out. Look, I'm not trying to lead you a merry dance, I promise you. I'll be blunt, shall I?'

'I would appreciate it.'

'I'm here in Edinburgh on a job of work, the nature of which is confidential. I have no intentions, honest or wicked, save what I've already confessed, to get to know you a bit better. I am—I am drawn to you. That's the description that I keep coming back to, whatever that may mean.' He shrugged, looking sheepish. 'There you have it.'

Drawn. The very word I had used myself to describe my reaction to him. It was reassuring and yes, it was slightly thrilling, to hear him articulate something akin to what I was experiencing. That he did so, I think against his better judgement, persuaded me that my instinct to trust him was sound, and that I could therefore indulge my wish to further our acquaintance. That sounds calculated, but it was rather caution born from experience. I cannot emphasise strongly enough how unusual this conversation was for me.

'What is the nature of your work?' I asked him.

'I'm a detective.'

'A detective! So you are a policeman after all!'

'Not exactly. I'm a private investigator.'

'Good grief!' I had not even considered such a thing and

was once again on my guard. 'What are you investigating? Not me, I presume, though it would explain the number of questions you have thrown at me.'

'I told you, I'm interested in you, it's just my way. As to why I'm here—it wouldn't be right to tell you that, not at the moment. My clients rely on my complete discretion.'

I could barely see his face in the flickering candlelight of the church, but my inner senses were on full alert. He was wary, but he was not lying. Despite what I have been accused of in the past, I am not a mind reader. I certainly cannot read people's thoughts precisely, but I am acutely sensitive, far more than most, to feelings, and at times, this gives me insights that have been seen as malign, even sorcery, when they most definitely are not.

My skill was more adept when a person was unaware of my interest. Rory Sutherland was very much aware that I was studying him, and his feelings were complex and confusing, as my own were becoming. Caution warring with heightened interest, mainly. 'If you are a detective,' I said, trying to focus on what he had told me rather than what I was experiencing, 'then why did you want to avoid that policeman? Don't the police and private investigators work together to solve crimes?'

He laughed at that, a snarling, vicious sound that was loud enough to echo, reminding us both of our surroundings. 'Solving crimes is something the police do selectively, in this city.'

The bitterness in his voice startled me. The black wave of anger and regret that enveloped him took me utterly aback and took me right back too, to the countless nights when my own anger at the injustice of my treatment was my only defence against despair. Before I knew what I was doing I stepped closer, putting my hand on his arm. 'Mr Sutherland, whatever it is that ails you, you can conquer it.'

His gloved hand covered mine. He looked at me with such bleakness that my heart contracted. 'The case I'm investigating now is of no interest to the police. What ails me is unfinished business that must remain unresolved for ever.'

We were close enough for me to feel the warmth of his breath, to smell the faint trace of soap on his skin. My gloved hand was enveloped in his, held but not constrained. I didn't feel trapped, and again I cannot say just how important and unusual that was. On the contrary, I wanted to close the gap further between us, to ease the pain that brought back so many memories of my own. 'The past, if that is what it is, is best left behind, Mr Sutherland.'

'Aye, I know that, it's why I shouldn't be in Edinburgh.'

'But you said your case…'

'Brought me here.' He gave me a strange look then turned away, making a pretence of studying the ancient stonework. 'It's the last place I should be, all the same. I love this city—sacrilege for a Weegie to say, but there it is. It's where I made my name, and it's where my name was blackened. If they find out I'm back…' His voice cracked. 'Well, I'll just have to make damn—blooming sure that they don't find out.'

'They? I don't understand, do you mean the police have forbidden—is your presence here illegal?'

'No. It's complicated. It's not the police, so much as—no, I'm sorry, I truly am, but there's no point in my saying any more.'

'But—but surely—you have told me almost nothing. Is your life in danger?'

'Ach no, it's not that serious.' Mr Sutherland turned towards me, trying and failing to summon a semblance of a smile. 'I'm sorry, I didn't mean to tell you any of this.' He was gathering himself together again, tucking away the dark emotions that had escaped his restraint, and my goodness that felt so horribly familiar. 'I have no idea why I just blurted that out. As you pointed out, it's all in the past now.'

But it clearly wasn't. Haunted. Hunted. No wonder I felt such an affinity with him. 'Who are these people?' I asked, with difficulty refraining from tugging at his sleeve. 'The ones who blackened your name? And why—how—if you did not commit a crime? I don't understand.'

He sighed heavily. 'My crime was not to listen to the advice I'd been given. To interfere when I'd been told not to. In short, I ruffled the wrong feathers, and the chickens came home to roost, so to speak.'

In short, I ruffled the wrong feathers.

Precisely what I had done, and with the same result. I very much wanted to know more, but I could tell from the way he set his mouth firmly that persistence would lead to resistance. 'I know what that's like,' I said, willing him to understand just how sincerely I empathised. 'It's clearly a painful subject, but if you wish to confide in me, I assure you, you can trust me.'

'Aye, I know, I can trust you. Intuition,' he added, before I could ask, 'I've good instincts in that department. But I've already told you more than I should have, and it's getting late. You shouldn't be out and about in this area, it's not safe. I think I'd best see you home.'

I remained rooted to the spot. 'But—but if you have been threatened—if it's true that you could be in danger—then this case that has brought you here to Edinburgh, it must be very important to you?'

'Oh, it is,' he said, giving me a look I could not interpret. 'Much more important than I thought when I took it on.'

I allowed him to accompany me to the Grassmarket, because he seemed determined that I needed chaperoning, and it was easier to accept that than to argue with him. We passed Flora flitting up Victoria Street on her way to earn her keep. I smiled, a friendly smile I thought it was, but it startled both her and Mr Sutherland, who asked if we were acquainted. I answered honestly enough that we were not. He saw me to the entrance of my close, and would have escorted me up the stairs to my rooms had I permitted him to do so. I bid him goodnight.

Once inside I opened my window without lighting the lamp, and spotted him immediately, on the other side of the Grassmarket gazing up at my tenement. He nodded, though I did not acknowledge seeing him, and then took himself off towards the Cowgate. Where was he lodging? What on earth had he done all those years ago, to result in his exile from Edinburgh? And what was this case of his that was important enough to make him risk returning? We had made no arrangements to meet again, but I retired to bed that night certain that we would.

Chapter Seven

Rory

Six weeks previously

I met Lord Westville in a hotel in central London. He was younger than I had imagined, in his late twenties, I estimated, tall, slim and very fair. Though it was a pleasant summer's day, his handshake was icy, and throughout our conversation he would every now and then give a violent shiver and complain about the room being cold. His eyes were the strangest colour, a blue so pale it was almost translucent, what diamonds would look like if they were blue, hard chips of precious stone glinting under his thin, arched brows. The Marquess was what passes for handsome in a man of his class, especially when what they call good breeding was accompanied by wealth. I found him as distasteful as all of his entitled ilk.

'I have spent a great deal of my life in sunnier climes,' he said to me, examining the contents of the teacup he had graciously allowed the maidservant to pour. 'If I am to settle in this country, I shall have to acquire a more suitable wardrobe.' He took a sip of his tea, shuddered and pushed it aside. 'That is one English habit I doubt I will acquire. You come highly recommended, Mr Sutherland.'

'Do I, now?'

'You are wondering by whom, and how I, who am almost a stranger to these shores, can have known how to set about finding you,' Lord Westville said, forcing me to reappraise the man. He smiled thinly. 'I am not the dilettante you imagine me to be, Mr Sutherland. My father was an extremely rich self-made man of independent means long before he inherited the Westville estates, and while it is true that I have been raised in what you might call the lap of luxury, I am not the idle type. My father instilled a strong work ethic in me. Diplomacy has been my calling, and it is one that has provided me with a great many contacts. I am told that discretion is your watchword, and discretion in this case is paramount.'

He had surprised me again. 'And what is this case, Lord Westville?' I asked him, pushing my own cup of tea aside, it being of the fragrant variety that tasted like perfume.

He steepled his fingers, studying me with those strange eyes from under deceptively languid lids. 'Tell me first what you have uncovered, Mr Sutherland, of my own circumstances? I give you credit, you see, for having carried out due diligence before this meeting.'

That was true enough, and I gave *him* the credit for that. 'Not very much,' I admitted reluctantly. 'Your father inherited the title and the estates from his distant cousin about seven years ago, but he remained abroad and has shown no interest in either. I understand the lands and estates are managed by a family lawyer.'

'His name is Eliot.'

His tone gave me pause. 'The way you said that implies you have some reservations about Mr Eliot.'

'You are on the right track, Mr Sutherland, but it is not the estate itself that causes me most concern. It is the…'

'Money,' I finished for him, since it was always at the root of everything.

'The crux of the matter, indeed. Filthy lucre, Mr Sutherland, and a great deal of it, which is why I must entreat you to tread very lightly with Mr Eliot. He must not know that I suspect him.'

'Misappropriation of funds, is it? That is not really my field of expertise, Lord Westville.'

'What I'm rather more concerned about is the misappropriation of a person. Or, more accurately, the absence of a person. That, I believe, *is* your field?'

'It depends upon the circumstances,' I said warily, but I have to admit I was instantly intrigued.

'Then let me enlighten you, Mr Sutherland, but first…'

'You have my assurances, Lord Westville, that whether I take the case or not, the content of this conversation will go no further.'

He smiled his thin smile. 'That I took for granted. What I was about to say was, first let us have something more refreshing to drink than tea.'

It was the kind of tale I'd have found difficult to believe, had Lord Westville not produced the evidence for me to read—including the will written by the cousin from whom his father had inherited the title. That previous Lord Westville had lived as a bachelor, but it transpired that he was a widower and moreover the father of a daughter.

'He secretly married a woman named Anne Little,' the

current Lord Westville informed me. 'And she, rather inconveniently for the infant, expired in the process of giving birth to her. The child was handed into the care of a couple, and a stipend was paid to them every month for the raising and education of her. When she was twenty-one, arrangements were made to pay the stipend directly to her.'

'Arrangements were made? Was she aware of who her father was?'

'Though she was baptised, and undoubtedly legitimate, I am afraid we must conclude that her father did not wish to know her,' Lord Westville said, a slight frown marring his pale brow. 'She was raised under the name Marianne Little, and if she ever enquired as to the identity of her benefactor, the arrangements ensured that she would receive no answer. Which makes her father's will very odd indeed. Lord Westville—my father's cousin, that is—really, there are too many Lords Westville in this tale—was extremely rich.'

'Railways, I believe, and canals.'

'Very good, Mr Sutherland, that is it exactly. Railways and canals and also coal. The lands, the estate and the title were inherited by my own father, but the money—and there is a vast amount of it—the money was left to the daughter.'

'Making her a considerable heiress, I take it?'

'Well now, here we reach the crux of the matter. It would make her husband a considerably wealthy man, but until she married, then she was to continue to receive her stipend, but nothing more.'

'And what was to happen if she didn't marry?'

'As I said, matters were to continue as before.' Lord Westville poured himself another glass of Madeira, shrugging at my refusal to join him. 'My own father did not, I'm afraid, cover himself in glory in this matter. He was not interested in the estates, though he was happy enough to assume the title. I fear we must conclude that Anne Little, the mother of our heiress, was of humble origins, and therefore not a connection my father would have wished to acknowledge.

'The will nominated Eliot, the lawyer, as both Executor and Trustee, which as far as the law is concerned, made him effectively legally responsible for the woman. She would of course have been oblivious to this, just as she had been oblivious of the fact that her father—our first Lord Westville—was previously, legally her guardian. And my own father—the second Lord Westville in this little drama—was happy to let matters be.'

At this point in the tale I was tempted to take a glass of the Madeira, even though it's not my kind of drink. However, I made do with a cup of coffee. 'Just to be clear then, as matters stand with you—the third Lord Westville—the woman in the case is still legally under the guardianship of Eliot, who is also her Trustee?'

'In the matter of her inheritance, that is correct.'

'Was she contacted, then? Made aware of her inheritance when her father died?'

Lord Westville shrugged, looking distinctly uncomfortable. 'You need to understand that these events are almost as new to me as they are to you. My father never mentioned her existence to me. The first I knew of her was when I met with Eliot last week. I've decided to move back to England for a while, at least, and intend to do what my father did not, get to grips with my inheritance. I am told that my cousin—for she must be some sort of cousin—has disappeared.'

'Disappeared! What do you mean by that—exactly?'

'Alas, I cannot be precise,' he replied, looking pained. 'I am reliant entirely on the testimony of Mr Eliot. He tells me that he attempted to contact her when her father died, in order to make arrangements to continue the stipend or to pass on her inheritance to her husband, were she married. Apparently she could not be found.'

'So he's not had any contact with her for—how long?'

'He was rather vague on the subject. It is about seven years since her father died and the trust was set up, delegating power to Eliot.'

'What age would the woman be now?'

'She was twenty-five or six when her father died, so that would make her thirty-three, I think.' He consulted a piece of paper, on which a number of dates were written. 'Yes, she was born in June forty-four, so just turned thirty-three.'

'She's most likely married years ago with a clutch of weans—children. And what has this lawyer been doing? Sitting on his backside twiddling his thumbs and making no effort to find her? There's more holes in his tale than a fisherman's net.'

'You express yourself more colourfully than I, but we are of one mind, Mr Sutherland.'

'Your own father, he wasn't exactly an old man when he died, was he?'

'He was fifty-two, in robust health until typhus claimed him, and importantly, persistently uninterested in Mr Eliot's management of his affairs. The circumstances are most—conducive—to exploitation, alas.'

'And has there been exploitation? Have you looked at the accounts?'

'It is a delicate situation. The money in question is not part of my inheritance, and I did not wish to make Mr Eliot suspicious. I have therefore feigned my father's indifference to the matter.'

'You did the right thing there, but we'll need to find a way to take a look at what he's been up to.'

'Thank you, Mr Sutherland. I am not an idiot.'

Clearly he wasn't. 'So you'll make arrangements, will you, to authorise me to do a bit of digging with the bank?'

'As soon as you agree to take the case and provided you can do so without alerting him.'

'I've a few contacts myself, obviously, that will help me find out if he has money problems. Or too much money. Talking of which, what happens if the woman isn't found?'

'Nothing at all. The money continues to be held in trust, unless she is dead, or declared dead.'

'She's been missing nearly seven years, after which, if no trace can be found of her, you can have the law declare her dead. And if she is already dead, then the money…'

'Unless she has legal progeny, then it will default to me,' Lord Westville said. 'Am I then also under suspicion?'

'Suspicion of what?' I countered. 'If you were in cahoots with the lawyer, then the last thing you'd want to do was find the woman. And if you wanted to pay lip service to trying to find her, you wouldn't have come to me.'

He laughed at that, a surprisingly hearty sound. 'Because you will succeed where others might fail, you mean? That was your forte, was it not, back in your days as a policeman north of the border? To go boldly where other men feared to tread? Until you fell on your sword.'

His words made my blood run cold. There had been a couple of times, when I first settled in the south, when my infamy lost me work, but few people in the south were much concerned with what happened *north of the border*.

I had made my name afresh, and put it behind me. Or so I had thought.

'You are surprisingly reticent, Mr Sutherland. You don't leap to your own defence?'

'If you believed the accusations, you would not be here, Lord Westville.'

'You were held in such high esteem, and your fall from grace was so very—so very complete—that it struck me as simply too dramatic to believe. A contrivance, in other words, Mr Sutherland. Am I correct?'

Aside from my da, he was the first person to give me the benefit of the doubt. Guilt made me cringe inside, for I'd judged him in a way he had not judged me. 'I thank you for your faith in me,' I said, swallowing the embarrassing lump in my throat.

'I hope it is not misplaced.'

'You do want her found, then?'

'Dead or alive. Married or unwed. One way or another, I wish the matter resolved for her sake as well as my own.'

His tone was cool, utterly lacking in emotion. Dead or alive, he said, seemingly quite indifferent to which. If this had been simply a matter of fraud, of a lawyer giving in to temptation and dipping into funds, I wouldn't have been interested. But the funds in question were huge and besides, it was really about a missing woman and her missing heritage.

I couldn't help but think of that other missing woman I had let down seven years before. My one failure. It was daft, there was no logic behind it, but from that minute, I linked the two cases in my head. I would find this heiress and remedy my failure in the other case. Bloody stupid thinking, completely illogical, but that's what I thought all the same.

Decision made, it was down to business. 'You're sure the

lawyer doesn't know you're set on this course?' I asked the man who was now my client. 'No,' I added hastily, 'forget I asked you that, you're not daft.'

'I am positive. If that changes, rest assured that I shall let you know. For now, I have him focused on my own concerns—the lands and the estates, I mean. Those, he has in fact managed competently. I plan to keep him busy while you investigate the other matter.'

'Good, make sure you do. Of course, it might be he's guilty of nothing other than a lack of care in trying to find the heiress himself.' I said it, because it needed said, though I didn't believe it.

Nor did Lord Westville. 'That may be the case, but there is, as we have both remarked, a great deal of money at stake.' He drained his glass. 'It sounds to me as if you have decided to take the case, Mr Sutherland. Or am I mistaken?'

I ought to have taken the time to consider, but I did not. The stakes were extremely high. It was, besides, a puzzle that might be tricky to resolve, something that might stretch me a bit. That's how I explained it to myself later, mind. At the time, all I could think about was, if I get this right, it will balance out that other one, at last. 'I'll need you to give me what little information you have on her.'

'I came prepared.' The Marquess pulled a paper from his pocket and handed it over. 'Here are the details of where the stipend was last paid to, and the address of the people who raised her. She was known as Marianne Little, but she was baptised Lady Mary Anne Westville. I have no desire for regular updates nor any interest in your methods. When you have significant progress to report, let me know.'

This suited me very well. 'And when I have an answer for you,' I asked him, 'what then?'

'Then your work will be done. I'll take care of the matter from there.'

With that, I was less happy. 'If I find her alive, what should I tell her? I need to tell her something.'

'Do you know, I haven't thought of that?' Lord Westville frowned down at his long-fingered hands. 'I suppose you must tell her the truth. I will provide you with copies of the will, her birth certificate.'

'It's going to come as a hell of a shock. Not only the money, but presumably all she thinks she knows about herself is wrong. She doesn't even know her own name.'

'Dear me, when you put it like that.' He shuddered dramatically. 'I detest emotional scenes. I suppose, as her only known relative, I should be the bearer of good news, but the problem is, the news as matters stand is not necessarily good.'

'You mean the money may not be hers, if she is alive but unmarried?'

'That is precisely what I mean. Contrary to what you may think, Mr Sutherland,' the Marquess said, looking pained, 'I have no desire to benefit from my predecessor's lack of foresight—I mean the first of the Lord Westvilles. Why he did not make provision for the possibility of his daughter eschewing the marital state, I do not know. *If* you find her, *if* she is alive, *if* she is a spinster, then she deserves her legacy. I do not know how I shall go about it, but I am sure the terms of the will can be altered. Until I have confirmation that this can be done, it seems to me that we should tread lightly. Say nothing, in other words, without consulting me.'

It pained me to be told what to do, but I knew he was right. Besides, it was quite a turnup for the book, hearing that he was promising to do himself out of a fortune, admittedly under highly unlikely circumstances. 'That seems sensible.'

He laughed lightly. 'Quoth he, through gritted teeth. I shall take account of your advice on the matter as we proceed, rest assured.'

I believed him, and so was satisfied. I had no idea where the quest would take me, what horrors I might uncover. Marianne Little was a name on a piece of paper, a lost woman I was set on finding. It was all about the money, I thought, and it was, in a sense. Lies and deception were at the heart of it, as they had likely been central to that other case of mine. And in both cases, it was the woman who had suffered. This time, I was determined to serve up justice. As subsequent events would prove, it would turn out to be far from straightforward.

Chapter Eight

Marianne

Edinburgh—
Sunday 5th August 1877

The view from Dean Bridge was the closest I had been to the industrial village which lay beneath, the mills and leather works which clung precariously to the banks of the Water of Leith. The works were Sabbath-silent today, but the peculiar odour which hung over the place like a miasma was still strong enough to make my nose itch.

'Can you smell it?' His voice made me jump as I hadn't seen him approach. 'Sulphur and lime,' Mr Sutherland said, 'it's what they use to cure the hides. Sheep fleeces, mostly. Sorry, did I startle you?'

'You did.' My heart was fluttering, though it wasn't so much with fright. He was standing close, but not too close, dressed in the same sombre clothes that were obviously a kind of uniform for him, his shirt very white, the collar very stiffly starched. In the unusually bright sunlight, his skin had a healthy glow. His eyelashes were very long, for a man. He had a most appealing smile. I returned it.

'We choose the strangest places to meet, Mr Sutherland,' I said, though the choice had been his. He had been waiting for me yesterday morning when I set out for work, drinking coffee in the tavern where Flora breakfasted each day. He had not pretended it was a chance encounter, nor had he wasted his time on niceties. I had been not a whit disconcerted to find him waiting for me, something that didn't strike me as strange until much later.

He wanted to see me again, he had said, because he wanted to continue our conversation, and he wondered if I would take the air with him on Sunday, assuming it was my day off. Which was why I found myself on Dean Bridge, dressed in my one summer gown, of pale green, with a matching bow in my straw hat, and a shawl. I had dressed for the weather, certainly not for the man, though he looked both relieved and pleased to see me.

'I wasn't sure you would turn up,' he admitted. 'I thought you might have changed your mind.'

I hadn't even considered it, though I knew I should have. For as long as I felt safe with him, I had decided to indulge my compulsion for his company. Today's arrangement had given me something to look forward to. Something pleasant. That was unusual in itself. 'I had no way of letting you know if I had,' I said to him. 'I wouldn't have known where to send a note.'

'I'm here. You're here. And the sun has joined us. We should make the most of it.'

'Having the sun on my face is something I never take for granted, Mr Sutherland,' I said, lifting my face to the warmth and closing my eyes for a moment. It was a mistake, for in that moment a memory pushed its way in, of an open window, myself leaning out, craning my face to the sunshine, drinking in the smell of new-mown grass far below, before I was yanked inside, the window slammed shut, one of the attendants swearing at me. All I had wanted was some fresh air!

I opened my eyes to find myself being scrutinised by Mr Sutherland. 'Are you all right?' he asked me.

'Fine. I'm fine,' I told him, without meeting his eyes. 'Shall we walk?'

He looked unconvinced, but he nodded. 'I thought we'd go down through the village,' he said, 'then we can follow the river for a bit, if you like. It's far from scenic, I'll grant you, but we'll also be far from the crowds in the parks taking the air, or walking in their Sunday best from church, and I thought—maybe I'm wrong, but I thought you'd like to see a different aspect of Edinburgh.'

'What made you think that?'

'You see a very different side of the city from the rooms you have in the Grassmarket—compared to the New Town where you work, I mean. I know from what you've told me that you could afford better, so that means it's a choice. Of course it could be that you want to keep yourself to yourself, neighbour-wise, and in the Grassmarket, nobody looks too closely into each other's business. But I reckon you like the buzz of it too, you like to watch and to speculate. You're curious about how other people live. Am I right?'

'You make a great deal of deductions about me, Detective Sutherland. You have a way of making a question of a statement.'

He laughed. 'And you have a way of not answering either. I'll assume I'm right.'

'About your choice of location for a walk, I'll give you that,' I conceded, unable to hide my smile.

We took the steep path down, walking side by side, our paces well matched. The chemical smell grew stronger, and then I ceased noticing it as we picked our way past looming mills, and a huddle of buildings and courts that proclaimed themselves to be Robert Legget and Sons, Tanners. The village was eerily quiet, though there was washing hanging on the lines outside a few of the tenements, and a dog barked as we passed. A narrow bridge spanned the Water of Leith, tumbling brown and foul beneath, yet upstream I was horrified to see a gaggle of ragged children leaping about in the poisonous shallows.

'Poor bairns, they'll be bound to catch something from that water,' Mr Sutherland said, 'and I don't mean a fish for their tea.'

We crossed the bridge to the other side where there were more poorly maintained tenements, what looked like a corner shop on the ground floor of one of them, more warehouses, another works of some sort. Though we saw no one, I was conscious of the presence of the workers and their families silently watching us. I began to feel uncomfortable. We did not belong here. We were intruders, sightseers, like the visitors to the institution from which I had escaped, who wandered through the gardens created by the inmates. Did the workers in this village feel trapped as I had, in a life defined by a never-ending routine? It was not the same, not at all the same, yet there were similarities.

'Aye,' Mr Sutherland said, picking up on some of my thoughts, keeping his voice low, 'it's not much of a life, is it? Mind, they wouldn't thank me for saying so.'

'Is there a school here for the little ones?'

'There is, though whether they attend or not, that's another question. The tenement in Glasgow I was raised in was a few rungs up the ladder from a place like this, but there were still a good few families who didn't think it worth sending their weans to school. My da, he knew it was important, thank the stars, but here—you'd think they'd be asking themselves, what's the point, wouldn't you? Let those wee terrors we saw enjoy themselves while they can before they're put to work, you know?'

He muttered something under his breath, shaking his head. 'I shouldn't make assumptions, but you can't help feeling the good people of Edinburgh are happy to have their industrial lungs and the people who work and live there hidden well away from view. Happy to let them police themselves too. They don't send the law in here, you know.'

'Is that why you chose this location?'

He stopped abruptly. 'Do you think I'm running scared from a few policemen on the beat? The chances are, they wouldn't have a clue who I am or more importantly who I was, but I don't want to take that chance. I'm persona non grata in this city, but it was once my city. I'm known here, which is why I'm careful about where I go, and why I'm constantly looking over my shoulder…' Mr Sutherland took a ragged breath. 'I'm sorry.'

'No, I'm sorry.' The temptation to comfort, to place my hand on his arm, was too much to resist. 'I am truly sorry. I do know what it is like to be constantly looking over your shoulder.'

His hand covered mine. Glove on glove, but I felt the heat of his skin. His expression softened. Inside, I felt a fluttering, anxious, sensation, a yearning to offer more, but more of what? He turned to face me. I wanted him to close the gap between us, though at the same time I dreaded it. He made no move, though I felt—oh, I have no idea if it was my own longing or his or both of us I felt, or indeed how long we stood there, our eyes locked, his hand covering mine, saying nothing but both of us aware—I am *sure* we were both aware—of the longing for more—more closeness. Warmth. Touch. Simple things, but they were far from simple.

He sighed, a long exhale, and the spell broke, enough for the longing to dispel, but not enough for either of us to release ourselves. His hand remained on mine. 'Look,' he said softly, 'the truth is, I wanted you to myself for a while, that's all. I lived and worked in this city for more than ten years. There's a lot of folks I'd rather not bump into, for my own peace of mind as well as theirs. We've all moved on, Mrs Crawford, and I'd like to keep it that way. Do you understand what I'm saying?'

Was it so simple? A moment ago, there had been such anger in his voice. Yet what he said now made a great deal of sense. He had not moved on, not as far as he wished, but who was I to dig up other people's skeletons, when I had enough trouble keeping my own in their cupboard.

Besides.

The truth is, I wanted you to myself.

Wasn't that what I wanted too, only I was not brave enough to say so? 'I understand,' I said. 'Let us enjoy the sunshine and forget the world for a time.'

He heaved a sigh, his frown easing. 'Let's try, any road.'

Chapter Nine

Rory

Edinburgh—
Sunday 5th August 1877

We walked on the narrow path, both lost in our thoughts. I heartily regretted my outburst, yet the mood between us was not as awkward as it could have been. The sun was shining, there were trees in full leaf, and the Water of Leith rushing past us on its journey to the Firth of Forth and out to sea gave the illusion that we were in the countryside.

It would have been the most natural thing in the world for us to walk arm in arm, if we had been what we must have looked, a couple with no more ambition than to take the Sunday air and enjoy a bit of peace and quiet. The fact that I very much wanted to do just that was one of the reasons I didn't suggest she put her arm through mine. I couldn't afford to indulge myself. It was simply wrong.

Even if it had felt right. Even if I had thought that she felt it too, when she'd touched me a few moments ago. Compassion changing to wanting. I wouldn't dare call it desire. I couldn't afford to go down that path.

So what path did I think I was treading then—and I don't mean the one that we were strolling on! Getting to know her? Making her feel at ease with me so I could assess how able she would be to deal with the real reason for my presence here? Aye, a good way to go about earning her trust, that would be, if I gave in to what I was wanting to do, which was to put my arms around her and kiss her. So I wouldn't give in to my impulses, tempted as I was—and I was very, very tempted, which in itself was very unusual. Boundaries are boundaries between my work and my private life, and I'd never before had any problem sticking to them. Likely I was imagining the feeling was mutual. If I could have convinced myself of that, the battle would have been won.

We left the straggling outskirts of the village behind at the bend in the river where the walls of the huge cemetery could be seen on one bank.

'What is that building?' Marianne—Mrs Crawford!—pointed up at the imposing classical edifice on the hill looking down at the village.

'It's the Dean Orphanage.' She had stopped walking, and was gazing fixedly at the building. It occurred to me, a bit too late, that it might remind her of the place she'd escaped from. I couldn't see much resemblance in style, but the fact that it was a large institution with extensive grounds could well be enough to trigger unpleasant memories. 'Maybe we should turn back,' I said.

But she stood her ground. 'It must hold a great number of children. So many little ones without any family.'

'Or alternatively, with family who have not the means to take care of them.'

'Not orphans, but it is what they will be called, just the same.' She gave a deep shiver, then turned her back on the building. 'It's not a happy place. Will we take a walk in the cemetery? At least there, the inmates are at peace.'

It's not a happy place.

I didn't want to spoil the mood, but I wasn't here for my own benefit. It struck me that this was as good an opportunity as any to sound her out about what she knew—or didn't know—of her own background. I was already worried about her. The way she disappeared into herself every now and then, like a light was switched off inside her. The way she snapped sometimes, if I pushed her. Not just touchy, defensive. You could almost see the drawbridge being pulled up. I needed to tread carefully, but I also needed to make progress.

'What is it?' She stopped, and I realised I'd been trailing behind her. 'You were miles away.'

'"It's not a happy place", you said, as if you knew what you were talking about. I was wondering why—were you an orphan?'

I thought she might palm me off, but she surprised me. 'I never knew my father, nor my mother either, which I suppose does make me an orphan, though I've never thought of myself as such and I was not raised in an orphanage.'

We had entered the cemetery through the main gates, but of one accord had immediately veered away from the wide paths to the perimeter. There was a bench against the wall, and we sat down. 'What happened to your parents?' I asked, hoping to fill in one of the many gaps regarding what I knew about her, and more importantly what she knew about herself. I was, I'll admit, also genuinely curious on my own behalf.

'I don't know. I was raised by a couple who had no children of their own. I was well cared for, given a reasonable education, but they did not care very much for me. I knew from an early age, that I was not their child, that they were being paid to look after me. And, yes,' she said, her gaze meeting mine, 'I was curious as to who was paying them.'

I hadn't voiced the question in my head, but it was an obvious one. Her eyes were more green than hazel today. Her hands were clasped in her lap. Her skirts were brushing my leg. We were not touching at all, but I felt as if we were, bodies and minds. I know, it's a ridiculous thought, but it's what I felt. 'That must have been painful though, growing up knowing you were—I mean, it sounds like they were more distant than they had to be.'

'They were kind enough, but I was not their child. At least I was not simply dumped in a place like that.' She pointed in the direction of the orphanage. 'Why should I care, if my family—whoever they were—did not?'

One thing I'd always been certain of in my own life, was that my parents loved me, and that I was very much wanted. If I'd been given away as she had—I simply couldn't imagine how I'd feel. Had Lord Westville, her father, cared? Was that a question she was going to ask when the truth came out? If she did, there was no answer. 'So what about the money then?' I asked, returning to surer ground. 'Did you ask them where the money for your keep came from?'

'A benefactor, that is all they would tell me. He wished to remain anonymous. I assumed it was a man. I assumed it must be my father, though I have no basis for that, it could have been his family, or even my mother's family. I assumed, when I was old enough to make such assumptions, that I must be the result of a—a misalliance, as they say.' Her mouth curled. 'That my parents were not married and that I was not wanted. Anyway, I never depended upon the money. I made my own living.'

'Looking after children?'

'Yes. I helped the school mistress in the local school from when I was about sixteen.'

'So your love of children goes back to then?'

'It does. I love to teach.' She gave me one of her tight little smiles. 'Governesses, nurses, nannies, are supposed to say that, but not so very many of them mean it. There are so few so-called respectable jobs open to women, and men assume that we are born with a maternal instinct. Many of them assume that it is our only talent, our only fate, to be a mother, or failing that, to care for someone else's children.

'But you're quite wrong,' she continued, 'if you're thinking I resent being forced to earn my living as I do. It is the other women I feel for, those who believe they have no choice since expectations of women are so ridiculously low. *That* I resent. For myself, from an early age I have enjoyed teaching little ones.'

'But you have opted to work for private families rather than in a school since you came to Edinburgh.'

'No, since before that. The school mistress was a lovely woman with the patience of a saint called Miss Lomond. It was she who suggested that I become a governess rather than a teacher. I was too young, you see, to be given any more responsibility, and the pay for such a junior position, for a woman, was not enough to support me. I had my stipend, but Miss Lomond pointed out that since I had no idea where it came from I would be foolish to rely on it.'

'That was very far-sighted of her.'

'Far more than I realised at the time.' Her smile faded, but she gave herself a wee shake. 'Sadly, like many middle-aged women from a respectable background with no desire to find a husband, Miss Lomond spoke from experience. Like me, she had had an allowance—from her brother, I believe. When he married, he decided that he could not afford to continue to support her as well as his family. I owe her a great deal.'

'Are you still in touch?' It was unlikely, but one thing I'd always wondered was why no one had made any attempt to have her released or even to visit her in the institution.

'She died ten years ago, of typhus. Now, Mr Sutherland, I've told you a great deal more than you are entitled to know, so I would appreciate it if you ceased to interrogate me as if I was one of your suspects.'

She jumped to her feet and set off at a pace along the path. I hurried after her, noting that at least she was not headed for the exit gate. That allowance of hers had been used to pay her keep in those places where the man who administered it had had her locked up. Even if she'd wanted to claim it after her escape she couldn't have, without giving away her whereabouts.

Did she know who it was that was responsible for her incarceration? It was one of the many things I still didn't know about Marianne Little. There were so many gaps, and I wasn't overly sure which ones mattered. I'd telegraphed my employer to let him know I'd found his relative, but I hadn't heard back from him yet.

I caught up with Marianne—I simply couldn't think of her as Mrs Crawford now. 'It is my turn to interrogate you,' she said. 'Tell me why you became a policeman—aside, I mean, from your enthusiasm for asking questions.'

'Oh, that's simple, I followed in my father's footsteps.'

'Really?' She stopped beside a massive tombstone with

a weeping marble cherub perched on top of it. 'But I am sure you told me he was from the Highlands?'

'They were short of numbers to police Glasgow, back in the day. He was a Highlander from the Isle of Harris, my da—*m'aither.* He was twenty-one when he came to Glasgow, and Gaelic was his native language. He was well built, like myself, and he was ambitious, and like I said, the authorities were desperate as the streets were getting out of control. He worked bloody—he worked hard. He was not long without English, he was clever, and he was good at his job, but he was always a teuchter, a Highlander who had come to Glasgow to put boots on his feet. He never made it past sergeant in twenty-odd years' service.'

'And yet you followed him into the police force?'

'It was all I ever wanted to do. I joined the Edinburgh force, though. A different city, and decades on from my da's time. I had it easier than him, but whenever I stepped out of line, I had the fact that I was a Weegie thrown in my face.'

'And did you step out of line often?'

'I was always on the side of justice.'

She laughed drily at that. 'As defined by you, and not the law?'

'That's one way of looking at it. It's a question of—of interpretation. I didn't think it was our job to lock up the people that the good citizens of Edinburgh would prefer to be invisible. Is a person struggling to make ends meet a vagrant? Is a drunk man necessarily a criminal? Just because a young woman's out on the streets after dark, does that make her a prostitute? Don't get the idea that I was the only officer who thought that way, we chose our battles, and there were a lot of grey areas between the right and the wrong side of the law.'

'I'm willing to bet you were a minority, however. Few people look beyond what they have been taught to see.'

She spoke bleakly. It took me a moment to understand the connection she must have made, with the upholders of law on the streets, and the upholders of law in that damned institution. She'd been a school teacher and a governess, and then she'd been labelled something else entirely. Now she was a governess again, and just as she was starting to recover from her years of incarceration and settle into that life, she was going to discover that she was another person altogether. It made my mind whirl, just thinking about it all, and I'd known the tale for a good few weeks now. I thanked the stars that the Marquess had as good as gagged me. If I'd lumbered her with everything I knew about her, she'd have collapsed under the weight of it.

'You're miles away,' Marianne—Mrs Crawford!—said, dragging me from my thoughts. Again.

'I was thinking about what you said.' Not exactly a lie, that. 'About people making assumptions, not looking beyond what they're expecting to see. It's easy to make fun of a constable on the beat as a big lump of brawn with no brain, focused on finding a drink when there's nowhere else open, and spending his nights courting chambermaids, but it's a hard and difficult job. You have to be as tough as the men you're policing.'

'You mean you were violent?' she asked me, her tone indicating disbelief that I found reassuring rather than insulting.

'I mean we faced violence. "Fists, feet and teeth" is what we were told to look out for. The teeth belonging to dogs, mostly but not always. I was forced to defend myself on occasion,' I added, because I felt the need to be entirely honest with her to make up for not being completely open, 'but I swear I never did any more than that.'

She gave me one of her looks, making me feel she was picking through my thoughts for the truth. I held her gaze, and it turned out to be the right thing to do, for after a moment she nodded, satisfied, and I felt that I'd passed a test. It made me wonder though, what she knew herself of physical violence. I couldn't bear the idea of it, as if being locked up hadn't been enough of a trial.

I wished then, fervently, that she'd trust me, that she'd let me know her, I mean really know her, and the strength of that rocked me, for it was way beyond my remit. I wanted it for myself, not for the work I was here to do. I started walking again, to give myself a bit of time. Once again, it was she who broke the silence.

'You loved your work, despite the danger,' she said.

Another statement, not a question, and she was in the right of it. 'I loved putting things right,' I admitted. 'I still do. I never saw the point in going after those who were forced on to the wrong side of the law to survive. It was the ones who deliberately chose to make a living that way I was interested in. Turns out I had a nose for sniffing those sorts of characters out, I had the right combination of brain and brawn. I didn't use violence, I told you that, but they had to know I could if I had to. As to brain—it's mostly about knowing who to look for, where to look, as well as trusting your instincts.'

'And you were good at it?'

'Good enough to make a name for myself.'

'Success made you unpopular,' she said.

Yet another statement, I noted. She was good at this, playing me at my own game. 'There are always some who resent the success of others. I've never been the type to socialise with colleagues, so that didn't bother me.'

'What then?' she asked, her eyes intent on my face.

I could have pretended not to understand her, or brushed her off, but I didn't want to, even though I'd never talked about what I felt about any of it before. Not even when I was pushed to. 'My cases were picked up in the press, the sensationalist ones at first, that report trials with lots of lurid detail. For some reason, they cottoned on to the fact that my name came up a few times, and they made something of that.'

'You were famous!'

I swore vehemently, fortunately in the Gaelic. 'I got a public reputation that I'd rather not have had, and that wasn't fair either, for there were many good men solving crimes in the city. I could have well done without it. All I wanted to do was get on with the job I loved.'

'So what went wrong?'

'The public, the press, the great and the good like it when you catch criminals, provided they come from a criminal class. They don't like it when you try to tell them that their friends and neighbours might be criminals too—and that's what I found when I started asking questions. However what's done is done and there's nothing I can do about it.'

I could feel her watching me. It made me uncomfortable. Even though she couldn't possibly read my actual thoughts, she was uncommonly good at sensing my feelings. 'I don't think you are capable of letting it go,' she said slowly.

I sighed, for it was dawning on me that she was right. 'It's not what I'm here for.'

'No, you have another case now that you can't talk about.'

We'd talked about it plenty, though she didn't know it,

and she'd given me a great deal to think about. 'Not yet,' I said, hedging.

'How long do you think it will keep you here in the city?'

'It can't take too much longer.' We had stopped walking again, though I hadn't noticed. We'd come almost full circle round the perimeter of the main burial grounds. I could see the gates in the distance. How much longer? Was it fair of me to keep what I knew to myself, even though that was what I'd been instructed to do?

I genuinely felt as if I was on the horns of a dilemma. On the one hand, she had a right to know. On the other, to know what, while the question of her inheritance was yet to be decided? On the one hand, she had a family and a name. On the other was what the world would make of it all. If all that was doing my head in, what was it going to do to her?

And in the meantime, there was the fact that I didn't want to think about it any more, not for now. The difficulty was, when I looked into those eyes of hers, and I stood close enough to smell the soap she used, but not nearly as close as I wanted to be, I wanted time to go to hell, and the job I was here to do, along with it. I wanted something more than the life I had, working, eating sleeping, happy to be a lone wolf. Looking at her, what I felt was terribly lonely.

It threw me. I didn't know what to do or to say, so I just stood there looking at her, with doubtless half at least of what I was longing for written on my face. And she just stood there too, looking back at me.

A clock began to chime. It must have come from the orphanage. We both started. 'We'd better get back,' I said.

'I had better go home,' she said at the same time.

And we left it at that, though neither of us wanted to. I knew that for certain.

Chapter Ten

Marianne

Edinburgh—
Wednesday 8th August 1877

The day started as it always did, with the horrible rude awakening, the cold sweats, clammy skin, the terror so all-consuming that I dare not open my eyes. Then the slow creeping in of reality. The Grassmarket view. Flora. Dressing. Breakfasting. As I stood just inside the close, preparing to take my first steps outside, I looked for him standing in the doorway of the coffee shop with his mug in his hand. Rory Sutherland beginning his day by looking out for me to begin mine.

I did not wave or nod or go over to talk to him, but if he had not been there I would have been disappointed. He made me feel not alone. Wanted? Of course I was valued by the mothers who employed me and by the children I cared for, but this was different. He wanted me for myself, not for what I could give him. That sounds strange, but it's what I sensed from him. What I felt for him.

I had dreamt of Rory Sutherland. Deep in the night before my usual nightmares took over, I had dreamt of him. Of us. I dreamt of the heat of his flesh, slick with sweat, merging with mine. His mouth. His tongue. His hands. I dreamt of the shuddering, clenching, thrill of him sliding inside me. I dreamt of my fevered response, so different from my daytime self, urging him on, urging myself on. I dreamt of the confidence of his touch and of mine. Knowing that what we did was what the other wanted. The certainty of it. And the pure, utter delight of letting go.

A sharp cry, a hand on my arm yanked me out of my daydream and back to the side of the road and saved me from walking straight into the path of a horse-drawn tram on Princes Street. I cried out, pushing the hand away, horrified at my own lapse. My saviour was a man, a perfectly harmless complete stranger who was more frightened by my narrow escape than I was. Muttering a rudimentary apology and my thanks, I hurried across the thoroughfare, thrown that I had so easily abandoned my customary caution. Was it really so necessary after all this time? Perhaps not, but I looked over my shoulder again before continuing, slowing to my usual measured stride.

My thoughts drifted back to last night. It was a dream, wish fulfilment, the product of my own suppressed desire, nothing more. Yet it had been so intimate, so intensely felt. I don't have visions, though that was how my insights have been described by some. I see what others don't, though they could if they would try harder. I see through lies and I understand acute emotions.

On occasion this led to something like a dream unfolding in my head, as if my mind was putting it all together into a story for me. The pictures were not always accurate. Sometimes they were what might happen, possibilities rather than certainties. That's what made me susceptible to being branded a liar, when they were used as evidence against me. All I ever wanted was to help people make better choices. If only I had been as perceptive when it came to myself, but I'd had no inkling, not until it was too late. I thought myself infallible. How wrong I was proven to be.

But last night was simply a dream, nothing more. A dream that had awoken a yearning, craving, longing, to have what I had dreamt happen for real. Or rather, it was Rory Sutherland who had awoken that feeling, and now it wouldn't go away. I tried to banish him from my thoughts, tried to calm my mind and cool my body, but had only part succeeded by the time I arrived at Queen Street. My reception at the front door, however, abruptly completed the task.

'Mrs Crawford! Thank heavens.' Mrs Oliphant herself beckoned me from the top of the stairs as soon as I set foot in the marble-tiled reception hall. I followed her into the main bedchamber, where she closed the door behind us and sank down on a *chaise longue*. 'I fear the baby is coming early.'

I untied my cloak and laid it on the bed. 'Have you sent for the midwife?'

'Not yet.' She laid her hand on her swollen abdomen, wincing. 'I wanted to be prepared. Oh, Mrs Crawford, do you think it's a boy? My husband will be so disappointed if it is another girl, when we already have three daughters and only one son.'

My heart sank at her plaintive tone. I could not know whether the baby was a girl or a boy, but I did know that if the child was female, this was not news my employer wished to hear. I sat down on the *chaise longue* beside her. 'You will know soon enough. Boy or girl, you should be preparing yourself for its entry into the world, not fretting about how your husband will receive the child. I will have one of the footmen send for the midwife.'

'Yes, yes, please do so.' Mrs Oliphant, to my relief, regained some control over herself. 'Do you think all will be well?'

'You have no cause to imagine otherwise.' I could not alter the outcome here, and my telling her anything at all would not help to prepare her for whatever nature had in store for her. 'You have had four perfectly healthy births, Mrs Oliphant.'

'I know, but I am forty next month, and this may be my last chance to give my husband the second son he desires so much. But you are right, of course.' She broke off as the pain swept over her, squeezing my hand tightly until it passed. 'You're right,' she said weakly. 'I will know one way or another in a few hours. If you will be so good as to summon my maid, Mrs Crawford.'

'And the children? The plan is for your sister is to take them temporarily, isn't that correct?'

'Yes, but she's not expecting them for at least another two weeks, when you were to take two weeks to yourself. What shall I do?'

'Leave it with me. I will send a telegram.' I gently pushed her back down on the *chaise longue*. Sweat had broken out on her pale brow. Her pains were coming worryingly fast. I rang the bell for her maid and hurried downstairs, calling for one of the footmen.

It felt like a very long day, though I finished early once I had seen the children off with their aunt. All four of them were excited to be going to Portobello and the seaside, heedless of the reason for their unexpected holiday. Mrs Oliphant, like all of the well-to-do mothers who employed me, had made every effort to disguise her condition, it being thought vulgar to appear pregnant, and indecent to talk of the origins of their progeny. The Oliphant children would doubtless be informed, when they returned from the seaside, that a little sister or brother had been delivered by the stork or found under a gooseberry bush.

The weather had held fair all week. It was a pleasant late afternoon when I walked home, and I decided to enjoy a moment in the sunshine, taking a seat in Princes Street Gardens. I don't allow myself to remember the past, for it was too painful, but the encounter with poor Mrs Oliphant had upset me. It shouldn't have, I knew better than anyone that men wield the power in this world and dictate what we should feel and when. I had bowed to convention, once upon a time, willingly. I persuaded myself that I wanted what he wanted. He wanted it so very ardently, or so I believed, and I had never felt wanted before, for myself alone. I trusted him, and I trusted what I sensed from him. Desire. Need. I detected no sense of danger, no sense of his treachery until it was too late. Far, far too late.

Chapter Eleven

Marianne

Five years previously

I had been locked up for nearly three years, initially in a small asylum in York from which I tried to escape, after which I was transferred to this enormous institution in the Scottish Borders. I had attempted to escape from here too, and lost the few liberties I had as a result. Of late, I had changed my tactics, trying to reconcile myself to the version of myself they presented to me. I tried to persuade myself that I was the person they claimed I was, in order to be able to set out on the journey they wished me to take, towards recovery. But buried deep inside me was a small, resistant core. My mind was not unhinged. I was not insane.

The doctor who had been newly assigned to my case was also new to the post of Physician Superintendent to the asylum. He was younger than those who had analysed, examined and pontificated about me in the past, one of those eager men whose good looks and good birth have instilled in them a confidence in their own abilities and charm that was often misplaced.

He set about measuring my head with his metal callipers without any preliminaries, contorting my neck and shoulders to ease his endeavours as if I were a life-sized doll stuffed with straw. When I protested, he seemed taken aback to hear me speak, and when I asked him to explain what on earth he was doing, he looked even more surprised. His ego and his enthusiasm led him to do as I bid him, however. He was without guile, but weighted with prejudice.

'The science of phrenology allows us to understand the workings of the mind,' he said pompously. 'From my readings of your skull, it is clear to me that you are not naturally inclined to evil. Though your nature is undoubtedly degenerate, it is not vicious. Rather, it is the sensual side of your brain which dominates and has contributed to your moral decline.'

This was so different from any past explanations I had been given, that I struggled to comprehend what he was saying. 'What has what you refer to as the sensual side of my brain got to do with my being locked up?' I asked baldly.

'Everything! I admit my approach is not conventional, or not yet, at least,' the doctor said, looking pleased to be able to expound. 'Let us consider your case history, Miss—er, Miss Little. You claimed to have visions of the future.' He drew the thick folder that documented my history in that place towards him, and flicked back through the pages. 'If we disregard the more trivial allegations, it came down to three main incidents. There was the woman you claim to have "saved" from marrying a bigamist.'

'He *was* a bigamist!'

'He always denied that, and the fact is, he did not marry the woman you claim to have saved.'

'He would have done, had I not intervened.'

'Then there was the more disturbing case of the illegitimate child...'

I ceased to listen as he droned on. I had tried countless times since my committal to make them understand what really happened in each instance, but the 'truth' that had been documented and used as evidence against me, the truth as presented by the man who betrayed me, his version of the truth always prevailed. My dossier proclaimed that I believed I could prophesy, and that I had used my prophesies vindictively. I could do no such thing.

The natural powers of intuition and deduction that I had had since I was a child had been turned into lunacy. My pitiful attempts to redress the balance of power, to arm vulnerable women with facts, to allow them to make better choices, had been translated as the vicious rantings of a madwoman. It would have been pointless to waste my breath attempting to defend myself again, and so I remained silent, staring at a point over the top of the doctor's head.

He was too absorbed in expounding his theory to notice my lack of response, or more likely he didn't care. 'I see from my predecessor's notes that you have lately been less resistant to the notion that these visions of yours were a figment of your imagination. That is proof that the regime here has tempered your mind somewhat,' the doctor said. He stroked his callipers as he spoke, as if they were a much-loved pet. The change in his tone alerted me. I started to listen again.

'The problem we have, however, is getting to the *root cause,'* he continued. 'Until we know that, we cannot risk releasing you, lest you lapse into believing you can foretell again, do you understand me?'

I prayed that I did not, but my stomach began to churn

in fear. I had assumed that if I continued with my charade of compliance and acceptance, I would eventually be deemed cured and then released, but this man appeared to be redrawing the rules, setting up new obstacles. I was so tired, so deeply humiliated, I was not sure I had the will to fight on.

'Do not despair.' The doctor misread my expression, putting aside his callipers to pat my hand. 'I believe, Miss Little, that I do understand the root cause, and shall be lauded when I am proved right. My analysis of your lunacy has shown to me that at the heart of these visions you claim to have, is a challenge to the sanctity of marriage.'

At the heart of these insights of mine was a desire for justice. The women I had helped, or tried to help, were being used, abused, lied to, robbed of their wealth, or in one case a child. 'I have no idea what you are talking about,' I said.

'Let me put it in simple terms. Your skull, Miss Little, tells me you have an overly developed sensual nature. This is something which has been overlooked. Though the evidence is there, it was misinterpreted.'

'What do you mean? What evidence?'

'The prophesy you made, that the man you claimed to have been your betrothed, would—let me see, yes, I have it here, "be the death of you".'

Francis. A wave of nausea made me feel faint. I pinched my nails into the tender flesh of my wrist. Pay attention!

'Now clearly, it was no prophesy, unless you are a ghost.' The doctor laughed at his own feeble joke. 'Until now, the main focus of your treatment has been to show you that these prophesies of yours were a figment of your imagination, but it is the content that interests me.

'You elected upon this unfortunate man as the answer to your dreams. You persuaded yourself that the feelings generated by your fevered imagination and overheated brain were reciprocated. The sensual nature which I have detected with my callipers, took hold of you. You could have what you had always wanted, a husband, a child. Then, when he rejected you, when he tried, in the most gentlemanly way, to refute your claim on him, your madness persuaded you that he was trying to kill you. Do you see?'

'I never thought he would murder me. That's not what I said.' Francis had told me he loved me. I thought I loved him. I was convinced he wanted me, convinced of his desire for me, else I would never have given myself so willingly. In the aftermath, for those fleeting few moments, he let his guard down and I sensed his true feelings. If I married him, I knew he would be the death of me. Not literally, but spiritually. As his wife, my life would be lost.

I had tried to explain this countless times. Two years in this hellish place had taught me to keep my mouth shut, for my words were invariably turned against me, but this was too much. 'Francis wanted to marry me,' I said, which was one fact I had never doubted. Not even now. 'I didn't make that up. I wasn't deluded. He was desperate to marry me, in fact. He was devastated when I told him I wouldn't marry him.'

Also true, and one of the things I had never understood. I had asked myself over and over, why had he turned on me, why had he betrayed me, why he had engineered my incarceration and why he paid to keep me locked up? What was his motive? Was it humiliation? Vindictiveness? How could his passion for marrying me have turned to this?

'It was you who were devastated, Miss Little,' the doctor reprimanded me. 'The feelings you attribute to him were your own.' He spoke in the condescending tone of a man speaking to a child. They all used that tone, doctors, orderlies, nurses, but on that occasion it grated almost beyond enduring. 'You were, let me see, almost twenty-six and already past your prime child-bearing years.'

'My what?' My nausea had metamorphosed into a burning anger, but I tried desperately to control it. 'What has my age to do with anything?'

'Hysteria,' the doctor said with a smug smile. 'The result of an empty womb. All of those visions of yours are connected in some way to the institution of marriage. An institution you, a confirmed spinster, despaired of joining. It is a pity,' he continued, looking not at me but at his own notebook, 'for I believe a child may have been the saving of you, a natural release, as it were. Alas, without that outlet your passion turned poisonous. You set out to ruin the happy marriages of others with your so-called prophesies, and when you tired of that, you turned your perverted desires on an entirely innocent man.'

'Innocent! Francis wanted to marry me!' Leaping to my feet, I could no longer contain myself. 'I refused him, and as a result of that refusal, he had me locked up.'

The doctor shook his head and tutted. 'Hysteria and delusion. We have our work cut out, I fear.'

'I am not hysterical. I am not delusional.' My voice rose with each exclamation, but I couldn't stop myself. 'He would have been the death of me. I am dying now, in this place.'

'That is quite enough, Miss Little. Listen to yourself. Have you any idea how ridiculous you sound, claiming that a perfectly respectable man wanted to kill you?'

'Why don't you listen! I didn't say he wanted to kill me, I said he would be the death of me.'

'And here you are, alive and large as life.'

'I am barely alive, thanks to him. Because I didn't marry him,' I said, catching my breath, sounding sullen to my own ears. A child sticking to a lie. But it wasn't a lie. When I refused him, he was beside himself. I was terrified and utterly taken aback by his white-faced fury. That was when my conviction took hold. When he left without laying a hand on me, I collapsed, and did not move for hours.

When I awoke and found myself alone, I thought him truly gone, I thought I had saved myself, but when he returned and instigated my committal, I realised my mistake. I had trusted him completely. I had confided in him, told him what no one else knew of my attempts to help people, of my ability to read them. And he used all of it against me.

The doctor, utterly indifferent to the anguish he had stirred up, was putting his callipers away in a leather case. 'Now, if you will control yourself, I will inform you of my treatment plan. Your case is more advanced than I had thought, but I am still of the opinion that my diagnosis is correct. I shall make my reputation if I can cure you.'

I was shaking, tears streaming down my face, but I forced myself to listen to his plans for me, all the time my mind racing. I would not waste any more time wondering why Francis had taken such a vicious revenge on me. What was clear to me now was that I had been right in a very different sense from what I'd imagined. I thought I had saved myself by refusing to marry him, but I was wrong. If I did not escape this place I would die none the less, either from the treatments or of despair. I would not let it come true. It was a warning, and I would heed it.

'Hysteria,' the doctor droned on. 'Thinning of the blood.

A cooling diet. Isolation to inure you to your cooled passions and empty womb. I do not believe it will come to surgery.'

'Surgery!'

'A most radical solution, and a last resort, for though it will definitely cure you, you may not survive. Hydrotherapy however, ice baths—yes, they might be of great value. Now, you have taken up a great deal more of my time than I expected, but I am confident that I have made progress. In time, a few years perhaps, when we are sure you are past the age where your womb is functional, then your release can certainly be considered. For myself, I have high hopes that my innovative work on you will assist in resolving many similar cases.' He smiled as if I should find that some sort of comfort.

'I shouldn't be here. You have no right to hold me. I demand you release me. I demand...'

He opened the door and the orderly who had been waiting outside took my arm. 'She may require a sedative tonight,' the doctor told him, though I was too faint with horror to require anything but to be supported back to my cell and left alone.

Days passed, and I continued to act out the torpor I was no longer feeling. I appeared to the staff languid, lethargic, co-operative, but inside, a fire was burning. I was not mad, therefore I could not be cured. What's more, I didn't want to be cured. I would not be the *case* that made my new doctor's reputation. I was determined that no matter how long it took me, I would escape the institution and the treatments forced upon me and I would disappear for ever from the clutches of the man who had had me locked up. All I needed was the opportunity.

Chapter Twelve

Rory

Edinburgh—
Wednesday 8th August 1877

The weather had returned to its usual miserable version of a Scottish summer, with a mizzle of rain drifting down. Every now and then the clouds would thin enough for the sun to make an effort to shine, long enough to make the cobblestones steam, and get your hopes up that it might win through, before the rain closed in again. I drank my coffee and pondered my next steps regarding the issue of Marianne—I'd given up completely trying to call her Mrs Crawford.

Sunday had unsettled me. I'm used to being on my own. I *prefer* my own company to anyone else's. Not on Sunday though. I hadn't wanted the day to end. And the things I'd told her, ordinary things about myself, but it hadn't only been facts. I'd talked of my feelings, and I'd told her a lot more than I'd meant to. Nothing that mattered, save that it did, because I never talked like that. It was one of the accusations that Moira was forever levelling at me—that I kept my own counsel on everything.

Moira! Now where had that come from? More than likely she still lived here in the city, which was something that ought to have occurred to me before now. I hoped she was married with a family, for it's what she had wanted. I hoped she was happy, to make up for the misery I'd caused her. I hadn't thought about her in years, which proved she was in the right of it when she ended things between us. Talking to Marianne had raked up a whole raft of memories I had no wish to be lumbered with. Maybe it was unfair of me to blame Marianne. Perhaps it was this city.

On Sunday, I'd put the fact that I shouldn't be here to the back of my mind, which was easy enough to do, far too easy, when I was with her. On Monday, I decided to take myself off to Portobello, think things over, untangle what was important for the case, and what mattered only to me. Even though the seaside had not the bustle of the weekend, there were plenty of women and their weans and their nannies or governesses or nurses or whatever the devil they were. The families who decamp out of the city to their big summer houses during the week, for the men must still go about their important business in the town. Would Marianne be part of the entourage if her current employer headed for the seaside? I still knew so little of her present life. Did that matter? To me it did.

Watching the waves creep up over the broad, damp yellow sand on Portobello beach, I'd let myself think about Marianne in exactly the way I'd told myself I wouldn't. I wanted her. Not in that way—or not only in that way! I wanted to get close to her. I wanted something I'd never wished for from a woman before. A friend? No, not that. A companion? That sounded far too staid and platonic. I didn't want platonic, even though that's all I could have.

I didn't know what I wanted, that's the truth, and that unsettled me all the more.

It was the waiting that was doing my head in, I decided. I wasn't used to waiting to be told what to do. On Tuesday I took another walk up the Crags, with the city spread out beneath me from the top, New Town, Old Town, all the way to Portobello where I'd been yesterday, and over to the other side of the Forth, and the East Neuk of Fife. Standing on the edge of one of the cliffs, I could trace the location of the many crimes I'd solved, including the ones that had made my name.

The view was like a map of my career as a policeman, the station, my old digs, the narrow, meandering streets of the Old Town where poverty and crime lived cheek by jowl, the wide boundary that was Princes Street and the gardens, the organised grid of the New Town, where I'd been employed privately when I was off duty to solve the crimes that never made it to the police.

It was a clear day, so I could see the sprawl of the docks at Leith where I'd found the body that put an end to my career here. All the old bile came flooding back before I could stop it. I'd been kidding myself, thinking I'd put it behind me. I'd been kidding myself, thinking I'd got over the shame of it, the sheer bloody pain of being exiled from the city I loved, from the work I'd loved and done so well. Too well for some.

It was the injustice of it that really stuck in my craw, when I let myself start thinking about it again. A dead woman whose murder was not even acknowledged, dead because she was somehow embroiled in something that the great and the good wanted kept hidden. No, I wasn't over it. I hadn't put it behind me, even though I knew that

I was teetering on the brink of ending up as she had, just for being here.

I'd walked away once. I could walk away again, I told myself. I was here for another case, and I didn't have the time to dally on resolving that old one. Not only was I risking my neck being here in Edinburgh, I was being paid good money to get the Marquess's case done and dusted. My reputation—the one I'd made for myself in the last seven years, with sheer hard graft—depended on my doing what I'd been employed to do.

And there was the rub. I was being employed to wait while Lord Westville tried to sort out the legal tangle, which left me too much time on my hands. Time to think about the old case. Time to think about Marianne. Time I could be using doing what I was most inclined to do, which was get to know her. Which was why I had tried to stay away from her.

Though I couldn't stay away from her entirely. I kept an eye out for her. Wednesday morning found me drinking coffee in a tavern in the Grassmarket. The woman Marianne called Flora came in and ordered her usual breakfast of bread, cheese and ale. She was a pretty lass, though she wouldn't be for much longer. Work such as she did would take its toll, one way or another. What chance had she to make a better life for herself? It had always been a sticking point with me back in the day, the way women like her were treated, but I'd never thought too seriously about what else they could do to survive. I'd never thought myself fortunate, simply because I'd been born a man and not a woman.

'There are so few so-called respectable jobs open to women.'

Marianne's words stuck with me, calling me out as thoughtless. For women like young Flora over there, falling asleep over her breakfast, there was plenty of work of the menial kind, but very little that would make any sort of decent living. If matters did get resolved, and Marianne had her inheritance, the last thing she'd do with it was set herself up in the lap of luxury. She was the daughter of a marquess, but she wouldn't play the lady, I was willing to bet. She'd go her own road. I'd like to see that.

That brought me up short again. It was none of my business what she did. I had no business in being interested in her. More than interested! I finished up my coffee and was on the brink of leaving, thinking that I'd catch her up as she walked to work, when *he* walked into the tavern.

I swore under my breath, for I recognised him straight away. He stood there in the doorway, surveying the room as if he owned it, which for all I knew he might well, by now. Judging by his clothes, Billy Sinclair had obviously gone up in the world since I last encountered him at the High Court, where he'd been in the public gallery for the trial of the docker who ran a very successful gang of thieves.

I'd suspected at the time that Billy was the brains behind them, and his appearance on the day confirmed it for me. There hadn't been time to follow up on that one though. Only a week later, I'd been giving my marching orders.

Billy sauntered over, stopping at Flora's table to drop a coin on to it—a coin that looked to me like silver. With a sinking feeling, I realised I'd been caught out. Billy, pulling up a chair to sit down beside me, nodded in confirmation. 'Katy over there has her head screwed on,' he said. 'She's planning her retirement from her current profession, if you know what I mean, and I'm her pension.'

The proprietor appeared with a cup of coffee and a bottle

of whisky. 'Just a splash,' Billy said, waiting for the man to return to his counter before addressing me. 'Mr Sutherland. I can't tell you how sorry I am to see you here.'

'Billy.' I smiled tightly, my mind racing. 'You're looking well.'

'I'm doing well enough,' he said. 'It's Mr Sinclair these days, but you can call me William.'

'What is it you want from me, William?'

'Straight to the point. I always respected you for that, Mr Sutherland.' He took another sip of his coffee laced with whisky. 'I'm here to give you a friendly warning. I don't know what it was you really did to get yourself in the bad books. I never believed what they put in the papers about you. Taking bribes!' He rolled his eyes. 'As if.'

'Thank you for the vote of confidence.'

He grinned. He had come up in the world, but he'd lost a few more teeth in the process. '*I* know you were set up. I don't know *who* was behind it, though I could take a good guess. Thing is, Mr Sutherland, seven years isn't long enough to make this city safe for you. You shouldn't be here.'

'I don't need you to tell me that, William.'

He laughed shortly. 'That's what I thought to myself when I was told you were back. He's too smart for that, I thought to myself. So he must have a good reason.'

'Is that what you're here to find out? Or are you here to find out for someone else?'

He bristled. 'I don't take orders from anyone these days. I came here out of the goodness of my heart, to give you a friendly warning.'

'It's news to me that you have a heart. Is that something else you've got your hands on while I've been away?'

'Very funny. I'm being serious. You rattled cages you shouldn't have rattled. They framed you, I know that, they dragged your name through the mud, but they left you with your heart beating. See, I happen to know that unlike me, you do have a heart. I reckon you'd like to keep it beating, too.'

'I appreciate that, William, and believe me, I share the same goal, but I've business here to conclude.'

He glowered. 'I hope you're not going to go about lifting up any old stones. Unfinished business, so to speak, especially if it involves me. Things here are ticking along nicely, since you left. We all keep our noses out of other people's business, and we all know when to keep our mouths shut. Something you never did learn, did you?'

'What was it you just said about keeping your nose out?'

He held his hands up as if in surrender, but his face hardened. 'Have it your own way, but don't say I didn't warn you. I'll give you this for nothing, because you and I go back a long way, and I owe you a few. As far as I know, I'm the only one who knows you're here. How long that will last I can't say, but no one will hear it from me. I'd be a bit less regular in your habits though, if you get my drift.' Billy scraped his chair back and got to his feet. 'Good luck to you, Mr Sutherland. I hope you don't need it.'

I paid for my coffee and hurried to the doorway, but there was no sign of him in the bustle of the Grassmarket. No one tells me what to do, I thought to myself, while at the same time thinking, I'd be an eejit to ignore what he'd said.

Back at my digs, there was a telegram from Lord Westville informing me to await further instructions. Fortunately the instructions in the form of an express letter had also arrived. Now that he knew his cousin was alive and unwed, the Marquess was determined to secure her inheritance. The process was complex, but would be complete within the next two weeks. He was, he assured me, as determined as I to bring Eliot to account, and was taking pains to ensure the man was fully occupied with estate matters, and under the impression that he was valued. In the meantime, I was to ensure his cousin came to no harm.

Chapter Thirteen

Marianne

Edinburgh—
Wednesday 8th August 1877

Those vile memories of the asylum had caught me unawares as I sat in Princes Street Gardens earlier that day. Usually I never allow them to creep up on me in the daylight. Was there a reason for that particular memory to have forced itself upon me? A reminder to trust no one? Or more specifically, not to trust Rory?

Rory was not Francis, the comparison was repellent, but I forced myself to compare them all the same. I had to, for the sake—literally—of my own sanity. Francis was the first and only man I had ever trusted, and that had proved a catastrophic decision. My judgement, my intuition, the tried-and-tested ability that I had relied upon my whole life had failed me.

I had trusted him with my heart and my body. I was on the brink of trusting him with the rest of my life when I finally saw through him. He betrayed me, yes, he did, but he could not have done so had I not failed myself. I had confided in him, I revealed my true self to him, and he turned it all against me.

Was I making the same mistake again, in thinking I could trust Rory? From the first, I felt I *could* trust him. With Francis—oh, I could not remember. Did I even ask myself that question? I was a different person then, singularly lacking any experience of being loved and embarrassingly ready, on reflection, to fall head over heels. Francis had desired me. He wanted to marry me. I sensed both those things so fiercely, and yet I must have been mistaken. He had kept his true, vindictive nature hidden from me until I refused to marry him and he revealed his true colours.

No, Rory wasn't like that. I felt none of that desperate need there had been from Francis, nor did I feel that I was being carried along by the force of his feelings. It was the force of my own feelings for Rory that confused me. He was an attractive man, why shouldn't I be attracted to him? But it was more than that. He listened to me—another thing that Francis had never done. He was interested in what I had to say—too interested, sometimes. He unsettled me, but not in a threatening way.

And then there was this persistent conviction I had, that I was meant to know him. I could trust him, but that didn't mean I would confide in him. I could acknowledge my attraction to him, but that certainly didn't mean I would give in to it, and I most certainly would never, ever fall in love with him or any man for that matter. So why should I not do what I believed I was meant to do, and indulge this compulsion I had for his company? My release from my duties with Mrs Oliphant for two weeks was fortuitous timing.

Having decided to surrender to my destiny, I was not in the least surprised to see Rory loitering near St Giles. I spotted him from the other side of the Lawnmarket, at the same time as he spotted me. 'I was hoping to bump into you,' he said, when I crossed the High Street to join him.

'I was hoping the same thing, though I'm not sure I wish to hold another whispered conversation inside the Kirk.'

'Nor I. It's a pleasant evening. I know somewhere close at hand where we won't be disturbed.'

He led the way down Victoria Street, and then at the head of the Grassmarket, turned left on to Candlemaker's Row and through the gate which brought us into the lower reaches of the graveyard attached to Greyfriars Kirk. Behind the walls, the noise and bustle of the city disappeared, leaving us alone in the peace of the old burial ground.

'I used to like coming here for a break when I found myself in the vicinity back in the day,' he said, leading the way along a path that led to the right. There's a spot up by the old Flodden Wall that I particularly liked. There's an odd little crypt, simply built like a stone outhouse. Trotter of Mortonhall, it says. I've often wondered who or what the family were.'

We reached the place a few moments later, and stopped to perch beside each other on one of the many overturned tombstones. Behind the walls of the cemetery some of the older tenements loomed, but inside the walls it was silent save for the birds and the rustle of the leaves in the few trees. I was angled towards him, my skirts brushing his leg. He had pulled off his hat and gloves, setting them down behind him, and was frowning down at his hands. His nails were neatly trimmed, his hands were very clean, but the knuckles were rough and scarred. 'Is life as a private detective as violent as it was as a policeman?' I asked him.

He shook his head. 'These are all old,' he said, indicating his hands. 'The people who can afford to employ me are very different from the types I was once employed to capture.'

'What sort of cases do you solve?'

'A multitude of different things, but in the end, it nearly always comes down to money. Money stolen. Money contested. Money made. Money lost. Though it's not nearly as boring as it sounds,' he added with a twisted smile. 'Usually there's a puzzle to be solved, and that's what I like. As well as putting things to rights, of course. I've an orderly mind.'

'Does your current case involve putting things to rights?'

I thought at first he wouldn't answer me, but after a moment he sighed heavily. 'I sincerely hope so.'

'Are you making good progress?'

He gave me a look I could not interpret. I had the feeling that he was on the verge of saying something, but then changed his mind. The man who solved puzzles for a living was a puzzle for me, and that, I confess, made me more determined than ever to try to understand him. 'It's been put on hold for a couple of weeks as a matter of fact,' he told me. 'There's a piece of the puzzle that needs clarifying. Until it is, the man who is paying me wants me to hold fire.'

'You find that—frustrating?' It was more of a guess than a supposition.

'A wee bit, because I don't like it when I'm having to wait on someone else doing something, but it's more—ach, I don't really like being told what to do, I suppose it's that,' he said, smiling ruefully. 'Though in this case, it makes sense.'

'But you are troubled, all the same?' I ventured, feeling on more certain ground.

'It matters. I want to get this one right. I mean, I want

to get every case right, but this one—it matters more than it should.'

'Are you worried that you will fail?'

He gave me another of those strange looks. 'I'm determined not to.'

'Is there a chance—?'

'I've said more than enough,' he interrupted, his tone making it very clear that the subject was closed. 'I don't fail. I never fail. That's why I'm in such demand.'

'You make a good living, then?' I asked, accepting the change of subject.

'More than I know what to do with, considering there's only me.'

'That might not always be the case,' I said, surprised to discover that I wasn't very keen on the idea I had mooted.

No more was he, for he shook his head vehemently. 'I'm not the marrying kind, if that's what you mean. I'm already married to my work, there's no room in my life for anyone else.'

'But what about family? You must have some?'

'None that I'm in touch with. I was an only child, and so too were my ma and my da.'

'M'aither?' I ventured.

'Not a bad attempt, but it's softer, and the "r" rolls. *M'aither.*'

I repeated the word, but with no greater success. 'Have you ever been to the Highlands?'

'Once, when I was wee, I went for a few weeks to stay on Harris with my—*m'aither's* cousins. I remember the beach, the sand like silver and the sea the colour of turquoise, with a mountain range on the horizon that was the mainland. I couldn't get my head around that, that I was looking down on Scotland. The sun shone the whole time we were there—or that's what I remember, any road. My da told me that was almost unheard of up there.'

His face had taken on a distant look. His smile had softened. Happiness warmed him, as if he was basking in the sunshine of the Highlands again. I wanted to step into that world with him. I wanted to feel the warmth of happiness make my skin glow. 'It sounds wonderful,' I said.

'There was a wee gang of us weans that played together every day. We built a fire on the beach, and cooked the biggest crabs you've ever seen in your life in an old pot filled with sea water. I hadnae a clue how to go about eating it, and they all laughed at me for trying to bite through the shell. Have you ever tasted crab? It's not a bit like fish. Sweet as a nut, it is. And mussels too, so soft, like a burst of the sea in your mouth, have you ever tried them?'

'You're making me want to.'

'Then there was the fish we caught from the end of the harbour wall. You could swim in the harbour too, the water was much warmer there, that's where I learned, but you had to be careful not to get caught out when the tide turned. That's one of the many things all the other weans knew but I didn't. I didn't know how to light a peat fire, or how to stack the stuff, or how to shear a sheep, or even the right bait for the fish, depending on what we wanted to catch. They made me feel a right eejit, a peely-wally wee runt from the city, but I learned fast. Not that I've had occasion to practise any of it since, mind.'

'It sounds idyllic, even though you were a—a peely-wally…'

'It means pale. I was wind-burned and sun-tanned by

the end of the holiday, so I stood out just as much, when I went home.'

'Why have you never gone back? You clearly loved your visit.'

His smile faded. 'School. Then work. Life got in the way. When my ma died, my da always said that we should pay another visit, but I never found the time.'

'You wish you had,' I said, though once again I didn't mean to say so aloud.

'But I didn't,' he said bitterly, 'and I try not to waste my time on what might have been. Look, Marianne, I don't know how we came to be talking about my childhood…'

Marianne. The way he said my name warmed me, though he didn't seem to have noticed the slip. Was it because I occupied his thoughts? Did he dream of me as I had of him—no! I could not allow myself to go down that path. 'I asked,' I said. 'I am interested.'

'I never talk about myself like that.'

The admission reassured me, for he loosened the guard I usually had on my own tongue. 'What did you wish to talk to me about then? You were waiting for me at St Giles. Couldn't it wait until the morning, when you take your coffee in the Grassmarket?'

To my surprise, he scowled. 'I won't be taking my coffee there in future. I've been spotted,' he added, in answer to my unasked question. 'Your Flora, whose name is actually Katy, reported me to a former acquaintance.'

'What!' Instinctively, I grabbed his arm. 'She told the police you are here? But how did she know who you are?'

'Not the police. She didn't know anything about me, save that I was a stranger and had become a regular at the tavern. She told a man called Billy Sinclair. He had his finger in a good many criminal pies during my time here, but essentially he was a thug. He's moved up in the criminal world since I left Edinburgh, though. These days, I reckon he pays others to do that aspect of his business.'

That Flora, who was actually Katy, was some sort of informer, I put to one side for later consideration. 'Did he threaten you, this man?'

'No, he had come to give me a bit of friendly advice, for old times' sake. To get out of Edinburgh, before someone else found out I was here, in other words.'

My fingers tightened around his arm. 'Mr Sutherland…'

He took my hand from his arm and enveloped it in his. 'Won't you call me Rory? I've already called you Marianne.'

So he had noticed! 'Rory.' Our eyes met, and I forgot what I was going to say. Through my skirts, I could feel his knee pressing against my leg. His head bent towards mine. My heart began to pound.

'Marianne.' With his other hand, he touched my cheek. The lightest of touches, tracing a path down to my jaw. 'I've been thinking.'

'Yes?' I leaned closer, the better to hear what he was going to say.

'What is it about you?' His fingers fluttered down my neck, settling on my nape, at the gap between my gown and my hair. 'You make me say things—tell you things—talk to you.'

I could feel his breath on my cheek. 'I've been thinking about that too.' My body was urging me closer, an irresistible force was tugging at me, so that when I spoke our mouths were almost touching. 'This is going to sound odd, but I feel we were meant to meet for some reason.'

'It doesn't sound odd.' His lids were heavy. His breath

was like mine, rapid, shallow. 'I mean it does sound odd, but it doesn't feel odd.'

I gave in to the temptation to place my free hand on his cheek, smoothing the palm of my glove over his skin, my heart beating faster as my touch made him shudder. 'I have two weeks' holiday, as of today.'

He groaned softly. 'I wish you hadn't told me that.'

'Don't you want me to…?'

'Oh, there's lots of things I would like you to do, Marianne.'

He said my name so softly. He leaned into me, closing the last tiny little gap between us. I felt the warmth of his lips on mine, the merest brush, and then he took my hand and leaned back. I was crushingly disappointed, but he didn't let go, unbuttoning my glove, peeling it back, finger by finger, and I forgot everything save the anticipation of what he would do next.

When he lifted my hand to his mouth, I almost cried out my pleasure at the softness of his lips on my palm, the gentlest of kisses, my fingers drawn into his mouth, relishing the heat that shimmered from his touch, making my stomach clench. I could see my wanting reflected in his eyes. I could feel my own yearning reflected back from him. What on earth was I doing? I asked myself, but I didn't really care.

Save that he had obviously asked himself the same question. He let me go reluctantly, but he let me go. 'We simply can't be doing this!' he said firmly.

Chapter Fourteen

Rory

Edinburgh—
Wednesday 8th August 1877

We simply can't be doing this!

Talk about an understatement! But by the sun and the stars, I wanted to. It took me all my willpower to let her go and to get to my feet, pulling on my gloves, as if they would somehow keep me safe. 'I'm sorry,' I said, my voice sounding as shaky as I felt. 'I truly didn't mean that to happen. I can't be letting that happen again.'

Marianne looked as flustered as I'd ever seen her, which was no consolation whatsoever. Her cheeks were flushed. There was a look in her eyes that told me she was as carried away as I had been, and as taken aback. Heaven help me, what I wanted to do was put my arms around her and kiss her and forget all about all the very, very good reasons why that was impossible. 'I'm sorry.'

I could see her visibly changing, pulling herself together, as she put her gloves back on. 'There is no need to apologise. It is not as if you forced yourself on me.'

'I would never…'

'I am aware of that.'

She stood up, shaking out her skirts. She was wearing the green dress again. The colour suited her. This was hardly the time for telling her so.

'All the same,' I said, because I couldn't get over how far I'd strayed from my own rules, 'I didn't mean to…'

'Nor did I, but I did!' She drew a breath, then continued in a softer voice. 'Forget what happened just now, it doesn't matter. I mean it's not relevant to why—to what I was trying to say.'

'You've lost me. No, wait. You mean when you said we were meant to meet?'

'Yes.'

We had met because I was looking for her. I couldn't say that, and even if I could have, it wouldn't have been completely true. I deal in facts, but I couldn't deny I had an inkling of what she was talking about. 'I felt it too, I'll admit, but I'm not sure where this conversation is going, Marianne.'

She wrinkled her nose and furrowed her brow. It made me want to kiss her, so I took a couple of steps away from temptation to look at the inscription on one of the nearby gravestones. *Here lies the mortal remains of...* The date was 1752. It was adorned with a skull and cross bones.

'They were more honest, back then,' Marianne said, joining me. 'Not a weeping angel or a grieving cherub in sight.'

'My thoughts exactly.'

'Really?'

She raised her brow. Just the one. I wished she wouldn't do that, I found it ridiculously alluring.

'What are you planning on doing for the next two weeks,

Rory, while your other case is in limbo? Will you remain in Edinburgh?'

'Where else would I go?' I asked, taken aback.

'I don't know, but since Edinburgh is dangerous…'

'No, no. I've no plans to go anywhere.' I was under orders to stay put. Then I remembered this morning, and Billy Sinclair's suggestion that I get out of town. 'I've been thinking about my old case.'

'Have you?' Marianne gazed at me, wide-eyed.

'I have, but I didn't mean that I was thinking of doing anything about it.'

'But don't you think that might be it? The reason we—that fate—no, I don't believe in fate—but don't you think all the same, that's why we met? I *knew* that you have not been able to forget about it, you as much as told me so on Sunday. And now you have two weeks, and I have two weeks. It is beginning to make sense.'

She smiled at me, one of those rare real smiles, the ones that reached her eyes, and her eyes were hazel that evening in the burial ground, and I wanted to kiss her again.

'Shall we walk?' I said, suiting action to words, and thinking fast. She was right, in a way. Ever since I'd come back to this city, that old scar had been itching. Even before, I'd made the connection between the unclaimed victim in that case and the victim in my current case walking beside me. Two lost women, only this one, thank the sun and the stars, was alive and kicking and very much determined she wasn't a victim. What a woman! I really admired her. Among other things.

We had come right round to the part of the graveyard that fronts the church itself. There was a bench, just on the other side of the door, and so I headed for it. If I did pick up the old case again, I could kill two birds with one stone, so to speak. Have one last go at finally finding out what had happened all those years ago, and at the same time, I could do what I'd been told to do, and keep an eye on Marianne. Which was also what I wanted to do, very much. Which rang a warning bell. Faintly, mind.

'Funnily enough,' I told her, as we sat down, 'I didn't take kindly to having Billy Sinclair warn me off this morning.'

'I gathered that.'

'Did you, now? And here was I thinking myself a man of mystery to you.'

She laughed faintly, frowning at the same time. 'You are, most of the time.'

'Not always though, clearly. You're very good at reading people, you'd make a good detective.'

'So you think I could help you, then?'

'Hang on, I didn't say…'

'But it's what you want, isn't it?'

I sighed. 'It wasn't my intention when I came here, but being back in this city made me realise how much grief that old case is still giving me. I thought I'd put it behind me. I don't think I have.' I hadn't meant to say that, but the relief of it! It shook me, I mean really shook me.

Marianne touched my hand. Glove on glove, and just for a second, not long enough for it to mean anything more than a bit of comfort, and it was. 'I want justice for her,' I said. 'The woman who was murdered. And for me, if I'm honest. Maybe justice isn't the right word. I want to find out what happened, I want to know why.'

'It's the not understanding that's the worst, isn't it? Why

me? What did I do to deserve this? And not being able to do anything about it. I know what that's like, Rory, I really do.'

I knew what she was referring to.

Why me! What did I do to deserve this!

My heart went out to her, and I couldn't say a word to let her know I understood. It wasn't only that I was under orders to keep my mouth shut for the time being, I knew, though I didn't like to admit it, that the Marquess was right. Better a whole story to tell her than half a tale. It touched me though, deeply, that she'd said that much. She understood. That touched me too. 'Thing is, Marianne, I'm not sure that I'd be able to get any further than before.'

'But if you don't try—though perhaps I shouldn't be encouraging you? How dangerous would it be, Rory?'

I tried to ask myself that, honestly. The problem was, I still had no idea who was behind what had happened all those years ago, who it was I'd be upsetting if I did resume my investigations.

'It's undoubtedly a risk,' I said, which was not a lie. 'And seven years is plenty of time for a trail to go cold. The dead body wasn't reported in the papers. All the stuff that they printed about me, that was all a smoke screen invented by someone. None if it had anything to do with what I was actually investigating.'

'You were wronged,' Marianne said, putting her hand on my arm again. 'For seven years, you've wondered why. You have the opportunity to put your mind at rest, Rory. Why wouldn't you take it?'

Her words went straight to my heart, for they were so obviously spoken from hers. She had also been wronged, and she didn't know why but she would, soon, she'd know that and so much more. My hand had wrapped itself around hers of its own accord. Our eyes were locked on each other. There was a stillness between us, as if we were scared to move. 'Marianne.' I said her name so softly, just because I wanted to say it.

'Rory,' she said.

Our lips touched. I hadn't meant them to. I hadn't meant to kiss her. I knew I shouldn't kiss her, but our lips touched, and she sighed into me when they did, and I felt my breath leaving me in a whoosh. A butterfly kiss. It took all my resolve to pull back. It was nothing, I told myself, though it wasn't.

'I can help you,' Marianne said. 'I don't know exactly how, but at least I'm a fresh pair of eyes and you've admitted yourself that I'm intuitive.' Our hands were still entwined. Our lips were still only a few inches from each other. 'Please, Rory. I'd like to—I want to.'

Two weeks, with the perfect excuse to be in each other's company. The Marquess might even approve. I couldn't have cared less about the Marquess at that moment. Two weeks with Marianne. The alarm bell sounded again, slightly more loudly this time. Was I playing with fire? But it was only two weeks. Two weeks to finally find out why someone had tried to destroy me. Marianne was right, that was the crux of it. And at the end of two weeks, she'd find out why someone had tried to destroy her. And who he was.

'You'll do it,' she said, though I'd said nothing. 'And you'll let me help you?'

I nodded slowly. 'But I'm not taking any risks, not with regard to your safety, do you understand?'

'Yes, yes.'

'No, I mean it. If I tell you something's dangerous. If I tell you not to do something. Or not to talk to someone. If

I tell you that it's not safe to stay involved, you listen and then do as you're told. Do you hear me?'

She opened her mouth to protest, no doubt to tell me she was perfectly capable of taking care of herself, but she met my eyes and thought the better of it. 'Why don't you start by telling me what happened, all those years ago?' she said.

So that's what I did. 'It began when a woman's body turned up in the docks at Leith,' I said. And that's how we decided to return to the scene of the crime the next day.

Chapter Fifteen

Marianne

Edinburgh—
Thursday 9th August 1877

The rain that morning was no more than a light drizzle, and by the time we reached the waterfront at Leith, it had all but ceased. We had taken the tram, rattling down Leith Walk from Princes Street, disembarking at Commercial Street, where we walked along towards the bridge over the Water of Leith.

It was a very different river here from the one we had followed tumbling along the banks of Dean Village. Wider, more like a canal, and emptying out into the vast complex of docks that surrounded the main basin and the harbour. I had not been here before. I had had no notion that the place, so near to the city, was so enormous.

'Stay close,' Rory said, 'and mind what I told you, keep your head down. The docks are rife with criminal activity. The chances of me being spotted by a former customer are far higher down here, which is why I've taken the precaution of changing my appearance. We'd stick out like a sore thumb otherwise.'

I was wearing my cloak with my hood pulled up. In a change from his usual understated neatness, Rory was wearing workman's boots, a rough jacket and trousers, a collarless shirt with a muffler, a cap rather than a hat, and no gloves. It ought to have looked incongruous on him, but I thought it suited him. He had not shaved, I noticed, his chin was dark with stubble, which also suited him.

I had dreamt of him again last night, my dreams even more real than before, for now I knew the softness of his lips, the warmth of his mouth. Enough to inflame my imagination. Enough to make me wake, racked with longing. Enough, looking at him then, my face shielded by the hood of my cloak, to make me want more.

We simply can't be doing this, Rory had said yesterday, though I was sure that he wanted to kiss me, kiss me properly, as much as I had wanted to kiss him. This conviction I had, that we were meant to be together had inconvenient side-effects. Was that all it was? What mattered most, and I was sure of this, was giving Rory something I would never have, peace of mind.

I would never really understand why Francis had me locked up, but yesterday it was so clear to me that Rory suffered as I did, with endlessly posing the question, *why?* If we could find the answer, what a huge relief that would be for him. The black cloud that I sensed hanging over him, the anger and the frustration would be gone. Someone had tried to destroy him. If we could discover why—oh, I so desperately wanted that for him.

So wanting to kiss him, wanting more than kisses from him, feverishly dreaming of what that would be like, must be a side-effect of my fervent longing to help. That made sense to me. Now that I understood it, I could control it.

The tingle I was feeling then, the excitement of being with him, the way I was so acutely conscious of the man beside me, that too was merely symptomatic of my fervent desire to help him.

If that manifested itself in desire for the man himself—then what if it did! It wasn't as if I was in any danger of acting on it. Fate—yes, I would credit fate with a role—had brought us together for one reason only, and we had two weeks to complete the task.

I turned my mind away from Rory to our surroundings. Behind us, Commercial Street was extremely busy, with drays, carts and carriages of all sorts jostling for position. People swarmed about, clerks with bundles of papers, dockers directing the carts in and out of the huge doors that were the entrance to the quayside, the occasional well-dressed man picking his way from his carriage to the steps of one imposing building or another. There were women too, with baskets and aprons, like everyone else rushing about their business.

'That's where all the port offices, custom house, all that sort of thing are,' Rory said. 'The commercial heart of the city. Where the money is.'

'So this case, do you think it is "all about the money" too?' I asked, following him in the opposite direction, to cross over the river.

'Somewhere along the line, it's bound to be, though I've no idea how. She was found on this side, but we'll get a better view if we cross over to the Shore. Are you sure you're wanting to do this?'

'Provided you are sure you will not be in too much danger?'

'Don't worry about me,' he said, which I knew was not an answer.

The waterside was lined with buildings, old and new, and there were a huge variety of ships, old and new, tied up alongside. Steam ships, paddle steamers, barges, and older clippers looking decidedly shabby and tired, surrounded by an army of little boats. Men were crying out to each other, we had to stick close to the buildings to avoid the endless flow of traffic, but above the noise I could smell the sea, and I could feel the salt of it on my face.

Rory's hair was wind-blown, fairer in the light down here, with streaks of gold I had not noticed before. His arms swung at his side. I hate to be held, but I wanted to take hold of his gloveless hand. I edged closer, so that my cloak fluttered against his legs.

He caught my eye, and smiled. 'You're enjoying yourself.'

'It's exciting,' I agreed, and it was, in a way I was not accustomed to. I was excited to be with him. I was excited to be out and about in a part of Edinburgh that was completely strange and new to me. I was excited by the thrill of the chase, even though we weren't chasing anyone yet, merely going back to the start of the trail, as Rory had put it.

I was excited by the prospect of helping him. I was exhilarated by his company, not being alone, not being lonely, engaged on something so very different from my usual line of work—much as I loved that. I was thrilled by the challenge of it all. My spirits lifted, and I smiled broadly at him.

He stumbled on the cobblestones. 'Have you any idea how much I want to…?'

Kiss you. Neither of us said the words, but we were both thinking them. Remembering yesterday. The kiss that was not nearly enough. We had come to a halt. Our eyes met again. I felt it again, that breathless tension, dangerous and exciting, pulling me towards him. I stood rooted to the spot.

He blinked, shook his head, started to walk again. 'Did I tell you that you've the makings of a good detective.'

I suppressed the completely irrelevant elation I felt at having my own tumultuous feelings returned, and followed his lead. 'You did. Yesterday.'

'So I did. You're good at reading people, that's what I said. You're a good judge of character. It's something I pride myself on, it's something I have to be good at in my line of work, but I like to have my judgement backed up with facts. With you it's more—more instinctive. You've a sense of whether or not people are telling the truth. Honestly, sometimes I feel like you can see right inside my head.'

'I cannot!' I exclaimed, immediately on the defensive. 'I told you yesterday that I find you almost impossible to read.'

'Most of the time, is what you said.'

'It's true. You keep your feelings closely guarded, most of the time.'

'And some of the time, with you I mean, when I should be keeping them to myself, I can't,' he said wryly. 'Though I should. I'm determined that I will.'

He was looking out at the docks, not at me, but I knew exactly what he was thinking, because I was thinking of it too. I spoke simply to break the spell. 'I have always been good at reading faces, even when I was a child. I remember one occasion when I was helping to serve tea to my foster mother's friends. I was handing round a chocolate cake, but when one of the women reached for a piece I said, no, you can't have that, you'll be sick again.

'At the time, I had no idea why everyone was embarrassed or why I was sent to my room. I presume she was expecting a child, though it may not have been that, but it's stuck in my head because I was punished so unfairly, simply for saying what was obvious to me. My foster mother accused me of listening at doors. She was never unkind to me, but she didn't like me. To use your phrase, it was all about the money for her.'

'She told you that?' Rory said, looking appalled.

I shook my head. '*I* told her that. Although she hid it well, I knew that it mattered more to her than me. She was furious.'

How could you possibly know that?

I winced, for her voice was loud and clear in my head, the first time I'd thought of that scene in years. I had said far more than I'd meant to or had ever said before. Not even to Francis had I confided this pathetic little tale. He had never shown any interest in my childhood. 'Anyway. I didn't know how I knew, but I knew and it was a very long time ago, and I don't know why I'm telling you.'

'Some people such as yourself, they're just better at piecing together what's in front of everyone's noses. I do the same, in a different way. I take all the facts I know, I add a bit of glue based on experience, and I get a picture. It's not a dark art, I don't *know* more than anyone else, but I'm better at working it out and making sense of it. I reckon you do the same, only it's not facts you use it's more what you feel from people. Would I be right?'

He was so perfectly right, I was temporarily lost for words. 'Do you find—have you ever had—has it ever got you into trouble?'

'Mostly, it's got other people into trouble. Criminals, I mean. What about you?'

I teetered on the brink of telling him. I came very close, because no one had ever understood that aspect of my character in that way, and it was such a relief, a pleasure, being understood. My intuition gave me the pieces. On occasion my sleeping mind was the glue that put them all together into a picture. It sounded so benign, yet it was those pictures that I had used to try to help people. Those pictures that I had described to Francis. And he had used those pictures, labelled them visions, and had me committed.

Horrified, I saw how close I had come to giving Rory the same ammunition. 'Why would you ask that?'

'It got you into trouble with your foster mother. I meant were there other times…?'

'We're here to try to find out why you were hauled over the coals for trying to piece together a picture of a murder, not to poke into all the incidents in the past where I have been hauled over the coals for—' I broke off, putting my hand over my mouth. What was wrong with me! I never lose my temper. I never speak without thinking! I took a calming breath. 'Your being hauled over the coals resulted in your exile from this city. The blackening of your name. A crime left unsolved. It's why we are here.'

I started to walk again, heartily regretting my outburst. Had I overreacted? This constant comparing of Rory with Francis in my head, I found it vile. Rory didn't deserve to be compared with that man, and I would happily never, ever think of Francis again. It was the institution that haunted my dreams, and my suffering there. Only since Rory had appeared had Francis also come back to haunt me.

Rory wasn't like Francis. Not even in the way he wanted

me. It was a longing that I felt from Rory, raw desire, but—but reined in, somehow, and—and sweeter? No, not that. I hadn't the words, but it was different. Or perhaps what I was actually trying to describe were my own feelings, not his. I couldn't read him when his guard was up. But when he touched me, or looked at me, when our lips had met—no, I wasn't mistaken, whatever I was feeling, so was he.

And just now, when *I* let my guard down, he hadn't derided me or mocked me. And yesterday, when I'd said that I was meant to help him, he'd accepted that. He wanted my company, he was glad of my offer of help, but would he wish either if he knew that for four years I had been incarcerated in an asylum? He was an unusual man, but I doubted there was any man unusual enough to consort with a woman who had been branded a lunatic. I had to be more careful.

'Marianne, slow down. Wait a minute.' Rory stopped at a gap between two ships on the quay. 'The spot we're looking for is over there,' he said, pointing at the opposite side. 'Do you see that inlet with the swing footbridge, just before where the main docks broaden out? It's known as the Rennie's Isle bridge. Her body was found lodged in there. Someone chose the wrong place to put her in the water.'

I shuddered. The screech of a steam train thundering past towards a much larger railway bridge further down made me jump.

'That line wasn't there in my day,' Rory said, shading his eyes to look at the engine. 'The docks it serves were only just being built. Do you see what I mean about the money that's pouring into this city?'

'It's the same in the New Town. In the three years I've been here, it has expanded at an incredible rate. It seems that every other day, a new circus or place is opened up, a new park or garden railed off. What now? Should we go over and take a closer look?'

'I don't see that we'd gain anything from it, I just wanted to remind us both what this is all about. She wasn't drowned, you know. She was already dead when they threw her in.'

'Poor woman.'

'Aye, no one deserves that fate.' He sighed, gazing over at the inlet and the little bridge. 'I wish you would trust me. You can, you know.'

'I do.'

'Then why is it you keep clamming up on me?'

I opened my mouth to contradict him, but could not.

'You can't deny it, because you can't tell a lie. It's been as clear as day to me from the start. You can dance around the truth, or you can keep something back, but you can't tell a lie. Your foster mother should have believed you when you said you didn't listen at doors, and she should have asked herself how a wee lassie in her care came to know that she wasn't actually cared for.'

'I was always treated…'

'Well enough,' he concluded for me, his lip curling. 'You deserved to be treated a lot better than that. Every wean deserves a bit of affection.'

His words brought a lump to my throat. 'You can't miss what you don't know, Rory.'

He frowned, looking deeply troubled. 'Do you ever wonder…?'

'What?'

'Nothing.' He reached towards me, then changed his mind. 'Like you said, we're not here to dig into your past, but mine. Or rather the poor woman that was found over there.'

Do you ever wonder...?

What? Better not to know. I followed the direction of his gaze, looking at the little bridge and the inlet it protected.

'She was caught up in the bridge itself, when it was swung open,' Rory said. 'I reckon whoever murdered her dumped her body in the docks over there, the big ones that were under construction at the time, and the tide moved her. She wasn't meant to be found but she was.'

'Are you sure she was murdered, Rory? It wasn't an accident, or—might she have jumped?'

'I *know* she was murdered. I'll explain later.'

'And she hadn't been missed? That's what you told me.'

'That's what got me at the time. No one cared. No one had even reported her missing.'

No one had reported me missing either. No one had wondered where I was, why I had disappeared. No one had cared enough. No, that was unfair. Those who might have cared were the women I had helped, but even had they been aware of my fate, they would have been helpless. 'You cared,' I said to Rory.

'Aye, and look what happened to me. Have you seen enough here? We're making ourselves a mite conspicuous. We'd best get a move on.'

'Must we take the tram back? The sun is out, why don't we walk back to the city and talk about our next steps?'

'Because I haven't worked out what they are, yet. But if you fancy a walk, we could head along the coast to Newhaven, it's not far. It's a wee fishing village. We'll be safe enough there.'

Chapter Sixteen

Rory

Edinburgh—
Thursday 9th August 1877

We walked back along Commercial Street, Marianne keeping a steady pace with her head down, me beside her keeping a look out just in case, though my mind was on other matters. The woman herself, specifically.

She was prickly as a hedgehog one minute, blurting out stuff she clearly didn't mean to tell me the next, and what she did tell me was making me feel like I'd been put through a wringer.

You can't miss what you don't know.

It made my guts twist, thinking of everything those words implied, and I'd come bloody close to blurting out that stupid question.

Do you ever wonder who your parents were?

Despite her avowal that she didn't care because they had given her away, I found it difficult to believe she hadn't wondered. But what was the point in stirring it up right now, when I was honour bound not to tell her what I knew, and anyway, their names weren't the point. It wasn't *who* her parents were that would matter to her, but why they didn't keep her. A dead mother was only one side of it.

What had her father been playing at? I could understand him getting someone else to care for his motherless child, but to have nothing more to do with her—that I didn't get. It didn't matter to me, I told myself for what seemed like the hundredth time, or rather it shouldn't matter. If the Marquess tasked me with the telling of the tale, I would be the bearer of facts, hopefully of good financial tidings, that was all.

Aye, right. I was getting in deep. Not too deep, not so deep I couldn't extricate myself when the time came, and I'd have to. I was committed to keeping an eye on her for the Marquess—which admittedly, I could do from more of a distance. But I'd committed to letting Marianne help me with this old case, and if I changed my mind it would look odd. What's more, I didn't want to change my mind.

Two weeks, that's all we had. I could almost hear the clock ticking, and I told myself that I was glad of it. There wasn't time, in just two weeks, for me to get myself in any deeper that I already was. Even if every moment I spent with her made me want more. Even if what I felt for her had a strength and a depth I hadn't felt before for any woman.

Two weeks wasn't going to be nearly enough with her, I felt it in my bones, but it would have to be. At the end of two weeks I'd lose her—literally. Marianne would become Lady Mary Anne. Titled, connected, rich and well above my station. I'd do well to remember all of that. And I would, I decided. Starting right there and then.

'You would never know that the docks are so close,

would you, or that the Firth of Forth was out there?' I said, pushing all of that to the back of my mind.

'I was thinking the same,' Marianne told me, smiling. 'Buildings on both sides, and the walls so high, I can't even see the masts of the ships over them.'

'You'll get a bit of a view back from Newhaven. Have you ever been there?'

She shook her head. 'I've never had cause. The families that employ me go to Portobello or North Berwick when they want to take the sea air.'

'I was at Portobello on Monday. I was thinking of you, watching all the weans with their nannies and governesses.'

'It is where Mrs Oliphant's children are now, taking a holiday with their aunt. She has her own nanny, which is why I am not required.'

'And you'll have another bairn in your charge, will you, when you go back to Queen Street in two weeks?'

'She will be in the care of a wet nurse for now, poor little thing. Her mother wanted a boy,' Marianne explained, 'for Mr Oliphant considers he already has a surfeit of daughters.'

The commercial buildings and warehouses had given way to a mixture of tenements and small shops. 'You don't like him, do you?'

'I make better work of disguising my feelings when I am with the family,' Marianne said, with one of her wry smiles. 'It's nothing personal, I have very little to do with him. I dislike the way he takes his wife for granted, and I heartily dislike the contempt in which he holds his daughters, at least two of whom are considerably brighter than his precious son, who will have the education *they* deserve.'

'They have you, though.'

'Only until their own governess returns, and when they are old enough, they'll be sent off to a school to learn how to be young ladies. I am not qualified to teach them those skills.' She pushed her hood back, smoothing her hair as she gazed around her. 'Ordinary families going about their business, though some of these children should surely be in school.'

'That would be a real challenge, if you were up for it,' I said. 'Getting them there and keeping them, I mean.'

'Oh, I would certainly be *up for it,* if what you mean is, would I relish it. It wouldn't only be a question of making the lessons interesting and challenging enough that they would want to stay, it would also be a case of persuading the parents that it was worth their while sending them there in the first place. In many cases, they would be giving up the few pennies the child could bring from doing other work.'

'You've thought about this.'

'A great deal. It's one of the ways I have of passing the time when I don't sleep. I could make such a difference to so many lives, given the chance. You probably think that arrogant of me.'

Don't sleep, I noted. What kept her awake? Memories? Fear of the dreams she might have? Or had she lost the habit of sleep in that place? Most likely all of it. 'I don't think you arrogant at all,' I said. 'I think it's admirable and pretty unusual that you have considered it. You've no knowledge of places like these, people like these. Don't take this the wrong way, but people raised as you were, in a respectable family, not the working type of family—families like these—people like you don't…' I bit my tongue, realising I was getting into a total fankle, and in danger of being offensive.

But she didn't take offence at all. 'Unlike people like you? You're right,' she said. 'And if I had stayed on at the school with Miss Lomond, I would have remained oblivious. I wouldn't have come across the women who opened my eyes. Women forced to earn a living doing the most appalling work.'

Her words gave me goosebumps, for I thought immediately of what Nurse Crawford had confided in me of the work she and women like her did to keep the institutions that employed them going. While those in charge played at god, these women swabbed down, mopped up, slopped out, fed, soothed and restrained the inmates. How they could endure it, hear the cries, witness the suffering, sometimes assist in inflicting it, and then go home to their own families with any peace of mind at all, I had no idea. No wonder some of them lost their humanity. And as for Marianne! That she had come through it all, and had brought a dream with her, put me in awe of her. And if the Marquess got his way, she could have her dream realised.

Don't worry. You'll have the money. You can make that dream and every other you've had come true.

The words were on the tip of my tongue. For the first time the sheer scale of possibilities that would be open to her took my breath away, putting all the other difficulties and emotional upheaval into the background. She'd come through so much, she could come through this and out the other side. She deserved this.

'What is it? What are you smiling at, Rory?'

'You're quite a woman,' I said, 'and if you look over there, you'll see the fishing harbour at Newhaven.'

Chapter Seventeen

Marianne

Edinburgh—
Thursday 9th August 1877

Rory's smile was infectious. For no other reason than that I was here with him, breathing in the fresh sea air, in a place I'd never before visited, my spirits lifted. I gave myself over to the moment. The fishing village of Newhaven was only a few miles from the city, but as we walked along the quay with the shuttered fish market behind us, it felt like another world. The air tasted of salt, and there was no pall of smoke hanging over us. The sun had still not made an appearance, but the sky was milky white and not dirty grey.

The tide was coming in, little waves creeping in through the neck of the harbour to lap at the hulls of the fishing boats that were stranded there, lying almost on their sides some of them, in the mud and silt, which gave off a stench of fish and seaweed. The empty boxes stacked outside the big doors of the market smelled of the day's catch—or maybe the previous day's. Across from us, on the harbour arm, there were nets drying, a clique of men working on them. The wind was blowing the wrong way for us to hear them talking, if they were talking.

It was peacefully quiet. We walked along the jetty to the neck of the harbour, where there was a commanding view out over the Firth of Forth. The flat kingdom of Fife was spread out before us, looking close enough to swim to.

'It's a shame it's not a clearer day, you can see all the way to Stirling from here sometimes,' Rory said. 'I reckon if I asked nicely, I might be able to persuade one of those men over there to gift us a crab, since it looks as if they're boiling up something to eat. You stay here, I won't be long.'

I watched him make his way back down the jetty to the harbour arm, not rushing but covering the ground quickly enough. I had the distinct impression that he'd been on the brink of saying something important to me just before we reached Newhaven, but then he'd changed his mind.

I couldn't fathom what he was feeling, never mind what he might be thinking, for his guard was up. Often, it seemed to me, he cut short his words, or changed them to say something else. He was careful. I supposed that must come from being a detective, or it might be that he had always been careful, and that was why he had become a detective.

There were times when my ability to read people irked me. I could be walking past someone and find myself assaulted by their anger or their foul temper. Grief was less common, but weariness and misery were sadly everywhere, and there was nothing I could do to alleviate any of it. I tried not to intrude, but it's difficult for me to switch off.

In the asylum there had been countless, terrible times when I wanted to cover my ears and scream for oblivion, to hide under the meagre covers and to stop listening to the outpourings of suffering and horror from the other inmates.

I ached to help them, to tell them, I hear you, for some of them could not even articulate what they felt.

I dared not speak though. Anything I said would be seen as further confirmation of my insanity. So I kept silent. In that diabolical place, I came to hate my intuition, for it multiplied my suffering, and burdened me with guilt for my enforced inaction. Only once, I had dared to use what I knew, and then I had acted without thinking, reacting to the threat, the immediate danger, screaming out the warning that stopped Nurse Crawford in her tracks as she began to unlock the cell door. I saved her life with my warning, and the risk I took in telling her was repaid in full when she gave me my life back.

Since my escape, I kept to myself everything I intuited, sensed, or unwittingly pieced together in every household I have worked. The women who employed me thought me perceptive, sensitive, trustworthy, but that is all.

How could you possibly know that?

I made sure that no one could ever throw that question at me.

You can't miss what you don't know.

My words this time. My hurt, that Rory's question had dredged up. I had forgotten it. It was his doing. He had a way of making my feelings spill out, things I didn't even know I was feeling, opening up wounds I thought long healed. Every time I thought I had myself under control, he overset me. He made me feel out of control. He made me want to lose control. But I wouldn't. I would never be such a fool again. I simply couldn't allow myself to.

I watched him chatting with the men on the other side of the harbour, his hands in his pockets, gesturing over to me. I was worrying too much. We were nothing to each other save two people with a shared purpose. In two weeks, he would go back to London, never to return. I resolved to stop worrying, to enjoy the moment.

He looked quite at ease, and not in the least in a hurry. I wondered what he was saying about me. Was I his wife? His sweetheart? His sister? No, not sister, and not wife either. As for sweetheart—no, we were not two innocents wooing. Acquaintance would be the most accurate, but we were surely far beyond mere acquaintances—had been since we first met. He was not employing me to help him, and we were not friends. Or were we? The only friend I ever had was Miss Lomond, but friendship felt far too safe a term for what I felt for Rory. One did not dream of making love to a friend.

He was coming back with a bucket. I had dreamt of him again the previous night, naked underneath me, inside me, making fierce, frantic love such as I had never made before. In my dream we were equals in passion.

'Success! And look, we're in luck, it's a beauty.'

My face was hot. Extremely thankful for the brim of my hat, I was happy to peer into the bucket and hide my face. Inside was the most enormous crab I've ever seen in my life. 'Good grief! Is it dead?'

'Cooked. It will be easier to eat if we leave it to cool.'

He set the bucket down. 'Do you think you could sit here? I have it on the authority of the fishermen over there that the sun will come out in a bit. Here, take hold of my hand and dreep down.'

I burst out laughing. 'I'll do my best, if you tell me how to—to dreep?'

'You don't really need to dreep. I just wanted to see your face when I suggested it. You dreep down a wall from the top, you know, sort of dropping and clinging at the same time to make the fall shorter. Here, take my hand and sit down there.'

I could have managed perfectly well, but I chose to let him help me, sitting down with my legs and skirts dangling over the wall. He sat beside me, close but not touching. He took off his cap, and pushed his hair back from his face. 'There, we're comfy now.'

'As *comfy* as we can be, perched on rock.'

'And look, the sun's coming out right enough.'

'And we have a crab for our dinner.' I was still struggling to compose myself, with him being so near. 'What more could we want?'

'A hammer for the claws, but I've found us a stone. You have a lovely smile, Marianne, did you know that? There, I didn't mean to make you blush, but it had to be said. When you smile—I mean properly smile, not that smile you use when you are pretending to smile—it makes your eyes glow.'

'Like a cat in the dark, you mean?' I said, trying to disguise my surprise and delight at the compliment.

'Like your eyes are smiling too. It warms me, when I'm on the receiving end of it which has not been often, mind you.'

The way he was looking at me was heating me from the inside. His own smile was so warm. 'You think I am ill tempered?'

'Crabbit, you mean? Like our dinner would have been when he was caught. Don't be daft. I think—I wish you could be happy, that's all.'

I could tell he had for once failed to guard his tongue,

and spoken what was on his mind. It took me aback as much as him. 'I am happy.'

Rory covered my hands with his. 'Are you, truly?'

He asked so earnestly that I took his question seriously. 'I am not unhappy.' I was not locked up. I was free. Provided I was never found, I was free. 'No, I am certainly not unhappy.'

His hands tightened on mine. 'That's pretty much what I would have said. I'm happy enough. I'm not unhappy. In fact, it wouldn't even have occurred to me to ask myself the question.'

'The why did you ask me?'

'I don't know. You make me think things I don't usually think. You make me want to do things I shouldn't want to do. I shouldn't be holding your hands. I shouldn't be sitting here beside you, thinking about kissing you. I shouldn't have told you that's what I'm thinking.'

'But you did.' And now I was thinking the same thing, when I should not be. It meant nothing. It couldn't mean anything. It was the day. The sea. The sun which was shining. The strangeness. It was Rory.

'When you look at me like that, I don't want to let go of you,' he said.

It was a question, though he didn't phrase it that way. 'Then don't,' I said to him.

I leant towards him. He leant towards me. My eyes drifted closed. I could feel the sunlight on my face, and his breath, and my heart was pounding so hard, and my belly was fluttering. And then his lips rested on mine, and I stopped thinking and gave myself over to sensation. It was a careful kiss. One I could escape from if I chose. Soft. His lips shaping themselves to mine without moving. And then it was less careful. Still soft, but more urgent. His tongue lightly touching mine. Our lips locked, kissing, and the kisses making me feel like I was melting, that I was liquid inside.

A whistle from one of the men on the other side of the harbour put an end to it. We sat staring at each other, our hands clasped, our breathing synchronised. The wind ruffled his hair.

'I can't believe we did that, in full view of those men,' I said, though I really couldn't have cared less.

'I can't believe I did that, when I've told myself countless times that I can't.'

I shouldn't have been pleased by this, but I was. It wasn't only me who was—not obsessed, but distracted. Often. 'Countless times?'

'A good many, at any rate. And when you do that thing, raise just the one eyebrow like that, you can have no idea what it does to me. I wish you weren't so bloody gorgeous.'

That made me laugh, breaking the spell, breaking our touch. 'I am thirty-three years old, and long past aspiring to be gorgeous. Not that I ever did.'

'Well, I'm forty, and long past the age of having my head turned, you'd have thought, but you're a fair way to doing it.'

'Has it been turned before?'

Rory pushed his hair back from his face again, and set his cap back on. 'I was engaged to be married once.'

I was entirely unprepared for that confession. 'You said you were married to your job.'

'I was. That was the problem. She was a good woman, far better than I deserved. That old case, it wasn't the reason for our parting, but it was the final straw.' Rory sighed, looking suddenly weary. 'We should talk about it, shouldn't we, the case, I mean? Not let ourselves get distracted. Let me see what I can do with this crab first.'

Rory made short work of dissecting the crab with the help of a stone and his pocket knife, throwing the waste to the gulls. It was utterly delicious, sweet and delicate white meat from the claws, stronger dark, juicier meat from the body which we scooped up with our fingers. We ate silently, each lost in our thoughts. If he was thinking about the old case, I was not. I was thinking about the kisses we had shared. I was thinking that he had matched my desire when he kissed me, just as he had matched my desire in my dreams. My desire roused him. His desire roused me.

'It's good, but not near so good as the ones I had on the beach on Harris.'

His words cut into my reverie. Mundane words, but the look he gave me made me wonder what he was thinking, if he knew what I had been thinking. It was another trick of his—not trick, I don't mean trick. Technique? He said one thing while thinking another.

'Sometimes I feel like you can see right inside my head,' he'd said to me.

I wished that I could do so more often.

'Here, use this.' He handed me his handkerchief, which I was obliged to use for my own was sodden. 'Did you enjoy it?'

'Isn't it obvious? It was wonderful.'

'It's even better when you have butter.' Rory threw the last of the shells from the bucket into the water, which had reached the wall on which we were sitting. The tide had come in, far enough for the fishing boats to bob about as if they were nodding. Across from us, on the other side of the harbour, the men looked as if they were preparing to go to sea. 'Will we stretch our legs while we talk? We can head along to Granton Harbour. It's only about a mile—unless you've walked far enough already?'

'No, I'm happy to walk and anyway, I've never been to Granton.'

'It's a port like this one, though much bigger. There's a new harbour that serves the fishing boats and the steamers out to Burntisland in Fife.' He got to his feet, holding out his hand. I took it and was pulled up effortlessly, though immediately released.

'You're not worried about being seen there?'

'I don't think so. I only told you the bare bones of the case the other day, I'll fill in the blanks while we walk.'

Chapter Eighteen

Rory

Edinburgh—
Thursday 9th August 1877

I was kicking myself for giving in to temptation, not even five minutes after I'd decided I wouldn't. I suggested we walk because if we continued sitting down together, I was pretty certain I'd give in and kiss her again. In public! With a crew of fishermen for an audience into the bargain! It wasn't so much the fact that I'd kissed her at all that shocked me to the core, it was how much I'd enjoyed it, and how much further I had wanted to go. It was the way she had kissed me back too, as if she felt the same. And there was no way it was wishful thinking, I was sure of it.

The old case was why we were here, I reminded myself as we made our way past the fishermen at the other end of the harbour, me giving them a look that made sure none of them made any comment on our behaviour. The sun had disappeared again, and there were clouds on the horizon. The breeze had picked up a bit too, as we began the walk along the front towards Granton. Marianne's skirts whipped around her ankles, but when I asked her if she'd changed her mind about the walk, she shook her head vehemently.

'Go on,' she said, in a way that made me think she was as keen as I was to distract herself. 'Forget what you've already told me and start from the beginning. Try to imagine you're writing a report or whatever it is policemen do. Did you have a notebook?'

'I did.' Concentrate, I told myself. Focus! 'They took it from me, but I wrote down what I could remember afterwards.'

'So your instinct even then, was that it was important and that you might need it one day?'

'I just knew the whole thing stank to high heaven. My policeman's instinct, if you like.' I tried to put myself back there. Tried to remember the man I'd been all those years ago. 'I told you I'd acquired a bit of a reputation for solving tricky cases. I was good at my job, and I *did* get to the bottom of the cases I was given, but I never liked the way the press reported them, as if I had a special talent or skill, as if I had some kind of magical powers, when all I did was use my head.'

'To make pictures that others couldn't.'

'Or didn't take the time to.'

'I think you are too modest,' Marianne said. 'Clearly you have a talent for detecting.'

'I have, I'll take that, but what I'm saying is, to me it's not anything extraordinary, and I didn't like that the press made out that it was.'

'So when the press made those false accusations, did they also cast aspersions on your previous successes?'

I took my time answering her, since it was clear she was making connections with the accusations that had been levelled against her. It made my heart ache, thinking what might be in store for her if the press got hold of that story. I'd been there, and if there was anything I could do to prevent the same thing happening to her—but what? And what business was it of mine? None, I knew that, but it wouldn't do either of us any good for me to lie to her. 'They implied that I must have been getting a helping hand, somehow,' I said. 'That I had been too good to be true.'

She nodded, a deep frown furrowing her brow. 'And the good you had done, or the harm you had prevented, the fact that you'd brought criminals to justice?'

'You're right, all that was forgotten, washed away,' I said bitterly.

Her lip curled. 'And your talent was used against you.' She turned away from me to face out to the Firth, where one of the Burntisland steamers was puffing its way across to this side. 'I know how that feels, Rory.'

Her voice was tinged with anger. Her gloved hands were curled into fists. I could see the memories chasing each other across her face as she turned to face me again. 'Years ago. Nine, ten years ago, long before I came to Edinburgh, I was employed as governess to two little girls in one of two large houses in a small town. I was on good terms with the governess from the other house. She was a little older than I and had unexpectedly come into a small inheritance. It was much discussed, as such things are, and everyone assumed that she would stop working but like me, she loved children.

'What she actually wanted was a child of her own. She met a man, personable, respectable looking, a stranger, though he claimed to have some connection with the town. I knew from the first—sensed from the first—that he was lying, though it took me some time to understand the extent of his deception. In a nutshell, he was after her money, nothing else. She wanted a husband and a child. But he already had a wife.

'I don't know,' Marianne said, when I opened my mouth to ask the obvious question. 'I cannot tell you how exactly I came to that conclusion. Things I'd heard him say, things he didn't say, things my friend told me about him. The way he hedged his bets when she spoke of where they would live. The persistent sense I had that he was holding something vital back. As I said, I don't know, but I woke up one morning and the picture was so clear in my head, I felt compelled to tell her.'

She drew a ragged breath. 'The courage she showed in confronting him—knowing that she was destroying her opportunity to have a family—oh, Rory, I almost wished I had kept silent.'

She turned away to face out towards the water again. I watched her struggle to control herself, desperate to put my arm around her, but knowing that was the last thing she wanted. All I could do was hand her my handkerchief, thankful for the small mercy that I always had a spare, for the other one had been used as a napkin earlier.

'I'm fine now,' Marianne said, looking far from it. 'I beg your pardon. I never talk about the past, it is too upsetting, but the parallels are so strong, I felt—because I do understand. As I said, my friend confronted him and he turned on her so viciously that she let fall it was I who had been the architect of his downfall. Needless to say, he then turned on me. He warned me that he would neither forget nor forgive what I had done, and then he disappeared, presumably back to his wife.'

'Poor woman. At least she was spared a bigamous marriage.'

'Yes, but at such a cost. It was a big scandal for a small town, and she found herself at the centre of it.'

'What happened to her?'

'I don't know. She left the area, her reputation in tatters, poor woman. It was so unfair, but at least she had her legacy.'

'And you?'

'Yes, I suffered too. The man found a way to tell the tale that made him the maligned and innocent victim, and I—I was accused of maliciously making it all up.'

I swore, invoking one of my da's most vicious Gaelic curses. 'It's outrageous. No wonder you have such a poor opinion of my sex.'

'Not all of you. I have a very high opinion of *you*.'

That stopped me in my tracks, and despite the sorry tale, it gave me a warm glow, distracting me for a wee bit. 'It's entirely mutual,' I said. 'It must have cost you to tell me. I appreciate it, I promise you.'

Her face crumpled, and she cursed under her breath, the first time I'd ever heard her do so. 'I wanted you to—you see I do understand.'

'And I can see you do. We've both suffered for having the courage of our convictions. You did someone a good turn, and it was turned against you.' I understood a lot more than she could have dreamed. It sickened me, for this sorry story must have been part of the evidence against her, the facts twisted and distorted to make her out as deluded. There was a gaping hole in the story as she told it, and that was how the tale got to the ears of the man who had her committed.

I wasn't going to ask her, she was in such a fragile state,

and it wasn't exactly pertinent. I couldn't help wondering though. Was it from the bigamist? A big scandal in a small town would be easy enough to dig up, but that meant Eliot must have known where to look. From where he paid the stipend to—right enough, that would be it.

Marianne straightened her shoulders and dabbed her eyes. 'I beg your pardon, you won't believe me, but usually I am not in the least emotional.'

'No more am I, save when I'm around you.'

'I'm not sure if that's a compliment or not.'

'It's a statement of fact,' I said ruefully. 'Shall we try to direct our emotions back to the murder case?'

'An excellent idea. Please proceed, Detective Sutherland.'

We had reached the long harbour arm at Wardie Bay, and I steered her towards it, away from the increasing bustle of the Granton seafront. 'I was on duty when we got a report that some weans had thought they had spotted a body caught under the bridge,' I told her, returning to the past. 'I took it with a pinch of salt but it turned out they were right. We had no idea who she was when we pulled her out, and she didn't fit with anyone we knew was missing, but that didn't count for much.

'She was pretty, she was young, and she was very obviously expecting a child. There was a gash on her head that looked suspicious to me. I put all of that in my report that night. The next day, I was called in and told it was an open-and-shut case. She was simply an unfortunate lassie who had found a way to deal with the shame of her condition, and the blow to her head happened when she fell in. Case closed, they said.'

'But you were determined to find out who she was?'

'They couldn't stop me doing that. It was my duty to try to put a name to her, let any family know, but they said it was best to let sleeping dogs lie. If anyone came forward to report her missing then fair enough, but until then she was just another tragic statistic. I thought that was unbelievably callous. At the very least some man somewhere must have contributed to her condition. It felt all wrong. Where she was found, it seemed to me that she'd been washed round by the tide from the new docks they were building and was likely put there by someone who intended to make sure she'd be lost for ever.'

We had reached the point on the harbour where the steamboat docked from Burntisland. There was a waiting room where we could have got a cup of tea, but neither of us were inclined to go in, so we started to retrace our steps. The weather had closed in. It had started to spit rain. 'I was told there were more important matters for me to investigate.'

'More important than a murder!'

'A woman, found in the docks, pregnant and with no wedding ring. The implication being that she wasn't respectable, perhaps a prostitute, and so not worthy of investigation. I know, it's wrong—'

'But it's how it is,' Marianne interrupted bitterly. 'Go on.'

'Another thing that makes a detective—or any policeman, for that matter—good at his job, is information. Knowing where to find it, I mean. The better you are at that, the quicker you are at solving crimes. The woman wasn't one of the street walkers in Leith, I knew who to ask to make certain of that. Besides, her clothing was well made, she looked to be in good health, and she wasn't under-nourished—so that was another dead end. Once again, I was told it wasn't worth bothering about. Then I was ordered to leave it, and given another couple of cases.'

'But you couldn't, because you smelled a rat, and because the more someone tells you not to do something, the more determined you are to do it?'

'That's about right. To cut a long story short, since we're running out of pier to walk and time's getting on, I went to my superior officer and made my case for murder. By then, she'd already been buried in a pauper's grave—mighty fast too. My superior was a good man, I could trust him, or so I thought. He promised he'd look into it. Two days later, he told me there was nothing to look into. Case dismissed.'

'But you didn't dismiss it.'

'I couldn't let it go, even though I was supposed to be—ach, it doesn't matter. Like you said, despite the lack of evidence, I was convinced I was right.' It was tipping it down all of a sudden. All around us, people were running for shelter. 'If we head up to Trinity we can catch the train back to the city. It's only a few hundred yards.'

We got to the station, standing under cover on the platform to wait for the train, which was fortunately due in a few minutes. 'You're drookit,' I said to Marianne. 'Soaked, I mean.'

'Drookit. I like that. What's wrong, Rory?'

I could have brushed her off, but I didn't want to. 'Raking it all up like this, it's a double-edged sword. I want to find out what happened, who murdered that poor woman and why, but it's making me think about myself. What if I'd done as they said, kept my mouth shut and stayed here? I was up for promotion again. I was earning enough from my private work to put money aside—that's one good thing about the papers making a fuss over me, it got me a lot of private work, and it paid very well. The plan was to buy one of the smaller houses in the New Town. I was due to get married. The day my superior told me the case was closed, I was supposed to be sorting out the final details of the wedding.'

I took off my cap to shake it out, and pushed my sodden hair back from my forehead. 'Looking back, it's obvious that I wasn't suited to settling down, but it was expected and I never questioned it. My ma had passed away a few years before, so my da was delighted at the thought of grand-weans. I was doing well. I was of an age to be thinking about taking a wife.

'And we got on, Moira—my betrothed and I. We were well suited, that's what everyone said. Her family was quite a step up from mine, but they never made me feel as if that mattered. Yet I simply couldn't see past that case. I became obsessed. It became an issue between us. In the end I—we—agreed there would be no wedding.' I winced, not wanting to recall that painful scene.

The train whistled, and a belch of steam preceded it as it screeched into the station. We had bought third-class tickets, right at the back in the last carriage. Marianne took my arm as we walked down the platform. We took our places on the hard wooden seats. The rain was coming in through the open windows. It was cold, my cheap woollen jacket was starting to smell damp.

'Is it a terrible thing to say, to think it might have been the making of me, rather than the ruining of me?'

Marianne turned towards me, frowning. 'How long have you been thinking in that way?'

'It's only just occurred to me.'

'And would it have occurred to you, if you hadn't come back here?'

'Probably not. And I still want to find who the woman was, if she was missed. Her family, if she has one, deserve to know her fate, at the very least. '

'Shall we give her a name, since no one else has? What shall we call her?'

I thought about it for a moment. 'Lillian,' I said.

'What about Lillian?' Marianne said at the exact same time.

We looked at each other and smiled. I leaned my head back, closed my eyes, and felt the tension leave me. I knew I shouldn't be here in this city. I knew I shouldn't be with this woman. But at that moment, all that mattered was that I was.

Chapter Nineteen

Marianne

Edinburgh—
Friday 10th August 1877

'She's beautiful,' I said to Mrs Oliphant, looking down into her new daughter's scrunched-up little face. It wasn't exactly true, I've always thought new-born babies look like a very tiny, very stern Queen Victoria, but it was a small enough lie for me to be able to pass it off. 'Have you chosen a name?'

'She is merely Baby at present,' my employer said. She was sitting up in bed draped in a selection of shawls, her hair hanging limply down from her nightcap. Though it was mid-morning, the curtains were drawn over the windows and the gas sconce was lit. There were dark shadows under her eyes, testament to what she had endured giving birth, and the sleepless nights that had followed despite having a wetnurse to attend to the little one.

The poor woman looked every day of her forty years, and despite the perfect little girl she had given birth too, quite miserable. 'My husband had decided on Simon, after his grandfather,' she told me. 'He is too disappointed to choose a girl's name.'

'Then why don't you name her?'

Mrs Oliphant sighed. 'You think me very feeble, don't you?'

'No!' I instantly regretted letting my impatience show. She had clearly endured enough of it from her husband, who had behaved exactly as I had predicted, when presented with another girl. 'I think your ordeal has taken a great toll on you, but look at what you have achieved.'

I settled the baby into her arms, and took the liberty of perching on the bed beside mother and daughter. 'You have brought a new, perfect life into this world. That's something your husband cannot do.

Her smile trembled. 'I have done that, haven't I?'

You can't miss what you don't know.

I was suddenly besieged with memories of my own childhood, memories I had no idea were locked away. 'Children sense far more than we realise,' I said, delicately touching the little baby's toes. 'I was raised by foster parents. I will always be grateful for the home they provided for me, but I knew, I always knew, that I was not loved.' I struggled on, a lump in my throat and my cheeks burning. 'I instinctively knew I was not wanted, Mrs Oliphant,' I said, forcing myself to meet her eyes. 'Though they were never cruel, always did the right thing by me, I could tell it was from duty, not love.'

'My dear Mrs Crawford, I had no idea. You are such a confident woman, so self-assured. And you are so good with the children, you always seem to know exactly how to deal with them. Even Ronnie heeds you, and the girls dote on you. To be honest, I have always been slightly in awe of you. I don't know how you do it, always knowing a step ahead what it is they want or need.'

'What they need before anything else is to know that they are wanted. That they are loved. Each and every one of them.'

'Including this little one, you mean?' Mrs Oliphant gazed down into her daughter's sleeping face, and gently stroked her plump cheeks. 'You're quite right, she is lovely. I will not have her brought up thinking herself unloved or unwanted. Even if her father does not care for her, I do. Oh, dear.' She fumbled in the sheets for her lace-edged handkerchief and dabbed at her eyes. 'I have become such a watering pot.'

'It is perfectly normal,' I told her, patting her hand—another thing I never usually did. 'Rest, peace and quiet from your very boisterous brood, will make all the difference. I take it that your husband…'

'He is staying at his club for a few weeks. He needs his sleep, and does not wish to be disturbed in the night by the baby crying.'

Since the baby would be spending the night in the nursery on the next floor, I doubted Mr Oliphant would be disturbed. 'Then you should make the most of this time to recuperate,' I said, 'and to enjoy this little one while you have her to yourself.'

'I shall call her Octavia,' Mrs Oliphant said, with a sudden smile, sitting up in bed, careful not to disturb her baby. 'After Octavia Hill, have you heard of her? She is a philanthropist who rents housing to the poor in London. I know of her only because I heard my husband telling one of his fellow businessmen that he was relieved that no decent Edinburgh woman would follow her lead.

'My husband owns a large portfolio of property in the Old Town. Slums, for want of a better word I am ashamed to say, and like to remain so, if he has anything to do with it. "Tenants find their level", that is what he is forever saying. His tenants don't deserve better, in other words. I can see I have shocked you.'

I couldn't deny that. 'I had no idea.'

'Why should you, your business is with me, and my business in domestic. The irony is that he won't for a moment guess *why* I have named her Octavia. It simply wouldn't occur to him that I would have taken it upon myself to find out about her namesake—for that is what I did. I went to the library.'

'Goodness, did you?'

'Now I have surprised you. I must say, I surprised myself. It was the day that my husband told me this was my last chance to give him a son. I had forgotten until now.' She reached over to clasp my hand in hers. 'I am glad you came to visit. You have reminded me of how fortunate I am to have little Octavia, and her sisters, and even her brother.'

'Perhaps your little Octavia will take inspiration from her namesake, when she grows up.'

'Perhaps.' Mrs Oliphant looked unconvinced. 'All my mother ever wanted for me was a good husband and a family. It's all I ever wished for too. I am fortunate, I have a beautiful home and am well provided for, I want for nothing, materially. Until now, like my husband, I have assumed my children will follow in their parents' footsteps. Ronnie is destined to take over his father's business, though it is already clear to me that Lizzie has a far better brain. And the girls will be found good husbands. Is it wrong of me—foolish of me—to wish for more for my daughters?'

'Neither wrong nor foolish,' I said, though I had little confidence in her wishes coming to fruition. Mrs Oliphant had been raised to bend her will to her husband. She knew nothing else. 'Lizzie is a very independent-minded little girl,' I said, brightening.

'Her father thinks her impertinent. I wish I had your strength of character, Mrs Crawford. You would know how to set a better example to my girls.'

'You have more strength of character than you realise,' I said, getting to my feet. 'Little Octavia is evidence of that already, for you have taken the naming of her into your own hands.'

'I have! And I shall stick to it too.'

'Excellent. Shall I put her back in her crib?'

'No, leave her with her mama.' Mrs Oliphant kissed her daughter on the forehead, then held out her hand to me. 'Thank you, Mrs Crawford, for the trust you have shown in me, and for giving up your own time to visit. I won't take any more of it, but if you could ask someone to send me up a tray of tea on your way out, I would be obliged.'

Rory and I had agreed to meet in Queen Street Gardens, because we could hope for some privacy there, the only other regular users of the garden, Mrs Aitken's family from Number Forty-Two, having decamped to North Berwick for the remainder of the month. When I arrived, he was already waiting on the bench where I had first encountered him, once again hiding behind a newspaper.

'Is there something wrong with the bairn?' he asked me, seeing my scowl.

'No, but there is something wrong with the baby's father.' I sank on to the bench, allowing my annoyance to take hold of me. 'Poor Mrs Oliphant dared to have a daughter and not a son, and her husband has had a tantrum and taken himself off to his gentleman's club.'

'At least while he is there, his wife will have respite from his company.'

I was obliged to smile. 'That is more or less what I said to her. Oh, dear, now you are thinking once again that I dislike men, which is not true, Rory. I like you.'

'That's what they call serendipity, for I very much like you.'

I could see from his face that he hadn't meant to say so, and though I knew I ought to wish he hadn't, I was very glad he had. 'I have never met anyone like you.' The words tumbled out before I could stop them.

'Serendipity again. I've never met anyone like you either. I think that every time I see you.'

'So do I.'

We were quite alone in the garden. My hand rested on his shoulder of its own accord. Then my lips met his of their own accord. Since yesterday, I had been longing for another kiss. The taste of him. The melting feeling inside, and the heat spreading through my body. I leaned in to cup his chin, smoothly shaved, sliding my fingers to the back of his neck to curl into his hair. His hat tumbled off.

Our kiss deepened, became more urgent, demanding, wanting. I gave myself over to the taste of him, the sweet, aching desire that was building inside me, making me feel as if my clothes were too tight, making me feel as if I couldn't breathe. One kiss merged into the next, into the next, and I was lost in a whirl of desire, wanting, aching for him to touch me, totally forgetting where I was.

Then his arms slid around me, locking me firmly in his embrace, and I jerked back, jumping to my feet. 'No!'

'Marianne! I'm sorry. I'm so sorry, I shouldn't have…'

I wrapped my arms around myself, taking another step back. 'It wasn't—I didn't mean…' I was shaking too much to continue. I turned my back to him, trying to banish the memory of those other arms roughly pinning me while the second man secured my arms behind my back. Of the reek of sweat and the stench of fear coming from the restraint jacket as they strapped me into it with ruthless efficiency. Of my helpless fall to the padded floor when they pushed me into the cell. 'Try escaping from that,' one of them shouted as the door slammed. Then came my screams, drawn from my depths, echoing over and over until I was hoarse.

But I didn't let them break me. That's what I reminded myself when I came to my senses again. It had been my first attempt to escape. It wouldn't be my last. And I had succeeded. I was free. I was in Edinburgh, and the only bars were the railings marking out Queen Street Gardens. I could smell new-mown grass. There were birds singing. I was free.

My heartbeat slowed. The memory faded. I turned around to face Rory. He was still seated on the bench, his eyes riveted on me. I thanked the stars he had not attempted to touch me. Mortification took over from horror. What must he think of me? 'I'm sorry.'

He said something under his breath I couldn't catch. 'I beg of you, don't apologise. Just tell me what I should do.'

'Nothing.' I studied him, clasping my hands together for they were still shaking. All I could sense from him was concern. He met my gaze frankly, allowing me to read him—at least that is what I felt. No disgust. No contempt. Just warmth and concern. 'You must think I am m—' I bit back the word.

'No!' He jumped to his feet and took a few steps towards me, then stopped. 'I don't think—you are not—I didn't mean to, but I frightened you.'

I don't think you're mad. You are not mad.

Was that really what he was going to say? 'It wasn't the kiss,' I said.

'I shouldn't have put my arms around you, is that it?'

He asked the question so gently, so carefully, yet still I had no sense of him judging or condemning, and though there was anger there, it was directed at himself. I wanted, suddenly, to tell him the truth. I wanted desperately to tell him, because I couldn't bear him to take the blame for what others had done to me. But even in my vulnerable state, I knew that would be a huge mistake. Knowledge was power. I did not think that Rory would abuse my trust, but I hadn't thought Francis would either. I had too much to lose. The life I had made for myself here. My sanity, if I was ever taken back to that place again.

'I'm perfectly fine now,' I said, returning to sit beside him. I had myself completely under control again. 'I don't like to be held, as you said.'

Why not?

I waited for him to ask the question, hoping he would not for I had no explanation I could give him. 'I'll remember that,' he said.

I was completely at a loss. Didn't he want an explanation?

'When you want to talk, I'll listen,' he said, 'I've told you, Marianne, you can trust me.'

His gentle tone and his understanding made my eyes smart with tears. This time I hadn't spoken aloud, yet he had still intuited what I was thinking. I wanted to trust him, I wanted to pour out the sad, sorry, horrific tale of my suffering. To what end? To label myself an escaped lunatic? To have Rory tactfully, but completely, withdraw from me? I wanted to help him. I wanted to be with him, though I knew I ought not to.

Totally conflicted, I changed the subject. 'Mrs Oliphant has named her baby Octavia, after a woman called Octavia Hill.' I recounted the tale, hands folded in my lap but not too tightly clasped, though I could not quite meet his gaze. 'I don't doubt her desire to give her daughters a different life, but nor do I hold out much hope that she will succeed. Do you want children, Rory? At some point in the future, I mean?'

He blinked, taken by surprise at my turning the subject, but as ever he took my question seriously, taking his time to answer. 'Like you, I think there are already too many children in need in this world.'

'Did I say that?'

'You implied it when you were talking about setting up your own school.'

'But when you were engaged to be married, it must have been in anticipation of having a family?'

'It's what Moira wanted, and my da was desperate for grand-weans. I wanted to please them, but I'm ashamed to say that I didn't think about it too deeply.'

'Did you love her?'

I thought he would tell me it was none of my business, which it wasn't. It didn't matter, I told myself, but I knew it did.

Rory looked troubled, picking up his hat and turning it around in his hands. 'I hadn't thought of her in a long time. Only since I got back to Edinburgh, and then last night, after I told you about her, I was going over that night when she broke it off. She said to me that if I loved her I would put her first. I'd forgotten that.' He put his hat back on. 'Truth is, she was right. I put my work first, always, and I couldn't see that changing. It was when I told her that, she gave me the ring back, and she was in the right of it. It seems I'm not the marrying kind. I didn't know myself as well as you did.'

'I'm not sure I know what you mean.'

'You told me you'd never wanted to marry. If I'd taken the time to think about it, I'd have reached the same conclusion but I didn't, I was too caught up with my work. And you know what's worse, Marianne? When I left Edinburgh, I was still too caught up with my own concerns, the injustice that was done to me, the injustice that was done to the woman we've named Lillian, that I barely gave the injustice I'd imposed on my da and Moira and her family a thought.

'They had expectations of me. They looked to me to make them happy, and I let them down.' He stopped, looking quite taken aback. 'I don't know where that came from. I didn't even know it was lurking there.'

'That's exactly what happens to me when I'm with you. I say things aloud that I mean to keep to myself, and I find myself thinking of things that…' Now it was my turn to fall silent.

'Thinking of things that you thought long buried? Is that it?'

'I didn't say that I had *never* wished to marry,' I told

him, proving his point. 'I said that I am now certain I never want to marry.'

'Meaning you did once?'

I was already heartily regretting saying anything, I certainly wasn't going to say any more. I didn't want to talk about Francis to Rory. I didn't want Rory to know about the needy, naive person who had been so desperate for love. I could tell myself that Rory's opinion didn't matter, but it would be a lie.

'Time is getting on. The clock is ticking,' I said. 'Tell me what progress you made this morning.'

Chapter Twenty

Rory

Edinburgh—
Friday 10th August 1877

I was gobsmacked, and by the looks of her, so was Marianne, at what she'd just confessed. She didn't want to tell me any more either, and I didn't know what I felt, but I couldn't leave it. 'Are you saying you were engaged to be married too?'

She sighed. 'A long time ago.'

'What happened?'

'Like you I realised, much later than I should have, that it was a mistake. I terminated the engagement.'

Did you love him?

I couldn't ask her that. I didn't want the answer to be that she had, but I wanted to know what had happened all the same. I was still shaken by the way she'd reacted when I'd put my arms around her. One minutes she had been kissing me passionately, lighting a fire in my belly, making me ache with wanting her, and the next minute she was looking at me as if I'd tried to strangle her. Had that been his fault? Had he hurt her?

'I don't know what you're thinking, Rory, but I would remind you, we're here to talk about your old case not my old love affair.'

The words hit me like a punch in the gut. 'It was a love affair, then?'

'I thought so at the time.' She lifted her eyes to meet mine, gleaming more yellow than green, and I recalled that phrase, *cat-like,* that the doctor I'd spoken to had used. 'I found I was mistaken,' she added, her tone strained, 'but not before I had surrendered—no, that's not right—not before I had indulged in the passion which I mistook for love. Now you have the truth, I expect you are shocked.'

'I don't know what I'm feeling.' I was struggling to take in what she was telling me, and more importantly, why.

'You must have known that you were not the first man I had kissed.'

Still that odd tone, and she was holding herself tight as a bow. 'I didn't care, Marianne. When I was kissing you, I wasn't thinking about who else you might have kissed. I wasn't thinking at all.'

'But afterwards…'

'Are you wanting me to criticise you for it?' I felt a flicker of anger. 'Are you wanting me to tell you that I think less of you?' My anger took root. 'Do you think that I'm a bloody hypocrite?'

'I don't!'

'No? Then why did you take that tone with me, when you told me that you're not a virgin—for that's what you meant, I take it? You were just waiting for me to judge you.'

'I was…'

'You misread my reaction. Do you know what was actually bothering me? I was wondering whether it was him who hurt you. Was it him who made you terrified of having someone's arms around you? That's what was bothering me.'

I knew I was reacting out of all proportion. It wasn't like me to get angry like that, but then everything I felt for Marianne was nothing like me and I was all over the place. Kissing her like there was no tomorrow one minute, and forgetting everything except wanting to go on kissing her. Then being stared at as if I was murderer. And now, when it hadn't even occurred to me to judge her, for I was very much intent on judging him, she was ripping up at me for doing just that.

I threw myself to my feet, cursing under my breath, angry and frustrated by the pair of us. 'I make my own mind up about people, I thought you knew me well enough to understand that. Do you think *I'm* a virgin? I'm forty years old, of course I'm not, and the women I've made love to—do you think I'm one of those men who thinks that only harlots can be passionate?'

Finally, I caught myself and bit the tumble of words back. 'I'm sorry. It's not like me to lose my temper. I didn't mean—I don't know where that came from. Again.' I caught my breath, trying to steady myself. 'I'm sorry. You'e right. What you did, who you did it with, it's none of my business. I just don't like the thought of you being hurt, that's all.'

You know that alarm bell that had clanged faintly a couple of days ago, when we talked about spending the next two weeks together? Well it clanged again at that, and I noticed it this time. I didn't like the thought of her being hurt. I wanted to be the one that stopped her getting hurt further. But if I wasn't careful…

I took a deep breath. I had to be careful or we'd both

make a mistake we might well rue for the rest of our days. She wasn't for me. I wasn't for her. That's the way it was, and that's the way we both wanted it to stay. We'd lay off the kissing. And I'd send another telegram to the Marquess, asking him to get a move on. The sooner Marianne knew the truth about herself, the better for both of us.

And if I kept telling myself that, I might start to believe it. 'Sorry,' I said. 'Rant over. Right then.' Time to do what I always do, and get back to work. I patted my coat pocket and drew out my notebook. 'Let me fill you in on what I've been up to, assuming you still want to know.'

She nodded. I sat down, making a point of keeping some distance between us, and opened the notebook, but her hand on my arm stayed me.

'I just want to say that I don't think of you like that at all, I promise you, Rory.'

'It doesnae matter.'

'Doesnae,' she repeated, with a valiant wee smile. 'Your accent becomes so much broader when you are emotional.'

'Aye, well, then I reckon I must speak broad Weegie or Scots when I'm around you, but I really am sorry I lost my temper.'

She had her hands clasped again, so tightly it was stretching her gloves at the knuckles. 'I am usually quite calm and collected too, but when I am with you, I am…'

'All over the shop?'

'Does that mean up and down? Yes, I'm all over the shop. I have known you just over a week…'

'Eight days. It's only been eight days.'

'It feels much longer, doesn't it? And we have less than two weeks left. Is that it? Do you think it's because we have so little time that we are *all over the shop*?'

'I don't know, it might be,' I said, because it was a straw I could clutch at. Twelve days left, maybe less if the Marquess could grease the legal cogs and get them to move faster. Twelve days, and we'd be going our separate ways. I didn't like the twinge I got in my guts at the thought. Part of me was thinking it might be a good idea to damn the Marquess and his orders to hell and just tell her the truth now. It would scupper any inappropriate hopes and desires I might be harbouring about us good and proper.

I wasn't just thinking of what it meant for her, but I was thinking of what she'd think of me, keeping it all to myself for so long. But I kept coming back to the fact that I'd not a whole story to tell her. And I was under orders to keep my gob shut. And they were sensible orders, what's more. So I turned back to my notebook once more, and the old case that had never failed to distract me, and I told Marianne what I'd turned up.

'The thing that always bothered me, as you know, was that our Lillian was a missing person that no one seemed to have missed. Widening the search, getting in touch with the police in the other big cities in Scotland, see if they knew anything about her, that was going to be my next step when my career came to a sudden halt. But this morning I had another chat with one of my own contacts here, the one who gave me the friendly advice a few days ago.'

Marianne, who seemed to be trying as hard as I was to forget, put her mind on the case, nodded. 'Billy Sinclair? You told me that he "owed you" a few favours, have I that right?'

'You have. He wasn't happy, but I told him this would be the first and last time. What he told me was what I'd already surmised. "You're looking in the wrong city," were

William's exact words. "You should look closer to home, Mr Sutherland."'

'Closer to home? Glasgow!'

'Exactly. And there's more. The reason William was persuaded to talk was because the man we're looking for is dead.'

'The murderer, you mean?'

'The man who put her in the docks. "An amateur, and a mere pawn". Again, I'm quoting William.'

Marianne's brow knitted. I had her full attention now. 'Does that mean someone was paid to do it?'

I closed my notebook again and stretched my legs out, still taking care not to brush against her. It was there all the time I was with her, that sense of her, awareness of her, even when I was totally focused on something else—well, almost totally. 'I think I was right all along. There could be only one reason for the pains they took to stop me investigating Lillian's murder, and that was because somehow, she was involved with someone important.'

'So it really was all about the money?'

'Almost certainly. The question is, whose money?' I said. 'And my nose tells me that we're getting close.'

'So we are headed to Glasgow?'

I hadn't meant for us both to go. But she was smiling at me, that real smile, and her eyes were warm and she'd shifted on the bench towards me, and though I meant to say no, *I'm* going to Glasgow, what I said was, 'Monday, if you're up for it. I've contacts there through my father who might help, I'll send off a few telegrams today, set the wheels in motion.'

Chapter Twenty-One

Marianne

Glasgow—
Monday 13th August 1877

The journey on the steam train from Edinburgh took two and a half hours. Rory said little for most of it, sitting quietly on the bench beside me, lost in his own thoughts. I had no idea what they were. Just outside Glasgow, our carriages were hauled up a steep incline by a rope powered by a stationery engine. I must confess, it made me extremely nervous, and I chose not to lean out of the windows with the other passengers to watch as the ropes were attached. I was simply glad when we reached the summit and could continue through the tunnel into the station under our own power.

Glasgow's Dundas Street station was smaller than Edinburgh's Waverley, and the platform swarmed with people from the busy train. The roof over the station prevented the steam from escaping, and as each new train pulled in, a cloud of black smoke was released, making the train, the people and the platform in the near vicinity disappear into darkness.

'You'll need to stay close,' Rory said. 'Do you mind putting your arm through mine? And hold on to your purse, for there are pickpockets everywhere here intent on making the most of the blackouts.'

I was more than happy to take his arm. 'I must confess, I'm feeling a bit overwhelmed. I'm not used to crowds like this. I feel as if I'm in danger of being swept along and separated from you.'

For answer, he pulled me closer. 'Are you regretting coming along?'

'Don't be daft,' I said, in a terrible attempt to mimic his accent. 'I want to see the city where you grew up.'

'It's five years since I was last back to attend my father's funeral, I wonder if I'll still recognise the place.'

We emerged from the station and Rory led the way to what he informed me was George Square. It was not the small, private garden I had imagined. On the contrary, it was a huge square set out with style and symmetry, featuring neatly kept lawns with small railings, and wide, paved walkways. There were trees and numerous statues, orderly flowerbeds and neatly spaced benches, and there were gas lights too, all around the perimeter.

A wide cobblestoned road separated the square from the mansions, hotels and commercial buildings which surrounded it. Hackney carriages loitered outside the Queen's Hotel. Horse-drawn trams and private carriages rattled along, but inside the square seemed an oasis of calm. Nannies strolled with their baby carriages. Men sat on the benches with their newspapers and pipes. A group of women stood gossiping. Above us, though the sky was dirty grey, the sun was streaking through.

'You're seeing it at its best today,' Rory said. 'Don't be

fooled though. A few hundred yards that way you'll find some of the roughest and most dangerous parts of the city. A few hundred yards in that direction is the River Clyde and the docks, and a bit further down river again, they build the ships and the steam engines that help Glasgow power the modern world.'

'I thought you loved Edinburgh the best.'

'Wheesht, don't be saying that here.' Rory grinned. 'This is my home town, of course I love it the best. While I'm here, any road. Come on, we've time to spare, will we take a stroll through George Square? When I was wee, it was a private garden. It's supposed to be open to the public now, but judging by the clientele, I reckon they mean only those and such as those.'

It seemed to me that he was right, when we crossed the road and entered the square. The men were all well-to-do in their business suits and top hats, the women clad in silk gowns and twirling frivolous lace-trimmed parasols that I couldn't help thinking would be filthy and painfully difficult for their maids to clean at the end of the day. Rory was attired with his usual understated elegance. I was wearing my green summer gown and with my favourite shawl and bonnet, an assembly that I had always considered my best, but as we meandered arm in arm around the square, I felt under-dressed, on the verge of shabby. I withdrew my arm from Rory's.

'What's wrong?'

'You're right, this square is for those and such as those. Shall we go?'

'You can't possibly be thinking that you look out of place. That gown suits you. I've always thought so. It brings out the colour of your eyes.'

'You have never said any such thing to me before.'

'I've thought it though, a few times.'

'It's the only summer gown I own.'

'Considering this is one of about ten days in the year that you would get the opportunity to wear it, to own another would be wasted.'

'If this one was a little smarter—' I broke off, embarrassed. 'Never mind.'

'I didn't think you set much store by clothes.'

Honestly! I wanted to roll my eyes. Sometimes Rory's powers of perception were irritating. 'I don't, usually. It would be wholly inappropriate for me to be better dressed than my employers.'

'But if you had the money…'

'I would spend it on more important things than silk gowns.' Looking up from the brim of my bonnet, I made the mistake of catching his eye. Blast the man, I could not lie to him. 'I'm not a governess today, but I'm dressed like one and you are not, and for the first time we are out in public in very respectable surroundings, not lurking in our usual haunts of graveyards and mill villages and dusty churches, and I feel I'm making you look conspicuous.'

I quailed as his face set, remembering his outburst in Queen Street Gardens when I had presumed he was judging me. 'I'm not saying that you are embarrassed by me, Rory, I'm saying that I am—I am uncomfortable. Though I know I shouldn't be. It's only clothes.'

'I've told you before that I think you're bloody gorgeous.'

My cheeks grew hotter. 'The point is, I don't think so. Now you'll tell me that it doesn't matter, but I think it does. Today, at any rate.'

Mortifyingly, I found myself on the brink of tears. Rory

ushered me over to one of the wrought-iron benches. 'We'll be late for your appointment with Mr Munro,' I demurred.

'This isn't like you.' He sat down, giving me no option but to follow suit.

'I know it's not.' I was nervous, jittery, and I couldn't understand why. It wasn't really my gown, that much I knew.

'Are you worried about meeting my da's friend?'

It wasn't that, though that might be part of it, in which case it wasn't a lie. 'How do you plan to introduce me?' I asked. 'Don't you think my presence might complicate matters, or make him more reticent? He's doing you a big favour, won't he be more likely to speak to you openly if I'm not there?'

I must have sounded convincing. Rory, in fact, looked relieved. 'I wouldn't be too long. I must admit, there's merit in what you say.'

'I will sit here and wait for you.' With the nannies, I was thinking. If only I had a charge of my own I wouldn't feel so out of place.

'Come on, I know where we can find you somewhere more comfortable.' He got up, holding out his hand and I allowed myself to take it. 'It's only five minutes away just off Ingram Street. I think you'll like it.'

He left me at the gates of a graveyard, with the promise that he would join me within the hour. St David's, the church which guarded the entrance, was in the Gothic style, squashed into a tight space that made it appear inordinately tall. There were three sections to the burial grounds, the main one long and narrow, enclosed by a high wall, with two smaller walled areas on either side of the church. The walls shut out the noise of Ingram Street. It was a quiet, gloomy place, but I felt immediately more at ease.

Rory had told me it was known as the Merchant's Graveyard. Reading the gravestones, I could see why. Sugar, tobacco, wool, the huge slabs of stone that covered the crypts proclaimed the merchant's trade, his wealth, his philanthropy and his stature. His wife and children were afternotes. There were other slabs laid neatly around the walls. Also buried here, Rory had told me, was the man that Madeleine Smith was accused of murdering twenty years before.

I had not heard of the case, but at the time it was apparently notorious, a respectable and very young woman who poisoned her lover, and whose love affair, documented in her passionate letters, scandalised Glasgow society at the time. Respectable young women didn't take lovers, they didn't declare their passion in writing, and they most certainly didn't commit murder. Madeleine Smith was not found guilty, though the peculiar Scottish verdict of not proven implied that the jury believed her to be so.

Rory said that Madeleine Smith's family stood by her, though the scandal forced them to move away from Glasgow. Her letters though, sounded like exactly the kind of thing that could have been used against her. I could easily have encountered Madeleine Smith in the asylum. We had both in our own way escaped that fate.

Unlike Greyfriars kirkyard, there was a uniformity to the tombs in Glasgow, and an austerity to the gravestones. I decided against looking for Madeleine Smith's lover's grave, and instead found a spot in the sunshine at the far corner of the burial grounds, and a convenient stone bench set against the wall. I was still on edge. In George Square, walking arm in arm, despite my shabby gown, Rory and I could have been a married couple taking a stroll together. We were not looking over our shoulders, either of us, and I was not having to mind someone else's children. For a moment, just a moment, I had allowed myself to dream that the illusion we were creating was real. That was what had set me on edge.

I was tired of looking over my shoulder all the time. What was I afraid of? Who could possibly be looking for me now, after all these years? Why should I feel safer in Glasgow than in Edinburgh? Was it an illusion, or was it Rory who made me feel safe? Rory, who was also looking over his shoulder for an enemy he couldn't name. Rory, who in ten days, possibly less, would be walking back out of my life to pick up his own. If we discovered Lillian's true identity, he might even resolve what I had come to think of as *our case* even sooner. And his other, suspended case? Was that what was preying on his mind during his silences? I knew so little about his real life, but why should I? When he was gone, it would be better for me not to be able to imagine. And he would be gone soon enough.

When he was gone, I resolved, I would be less afraid. Restlessly, I began to circle the burial ground in the opposite direction. When he was gone, there would be no more blood-stirring kisses. I wouldn't have him to look forward to seeing, to talk to, but I could make another friend, couldn't I? Not one like Rory, but…

There was no one like Rory, that was the problem. I stopped in front of a tomb commemorating Andrew Buchannan, tobacco merchant and Lord Provost of Glasgow. I could not possibly be so foolish as to imagine myself to be falling in love with Rory. I forced myself to try to recall how I had felt that one fatal time I had fallen in love.

Anxious. I was always anxious. Eager to please. Thrilled when I did please. Devastated when I did not, and anxious—anxious again!—to make amends.

There must have been more to it than that. Passion? I sat down on the obliging tobacco merchant's grave and tried to remember. There must have been passion. There had been, on his side, and I had wanted what he wanted. Until afterwards, when I had wanted the opposite of what he had wanted.

Sighing, I pushed these unpleasant memories to one side. It sickened me to compare Rory and Francis, so I would not. I must have loved Francis, for I had agreed to marry him and I had made love to him, but what I felt for Rory was very different. Passion? Undoubtedly. Just thinking about his kisses set me on fire.

The restraint that he showed too, the sense that he was holding himself on a tight rein, made me want to unleash him. But it wasn't only passion. Rory listened to me. Rory was interested in what I had to say—too interested for comfort at times. And he was careful with me too. He knew when to stop pushing me, when to restrain his curiosity. And he didn't judge me. Though he didn't know me. And I'd make sure he never would.

Ten days, perhaps less. Not enough for me to care too much, not enough for me to miss him too much, not enough for him to become a part of my life. Not that I wanted that, any more than he did. I was in no danger from Rory, so there was no danger in my being with him. In my wanting him. And my longing for his company, that was precisely what I'd said the other day, a side-effect of the clock that was counting down the days until we went our separate ways.

A signal to make the most of them? My edginess gave way to a different kind of tension. I got up and began to make my way towards the entrance. Rory was walking towards me. He waved, and my heart leapt.

Chapter Twenty-Two

Rory

Glasgow—
Monday 13th August 1877

When I saw Marianne walking towards me, my heart lifted, and that worried me, but then she smiled, and I forgot to worry, and hurried towards her, smiling back.

'Do you have good news?' she asked me. 'Could Mr Munro help?'

'I'll tell you in a moment. Are you feeling better now?'

To my surprise, she slipped her arm through mine. 'It's odd, isn't it, being in a very different city together. You don't have to worry about being seen by the wrong person in the wrong place, and I—oh, I think it is time that I stopped worrying and began to enjoy my freedom.'

Freedom. I waited, wondering if she'd even noticed the slip, but she didn't. 'Go on then,' she said, 'tell me what you have found out, it's why we're here after all.'

'Is there anywhere we can…?'

'Sit and be private? Yes.'

She led the way to a stone bench on the back wall, in full

sun. I took off my hat and gloves and handed her the slice of fruit cake I'd brought her, wrapped in paper. 'I thought you might be hungry. You can eat it while I talk.'

'Thank you! I didn't think I was hungry, but now you mention it.' She took her gloves off, crumbled a bit and popped it in her mouth. 'Delicious.'

She crumbled another bit and held it out to me. I don't like fruit cake, I've always found it claggy, but I took it, surprising us both by guiding the cake and the tips of her fingers into my mouth. Her eyes widened. She withdrew them slowly, letting my lips linger. I turned her hand over to kiss her wrist, feeling the flutter of her pulse on my lips, feeling my own heart thump, and her fingers ruffling through my hair.

There were birds singing somewhere. There wasn't a breath of breeze. The sun baked down on us through the grey-blue sky. I looked up to find her eyes fixed on me. Her lips were parted. I think it was she who moved towards me, but I wouldn't swear to it. Then we kissed. Sweetened by fruit cake, warmed by the sun, it was a delicate kiss, though not careful. I knew how much she wanted me, from that kiss. I ached with wanting her. Which was why I ended it, though slowly, mind. Very slowly.

We stared at each other. Entranced, mesmerised, I don't know what it was. I didn't want to break the spell. I wanted to kiss her again. If she'd made a move, just the tiniest move—but she didn't. So I took a long overdue breath, and I sat back, but it was Marianne who spoke.

'We've not got long left,' she said.

'I know.'

'Ah know.' She smiled, one of her real smiles. 'You feel

it too, don't you, just as strongly as I do. The clock ticking. The need to—to…'

'Make the most of it. How could you doubt it?'

Her smile faltered for a moment, but then she rallied. 'I don't. I wish…' She reached for me, taking my hand and placing it against her cheek. 'Oh, Rory, I wish that we could stay here for just a little longer. In this city, I mean, away from Edinburgh. Where we are safe.' She kissed the palm of my hand, and I should have been glad that she let it go then, but what I wanted—well, it's obvious what I wanted. 'We've become distracted again,' she said.

'It's too easy done. I've never had that problem before. Let me think.' I moved away from her to do so. Then I recounted what Gordon Munro had told me. 'The problem is,' I said, 'the family he thinks are Lillian's have been on holiday doon the watter. On the Clyde Coast, that is. They're not due home until tomorrow morning, so we'll have to come back another day.'

Marianne was silent for a moment, biting her lip—which I had to stop watching for what it was making me want to do. 'We don't have long,' she said. 'Going back to Edinburgh, then coming back here again, it seems such a waste of time.'

'What are you thinking?'

She was blushing faintly—though that might have been the sun. 'I'm thinking that fate might have taken a hand. We could stay here in Glasgow.' She was definitely blushing. 'If you thought it was a good idea.'

I thought it was a terrible idea—or that's what I told myself I was thinking. My body, on the other hand, leapt at it, in every embarrassing way. And was it such a terrible idea after all? We would save ourselves a journey. We could take separate rooms in a hotel. We could take separate rooms in a separate hotel—that would be safer. Then I remembered that Marianne had been a bit overwhelmed when we arrived, that Glasgow was completely new to her, and it not being new to me made me wary of leaving her in another hotel, no matter how respectable it might be. So the same hotels, but different rooms, then?

'What do you think, Rory?'

'The Queen's Hotel,' I said, my mouth running way ahead of my mind. That's the one on George Square, right beside the train station. It has a good name.'

'Is it expensive?'

'This is my case, so I'll take care of it. And I won't have you arguing. Think about it, Marianne, you're more or less working without a fee. Unless Mrs Oliphant is paying you for your holiday…'

'She is very generous, but it wouldn't even occur to her to do so, and even if it did, I doubt Mr Oliphant would agree.'

'Forget about him, and everything else. I'll take care of any expenses while we're here, and that isn't up for discussion.'

'Can you afford it?'

'Easily,' I said, ridiculously touched. 'I'm not rich, but I'm very comfortable. I do well for myself.'

'And there is only you,' she said, with an odd smile.

Only me. I'd always relished that before. Only me, without Marianne—was I kidding myself, staying overnight here with her? In separate rooms, I reminded myself. And I might be comfortably off, but compared to the wealth that was hopefully coming her way, I was a pauper.

If anything happened between us, would she think I was

making a play for her money? It hadn't occurred to me until then, but now it did—like that man she told me about, the bigamist who had tried to marry her friend. But then I had no intentions of asking her to marry me. The very idea of it made me laugh. Or would, if I thought about it. Which I wasn't going to do.

I got up, holding out my hand to help her. She took it, and she slid her hand into my arm, as if she'd been doing that for weeks. We hadn't even known each other for two weeks. No one could fall in love in two weeks. I had never been in love. I was forty years old. If I'd been going to do it, I'd have done it by now.

'Do you fancy coming with me on a wee trip down memory lane?' I asked her.

She gave a skip, beaming up at me. 'You read my mind. That is exactly what I would like to do.'

Glasgow was changing under our very noses, was how it felt to me. My eyes were out on stalks on the journey to Partick, I couldn't get over the number of big new tenements that were popping up, at the way the streets had broadened and bustled even more. We got off the tram at Partick Cross, and I stood for a moment, Marianne on my arm, looking about me in amazement. More tenements, a mix of red and blond sandstone, with shops under them, their awnings out, goods stacked outside, all the way along Dumbarton Road.

We walked along, dodging the multitude of people going about their business, and I filled Marianne in on the changes. She was like me, her eyes darting from one place to another, wide with interest, and every now and then she'd look up at me, check up on me, then nod to herself, as if I'd passed some sort of test.

'I'm fine,' I said to her, catching her out, just as we turned into Keith Street, and then I was brought up short.

'Is this it?'

'It is, and it isn't.' I began to walk slowly down the street. 'That flat there, on the second floor, was ours.' It looked shabbier than I recalled, against the newer buildings that had gone up since. 'And here,' I said, standing in front of the next block, 'this used to be a wine merchants, and there was a dairy further down.' The old buildings, thatched cottages and two-storey houses were falling down, their roofs sagging, their windows boarded up. The church was still there, and the old Quakers Graveyard, but all around it the buildings were falling down or being pulled down.

'Your father isn't buried there, is he?' Marianne asked, looking at the tumble of ancient graves.

'No, that's not been used for about twenty years,' I said. 'He's over in Govan with my ma. Across the other side of the Clyde.'

'Do you want to pay your respects?'

'I'd rather recall happier times. We *were* happy here, you know.'

'Yes.' She smiled, pressing my arm, which she hadn't let go the whole time we'd been walking. 'Show me more.'

So I did. The big police station on Anderson Street where my father was stationed for a while when he was with the Partick Burgh force. The school I went to. The grocer shop where my ma used to send me for bread and milk in the mornings. The cricket ground at Hamilton Crescent. 'Though that wasn't there when I was a wean. We played out in the back courts, along the banks of the Kelvin, and what is now the West End Park.'

I didn't want to go further along to Thornhill, where my da had moved when my ma died. Instead, we retraced our steps to walk into the park, over the old Snow Bridge, with the massive edifice of Glasgow University rising up in front of us. The day had turned sultry, but the weather had still brought out the Weegies in force.

We passed couples like ourselves, who nodded a greeting as they passed. Men doffed their hats. Weans screamed and shouted on the banks of the Kelvin, just as they always had. The river was too low for the mills to be running. Further in, at the pond, there were nannies and governesses from the posher bit of the West End, and on the steep banks of the grass rising up to the terraces that were being built there, younger people sitting taking in the sun from all walks of life.

The view from the top of the hill was as breathtaking as ever, with the sweep of Park Circus behind us, the West End Park spread below us, and over on the other side, the University. 'My goodness,' Marianne said, 'it is quite beautiful. And so grand.'

'Here, it is. If you look over there, you'll see the Clyde, and the shipyards I was telling you about. That's what all the new tenements in Partick are for, to house the ship builders.'

'It's quite a contrast, isn't it.' She was looking at Park Circus, the elegant town houses, the imposing porticoes. 'This is like Edinburgh's New Town. And the park there, acts as the border, like Princes Street Gardens, save that people here seem to mix more than they do in Edinburgh.

I like it here. I mean this city. I don't know why, but I feel comfortable here in a way that I don't in Edinburgh.'

'Glasgow's a friendlier city, but you weren't at all comfortable this morning.'

'I was overwhelmed.' She walked away, over to the edge of the hill where we were standing, and leaned on the railings, looking out over the west of the city. 'Don't you miss it, Rory?'

I hadn't, until she asked me. Joining her at the railings, I focused on the ribbon of the Clyde, where the cranes for the engineering works were spread out, more of them than I remembered, bigger than I recalled. 'I left for Edinburgh to join the force twenty years ago. I've never worked here, never made my own life here, never thought to either.'

'Is there a demand for your sort of work here?'

'Funnily enough, my da's friend from the force said there was good business to be had, for the right man.'

'And are you the right man?'

Glasgow was only two hours from Edinburgh by train. Two hours from Marianne. But why would Marianne remain in Edinburgh, if she had the funds to go wherever she chose? And why would I imagine Marianne's whereabouts would be of any interest to me, after she'd found out…

'Rory.'

She tugged at my sleeve, raising her eyebrow at me. Just the one. And I lost my train of thought. 'Have you any notion what that does to me?'

'I don't know what you mean.'

'This.' I traced her brow with my finger. Then I let my fingers flutter down her cheek. Then I leaned over, and I kissed her. Her lips were warm. Sun-kissed, I thought hazily, the thought rousing me even more. She lifted her hand to my cheek. Smoothing it down, the palm of her glove cupping my chin.

I whispered her name. I didn't know it was a question. I hadn't meant it as a question, but she answered me all the same. 'Yes,' she whispered. 'Oh, yes.'

Chapter Twenty-Three

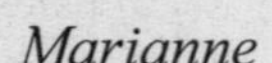

Marianne

Glasgow—
Monday 13th August 1877

I barely recall the journey back from the West End Park to the Queen's Hotel. We walked until Rory found us a hackney carriage. We sat side by side. I looked out of the dusty window, but I didn't see anything. My hand lay on Rory's leg. He unbuttoned my glove and eased it off slowly, finger by finger. He had removed his own glove. He traced circles on my palm.

All of my attention was on his hand, on the circles he was drawing, circles that were sending shivers up my arm, making my body thrum, making my nipples ache for his touch, making me feel as if I couldn't breathe. Making me want to moan my pleasure. I bit my lip, and he continued stroking my hand. I didn't dare look at him. I never wanted that journey to end. I was desperate for it to end.

When we arrived, and it did end, I did moan, softly. I heard the intake of his breath in response. I dare not look at him. I knew he was as aroused as I was. I knew, though I hadn't touched him. I don't recall descending from the coach or him paying the driver. I waited, barely aware of our surroundings.

But when the carriage pulled away and we ascended the shallow flight of marble steps to enter the hotel's reception area, Rory pulled me to one side. 'Marianne, I want…'

'So do I.'

He laughed shortly, his cheeks warm. 'Two rooms. I'll get two rooms. Then it's not too late to change your mind.'

'I won't, Rory.' Now that my decision had been made, I felt so certain. 'I won't change my mind.'

I thought he would kiss me there and then. He shuddered. He shook his head. He made to say something. Then he headed over to the reception desk. Five minutes later, we were being escorted up the stairs by a liveried porter who seemed to take our lack of luggage quite for granted, muttering about the shocking state of the Edinburgh railway, the vast numbers of passengers and the lack of railway porters.

Rory nodded in agreement, though I knew his mind was on me, almost entirely on me. He barely contained his impatience as the porter showed us the two adjoining rooms, one for Mr Sutherland, one for his good lady wife, and the little sitting room that separated them. Happy that he had earned the tip Rory slid into his waiting palm, the man finally departed.

And finally, belatedly, my nerves began to make themselves felt. 'I've never in my life been in a hotel before,' I said, going over to the sitting room window and staring out at the view of George Square. 'Do you think they believed that we are married?'

'If we'd been any younger, they might have been more sceptical. I'm not much interested in what anyone else thinks, however.'

'But you're nervous!' I exclaimed, unthinking.

He laughed shakily. 'Do you think I make a habit of this sort of thing?' He set his hat and gloves down on the table, and pushed his hair back from his brow. 'I've never in my life—not like this. And I'm thinking—or at least I'm trying to think—to tell myself—that we shouldn't.'

But I felt that this was meant. Our one chance. Fate had intervened. And I wanted so much, so desperately, for this to happen. Now. As did he, I was sure of it.

I set my gloves down beside his. I took off my bonnet. I draped my shawl over a chair. I went to him, putting one hand on each shoulder, and I leaned into him. 'I want you, Rory,' I whispered. 'I have never wanted anyone like this.' The truth of it made me light-headed. Whatever this was between us, it was like nothing ever before. The delight of that, and the relief made me giddy. 'And you want me too, don't you?'

'You know I do Marianne, every bit as much. And I've never…'

'Never,' I said, leaning closer.

'Never.'

Our lips met. This kiss was different. I felt the jolt of connection, joining, merging, the rightness of it, deep inside me. It was a kiss like nothing I'd ever felt before. Elemental. I didn't speak, but I said his name in my head, over and over. And he spoke to me in the same language. Mouth, minds, touching, melding.

Rory, I thought, raking my fingers through his hair.

Marianne, he said, pulling the pins from mine, running

his hands through my thick tresses, uncut for so long now that they hung down my back almost to my waist.

Rory. Pushing his coat back, I felt the heat of his skin through his shirt and waistcoat. The flex of his shoulders as I stroked, then the hiss of his exhaling breath.

Marianne. His mouth on my neck, kiss after kiss, fluttering down my skin, while he pushed back the neckline of my gown, and there were more kisses, on my collarbones, across the top of my breasts, making me sigh his name again.

His coat fell to the floor followed by his waistcoat, his collar and necktie. Kissing, we made our way to one of the bedchambers. Still kissing, we pulled the curtains closed. In the soft afternoon light, we stopped to look at each other for a moment, just a moment.

More?

Yes.

Oh, yes.

Passionate kisses now, but he was careful not to embrace me, his hands on my arms, on the fastenings of my gown, smoothing over my breasts, making my nipples harden and peak beneath the layers of my undergarments. I yearned for him. I ached for him. I was frantic for him. My desire for him staggered me, it was so new, so different, as if this was what I had always been waiting for. This man. This moment.

'Marianne.' His voice took me aback. His eyes were dark, his lids heavy, his breathing ragged. 'I need to know—are you certain?'

'You know I am.'

'If you change your mind…'

'I won't, Rory.'

He studied me for a long moment. Then he kissed me again, slowly this time, taking his time, but when I tried to deepen the kiss, he drew back. 'There's no hurry,' he said, and it confused me, for I thought there was always a hurry. There always had been before. My body was clamouring, roused. I remembered what I had forgotten. That I had reached this point but no further. That the rush there had always been had left me disappointed. I had been so sure that there was more, but there never was.

"Trust me,' Rory said, kissing me softly again. 'Will you trust me?'

I knew I could. I *knew.* I nodded, overcome, unable to speak.

He turned me around, pushing my hair over my shoulder to kiss my neck. He began to unbutton my gown, his mouth feathering kisses on each bit of skin he revealed. I gave myself over to him. He unwrapped me, layer by layer, and I stood pliant, though every touch, every kiss aroused me more. My gown slid to the floor. He reached around me to unfasten my corset, carefully working to untie the knots. Behind me, he was all but fully clothed, careful to keep a distance.

Trust me.

I resisted the urge to lean into him.

My corset fell to the floor. His arms were around me, but carefully, his hands cupping my breasts, his thumbs stroking my nipples through my chemise, drawing a long moan of pleasure from me.

Marianne. Marianne. Marianne.

The way he said my name roused me more. I could no longer resist leaning back into him, my petticoats against his thighs, his soft cry of pleasure as I nestled closer, emboldened by his arousal. My petticoats were next. I stepped out of them. He turned me back round to face him at last, and our mouths met again. Frantic this time. Not slow. Frantic. Still he did not embrace me, but I wanted to be closer. Pressing against him again, I felt him hard against my belly. His hands cupped my bottom, pulling me closer. Hot. I was so hot.

I tugged at his shirt. He pulled it over his head. I studied him. Taking my time. This was new. All of this was new. The way he watched me watching him. The anticipation, sharp between us, shared between us. I smoothed my hands over his skin, encouraged by the sharp intake of his breath, feeling the ripple of his muscles under my touch. Smooth skin. Rough hair on his chest. The dip of his belly. A scar, a long thin scar on his abdomen.

'Knife,' he said, as I traced the curve of it.

His skin was burning. I wanted to feel his arms around me, but I was afraid, and so I wrapped my arms around his waist instead. I burrowed my face into his chest, my smooth cheek, his rough hair, his nipple peaking under my palm, the smell of his soap, a faint tang of sweat. His hands smoothed my hair. He said my name and I looked up, seeing such tenderness in his expression. I slid my arms up around his neck and burrowed closer. Then our lips met again and we fell back on to the bed, still kissing. But though he had kicked off his shoes he was still wearing his trousers. I was frantic, but I wasn't sure what to do. What he wanted.

'Nothing,' he said to me, pushing my hair back from my face. 'I don't want anything. Trust me.'

I did, but I didn't understand, and I must have said so, for he smiled, a smile that I had never seen before, a smile that made my insides tense further with desire. Then he began to kiss me. My lips. My neck. My breasts. Taking my nipples in his mouth, teasing, sucking, licking, driving me wild, and stilling me with his hands. My belly. He knelt down and eased my legs apart. I grabbed his hair. He looked up. Another of those smiles. 'Do you want me to stop, Marianne?'

'No. No, no, no.' And as he kissed me again, his mouth soft and hot between my legs, 'Yes, yes. Oh, Rory, yes.'

His kisses made me feel like molten metal, melted chocolate, bubbling, burning sugar. I was a tightly coiled clock spring, I was a bow stretched too tight, I was clinging to a cliff face, my whole body tensed, and then I was shattered int a million pieces of pure and utter delight, spinning and spiralling out of control, as wave after wave of pleasure picked me up and tossed me in the air and then let me fall.

I was calling out his name, I was clutching at his hair, at his shoulders, my legs were wrapped tightly around his body, and then I was trying to pull him up towards me, to find his mouth. Such kisses. Such bliss. I was lying on top of him, my breasts flattened against his chest, kissing him frantically, saying his name urgently, his hardness pressed to the throbbing heat between my legs. He was still half dressed.

'Rory.' I tugged at the waistband of his trousers. He removed my hand and eased me on to my side. 'Rory?'

'I can't.' He sat up. 'It's not any lack of desire. I've never wanted anything so much in my life, but I simply can't—must not.'

'Why not?' I sat up too, pulling the sheet over my nakedness. 'What did I do? What's wrong?'

'There's nothing wrong. This couldn't feel more right, and that's the problem.'

The words frightened me, for they echoed what I was feeling. Instinctively, I shrank away from him.

Rory rolled out of bed and pulled on his shirt. 'I'm sorry.'

'You're *sorry*?'

'I don't mean that, not the way you think.'

'Then what do you mean? No, never mind. It's best if you leave me alone now.'

He took a step towards me then changed his mind. 'You're right.'

The door closed quietly behind him. I felt as if I'd been dropped violently from a very high, blissful place, to a very cold, rocky one. Tears burned my eyes. I burrowed my way under the sheets, digging my nails into my palms. I wasn't hurt. I wouldn't cry, but I had been *such* a fool.

Chapter Twenty-Four

Rory

Glasgow—
Tuesday 14th August 1877

Mr and Mrs Soutar lived in one of the newer, larger tenements in Shawlands on the South Side of the River Clyde. Mr Soutar was employed as a senior clerk in the local Camphill Bakery, while his son, Oscar, was an office junior in the Bank of Scotland in Queen Street. It was a delicate situation, and though Marianne and I had discussed how we'd set about it, as we reached the entrance to the close, I was on edge.

'After seven years, if we are right, we may be able to give this family some answers if not all,' she said to me, as I raised my hand to knock the door. 'This is the reason we are here in Glasgow, we must give it our full attention.'

It was the first oblique reference she'd made to last night. Though I'd ordered a dinner to be sent up to her before I went out for a walk to try to sort out the mess my head was in, she hadn't eaten a thing by the time I returned. I hadn't seen her until this morning, when she'd emerged from her room carrying her bonnet and gloves, and determined to talk to me about this visit and nothing else.

I introduced Marianne as my female assistant, for she'd had none of it when I suggested she could pretend to be my wife, and the Soutars seemed to accept this, son Oscar chiming in that he'd been reading all about Mrs Paschal, in Revelations of a Lady Detective. It took me a moment to work out he was referring to a work of fiction.

It was a heart-wrenching hour that we spent with the Soutar family. We already knew from my da's friend that Ada Soutar, their eldest child, had been reported missing around the same time as Lillian's body was found. Mr Soutar told us how much Ada had loved her job at Copland and Lye, one of the posh department stores on Sauchiehall Street that specialised in ladies' apparel.

She was always well turned-out thanks to the staff discount she got, her mother said. She was vain, her father said, and spent too much on frippery, but we must not be getting ideas, his daughter was a respectable young woman. Then he got upset, poor man, though he tried to hold himself together, blowing his nose and coughing, and saying he'd caught a cold paddling in the Clyde at the West Bay lido in Dunoon, which, to be fair, was highly plausible.

Mrs Soutar insisted on making us tea. After she brought in the tray, her husband produced the photograph of Ada, taken on her twenty-first birthday. She was looking primly at the camera, as they all do in those photographs, but you could see she had been a bonny lassie. The same bonny lassie that we'd pulled from Leith Docks, cut off in her prime of life, bearing another life that would never see the light of day. I had to clench my fists to mask my anger. A glance at Marianne showed me she was feeling the same surge of emotion. The waste of it. The pity of it. The senseless loss.

Which made me forget what I was feeling and turn my attention back to the ones who had suffered far more. We sombrely told them, the Soutar family, of their loss, and it was one of the hardest things I've ever had to do. The tea remained untouched on the tray. We sat with them as the shock gave way to grief. We told them only what we'd agreed, Marianne and I, almost exactly what I'd been told to think had happened all those years ago. Ada had died by accident. She'd tripped and fallen into the docks. She'd hit her head. She hadn't suffered. This last element wasn't true, but there was nothing to be gained by hurting them further. They didn't ask too many questions, the family, and for that I was grateful.

When we left them, Mrs Soutar and Oscar were crying unashamedly. Mr Soutar, with his eyes red-rimmed, took both my hands in the fiercest of grips. 'Thanks, Son,' he said. 'We'll be able to get her a headstone now.'

Both Marianne and I were silent on the journey back into town, and I knew that she was thinking, like me, of the bereaved family we'd left behind. In the waiting room at Dundas Street station, I ordered us both another cup of tea we didn't want, and buns I knew we wouldn't eat. We were both of us aware of the conversation we knew we had to have too, but neither of us had the appetite for that either.

I told myself it was because I wasn't sure of my state of mind, but it was the opposite of that, and I was equally sure that the last thing I should do was discuss it. As to Marianne, for once I hadn't a clue what she was thinking, and as she was clearly determined that I shouldn't, I knew her well enough not to push her.

'Well, we've done what we had to do,' I said. 'I'm glad you were with me. I reckon it made all the difference to Mrs Soutar.'

'We did the right thing, didn't we, in telling them their daughter was dead?'

'I had the proof the minute I saw the photograph.' I shivered, remembering the same woman lying prostrate on the side of Leith dock.

'Don't dwell on that, Rory,' Marianne said. 'Ada's family can grieve for her now. You heard her father. They will have a headstone erected for her in their church graveyard. She was much missed. She won't be forgotten. You have given them that much.'

'*We* have.'

'I have contributed very little.'

'That's nonsense. I wouldn't even have gone back to the case if it weren't for you.' I reached for her automatically, it had become a habit with me so quickly it was scary. Midway, I remembered, and I picked up my teacup instead.

She pretended not to notice. 'What next though, Rory?'

'I don't know. We know more about Ada, also thanks to you.'

'The "fancy rich gentleman admirer" that her mother told me about when we were in the scullery together. They must have had somewhere where they met regularly, don't you think?'

'It could be he had a flat, or rooms in the West End. Ada let fall to Oscar that she'd been taking walks in the Botanic Gardens. He couldn't understand why she'd go all the way from the South Side to the West End, when there was a big new park on her doorstep.'

'And Mrs Soutar was convinced that he was a successful

business man, something to do with property. She couldn't tell me how she arrived at that conclusion. It must have been something that Ada let drop, or that she overheard, and she put two and two together.'

'A bit like you do yourself,' I said. 'And you managed to get Mrs Soutar to admit she knew her daughter was expecting a baby. Neither the father nor the son had any idea about that.'

'Mrs Soutar was very keen that they never do. She has kept that secret for so long, if her husband found out now, it would make matters between them unbearable.'

'Soutar won't hear a bad word against his daughter,' I said. 'Every time I tried to ask him if she was walking out with anyone he bristled. Too much, actually. I reckon he must have some idea, after all. Maybe he noticed more than his wife realised and like her, kept silent.'

'Poor Mrs Soutar is heartbroken. The last thing Ada told her was that she was going to find the baby's father and force him to take care of her. She made her mother promise she'd keep the situation secret until she came home. But of course she never did come home.'

Marianne's eyes filled with tears. I wanted to comfort her, but she was already dabbing at her eyes, glaring at me as if to say, don't you dare. 'Did Mrs Soutar rate her daughter's chances of success?'

'The fact that Ada wouldn't tell her the man's name made her suspicious. I think that both she and Ada suspected it was not his real name.'

'So he was likely married?'

Marianne nodded. 'I'm afraid that makes horrible sense. It was Ada's words. She wanted him to "take care of her".'

'Not marry her, do the decent thing? You're right, the words are telling.'

'What do you think she did expect though, if not marriage?'

'Money? Somewhere decent for herself and the bairn to live? I don't know, it could have been anything.'

'But what she actually got—oh, Rory, she didn't deserve that.'

'No. My sex never cover themselves in glory, where you are concerned, do they?'

She flinched, paled. 'I don't blame you for last night, if that's what you mean. There is no need to inform me once again that you are sorry.'

'I didn't mean—I was referring to the bigamy case you told me about. As for last night…'

She shook her head violently. 'We are discussing Ada.'

We would need to discuss Marianne and Rory soon, but she was right. 'So, we've got a man who's more than likely married, who might be a property developer, who did a bunk when he discovered that Ada was expecting his child.'

'Does did a bunk mean he ran off?'

'It does.'

'But if he was well to do, why didn't he "take care of" Ada and the child before he left?'

'It's a good question. Perhaps he didn't know about the child. What's clear to me now that we've met them is that the Soutar family are not likely to benefit from knowing that their daughter was murdered.'

Marianne had been turning her cup around in its saucer without drinking the contents. At this, she looked up. 'Even if we discover who did it?'

'It's not going to bring Ada back, is it? As things stand,

no matter what they suspect, they can paint a picture for themselves and their family and friends too, if they want, that doesn't slander their wee lassie. Think about it, Marianne, they didn't ask us what she was doing in Leith, or even Edinburgh, for that matter. Mrs Soutar told you some of her thoughts, but Mr Soutar went out of his way *not* to ask. That's what been bothering me, now I come to think of it. It was his lack of questions.'

'So he does know more than he admitted to?'

'Like I said, he probably noticed Ada was pregnant, but he was sticking his head in the sand, hoping that someone else would deal with the situation.'

'Which poor Ada was trying to do. But what about poor Rory?' Marianne asked with a sad smile. 'You still want to know the truth, don't you? To know why your name was blackened? After all this time…'

'After all this time,' I said slowly, 'I'm beginning to think it doesn't really matter that much at all. We've given the family some peace of mind, so they can stop wondering. Right now, I'm thinking that might be enough for me too.'

There were other things on my mind. One in particular, sitting opposite me. Whatever we said at the time, what happened between us yesterday mattered a great deal more than it should have, and it had to be dealt with. I checked my watch and saw to my relief that our train was due. 'It's time we went. Mind now, the platform will be busy.'

'I am prepared for it this time, thank you.'

She marched off, making it clear that she too had been thinking about last night, and she wasn't' ready to talk about it either. I threw some coins down on the table, cursing under my breath for she was almost immediately enveloped in a cloud of smoke. I grabbed hold of her, just as she clutched at me. 'Rory.' She sounded relieved but unsurprised. She tucked her hand into my arm.

We travelled First Class. It was a calculated risk, for there might be a fellow traveller that recognised me, but I hadn't slept a wink last night, and I doubted Marianne had either. The last thing we needed was two hours on a wooden bench exposed to the driving rain that was falling that typical summer's day. We had the carriage to ourselves.

Marianne pretended to be asleep. I passed the journey trying to decide what to do or not do about the tangle I'd got myself into, and in the end I opted to wait until I got back to my digs. If there was a telegram from the Marquess then that at least took one of the decisions out of my hands. It was procrastinating, but I told myself it wasn't, and turned my mind back to Ada Soutar's murder.

Money, as usual, was what it almost certainly came back to. Someone from Edinburgh with enough money to invest in building property in the West End of Glasgow. Someone who maybe had installed his lady friend in one of them. Someone who had completed his business in Glasgow, and scarpered back home, maybe in the knowledge that he was leaving his lady friend carrying his child and his empty promises behind, maybe oblivious to the situation. Someone wealthy and powerful enough to pay someone to make the problem go away. And to have me dealt with as well, when I looked like I might be getting too close—not that I had, but I would have if they'd let me, they had been right to worry.

Edinburgh was a big city and I'd been away seven years, but I doubted the cream at the top of society had changed much. By the time we reached Waverly, I had drawn up a list in my head of possible candidates. Would I do anything to pursue it? Seven years, I'd been waiting to get this close.

Seven years, I'd been nursing a grudge, letting it gnaw away at me, and wondering why what had happened to me had happened. The list in my head was a short one, but what good would it do me? There was no evidence. What's more, after seven years I was scunnered thinking about it. I had other, more pressing matters on my mind.

Marianne wanted to make her own way home. Like me, she clearly wanted to be alone with her thoughts, so I didn't protest, much as I wanted to. I knew I had some life-changing decisions to make, and we'd reached a temporary impasse between us, but the moment she started to walk away, all I wanted was to have her by my side.

I didn't go straight back to my digs. I decided that after all I didn't want a telegram or lack of a telegram from the Marquess to decide my fate, I wanted it to be my own decision. So I took myself off, up Salisbury Craggs in the rain.

I reached the top in record time, head down, marching up, until I arrived out of breath and soaked to the skin. There was no view to speak of today, you could hardly see Duddingston, never mind Leith, so there was nothing to distract me, and not a soul about save for the gulls and the crows.

First things first. There was no denying it, no dancing around it, no more trying to kid myself on. I was in love with Marianne. Deeply, head over heels, desperately in love with Marianne for ever. How did I know, when I'd never been in love before? I just did, simple as that. What happened to all my, I'm too old to fall in love, I'm not the type to fall in love reasons? Easily answered. I'd never fallen in love before because I hadn't met the right person. If I hadn't met Marianne, I would still be the type that didn't fall in love. She was the only one for me. No one else would do. Like I said, simple.

Simple if only it wasn't such a bloody tangle. I was in love. The one straightforward thing I could say to her. I love you. God help me, I'd near enough said it yesterday when I was making love to her. And I'd been making love. That was the thing that hit me like a ton of bricks afterwards. I mean, really making love, to the woman I was in love with. I closed my eyes and lifted my face to the rain, and I let myself wallow in every perfect moment of it.

And it had been perfect, for her as well as me. That's not me bragging, that's just something else I knew in my heart, as if she'd told me herself. It had been perfect. Like nothing else before for either of us. It was it being so perfect that made those other times so irrelevant. I didn't want to think of her with another man any more than I wanted to think of myself with another woman, but it didn't matter. For me, she was the only one, as if there hadn't ever been anyone else before. And there wouldn't be anyone after.

Not even her?

Especially not her! I came out of my dwam to find it was tipping it down again, so I cowered under the crags for shelter. Time to come back down to earth. What the devil had I been playing at yesterday? Or with? Fire, that's what, and now I'd been well and truly and deservedly burned, for I'd paid no heed to the many warnings I'd issued to myself.

I'd known that it was a mistake to stay over in Glasgow, but I'd done it anyway. I'd known that I was lying to myself, when I agreed we were only 'making the most of the situation'. How many times since we first met had I sworn to myself that I wouldn't kiss her again, then by some tortuous logic, allowed myself to carry on in her company until

I couldn't resist her. Me, the detective who prided myself on being able to second-guess everyone's motives, I'd been blind when it came to myself.

But there's only so much self-lacerating you can do. It was done, and I'd done it to myself. Question was, what to do for the best. No, the first question was, what was Marianne thinking? How did she feel? She didn't love me. Did she? She certainly didn't want to love me. And even if she loved me now, at this moment, would she still love me after she found out the truth? Would she think I'd been pretending to fall in love with her when all the time I was actually in love with her inheritance?

No way! Bloody hell, surely she couldn't believe that of me. But if I asked her to marry me before I told her about the money—no, I couldn't do that. Then if I asked her to marry me after I told her about the money—no, I couldn't do that either. What's more, I was losing sight of something even more important. This was about Marianne, and who she was, and the shock she was going to get when she found out. When I told her. That was one decision made. Whatever the Marquess decreed, I was going to be the one who told her. I owed her that.

In the end, it actually was simple. There was no hope. Even if she would have considered marrying me right now, with none of these other things hanging over us, I doubted that she would consider it. She'd been crystal clear that she didn't want a husband, just as I had been crystal clear that I didn't want a wife. Unless it was Marianne.

I was going round and round in circles, and my head was aching as if I'd dunted it on the crags. And here's the thing—yet another thing. Marianne wasn't Marianne. She was Lady Mary Anne Westville. Heiress. Who, if all went well, would do wonderful things with her money, and who deserved to be free to do whatever she wanted, after all she'd suffered. Whatever her plans were, I would play no part in them.

Yesterday, I shouldn't have made love to her, but having done so, I shouldn't have said I was sorry afterwards. I wasn't sorry. It was wrong of me, and the memories would likely eat me up later, but I wasn't sorry. In my own way I'd demonstrated how I felt. I'd always have that.

There was a crack of thunder, followed quickly by a fork of lightning over Duddingston way and another long roll of thunder. We were in for a spectacular storm. The sensible thing now would be to sit it out, but I seemed to have turned into someone incapable of being sensible, lately. I pulled up the collar of my already sodden coat, and began to head back down the hill.

Chapter Twenty-Five

Marianne

Edinburgh—
Wednesday 15th August 1877

Ever since Monday in Glasgow, I had had a crushing sense of an imminent ending. Now we knew that it was Ada Soutar who had been murdered, and at least part of the reason why, we were close to resolving Rory's old case. Soon he would have answers to the questions that had tortured him for seven long years, or he would know that he would never have answers. If he chose to pursue the matter, that was.

In the tearoom at Dundas Street, he had not seemed particularly eager. After all this time haunted by his failure to solve the case and the blackening of his name, Rory had seemed almost dismissive of his own involvement. Ada's family could grieve. That was enough, he seemed to be saying. He could stop searching for answers. He could leave Edinburgh. Which would be for the best. That's what I told myself over and over during my sleepless night. It would be better for both of us if he left Edinburgh.

I did not love Rory. I would not love Rory. I would never, ever, let myself fall in love again. But I had come perilously close. It terrified me, how close I had come. And he had too. His face, when he left the hotel bedroom on Monday, spoke of how much he felt, and how much he regretted. And his words.

I've never wanted anything so much in my life.

This couldn't feel more right, and that's the problem.

Those were *my* thoughts, though I hadn't known I was thinking them until Rory spoke them aloud.

The man I thought I loved had turned on me because I would not marry him. I would not surrender my freedom to Francis, bind myself in marriage, become his. But he had made me his anyway, his prisoner, his madwoman. Love had almost killed me.

I would not love Rory. I did not love Rory. Rory did not love me. On Monday, in the hotel in Glasgow, I thought he might. I thought he was on the point of speaking of it. I *wanted* him to speak, and that's what terrified me more than anything, that I wanted what would destroy me. Rory wasn't Francis. Rory *wasn't* Francis. All of my instincts told me that I could trust Rory, had told me so from the start. When Rory kissed me, I *felt* his longing for me. When he was with me, I was sure it was because he wanted to be with me.

This couldn't feel more right.

I felt exactly the same.

And that was the problem. My instincts had let me down with Francis. The one and only time I had been utterly wrong, and the one and only time when I relied upon them to guide me. I couldn't trust myself. I couldn't take the risk that I might be wrong again.

At least my wakeful night had spared me my usual dreams, my usual waking terror. In fact, it had been two or three days since I had woken with the smell of the institution in my nose, my sheets clammy. My dreams had been of Rory these last few nights, not the asylum. A few weeks ago, two weeks ago, as little as a week ago, I'd have given a great deal to pass one night without my dreams of that place, without having to wake terrified, clammy, imagining myself back there. I had done so for the last few days, and I hadn't even noticed!

I rolled out of bed and opened the window. It was still raining, though softly now after last night's storm. The cobblestones on the Grassmarket were shining, slickly wet and treacherous. I was later than usual, for there was Flora, plaid wrapped tightly around her, hair in soaking rat's tails, heading into the tavern. Surely she could not have had much business in last night's foul weather? Poor woman. If I was in her situation, I would be sorely tempted to earn money from Billy Sinclair.

My stomach rumbled. I closed the window and made my coffee, forcing myself to eat some bread and cheese. There was a possibility Rory might be thinking himself in love with me. And oh, if he was—my heart fluttered wildly.

But if Rory found out he was in love with an escaped lunatic, that would quickly put an end to it. I would never trust anyone with the truth about myself again. Rory already knew far more than I should have told him. I would not give him any more power over me. No more kisses. No more thinking about kisses. No more dreaming about making love to him, or remembering those perfect, wonderful, blissful hours in Glasgow when it had been just the two of us. The lovemaking that had been such a revelation. The lovemaking that had introduced me to a whole new world of sensation. The love that Rory had made to me, giving without taking.

Oh, Rory.

Oh, Marianne, get a grip of yourself!

I set my coffee cup down, and jumped to my feet. I needed him to leave Edinburgh. I needed to tell him to go. I sat back down again. Wouldn't it be better if I never saw Rory again? My heart sank. Never?

One last time. Then goodbye. Resolved, I dressed myself and prepared to seek him out to tell him so. I still had no idea where his lodgings were, but Flora might be able to help me. I was pulling on my cloak when there was a rap at my door that made my heart leap in fear. No one ever knocked on my door except the landlord, and my rent was not due. I stood stock still, willing whoever it was to go away. They rapped again.

'Marianne. Don't be afraid. It's Rory.'

Relief flooded through me. I threw the door open, but seeing him standing there, I was flooded with a very different emotion. 'What do you want?'

'I need to talk to you. I know you don't want me here, I know this is your sanctuary, but I need to talk to you, and in private. It's important. May I come in?'

I didn't love him, I told myself as I stood back to allow him in. But my heart was telling me I did. Deluded heart.

He was looking about him, though he was pretending he wasn't. My rooms that were mine and mine alone, were being surveyed. 'You have quite a view from here.'

I crossed my arms. 'I was on the point of going out.' To look for him as it happens, but I wasn't going to say so.

'What is so important—oh! Rory, have you found out who the father of Ada's child is?'

'What? No. I've a list of possible suspects, but I've decided not to pursue it.'

'Not pursue it! You've spent the last seven years wondering…'

'And I reckon I'll never know. I can suspect all I like, but we've not a scrap of evidence to link anyone to Ada's death. We've given her family an ending, and they can grieve now. Whoever was behind it…'

'Is getting away with murder! And with blackening your name. Destroying your career. You've been wondering and wondering why and who, Rory, for all those years.'

'I've realised it doesn't matter any more. I've made my life somewhere else. I don't want to go backwards. Whoever ordered Ada Soutar's death will pay in the end. Bad things eventually happen to bad people. But me—it's time I put the whole thing to bed for good. I'm done with it, and I actually feel relieved.'

'So you're leaving.' I had what I wanted, and now I didn't want it. He said nothing for a moment, words forming and being rejected as he gazed at me, and my stomach roiled, for it was such a look. 'What is it, Rory?'

'I've had a telegram. It's not Ada Soutar that I'm here to talk to you about, Marianne. It's my other case. The case that brought me here.'

My legs turned to jelly. I had no idea what he was going to say, but I knew I didn't want to hear it. 'You said it was suspended for two weeks. You said that you were waiting on something. A piece of the puzzle that needs clarifying, that's what you said.'

'It's sorted now. Marianne, the case…'

'Has something to do with me.' It was his face. The tone of his voice. No, it was more than that. All the pieces slotted together, all the clues that he'd given me that I hadn't realised I'd picked up, filed away, until I could make sense of them. The odd times when I'd thought he was on the brink of telling me something important. And the questions he'd asked me. I'd even accused him of interrogating me once. I sank on to the chair. My coffee cup still lay half-full on the table.

'Marianne, you're white as a sheet.'

I had been right to be wary. I had been right not to trust myself and right not to trust him. I had been looking over my shoulder all this time and it turned out the person they had sent to find me was Rory!

Chapter Twenty-Six

Rory

Edinburgh—
Wednesday 15th August 1877

I'd already decided there was no future for us, of my own accord. When I read the telegram from Lord Westville, that confirmed it. When I came here, I knew it. But seeing Marianne's face when she realised she'd been my quarry all along—that was when it really sank in. That was when I realised that right up until that point, I'd still been hoping there was a way for us to be together, fool that I was!

'Who sent you?' she asked me, whey-faced, her lovely eyes wide with fear, her hands gripped tightly together, knuckles white.

'It's not bad news,' I said hastily, appalled by the notion that must be crossing her mind, that I'd been sent to lock her up again. 'I promise, you're not in any danger.'

'You promise!'

The look she gave me then. She'd trusted me, and as far as she was concerned, I had been lying to her all along. I drew up a chair and sat down opposite her. I was really struggling not to tell her what I was feeling. I mean, really struggling. As if that would make things any easier. More like a bloody sight worse.

I'd been awake all night trying to work out the least painful way to explain, but I decided that the best thing was simply to get it over with. So I told her, about my meeting with Lord Westville and about the woman he had employed me to find. 'She'd be a distant cousin of his—of my client's I mean,' I said, trying to keep my voice level. Trying, too, to keep my own feelings in check, for I didn't want her sensing them, and I didn't want what I was feeling getting in the way of what I was telling her. This wasn't about me. Or us. It was about Marianne.

She had herself in check again, holding herself painfully rigid. 'He had no idea she existed, this distant cousin, is that what you are telling me?'

'None at all. I was sceptical when he told me at first, but what he told me of his own father convinced me.' I waited, giving her plenty time to sort through what I'd told her before moving on. I'd never seen her so tightly wound.

'So your Lord Westville's father knew of her, but he had no interest in her fate. And *her* father had no interest in making her acquaintance, even after he had paid someone else to go to the trouble of raising her. Am I correct?'

That cold tone. Those measured words. I wanted to tell her she had it wrong. I wanted to tell her that her father had cared, but I didn't know what he'd felt, and it wasn't my place to make her guesses or suppositions for her. 'Yes, but *my* Lord Westville, as you call him, employed me to find her.'

'And how did you set about doing that?'

I told her all of it. Asylum to asylum. Then Nurse Crawford. My voice cracked a couple of times. Marianne was retreating further and further into her shell before my very eyes. I swear, it was like she was turning to stone. 'That led me to Mrs White at the employment agency in Edinburgh. I pretended that I was looking to employ a children's nurse hoping to find more information, but I was given short shrift. She was clearly protecting you.'

'I owe Mrs White more than I can put into words.'

'It wasn't difficult though, to find you in this city without her help. There was the name you'd assumed. And as you've told me yourself, you're good at what you do.'

'As are you, clearly, Detective Sutherland,' she said coldly.

'Marianne, do you understand the implications of what I've told you so far? Your real name is Lady Mary Anne Westville. You're the legitimate daughter of a marquess.'

'You have discovered that I am also an escaped lunatic.'

'There's nothing wrong with your mind! You must know that I've never for one minute thought that you were locked up for genuine reasons. I think that you're the strongest, bravest woman I could ever wish to meet. Even before I set eyes on you, I was in awe of you. To have come through what they did to you, to keep your mind perfectly sane, to have the confidence and belief in yourself—Marianne, I swear to god, that's what I think, and more. You're an amazing woman. I told you that before, and I meant it. I still mean it.'

I could see her throat working. I could feel tears smarting in my own eyes, but I held her gaze. I wasn't ashamed of what I was feeling. I wanted her to know that. Finally, she gave a little nod, picked her cup up and found it empty.

'Shall I make another pot?'

'Please.'

I was glad of it, something to do for her and a breather for both of us. I'd always known this would be difficult, but watching her was proving an agony. And there was a lot more to come. 'Do you want me to get you something stronger?' I asked, setting the fresh cup down. 'I could nip across to the White Hart.'

She shook her head. She lifted the cup, her hands shaking, and took several sips. 'You know that if it ever came out that I was committed to an asylum...'

'That you were wrongly held against your will...'

'Does he know, this man who has employed you to find me?'

'He knows the bones of it.'

'And what did he...?' Her mouth wobbled, and she took another sip of her coffee. 'It doesn't matter. I am not interested in meeting him, any more than he will be interested in meeting me.'

'You're wrong, Marianne. He's your family, and...'

'My mother died giving birth. My father gave me away. His heir was so indifferent he never even mentioned my existence. I was not wanted, Rory. The message could not be clearer.'

I wanted to argue with her, but it would be a distraction, and I wasn't at all sure of my employer's feelings. The Marquess was set on justice, for getting Marianne her inheritance and making Eliot pay for what he'd done to her, but of his intentions regarding the woman who was his kin, he'd said nothing since I'd told him she was alive. Why should he? As far as he was concerned, to me, Marianne was merely a case to be solved. If he ever knew—I shuddered. He wouldn't, and it was beside the point.

'Lord Westville, your cousin, is on your side,' I said, which was true enough. And what's more, he was going out of his way to get her legacy for her, which must mean something.

But Marianne's lip curled. 'Lord Westville, my cousin! Mrs Oliphant will be delighted to discover that she has a marquess's daughter for a governess, don't you think? Lady Mary Anne Westville! That's not me. I have a name, I chose it myself, and I intend to keep it. Are you finished with your revelations, Rory? Now I come to think of it, why did you save them for now?'

It was the question I'd been dreading. I had resolved to stick to the facts, but I couldn't help but tell her something closer to the truth. 'I was tasked with finding you, but as to telling you—it was complicated. I was told to say nothing until what I referred to as the final piece of the puzzle was resolved, but it wasn't only that. There was so much I knew of your heritage that was likely to come as a huge shock to you, and from the first time we spoke, I felt…'

'Don't!' She jumped to her feet and hurried over to the window, throwing it open. 'Please don't, Rory. We—I—whatever you are feeling, I don't want to know.' She turned back around, but kept her distance, her hands clasped at her breast, her eyes pleading. 'You were right, what you said when we—after we—you were right. It was a mistake.'

'I didn't say that.'

'You said you were sorry.'

'I was, but not…'

'Please! We have been foolish and irresponsible, and it is as much my fault as yours. It was I who insisted that I was meant to help you. I who inflicted my company on you.'

'Inflicted! I clutched at any excuse to spend time with you.'

'Even though you knew me for an escaped lunatic.'

I opened my mouth to chastise her again, then I closed it. Her eyes were bright with tears, but her mouth was trembling in an attempt at a smile. 'Your sense of humour is part of your charm,' I said. 'One of the many reasons I was drawn to you.'

'Oh, Rory.'

She turned her back on me again, but not before I caught a glimpse of my own feelings reflected in her face. Or thought I did. And I tried to tell myself it didn't matter, but it did. It did my heart good, even if it changed nothing. Then she turned around, and it was clear that she had herself back in check, and that brought me back down to earth.

'You could have told me before now.' Her tone was businesslike. 'As I recall there were several occasions when you were on the brink of telling me the truth, but you changed your mind. Why?'

'I didn't have the full story and I was told to wait until I had it.' The facts, but not the truth. I couldn't leave it at that. 'I was to keep an eye on you, make sure you didn't come to any harm, and I was very happy to do that, because it was what I wanted, to spend time with you.'

'So you lied?'

'I have never lied to you. I've not been completely honest with you, but I've never lied.'

'Did you think I needed protecting, Rory, was that it? Did you think that I wasn't strong enough to deal with what you had to tell me?'

'You're strong, all right, but that place still haunts you, and no wonder. Then there was the fact that you had built a new life for yourself…'

'One I'm perfectly happy with.'

'That too. And I can relate to that. So I decided to wait

until I was in possession of all the facts. After Glasgow though, I'd decided to tell you anyway. It just so happened that when I got back to my digs, I had a telegram telling me to go ahead.'

Marianne narrowed he eyes at me. 'What else do you have to tell me?'

For a wee tiny moment, I wanted to end it there. I'd already put us both through the wringer, but we weren't even halfway done. I fingered the telegram in my pocket.

Legal matters resolved. Inform my cousin of her good fortune. Then return immediately to London to address the matter of retribution regarding Eliot.

Twenty-three words, ten of them instructing me to turn Marianne's world upside down. And the other thirteen forcing me to part from her, even though I'd already decided I needed to do that. Twenty-three in total. I'd choose my own with care.

'Rory?'

First things first. 'Your father didn't raise you, Marianne, but he did make provision for you.'

'The allowance that was paid to my foster parents, and then to me.'

'It was much more than that.' I took a breath. 'He left you a fortune.'

'What do you mean, a fortune?'

Keep it simple, I reminded myself. Stick to the facts. I told her the sum that Lord Westville had given me. She had the same reaction that I'd had. Her jaw dropped.

'Exactly.' For the first time, I hesitated.

Needless to say, she pounced. 'What?'

'There were conditions attached.' I told her, sticking to the facts again. Marianne turned paler and paler before my eyes. 'Do you understand what I'm telling you?' I asked, when the silence became unbearable.

'The man you tell me is my father left me a fortune, but though he had never met me, he believed me incapable of administering it, or perhaps he thought I'd fritter it away over the next hundred years, which is what it would take, given the huge sums involved. For whatever reason, he decided that I needed a sensible male to look after it for me. A husband, in other words. Do I have that right?'

'You do. And until you married, a trustee.'

'When did he die, Rory? The man you tell me is my father?'

'About seven years ago.'

I hadn't thought she could turn any paler, but she looked like a ghost now. There was something wrong. Something I didn't understand.

'And the name of my trustee?' Her voice wasn't much more than a whisper.

A horrible premonition took hold of me. 'Francis Eliot.'

I leapt to my feet, thinking she was about to fall off her chair, but she shrank from me. 'Don't touch me!'

It was a kick in the teeth, that look, those words, but I bit back everything I was feeling, and made myself sit back down, let her be, trying desperately to keep a rein on myself.

'Francis Eliot was the man who had me committed. I presume you knew that, Rory?'

I nodded, afraid to speak. I felt almost as sick as she looked.

'But what you didn't know—ah, but I can see you have

now put two and two together. Francis Eliot was the man that I…' She broke off, pushed her chair back but changed her mind about getting up. 'Francis Eliot was the man who wanted to marry me. So you were right all along, Rory. It really was all about the money.'

The last vestiges of colour drained from her face. I was on my feet as she began to topple sideways.

Chapter Twenty-Seven

Marianne

Edinburgh—
Wednesday 15th August 1877

I woke up on the floor, cradled in Rory's arms. For a blessed, wonderful, magical moment I lay there, drinking in the tender expression on his face, bathed in the warmth of the love that emanated from him, soothed by the gentle touch of his hand stroking my brow, and his embrace keeping me safe. Rory loved me. I loved him.

'No!' I yanked myself free and struggled to my feet. A wave of nausea hit me, but I pushed him away, clutching at the chair instead. It all came flooding back to me then. I sank on to the chair, waving Rory away. 'Sit down. Keep away from me.'

He did as I bid him, though he looked as sick as I felt. I poured the dregs of the coffee, aiming for my cup and only managing to get some of it in. It was cold and much stronger than I'd have made. I gulped it down. The harshness of it in my throat, hitting my stomach, steadied me.

Across from me, Rory's hands were shaking. He clasped

them together on the table. His frown was so deep it drew his brows together. 'So that's how Eliot gathered the evidence that was used against you…'

'He used my own words against me. Like an idiot I trusted him.'

'Oh, Marianne…'

I shrank back, though he'd made no move to reach for me. 'Did you suspect him from the first? Or was it when you saw his name on my papers in the asylum?'

He cursed under his breath. His father's language, but he made the soft Gaelic sound vicious. Then he gave himself a shake and began to speak in a tone I recognised, drained of emotion, reined in tight. 'Lord Westville and I—we've been very careful to make sure Eliot knows nothing of our suspicions, but, yes, we did suspect him from the first. He was the obvious candidate.

'It's a great deal of money and he was left solely in charge and unsupervised, so it was easy for him to take advantage. Eliot's family have served the Westville family for many years. Lord Westville—your father—left him a token sum in his will, and a hell of a lot of responsibility. I reckon he resented the fact that you, who'd never even been acknowledged by his employer, had been given what he could have put to better use. So when the next Lord Westville, my client's father, showed no interest in you or the money, Eliot decided to appropriate it.'

'By appropriating me.'

Rory winced, then nodded.

'And when I refused to be appropriated…'

'He came up with an alternative.' He turned green. Pushing back his chair, he strode for the scullery. There was silence, then a clattering. When he returned, his face was damp. 'I'm sorry.'

'Not as sorry as I am.' A cold rage had seized me. 'I gave him the evidence of my own free will.'

'And he contorted it and turned it against you. It's not your fault, Marianne. Men like that are utterly selfish. Once he got his hands on the capital, he thought of it as his own, to do with as he pleased.'

'And provided I remained safely out of the way, and your client's father remained indifferent to my fate, he did just that. Did he attempt to find me after I escaped?'

'I don't know. I doubt it.'

'No, your right. I was even less of a threat to him, as an escaped lunatic, wasn't I?'

Rory flinched. 'He knew you wouldn't want to be found.'

'And by escaping, I'd saved him the expense of keeping me in the institution,' I said bitterly. 'How unfortunate for him, that your Lord Westville's father died prematurely. I'm afraid he has still managed to spend some of the money or rather lose some of it, in poor investments. He's greedy, but he's not canny.'

'I don't care! I'm not interested in the money. Why the devil would you think I'd want it after all the pain and suffering it has caused me?'

'But this is about more than the money. I told you, I distinctly remember telling you that day in Greyfriars, that it was about putting things to rights. Giving you answers to the questions that you've been asking yourself for years. And making Eliot pay, Marianne. You want that, don't you?'

Eliot. Francis Eliot.

The name made me sick to my stomach. I stared at Rory, my head reeling. What I wanted, what I desperately wanted, was to be in his arms again. To wrap my body around him. To forget all of this, all that he'd told me, everything. To see that look on his face. Tenderness. Love.

No, it couldn't be love. Right from the very start Rory had been lying to me. More importantly, I had been lying to myself, telling myself we were meant to be together, finding reasons to justify my desire, fooling myself into thinking that he wanted it too. It was all a lie. I hadn't learned from my catastrophic mistake, and this time it hurt so much more. This time, even though I knew Rory must have been pretending, just as Francis must have been pretending, this time my own feelings persisted.

I had fallen in love with Rory. Too late, I saw it so clearly. Rory wasn't Francis. I had recovered from what I felt—from what I thought I felt—for Francis in an instant. As I looked at Rory across the table what I felt, to my horror, was a conviction that I would never get over him.

It's why I told him then, all of it. The sad story of a poor nobody who had been so easily wooed by a vile, twisted, money-grabbing lawyer. As soon as I began to speak, the dam burst and it all came flooding out. How flattered I had been to have such a personable, charming man pay attention to me. How naive I had been, imagining that Francis saw something no one else had in me. How clever he had been to see that I had never been loved. How manipulative I knew now he had been to endear himself to me.

'I was convinced that he loved me. I sensed his desperate need of me from the first,' I said, forcing the words out, lacerating myself with them, and Rory too, set upon teaching us both a lesson we would not forget. 'The clues were all there, but for once I failed to make a picture of them. "I couldn't believe it when I discovered you were not already married", he said to me. "You have no idea how much I need you. No idea how much I want you." Looking back, I can't recall that he ever told me he loved me. I thought he did.'

Rory listened, frozen in his chair, saying not a word.

'I let him make love to me.' I continued, though the memory made me want to retch. 'I *wanted* him to make love to me.' Had I? It had been nothing like the wanting I'd felt for Rory. And it had been disappointing, though I had not dared say so, even to myself. I had had nothing to compare it with. Now I did. Now I knew. Rory.

Oh, Rory.

Francis! I made myself recall his face. Francis, my betrayer. 'I trusted him.' Here, I was on horribly solid ground. 'I told him about my insights, I told him some of the pictures my mind made for me. He was so interested. Fascinated. I'd never told anyone before. Then when I declared I could not marry him, he took what I'd told him and he made his own version of it all. "If I can't have you, I'm going to make sure no one else can." Those were the words he threw at me that night. I had no idea what he meant. I had no notion. None! All the time I was locked up, when the doctors were telling me that I was mad, when I was trying to tell them, to explain, the one thing that almost drove me mad was not knowing why. What had I done to make him hate me so much. And now I know.'

I hadn't meant to cry, but when the tears came they flooded my eyes and streamed down my face. I scrubbed at them, but more came and with the tears the memories I thought long lost. '"I won't let you ruin me," Francis told me. And he said that I was ruined for any other decent man. He said that no other man would have me now. As if I cared. As if I would be so stupid as to ever want another man.'

Except I had indeed been so stupid and the evidence was sitting opposite me, looking at me as if his heart was breaking.

No! If anyone's heart was breaking, it was mine. My tears dried. I dabbed my face with my sodden handkerchief. 'I would like you to leave now,' I said, my voice hoarse with crying.

'I can't leave you like this, Marianne.'

Rory looked wretched. Well, and so he should! 'There's no point in you remaining. You may return to your client and tell him that you've done what he paid you to do.'

'It's not as simple as that. There's your inheritance to be considered. Think of all the good you could do with that money. You could open as many schools as you wish. You could give so many wee lassies an opportunity they'd never get otherwise. If you wanted to, you could even help Flora escape her sordid life.'

I hated that he understood me so well. I had allowed that. I had let him into my mind and my thoughts. And my heart. 'Her name is Katy, not Flora,' I said.

He chose not to engage with this petty line of conversation. I wanted him to argue with me. I wanted him to get angry. I wanted him to be unreasonable. I wanted him to behave as Francis had, lobbing accusations and insults. Rory remained in his seat. He was hurt and he was angry, but not with me. 'What made you change your mind about marrying him?' he asked. 'It must have been something more than you waking up one morning and realising you didn't love him.'

'Does it matter?'

'Only to me, and you've made it pretty clear that I don't count.'

I should have been pleased to hear him say so. I didn't have to tell him, but I did. 'After the first time. The only time we—he—I felt there was something wrong.' I closed my eyes, not wanting to recall, but my mind produced a vivid memory. 'He was—he was jubilant.' And I had been—deflated? No, disappointed.

'So you sensed, though you didn't know you knew, that he was leading you on?'

'I wanted to believe that someone loved me. I had never been loved so I was ripe for the plucking.'

'Ach, don't say that, Marianne.' He pushed his chair back, made to move towards me, but I warded him off. 'Don't take the blame for what that man did to you, do you hear me?'

'It was my fault! I knew, you've just pointed out that I must have known, and I didn't listen to the warning bells until afterwards. And then—and then I knew he would be the death of me.'

'You thought he'd kill you?'

I shook my head. All those times I'd tried to explain, and no one had listened. What was the point of explaining again? Still, I wanted Rory to understand. Even though it didn't matter. 'I thought that if I married him, it would kill me—inside.'

'Your spirit? That he'd crush your spirit?'

Tears welled up again. I wished fervently now that I had not told him, that he had not understood. It didn't matter because he didn't love me, and even if he did, it didn't change anything. 'I thought I'd saved myself,' I said, the words uttered of their own accord. 'By refusing him. But I didn't.'

'You did, though. You survived three years of incarceration. You escaped. And now look at you. You're a wonderful woman, Marianne.'

I wouldn't listen. I wouldn't believe him. I shook my head fiercely.

'You knew,' Rory insisted. 'Your instincts weren't wrong. You knew he was desperate to marry you. You knew that he needed you. Both of those were true. What you got wrong were his reasons. And now you're thinking that I'm like Eliot, aren't you, history repeating itself? I turned up out of the blue, and I pretended to be taken with you. Not because I was, but for my own reasons. You're thinking that I pretended that I wanted you, because it suited me to get to know you, to make sure that you were who I thought you were.'

'You're a detective on a case!'

'And what I was feeling for you—as a detective on a case—was morally wrong. I've known that. I've fought it. But I kept giving in to it, even though I knew I shouldn't.'

'So that's why you were so sorry in Glasgow. Because you broke your own rule book.'

'I wasn't sorry for what we did. I'll never forget what we shared together. I was only sorry that it could come to nothing.'

'Because you'd eventually have to admit you'd been lying to me.'

'I wasn't lying! Whatever you want to tell yourself, what happened between us it's something special. But we've no future together, I've known that from the first. You made it clear that you're not interested in marriage…'

'As did you!'

'I've never been interested in marrying anyone until…'

'Until you met an heiress! Ah no, that was unworthy of me.'

'It makes no difference,' Rory said, after a moment. 'You don't believe a word I say now, and I completely understand why. As far as you're concerned I've been lying to you, and after what you've told me about Eliot...'

'You're not Francis.' I hadn't meant to say so, but I couldn't help it.

However, he shook his head. 'It makes no difference. You don't trust me, and why should you. Fact is, what I've just told you puts us poles apart. I'm a detective...'

'And I am an escaped lunatic.'

'You're a survivor, is what you are! You are...'

He broke off, shaking his head again. When he spoke next, the emotion was stripped from his voice. He sounded intensely weary. 'You're a peeress in your own right. You've a title, a family, and a fortune. You don't have to have anything to do with Lord Westville if you don't want to. He's your kin, and he's sorry for how you've been treated, and he wants to make amends, but he's not the type to force his company on anyone. He's a cold fish, but he's a decent man. But whatever you do, Marianne, take the money. Not for yourself, but for what you can do for others.'

He picked up his hat, looking at it as if he had no idea what it was. 'Where are you going?' I asked, panicking, speaking without thinking again. I wanted him to go, didn't I?

'London. Lord Westville wants Eliot dealt with before he becomes suspicious. We want to make sure he doesn't make a bolt for it.'

'Will he go to prison?'

Rory set down his hat again. 'You want him to pay, don't you?'

'You've asked me that already. I never thought it possible until today.' I thought of it then however, and my hands curled into fists. I imagined Francis locked up in a cell, as I had been. I imagined him, unkempt, dirty, dressed in rough clothes, doing menial work. 'I don't want him to hang.'

'Nor do I,' Rory agreed grimly. 'It would be over too quickly.'

'Will I have to speak against him in court?'

'Possibly. If you want to.' More pieces slotted together to show me another picture. The way he had spoken of his own experience, his name dragged through the mud in the press. The shame and humiliation. Each time, it had been there—empathy. Understanding. Sympathy. No wonder he had wanted to protect me.

By lying. I hardened my heart. 'I want to think about it. All of it.'

'Of course you do. It's a lot to take in. There's no need to be making any decisions right now. I'm thinking,' Rory said, picking up his hat again, 'that I'd best go.'

'You're going to London now? Today? Do you intend to come back?'

'I reckon Lord Westville will want to take it from here. I forgot, he said to tell you he would write.'

So this was goodbye. It was what I wanted, wasn't it? Rory had lied to me. He had betrayed me. He had *made* me fall in love with him. He'd made me believe that he had fallen in love with me. And he hadn't, he really hadn't, even though the way he was looking at me now, with such yearning, and even though I could sense it, he'd never said, I love you. Not aloud.

He was on his feet. I pushed past my chair and threw myself into his arms. It may all be a lie, but I loved him all the same. He pulled me so close, achingly close, and when he realised his mistake, when he would have released me, I put my arms around his neck and pressed myself tighter.

Hold me, hold me, hold me.

His arms went gently around me again. He burrowed his face in my hair.

I love you.

He didn't say the words.

I love you.

I didn't say the words. I turned my face up towards his. His lips met mine. Our kiss spoke. Longing. Such longing. Our lips clung. Then gently, he eased himself free of me.

'If you ever need holding again,' he said, giving me a business card. 'Just holding. Any time. Always. You only have to ask and I'll be there.'

I needed holding now.

'Goodbye, Marianne. Take good care of yourself.'

The door closed behind him. I heard his footsteps on the stairs. I ran to the window and leaned out, watching him cross the Grassmarket in the direction of Victoria Street. I watched until he was just a speck, but he didn't once look back.

I had made a huge mistake. No, I had done the best and only thing possible. I collapsed on to the floor then. I didn't cry. I sat there, my back against the wall, my legs stretched out in front of me like a lifeless rag doll, like a wrongly incarcerated woman in her cell.

I didn't move until night fell. Then I crawled into my bed and lay wide awake, staring at the ceiling. I would reclaim my life. I would carry on as before. I'd been perfectly content before. I hadn't been unhappy. I loved Rory but it didn't matter if I did because no matter what I thought I felt, he couldn't possibly love me. If he did, he wouldn't have left.

My twisted logic was giving me a headache. I wanted to run. I had done it before. I could do it again. No, I would remain in Edinburgh. I'd remain in the city where he wasn't welcome. Not even by me.

I got up as the grey dawn gave way to a watery sun, weighted down by the knowledge that whether I wanted it to or not, my life would never be the same again. There were decisions to be made, life-changing decisions that didn't only affect me. This was the first day of my second new life. I had never been so miserable.

Chapter Twenty-Eight

Marianne

Glasgow—
February 1878, six months later

'You really do have a magnificent view from here. The city spread out for your delectation and delight, Cousin.' Lord Westville turned away from my drawing room window, smiling his thin smile. 'You will be able to oversee progress on your good works from here.'

'I don't consider my plans to be charitable,' I said to him. 'I see them more as efforts to redress imbalances.'

'Now that your inheritance is yours, you can redress a great many.'

'I must thank you, Lord Westville…'

'You must not,' he said, looking pained. 'Call it my contribution to redressing an imbalance regarding you. You have been treated most unjustly by our family. If my father had shown an ounce of interest in you, that villain would never have had the opportunity to exploit…'

'You are not responsible for what Eliot did to me. He is paying for it now.'

'And will do, for the rest of his life thanks to Mr Sutherland's testimony. And yours, of course.'

As always, the mere mention of Rory's name made my heart flutter, and as always, I ignored it. I had written my testimony for him, and he had given it in court on my behalf, anonymously, but the judge had been more interested in the money.

'My dear Marianne—may I call you that?' Lord Westville had taken a seat next to mine. 'It seems wrong, I know, that so little weight was attached to the crime of having you wrongly incarcerated, and so much to the misappropriation of funds, but the end result is that Eliot will never be free again. The law is not always just, I am afraid.

'Mr Sutherland himself was most—really, he was quite beside himself on the subject. And I—he has told me sufficient of what you suffered, Cousin, to stir me into action. As a peer of the realm, I have the right to put forward changes to the law. I don't know if I will succeed, but I intend to try to make it more difficult for anyone to be committed as you were, with no right to review.'

'Would you be able to make a stronger case using me as an example?'

Lord Westville raised a brow. Just one. I wondered if it was a family trait. Rory found my brow alluring. I mustn't think of Rory.

'Mr Sutherland was at great pains to keep your name out of the case,' the Marquess said. 'If you chose to help me I could not guarantee your anonymity.'

'I hope that Mr Sutherland knows how much I appreciate his efforts,' I said, choosing my words with care. 'You will tell him, Lord Westville, won't you, how much I appreciate it? But I also feel—I'm stronger now, and if I can use my experiences to help others—unless you would rather not associate…'

'I beg you to believe, that I give not a fig for what people will say. I am honoured to claim you for my kin.'

'You are very good to say so.'

'I never say what I don't mean.' Lord Westville studied me for a moment, his pale blue eyes intent on mine. 'Mr Sutherland assured me that you were an astute judge of character. I consider myself one such too. You have a strength and a fortitude, a singleness of mind that I very much admire. Your experiences could have made you bitter. They could have broken you. I believe, however, that they have made you into a very remarkable woman.'

I felt myself blushing. Though his expression remained cool, his eyes detached, I sensed that he meant what he said, and detected a glimmer of humour in his icy eyes. 'You like to confound expectations,' I said.

'That's better! I do, very much. I shall take pleasure in owning you, if only you will permit it. You would wield a great deal more influence if you claimed your rightful title, you know.'

'If I had continued to reside in Edinburgh, perhaps. Here in Glasgow, they consider the aristocracy sleekit.' I smiled, seeing his confusion. 'Sly. You see, I'm learning the lingo. I shall earn more respect as plain Mrs Crawford.'

'You couldn't bring yourself to claim Miss Westville? No, I should not have asked.' Lord Westville got to his feet. 'I must go, I have an express train to catch, but if you are serious about assisting me…'

'I am, very serious. If we can prevent one person enduring what I did then it will be worth it.' I got up and held out my hand. 'Thank you again, for all that you have done.'

To my surprise, he retained my hand. 'Mr Sutherland gave me strict instructions not to try to interfere with how you spend your inheritance. "Trust her, she knows her own mind"—to use his own words—"she'll do a power of good." I shan't interfere, but if I can be of help at all I trust that you do know you can count on me, Marianne?'

His hands were as cold as his eyes, but I sensed a genuine warmth emanating from him that brought a lump to my throat. 'Rory—Mr Sutherland—will you tell him that I am taking my cue from Octavia Hill? He'll understand.'

'I shall tell him if I see him, but now that your case is closed, our paths are unlikely to cross.'

'Oh. I see.' I couldn't keep the disappointment from my voice.

'You could tell him yourself. Write to him, let him know your plans, I am sure he would be interested, and I believe you have his business address?'

I snatched my hand away. 'You will miss your train if you don't hurry.'

'Indeed.'

I escorted him out to the hallway, where he took his time with his hat and gloves. 'I have been inept,' he said, pursing his thin lips. 'If I gave you the impression that Mr Sutherland urged me to tell you to write, that is. I asked him, you know, if he had a message for you, but he was quite adamant. "What I said to her still stands," he said. "I've nothing to add." Ah. Yes. I can see you do understand. If you will permit?'

Lord Westville saluted me chastely on the cheek. 'It has been a pleasure, Marianne. One I hope we will repeat soon. Until then, au revoir.'

I watched from the bay window as his carriage made its

way down Park Circus, but I wasn't thinking of my cousin. My thoughts were only of Rory.

What I said to her still stands. I've nothing to add.

I pressed my head against the window pane, gazing out beyond the park that spread before me, to the misty curve of the River Clyde and the hazy cranes of the shipyards. Rory's Glasgow. I felt closer to him here, but that wasn't the only reason I had moved from Edinburgh. I felt at home here. Here in the city, for less than a day, I'd been truly myself, with Rory. I loved him so much.

Did he truly love me? Six months ago, I had been so confused. Terrified by my previous experience of what I thought was love, I had clutched at every possible reason to reject Rory. I'd always known that Rory wasn't like Francis, that my feelings for Rory were different, but I hadn't understood that his feelings were different too.

Rory always put me first. Even though he had not been honest with me, it was because he put me first. He knew the worst of me from the outset, and he saw it as the best of me. He saw me for who I was, and he never once tried to change me. He trusted me, before I could trust myself. He believed in me, before I believed in myself. I knew those things now. I'd had six months to learn them.

Was that what defined love? He'd been right about my insights too. I did sense Francis's true feelings, but I misunderstood his motives. Francis *would* have been the death of me, one way or another.

I had saved myself though, and now I had the power to save countless other women and children—or to provide them with the opportunity to save themselves. I had not forgotten my experiences in the asylum, but my dreams these days were of Rory, not of that vile place. Or not often. I was looking forward now, not looking back. I was often happy. But not always. Always, I missed Rory.

Did he miss me? He hadn't said the words I love you aloud, but he had made love to me. He had shown me he loved me by leaving me to be me. And that last time, that last kiss. *I love you.* I heard it, though he had not spoken it.

I missed him so much. The ever-present ache became an intense longing. I didn't need him in order to survive, I didn't need him to make the most of my life now, to make decisions for me or to guide me. I didn't need him, but I wanted him. Did he want me?

I'd never felt safe in anyone else's arms. Rory had given me my freedom. I was free to share it with him, if I had the courage. Because I believed him. Because I trusted him. I always had. It had been trusting myself that was the problem. It seemed so simple, all of a sudden, but it had taken me six months to see that. Six months, and Rory had not once tried to get in touch. Not for the lack of love. Because he loved me. Because he understood me.

If you ever need holding again. Just holding. Any time. Always. You only have to ask and I'll be there.

I didn't want to wait another day, never mind another six months. I raced to my bedroom and grabbed a hat and cloak, then ran all the way to the nearest telegram office. I needed holding. It was time to ask him to keep his promise.

Chapter Twenty-Nine

Rory

Glasgow—
February 1878

I was glad that the Caledonian Railway took me direct to Glasgow rather than Edinburgh. That city had no appeal for me now that Marianne wasn't there. With every passing mile, after we steamed over the border, I felt as if the pistons of the engine were singing I'm coming home, I'm coming home, I'm coming home. Home! I'd never thought of my house in the London suburbs as home. It was a decent house in a good neighbourhood. My ma would have thought it a palace. I'd been content enough there before I met Marianne. Since Marianne—oh, since Marianne my world had changed.

For a start, I'd put the case of Ada Soutar well and truly to bed. I had my suspicions about who had been behind her death, who had been behind blackening my name, but I'd given up any notion of doing anything about it. Giving the Soutars answers, even though they weren't really answers, had proved to be enough for me. I was done with looking over my shoulder. Marianne had taught me that. I was done with the past. I was done with being feart of going back to Edinburgh too. What benefit would there be for whoever had it in for me, to finish me off now? They'd risk being collared for a second crime. I had the Capital back, if I wanted it. Point was, I didn't want it. Marianne wasn't there.

I tried to get on with my own life. No, I *got on* with my own life. New cases. Some good ones, thanks to the Marquess, but work wasn't the be all and end all it had been for me before. I missed her. Not consciously all the time, but there was a gap beside me, and I was constantly aware of it. A place where I felt she should be. I missed her like hell. I loved that woman. By the sun and the stars, I truly believed that I loved her more with every passing day. Every day that we were apart I missed her.

I tried not to think too far forward, for the notion of missing her for the rest of my life would have scuppered me. I missed her, and of course I wondered if she was missing me, but what I wanted more than anything was for her to be happy. I wanted her to learn to enjoy her freedom. I wanted her to make something of herself. I knew she would. She simply needed time, and that's the one thing I could give her. As long as she wanted. For ever if she needed it.

That was what I told myself, but when the telegram arrived, I knew before I opened it what it would say, and I knew then that I'd been right not to give up hope.

I need holding.

Three words.

I was packed and on the express train north first thing the next morning.

The train was pulling into the station. My heart was hammering harder than the pistons of the engine now. There was so much we'd need to talk about, but what I knew for certain was that we'd finally talk about the most important subject of all. I loved her. She loved me. We'd not spoken those words but they were suspended there, in the three-word message in the telegram that I was clutching inside my coat pocket like a talisman.

I'd already arranged to have my bags sent on to the Queen's Hotel. I didn't know if Marianne would be waiting for me. She knew I was coming though, so I hoped. I threw open the door of the First-Class carriage and was caught up in the belching black smoke of the still-slowing engine. She didn't need me, Marianne, but she wanted me, so I hoped she'd be there.

I pelted down the platform, first out of the train, first to the waiting huddle of people looking anxiously for their friends and family. I saw her before she saw me. She was wearing a new cloak in emerald-green, with the hood pulled up over her hair. She was standing stock still, eyes wide, emanating anxiety. And then she saw me, and I slowed down to walk, because I wanted to remember this moment for always. I wanted to remember every step.

The hiss of the steam coming from the trains. The smell of the smoke. The soot settling on my face. The shouts of the porters. The other people waving, calling out greetings. And her face. Her smile dawning so slowly, creeping up to light up her eyes. The half-step she took towards me. My name on her lips. And as I got closer I felt it. Saw it light up all of her. Felt it light up me too. Perfect, perfect love.

I took her outstretched hands in mine. Her gloves were new, dark leather, neatly fitted. Her fingers curled around mine. But we didn't say it then. We'd waited so long, but we didn't dare say it yet. 'I know a place,' I said, and she nodded, as if she knew what I was on about, though how—but maybe she did.

There was a hackney carriage waiting outside. It had been snowing, fresh snow, so fresh that George Square was carpeted in white. It wouldn't last, but for now it looked almost perfect, only one set of footprints streaking across it. Our carriage made fresh tracks. The streets we passed through were hushed, or so it seemed to me, though they couldn't have been, there must have been the usual bustle of the East End.

Maybe I didn't notice because all I could see, all I could think about, was Marianne sitting silently beside me, her hand in mine. The journey must have taken a good while, but I didn't notice that. There was the Cathedral, soot-black and stark against the snow. The Royal Infirmary beside it. And then the gates of the Necropolis, where we got down and I paid the driver off.

I led her up the steep paths. 'Top of the world,' I said to her, indicating the view spread out before us. The skies had cleared—of course they had! 'Our world, any road.'

'Ours?' She sounded breathless. The first words she'd spoken, and it was a question. It shouldn't have been, she must have known why I was there, but it was.

We were at the highest point of Glasgow's biggest graveyard, surrounded by memorials to the great and the good. The sun peaked through the clouds, and far away you could see the River Clyde. Closer to hand were the factories and works of Glasgow's industrial engine. The houses for the people who worked there. The city itself, where the money was. 'Our world,' I said, getting down on one knee and taking her hand in mine. 'I love you,' I said, putting all my heart into it. 'I love you with everything I am. I love you for all that you are, just exactly as you are. I can get by without you, Marianne, but I don't want to. Whatever we do, however we do it, I want us to be together. Will you marry me?'

She dropped on to her knees beside me and threw her arms around me. 'Will you hold me, Rory, like you promised?'

I put my arms around her. I pulled her close, careful still, but she wriggled even closer. 'I love you,' she said. 'You know that, don't you?'

I had a lump in my throat, so I nodded.

'I didn't know,' she said to me. 'I thought I was in love before, but I was so wrong. And I was frightened to trust myself. Frightened of what you made me feel. You mattered so much, and in such a different way, but I didn't trust myself.'

'You do now, though?'

'Oh, yes. It took me a while,' she said, pushing my hat off and running her fingers through my hair. 'But you gave me the time I didn't even know I needed. I love you, Rory Sutherland.'

'I love you, Marianne—it's just struck me. I don't know—is it Little, Crawford or Westville?'

'What about Marianne Sutherland?' she said, with a smile that went straight to my groin. 'The answer is yes, Rory. I will marry you, with great pleasure.'

I couldn't wait any more, and nor could she. Our mouths met in a kiss that was desperate and without finesse. We kissed, kneeling in the snow in a graveyard, with the sun weakly shining on us. We kissed frantically, our tongues clashing, our hands fevered, hampered by cloaks and gloves and hats and the cold. Then our kisses slowed, became tender, and I told her with my heart and my lips, how much I loved her, and she told me too, how much she loved me, in the same way. And nothing, nothing had ever felt so perfectly right.

Chapter Thirty

Marianne

Glasgow—
March 1878, six weeks later

We had the simplest of ceremonies, in the simplest of churches in Govan, where Rory's parents lay buried in the churchyard outside. We made no announcements, though we sent a telegram to Lord Westville and received three words in return.

At Last. Congratulations.

'We are married,' I said to Rory as we stood together at the window of our flat in Park Circus, looking out at the driving rain. 'I can't quite believe it.'

'Nor I. These last few weeks have seemed like an eternity.'

'I know.' It had been Rory who insisted we wait. Rory who asked me at least once a day, whether I was certain this was what I wanted. Rory who assured me each day that he could wait as long as was necessary. I told him that with every passing day I was more sure, and less inclined to wait. But now the moment was here, now the gold band on my finger proclaimed me his wife, now that we were alone in this place that would become our home, I was besieged by nerves.

'Don't fret,' he said, taking my hands in his.

'What if I don't...?'

He kissed the rest of my words away. A gentle, tender kiss, the same kind of kiss he had bestowed on me every day for the last six weeks. Reassuring. Pledging his love. 'You are everything to me,' he said. 'My only worry is that after all this time, I'll be the one who won't—who will lose control too early.'

His words gave me confidence. My nerves turned into anticipation. 'I want you to lose control.'

He inhaled sharply. He gave me one last, assessing look. Then he pulled me into his arms, and our mouths locked. Heat seared through me. At last, our kisses were without restraint. Deep kisses that lit flames inside me, made me molten, made me raw with desire. Kisses that had no trace of gentleness, but that roused and demanded a response, that made every bit of my body throb with wanting more.

It was the middle of the afternoon, but we were in our own flat, on our own. We neither of us made any attempt to reach a bedroom. Rory let me go only to pull the long, elegant curtains over the windows before he returned to my waiting arms, to my eager body. His fingers shook as he undid the fastenings of my gown. My own shook as I undid the buttons of his waistcoat.

We shed clothes equally this time, not like the last time, shared kisses equally, hands smoothing, caressing each newly exposed piece of skin. My petticoats. His shirt. My boots, then his. My stockings, then his. I kissed the scar on his abdomen. He teased my nipples into aching, hard peaks. And all the time we communed.

Rory.

Marianne.

I love you.

I love you.

I want...

This?

Yes.

This?

Yes. Oh, yes.

And this?

Yes!

I thought I would melt with desire. His breathing was ragged. So too was mine. He undid the string of my drawers. I was naked before him. He gazed at me for a moment and I relished his gaze, the hunger in him reflecting my own, the colour slashing his cheeks. The pinpoints of his pupils.

So lovely.

He dipped his head to take one of my nipples into his mouth. I groaned aloud, arching backwards. His hand slid between my legs, slid inside me, and I clenched around him. Melting. Desire building and building as I clutched desperately to maintain an element of self-control.

Let go.

Not yet. Not yet.

I tugged at the waistband of his trousers. He released me to finish undressing himself. When he made to pull me back into his arms, I shook my head. I drank my fill of him as he had me. His hard-muscled body. The smattering of hair on his chest leading my eyes down, past the scar, past the dip of his belly, to his aroused member. I wanted to touch him. I had never before—so I wanted to touch him. He took my hand, wrapped my fingers around him. I felt him throb at my touch. Heard him moan at my touch. My name, a soft exhalation of desire. I stroked him, relishing his moaning response, but then his hand stayed me.

'No more.' He spoke as if through gritted teeth. 'Can't wait.'

'Don't.'

Kisses again, as we sank on to our knees. More kisses as we fell on to the floor. His member was pressing into my belly. His fingers easing inside me. I was losing control. Wave after wave of desire gripping me as he kissed me and stroked me, but still I clung on, wanting, wanting, wanting, restless with wanting, until he pulled me astride him, and I let go of all control as he entered me, his own hoarse cry echoing mine as he bucked under me, going deeper.

Wave after wave engulfed me. I heard myself crying out my pleasure, felt him inside me, barely moving, saw his desperate attempt to control himself etched on his face, and then he thrust, thrust again, and I moved with him, taking him inside deeper, faster, until he too lost control, and I toppled on to him, clinging for dear life, sweat-slicked, sated, floating.

'I love you.'

A slow, delicious, sweet kiss.

'I love you.'

He held me close. And later, after we made love in our bed, he held me close again. And when I woke to my first morning as his wife, he was still holding me and I knew not only where I was, but that it was exactly where I needed to be.

Epilogue

Rory

Glasgow—
July 1878, four months later

The day began as it always did. I woke slowly, and the first thing I was aware of was Marianne. Usually she was nestled against me, her hair tickling my nose. Sometimes her head was still resting on my shoulder, just as it had been when we'd fallen asleep, one of her legs between mine, her hand resting on my chest. On the morning of our fourth month as husband and wife, she was curled into my back, her mouth on the nape of my neck, and her hand—she was stroking me. Not asleep, then, my wife.

I gave myself over to the pleasure of her gentle, sure touch until she whispered my name, and I turned, and she pulled me on top of her and I slid inside her. I can't get used to that. I never want to get used to it. The sheer delight of being inside her, of her legs wrapping themselves around me, of her urging me on with her mouth and her hands. The way she tightens around me. The soft moan she lets out. The way she says my name. It tips me over every time. Every sweet, wonderful time.

We had breakfast together, as we do every morning, even when I've an early start. Coffee and bread and butter, eggs sometimes, sitting in our fancy wee dining room in our dressing robes, staring at each other across the table as if we can't believe our luck. Which I can't.

We don't keep a servant, but we have a couple of women who come in later to clean and to cook dinner. Women Marianne knows from Partick. Women who worship the ground Marianne walks on. As do I. At breakfast, we plan our respective days, but that morning it was all arranged, so we put on our best clothes—nothing too good mind, Marianne doesn't have a taste for the fancy and I've always been a plain dresser.

It was a lovely morning, considering it was July in Glasgow and Fair Friday to boot, which I don't recall ever being dry when I was growing up here. Marianne tucked her hand into my arm as we made our way out, smiling up at me in a way that made me want to take her right back inside and make love to her again.

'Happy fourth month of marriage,' she said to me.

'I couldn't be happier, you know that?'

She laughed. 'You say that every day, and then the next day you say it again.'

I did kiss her then, just a quick kiss, but I couldn't resist her. 'I'm planning on saying it every day for the rest of our lives. I love you.'

'And I love you.' She tugged me forward into the West End Park. 'But if we're going to walk all the way to Partick, we'd better get a shifty on.'

I burst out laughing.

'Don't I have that right? Get a shifty on?'

'You've got it right, but it sounds so funny in your accent. We'll make a Weegie of you one day, but not yet.'

'Thank you for taking the time away from your case, I really wanted you to be with me today.'

'I wouldn't miss it for the world, and Gordon Munro is more than happy with what needs to be done in the office today.' I had been delighted to employ my father's old colleague into my business. As the man himself had suggested, there was plenty of work in the city, so much that we were actually considering taking his son on too. And unlike the police in the capital, my name here was neither poison nor mud.

It wasn't even eleven, but there were already plenty of people in the park taking the air, and plenty of them on nodding and greeting terms with Marianne. She smiled sunnily at mill workers on their break, and stopped several times to exchange banter with weans. 'It's as well we don't have to be there until noon,' I said to her.

'I'm thinking Rory, that it might be a good idea to speak to some of the mill owners along the Kelvin. The school they have for the little ones isn't nearly big enough, and if there was a nursery, then it would mean that some of the women could go back to work if they wished, earlier. Do you think I'd be standing on too many toes doing that?'

'Has it ever bothered you, standing on toes?'

'Well, no, but it is much easier to make progress if one doesn't.'

'I think it's a wonderful idea, but I was hoping you'd take a couple of weeks off before launching yourself into another project. It's the Fair. I thought we'd take a bit of a holiday ourselves. What do you think?'

'Shall we go—what is it?—doon the watter?'

'I was thinking somewhere a bit further north. With golden beaches and...'

'Harris!' She gave a leap of excitement. 'Rory, are we going to Harris?'

'I'd like to introduce you to my family, at long last. We leave tomorrow.'

Her eyes were sparkling as we walked the rest of the way, out of the park over the Snow Bridge and along to Partick. The new block of tenements was on Anderson Street, a couple of blocks from my own childhood home. Blond sandstone, it had its own bathhouse out in the back courts, and above the entrance to the freshly tiled close, a plaque.

Marianne was immediately lost to me in the crowd of women waiting to receive her. I watched from a distance, my heart bursting with pride. There was Katy, formerly Flora, in her smart new outfit, the housekeeper in charge of this experiment. There were Mr and Mrs Soutar and Oscar, pointing up at the plaque, surrounding by what must be their friends and family from the South Side. And Mrs Oliphant, standing nervously to one side with an outsize pair of scissors to cut the ribbon. A stamping of feet, a few whistles, and my wife stepped out in front of the crowd.

'Ladies—and of course gentlemen,' she said, with a bow at the few men there and a smile for me, 'I won't bore you with speeches. I just want to say a huge thank you to everyone for all the help and support you've given me in making this project happen. I will now ask Mrs Oliphant, to whom I owe a great debt for drawing my attention to the work of Octavia Hill, to perform the opening ceremony.'

Mrs Oliphant, looking so nervous I thought she might faint, stepped up to the ribbon and with some difficulty sawed it in two. 'I now declare the Ada Soutar Residential Rooms for Women open.'

There was tea and cake for everyone, and lemonade for the weans. I don't know how many times I assured someone or other that I was very proud of Marianne—indeed, I'd never tire of telling the world that.

'Are you happy?' I asked her, when I finally got a moment alone with her.

'I couldn't be happier,' she said, handing my own words back to me, and meaning them too.

I kissed her then, a chaste wee peck on the lips, but it still got us a cheer. 'There's only one thing missing, to make the day perfect,' I said.

She took one look at me. She smiled, a slow smile that did sinful things to me, and that I'd come to know very well these last four months. 'I think that can be arranged,' she said. 'Give me ten minutes and we'll head home.'

'Make it five,' I said, grinning.

* * * * *

Historical Note

First of all, a huge thank-you to Early Police historian Dr Elaine Saunders—@hertfordshirehistory—for all her advice and guidance on the police service in Rory's time. I've only used a fraction of the answers she gave me to my many questions, but she gave me an invaluable insight into the kinds of crimes Rory would have been tackling in Edinburgh, and the kinds of prejudice that his father would have encountered at the time, when Highlanders really were seen as coming to Glasgow and joining the police simply to 'put boots on their feet'.

Clive Elmsley's excellent book *The Great British Bobby* gave me an insight to the life of a police detective. Rory's 'fist, feet and teeth' quotation is taken directly from one of those real detectives quoted in Elmsley's book. Private detectives like Rory really did exist at the time, and they were often used to investigate crimes which the great and the good wished to keep out of the press.

Marianne's main place of incarceration was inspired by a tour led by Mostly Ghostly of the Crichton in Dumfries, which I took with my sister Johanna. I am afraid I've used and abused the Crichton in this book, for it was in fact very much a forward-thinking institution for its time, though there were locked wards such as the ones in which I placed poor Marianne. The coffin cart which Marianne sees as she escapes is real, and on display in the crypt at the Crichton.

The story of Angus Mackay's escape is one that I also heard on the Mostly Ghostly tour. It happened in 1859, a few years too early for Marianne's escape, but it was too good a story not to use. Sadly, Sarah Wise's book *Inconvenient People, Lunacy, Liberty and the Mad-Doctors in Victorian England* documents cases very similar to Marianne's.

I have borrowed a story from another tour I took recently, of Glasgow Central Station, with my sister Fiona—I have very tolerant sisters…they're always happy to come along while I play the geek, provided lunch is involved. It was here that I heard the story of pickpockets hanging about the platforms waiting for the moment of darkness caused by steam enclosed under a station roof to take the opportunity to pinch both the purses and the bottoms of the female passengers.

As you'll know, if you're read some of my other books, I have a deep and abiding love of both Edinburgh and Glasgow. This time I wanted to showcase the 'hidden gems' in the cities, and some of my own favourite places to wander.

The obstetrician and pioneer of chloroform James Young Simpson really did reside at Number Fifty-Two Queen Street, and the gardens—if you have a key!—are a lovely spot to have a picnic. Dean Village, which is now a heritage site, was very, very different in Marianne and Rory's day, and I'm not actually sure if you could have walked along the Water of Leith back then—though you can now. The Dean Orphanage is now part of the National Galleries of Modern Art. Dean Cemetery is a wonderful place to wander, full of fascinating graves and memorials—including one for one of my own favourite artists, John Bellany.

And finally I should say a word about Rory's language, which is very much *not* Victorian, but fairly colloquial Weegie and Scots. I chose to do this partly to make his speech quite distinct from Marianne's, but also, to be honest, because some of the words he uses are my favourites. Thank you to my family WhatsApp group for the many suggestions, including all those that didn't make the cut—sorry, Mum, but 'oxter' was just a step too far.

As ever, I've done a ton of reading and research for this book, and shared most of it on social media. And, as ever, all mistakes and inaccuracies are entirely my own.

Rescuing The Runway Heiress

Sadie King

MILLS & BOON

Sadie King was born in Nottingham and raised in Lancashire. After graduating with a degree in history from Lancaster University, she moved to West Lothian, Scotland, where she now lives with her husband and children. When she's not writing, Sadie loves long country walks, romantic ruins, Thai food and travelling with her family. She also writes historical fiction and contemporary mysteries as Sarah L King.

Visit the Author Profile page
at millsandboon.com.au for more titles.

Author Note

Readers of *Spinster with a Scandalous Past* will recognize Samuel, the cheerful, sociable opposite of his brooding older brother, Isaac, who is the hero of that story. Readers may also recall that in that novel, Samuel has his hopes of romance dashed. When it came to deciding who to write about next, Samuel was the obvious choice as I really wanted him to have his own happy ending.

A visit to the Cumbrian coast in autumn 2022 led me to explore the area's murkier history, the smuggling and the illegal distilling that went on in the Georgian period. At the same time, I'd been reading a lot about the period's famous actresses, such as Sarah Siddons and Dorothea Jordan, and I knew I wanted to write about a heroine who had the theater in her background. All these elements came together in Hope—a strong, brave and resilient actress with a troubled past.

Samuel and Hope find themselves in close confines at Hayton Hall, and they both have their reasons not to be honest about who they really are. Theirs is a story of secrets, lies and sizzling attraction, and it was an absolute joy to write.

DEDICATION

For David

Chapter One

September 1818

A loud cry pierced the cool, still air of the early autumn evening, causing Samuel to startle. He had been enjoying his usual slow promenade around Hayton Hall's fine gardens, appreciating the quiet calm, observing the changing light and admiring the late blooming plants as one season ebbed into the next. Or at least, so he told himself. He found that he told stories to himself frequently these days, as though such works of fiction, if repeated often enough, could eventually embody the truth. He'd tell himself that he was simply a country gentleman, relishing some moments of peaceful solitude before retiring for the night. That he took just as much pleasure in doing his duty as he always had. That he was his own man, in charge of his own destiny. That he did not mind being alone. That he did not spend most evenings walking in that garden, listening to his doubts as they whispered to him, about just how bleak his prospects now seemed.

Samuel looked around him, shaking his head at himself in an uncomfortable acknowledgement of the darker turn his thoughts had taken before that brief, shrill noise had intruded. The gardens of Hayton Hall fell back into silence once more, readying themselves for the impending dark as, above them, the sky's pink hues deepened. His gaze shifted towards the wood beyond, its trees still thick with summer's lush green foliage, the leaves only now hinting at beginning to turn. He stood still for several moments, listening for anything which might betray the origin of such a sound. All he could detect, however, were the occasional caws of the crows as they came home to roost for the night.

'You see, Samuel,' he muttered to himself, 'you've naught but the birds for company.'

Naught but birds, and his servants, of course. Or, rather, his older brother's servants, since it was Sir Isaac Liddell who was the master here. Samuel was merely the caretaker, appointed to look after the family estate while his brother travelled with his new bride.

As Samuel turned his back to the woods and continued his gentle promenade, he found himself counting the weeks since Isaac and Louisa's departure, and considering how much, and how little, had changed since. At first, he'd embraced the responsibility his brother had bestowed on him with his usual cheerful enthusiasm, but although he believed he'd discharged his duties competently, he'd quickly wearied of just how solitary and tedious running a country estate could be. It pained him to admit it, but he resented how it tied him, quite literally, to its acres. He'd never have thought it possible, but he was tired of the sight of his ancestral home. Tired, too, of his own company.

Yet solitude, he'd discovered, was infinitely preferable to being the subject of ceaseless gossip. As happy as he was for his older brother, he could not fail to acknowledge that Isaac had left quite a scandal in his wake, and the news of his elopement with a woman who'd borne a naval captain's child out of wedlock had quickly spread. For the first time in his life, Samuel had become disenchanted with Cumberland society, as he found himself either invited to dinner parties to answer questions about the scandal, or not invited at all. In the end, declining such invitations had been a blessed relief, but it had made his world grow smaller still. It was hard to believe that last year he'd been on the Continent, enjoying picnics on the shores of the Swiss lakes and attending lavish dinner parties in cities like Geneva, Milan and Venice. It was hard to believe that he'd been surrounded by so much culture and good company, and yet now…

A crow cawed again, taunting him.

Resigned to his lonely routine, he sauntered back towards Hayton Hall, to the servants waiting to greet him, to offer their deferential smiles whilst always keeping their distance. They played their roles as well as he knew he had to play his. He'd seen that clearly, the first and only time he'd ventured to suggest that Smithson, his brother's butler, join him for an evening brandy. The ageing man's jaw had just about hit the floor, and Samuel had reddened at his transgression, unable to decide what was worse—the awkward excuses the butler offered as a refusal or the look of pity in his eyes.

Since then, he'd not strayed from his side of the line which divided servants and masters, even though he was not master of anyone—not truly. It was just a part he had to play for a little while longer, until the real master of Hayton Hall returned. Then he would revert to his real role, that of the younger brother, free to do as he pleased, to spend his time and inheritance as he wished. Of the unattached gentleman, untroubled by land or titles.

Or, more realistically, of being the less attractive prospect, the wrong brother. Or at least that was what his rejection by a certain young lady that summer had taught him. As he drew nearer to Hayton Hall he shuddered—at the cooling air, perhaps, or at the memory of her bright red hair, the smattering of freckles across her nose, her broad smile. Remembering her biting words to him that afternoon as they'd walked together and he'd dared to suggest he was fond of her, that he would like, with her father's permission, to begin a courtship.

'Why would you think to even ask such a thing? When I am my father's only daughter, and you are a younger son. When you have no property, no title...'

Samuel grimaced, his mind suddenly filled with the images of her usually pretty face contorted into a look which was part-offence and part-mockery as she quashed his hopes and stamped upon his heart. He held no affection for her now; he'd seen her true fickle nature too clearly for that. But her rejection of him had been thoroughly humiliating and whilst the hurt he'd felt no longer burned his insides, it still stubbornly smouldered somewhere within him, its embers always ready to be rekindled in his quiet, contemplative moments. And, as God only knew, he'd had too many of those during the preceding weeks.

'Pull yourself together, man,' he muttered under his breath, reminding himself that in the coming days his solitude would be over. His friend Charles Gordon had mercifully responded to Samuel's plea that he should visit, gladly accepting and venturing to suggest that he bring his sister with him too. He had much to look forward to, Samuel reminded himself. He'd met Charles during his Continental travels, taking an instant liking to the man's convivial demeanour and outrageous sense of fun. Seeing his friend again would lift his spirits, and he was intrigued about making the acquaintance of Henrietta Gordon, especially since, until Charles had mentioned her in his letter, Samuel had not known about the existence of a sister at all.

Another loud yell breached the silence. It was deeper this time, longer and angrier, almost a roar. Samuel spun around, his eyes darting warily back towards the wood. Up in the trees the crows began to squawk frantically, and it occurred to him then that it could be a fox. He decided he would mention the noise to his brother's steward; the estate's tenants would need to be put on their guard, especially those who raised sheep.

Then, before he could think any more about it, a final cry rang out. This one, however, put paid to any theories he'd entertained about foxes, instead betraying its origins as being unmistakably human. This one, he realised as he ran instinctively towards the trees, was not a scream or a roar, but a plea.

'Help!'

As she lay on the ground, pain pulsing through her as she watched a murder of crows circling overhead, all Hope Sloane could think was how much easier her bid to escape would have been if only she'd had a breeches role. Men's clothing was without doubt far more suitable attire for dashing across the countryside than a flimsy gown of muslin and lace. However, if there was one thing that life had taught Hope, it was that you played the hand you were dealt, and you seized your opportunities when they came. And so she had, running for her life across fields and through woodland, hoping she could get far enough away before falling under the cloak of inevitable darkness.

Unfortunately, the only thing she'd fallen upon was the uneven, branch-strewn ground. She hadn't gone down quietly either, letting out an almighty scream at the pain as it seared through her. Truly, she could not have announced her whereabouts more clearly if she'd tried. She could only hope that her disappearance had not yet been discovered, that there might still be sufficient distance between herself and those who sought to capture her.

Namely her father and the man to whom she'd been promised as though she was nothing more than contraband to be smuggled and traded.

Hope shivered, the short sleeves and thin fabric of her gown doing nothing to ward off the early autumn chill. They'd made her put on this gown, her father and the man. They'd insisted that she should look nice and tidy her hair and make an effort. She was going to celebrate with them, they'd told her, for in a matter of days she would be wed. The following day she would depart for Scotland, where she would smile and make her vows before God, or risk her father's wrath. Then she would go to live with this man, the one her father called George, although she had not cared to even know his name. She would spend the rest of her days on his farm near the Solway Firth, only leaving the place to run whisky over the border and into England by wearing a belly canteen which made her look as though she was heavy with child.

'Except when you're actually having a bairn, of course,' the brute George had said as he leered at her, placing an unwelcome arm around her waist and pulling her roughly towards him.

Both men had laughed and raised their mugs in a toast while Hope had bitten her tongue, resolving to say nothing and to bide her time. Foolishly, after making her change her clothes, they'd left her unbound, instead ordering her to wait on them hand and foot. Recognising the opportunity for what it was, Hope had turned on the charm, forcing a smile on to her face for George's benefit while she'd plied both men with more and more drink. There was no stronger liquor in Cumberland than that which came from her father's stills. All she'd had to do was wait until they passed from stupor into slumber. The moment they did, she'd hurried to escape.

Hope shivered again, wincing as she pulled futilely at the muslin sleeves as though they could somehow be stretched to cover her bare arms. Forcing her to wear that gown had been a form of mockery, she knew that. It was the gown she'd been wearing when they'd grabbed her that night at the theatre, not long after the play was over. It was her Lady Teazle gown, a beautifully embellished but ultimately thin piece of frippery befitting the flirtatious and spendthrift gentleman's wife she'd played in Sheridan's *The School for Scandal*. It was a relic from a life she might never know again, thanks to her own naïve foolishness.

Why had she not tried to excuse herself, when she learned her theatre company were to tour in Cumberland in addition to their usual destinations in Westmorland? Why had she not feigned illness, or injury? She was an actress, after all.

Why had she ever thought that several years of absence and a stage name would be enough to protect her from recognition? Why had she fooled herself into thinking she could slip in and out of Lowhaven, undetected by her father's many spies? Why, on that day five years ago when she'd crept out of her family's damp cottage for the final time, had she believed that running away to Yorkshire would ever be far enough?

Hope's teeth began to chatter. And why, she asked herself for the umpteenth time, had she not taken a breeches role? She was going to freeze to death in that ridiculous gown! A potent mix of anger and anxiety coursed through her veins as she forced herself to sit, desperation and determination gripping her as she realised she must drag herself, somehow, towards shelter.

Using all the strength she could muster, she tried to pull herself to her feet, only to fall down once more as a dizzying pain in her head overwhelmed her, and her right leg refused to bear her weight. Furious now, she pounded her fists into the ground, letting out a loud, guttural cry—at the pain, made worse by the sudden movement, and at her predicament. At the unfairness of it all.

She'd run away once before; back then, she'd had more time to think and to plan, to pack clothing and gather coins to aid her escape. She'd got on one coach, then another; she'd put many miles between herself and Cumberland and carved out a life she could call her own. A life which was not beholden to the whims of cruel men, or to the tides of fortune which dictated whether she escaped the grasp of constables and excisemen, or found herself in gaol, facing the noose. A life in which she'd played many different parts, and lived many colourful lives. A life she could enjoy once again, if only she could get herself out of this terrible mess.

Above her the crows still circled, their squalls growing louder and more urgent as though they too understood the severity of her situation. Hope cast her eyes around, trying to get some sense of where she was. Trying to ignore the way pain spread from her head to her neck as well as searing up her leg. Through the trees, she caught glimpses of stonework in the near distance, and her heart began to race at the prospect of having stumbled upon a house, upon the possibility of rescue and shelter.

Play the hand you've been dealt, Hope, she thought to herself as a fresh wave of dizziness threatened to consume her. *Play the hand, even if it means placing yourself at the mercy of fortune's tides once more.*

At the top of her lungs and with the last vestiges of her strength, Hope mustered one final cry.

'Help!'

By the time Samuel found her, the crows had fallen silent, and so had she. Above him, the sky was ink-blue and the sun was long gone, leaving the woodland to languish in the gloomy shadows of its many trees. He bent down at her side, his instincts racing ahead of his thoughts as he tried to assess the situation. The woman before him lay very still, her eyes shut, her arms perishingly cold to the touch. Little wonder really, he thought, since the evening gown she wore was completely unsuitable attire for wandering about the countryside at dusk. She needed warmth, and the attention of a physician. Whoever she was, and whatever had happened to her, it was clear that something was gravely wrong.

Carefully, he lifted her off the ground, simultaneously concerned and reassured by the brief groan which escaped her lips in response to the movement. At least she still lived, although how badly injured she was, he could not tell. Holding her in his arms, he walked back towards Hayton Hall, calling out for his servants once he reached the formal gardens he'd been sauntering around just a little while ago. The noise he made seemed to rouse her slightly, and she began to murmur again—pained moans littered with sobs, and in amongst all that, a few words. Words which seemed to distress her greatly.

'No…not going with him…' she whimpered.

'Hush,' he replied softly, anxious to reassure her. 'You're safe now.'

The woman's eyes rolled and closed once more and, to his horror, he sensed her grow limp in his arms. With increasing urgency, Samuel hurried towards the door of Hayton Hall, from which several servants were rushing towards him, their brows furrowed as they responded to his calls.

'Prepare a bedchamber!' Samuel barked his orders, playing their master once more. 'Fetch some water and light a fire! This lady needs our help.'

Chapter Two

Hope's eyes fluttered open, the brightness of the midday sun immediately overwhelming her blurry vision. She blinked several times, trying to see better, trying to understand where she was. The bed she lay in was large and soft, her head resting upon a pile of pillows as she remained tucked beneath crisp white sheets. She shifted her gaze, wincing at the discomfort that this slightest movement of her head caused as she observed the light streaming through lattice windows, illuminating a room dominated by dark furniture, wooden panelling and heavy tapestries. An old and very fine room, to be sure, but where? And how had she ended up here?

She licked her dry lips, conscious suddenly of feeling desperately thirsty as she tried to remember what had happened. She'd been in some woodland, running as fast as she could. She'd slipped and she'd fallen—she'd felt pain everywhere. She'd cried out, and then…

A voice—deep and reassuring. A tide rolling in, lifting her off the bracken-strewn ground and carrying her away, its undulating waves rocking her, conspiring with sleep to distance her from her pain. Except it hadn't been the sea at all, had it? It had been a man, the one the voice had belonged to, taking her into his arms, offering gentle words to calm her as he carried her away from the woods. She'd been found, but by whom? Where on earth was she? And, more to the point, was she safe?

Or had she been found by yet another of her father's many acquaintances? Had he been alerted to her whereabouts? Was he on his way to take her again, right now?

Hope's heart began to race, and in a sudden panic she tried to pull herself upright. Pain shot through her back and her neck, causing her to cry out. Her head throbbed; she touched the back of it gingerly, wincing as her fingers grazed over a swollen lump. What had she done to herself? Just how badly injured was she? The heat of coming tears burned her eyes and she blinked furiously, forbidding them to fall. Crying would do no good; it never had.

Crying hadn't helped on the day that she'd found her mother's lifeless body strewn across her bed, having finally succumbed to laudanum's charms. Nor had it helped her stop herself from being drawn into her father's underworld of illicit stills and free trading, a world in which she'd never been able to decide whose wrath she feared more, that of her kin or that of the law. Her tears and her pleas had not prevented her father from trying to force her into a marriage, either five years ago or yesterday. The man was immune to tears, and so should she be. The only thing which had helped, then and now, was running away.

She had to run. But first she had to get out of this bed.

Pushing the bedsheets away, she forced herself upright, gritting her teeth as a fresh, sharp agony stabbed at her lower back. Glancing down at herself, Hope was surprised to see that the pretty, thin gown she'd been wearing last night had gone, along with her stays, leaving her wearing only her white linen shift. She felt her cheeks redden at the realisation—who on earth had done that? Not the man who'd carried her, surely? No matter, she decided. She would run across the countryside wearing her undergarments and no shoes, if she had to.

Persevering despite the pounding which grew in her head, Hope shuffled to the edge of the bed and let her toes touch the floor. Her right ankle began to throb and she looked down to see that someone had covered it with a bandage. The rug below her feet felt soft and reassuring as she pressed against it. However, her injured ankle protested, a sudden pain shooting through it and causing both her legs to buckle. Before she could stop herself, she was falling down, landing on the floor with a hard and graceless thud.

'Ow!' she cried out and this time, despite herself, the tears did fall.

Clearly the commotion she'd caused had been heard. Beyond the bedchamber, someone else in the house stirred, and all Hope could do was sit helplessly on the floor, tears flooding down her cheeks as footsteps approached. Quick, frantic footsteps, growing louder by the second. Then, after a moment, the door creaked open and a face peered around it. A man's face, etched with concern, his brow furrowing as he spied her on the floor.

'What the devil are you doing down there?'

He was impeccably dressed; that was the first thing she noticed. As he strode towards her, she drew her first, hurried conclusions about him, taking in his tidy, sand-coloured hair, his high collar and cravat, his immaculate blue coat. A gentleman, certainly, although that was no surprise to her really, considering the fine surroundings she'd awoken in. She stared up at him, meeting his grey-blue eyes for the first time and finding, to her great relief, kindness there. Whatever he saw in her gaze was presumably less reassuring; she watched in confusion as he hesitated, averting his eyes and half turning back towards the door.

'Sir?' Hope croaked, her mouth desert dry.

'Forgive me,' the man said, still looking away. 'I should not have burst in like that. I shall fetch a maid to attend to you.'

A maid to attend to her. Yes—he was definitely a gentleman. Hope glanced down, her confusion clearing like mist as she caught sight of the linen shift she wore once more. Ah, of course. Now she understood his hesitation.

'Thank you, sir. Also, if it is not too much trouble, I would be obliged to you for some water,' she added politely, instinctively slipping into the voice she'd used on stage just days ago—soft and refined, clear and articulate. She didn't know why. Perhaps because she feared that even a word spoken in her own voice, laced as it was with the Cumberland accent, would tell him exactly who she was? Or perhaps because sitting here, in this grand room, speaking to the well-dressed gentleman who'd saved her life, she felt that she ought to smooth over her coarse ways?

She watched as the man glanced at the water jug sitting atop the table. He sighed heavily before turning back around and stepping towards her once more.

'This is ridiculous,' he muttered as he bent down, gently lifting her off the floor and placing her back upon the bed. Despite the discomfort that the movement caused, the brief feeling of his arms around her was warm and strangely reassuring, bringing back those vague, confused memories of the previous night. She did not even need to ask if he'd been her rescuer; instinctively, she knew that he had.

'What is ridiculous, sir?' she asked him.

The man walked around the bed and poured some water into a cup. 'Fetching a maid to help you when I can just as easily do it myself,' he replied, handing the cup to her. 'Anyway,' he continued, 'you did not answer me. What were you doing on the floor?'

'I was trying to get up,' Hope replied between thirsty sips. 'I am grateful to you, sir, but I am sure I have been a burden for long enough. If you could see to it that my dress and shoes are returned to me, I promise I will leave within the hour.'

'The devil you will,' the man replied, frowning at her once more. 'I'm afraid you're not fit to go anywhere right now. Your right ankle is badly injured, and you've suffered a nasty blow to the head. I don't know what happened to you in the woods, but my physician says you're purple and blue with bruises.'

'Your physician?' Hope repeated, her heart pounding once more. She pulled the bedsheets tighter around herself, as though they could protect her. As though anything could protect her.

'Yes, my physician. He attended to you last night. He assures me that your ankle is not broken, and that all your wounds will heal. But he says you must rest.'

Hope, however, was not listening. 'Did you say anything to him about me? Did you tell him where you found me?' she asked, her questions rapid as she began to panic. Did her father know any physicians? Was it possible that this physician knew who she was? Might he betray her whereabouts?

'I told him that I discovered you lying injured in the woods,' the man replied. 'That was all I could say, since I do not know anything about you.' He paused, holding her gaze with his own for a long moment. 'I dare say that's something we ought to rectify. Perhaps you'd like to begin by telling me your name and whether there is someone I should inform of your whereabouts.'

Hope's heart raced even faster, the pain in her head reaching a crescendo as she felt the room begin to spin. 'Someone you should inform?' she repeated.

'Of course,' the man said. 'Surely a lady such as yourself has loved ones who are desperately worried about you? They'd be welcome to stay here too, of course, while you convalesce. Indeed, that would be best, for propriety's sake. I will have to ask them to arrange for some of your clothes to be brought to you. That gown you were wearing last night is unfortunately beyond repair.' He gave her an affable smile, but she could not mistake the curiosity lingering in his eyes. 'I do wonder what you were doing, wandering in the woods by yourself in such a fine evening gown.'

Hope drew a deep breath, trying to calm herself, trying to read between the lines. She thought about the way he behaved towards her—calling her a lady, talking about her fine gown, panicking at the impropriety of being in the same room as her while she wore only a shift. Did he think she was like him? Had he mistaken her for a gentleman's daughter? For the offspring of some grand duke, or of a wealthy merchant?

Hope sipped her water again, buying herself some time as she considered her options. Telling this man the truth about herself was out of the question; the nature of her father's business, such as it was, meant that he was known across Cumberland society. It was well known that Jeremiah Sloane supplied his contraband to many of the fine houses, and many of the magistrates, thus ensuring they happily continued to turn a blind eye to his activities. For all she knew, this was one such house, and one such gentleman. And yet she knew she had to tell this man something. If she had to remain here for the moment, she needed him to understand her requirement for secrecy; she needed him to help her hide. Surely, she reasoned, she could come up with a story which explained why, one which met with the assumptions he seemed to have made about her. Surely she could create a suitably genteel and imperilled character for herself. She was an actress, after all. This would simply be another role for her to play.

She cleared her throat. 'Please understand, sir, that no one can know I am here. Promise me that you will not whisper my whereabouts to a single soul. It is bad enough that your physician and your servants already know…'

Her plea seemed to grab the man's attention and he drew closer, his sympathy evident in his expression. 'Of course, I promise I will say nothing. And please, do not worry—my servants' discretion can be trusted, and my physician is a good man. Besides, no one even knows your name—including me.'

Hope gave an obliging nod. It was the sort of nod she'd cultivated on stage when playing high society types—subtle and reserved. 'My name is Hope…' She paused, searching for a family name. 'Hope Swynford.' Inwardly she groaned; that name was uncomfortably similar to her stage name, Hope Swyndale. She might be a decent actress, but it was already becoming apparent that she was a hopeless playwright.

'Ah! Like the third wife of John of Gaunt,' the man said, a grin spreading across his face. It was a handsome face; she noticed that now, her attention drawn to his blue-grey eyes, sparkling with interest, to his straight nose, his fair complexion, his full lips…

'Oh, John of Gaunt—yes, indeed,' she replied, forcing herself to concentrate on their conversation. She knew that name from a play by Shakespeare, but could not recall which one. Nor could she recall a wife, much less three of them. What on earth had got into her?

The man extended a hand towards her, and she accepted it gingerly. His fingers were gentle and warm, just as his arms had been both times she'd found herself within them. 'Delighted to make your acquaintance, Miss Swynford,' he said. 'My name is Samuel Liddell.'

She offered him a polite smile. 'It is a pleasure to meet you, sir, and thank you once again for coming to my aid. I believe you saved my life.'

'I was glad to be of assistance to you.' He let go of her hand, his expression growing serious once more. 'Perhaps, Miss Swynford, you might tell me what happened to you last night, and why you do not wish for your whereabouts to be known. I would like to help you, if I can.'

The look in his eyes was so genuine that for a brief moment Hope considered telling him the truth. Perhaps this Samuel Liddell really was a good man, perhaps he knew nothing of her father. Perhaps he would be willing to help Hope Sloane just as much as he wished to help Hope Swynford. Yet, as much as she wanted to be honest, she knew that it was not worth the risk. If life had taught her anything, it was that the only person she could really trust was herself.

Hope drew a deep breath, committing herself finally to her deceit. 'I am running away from my uncle, sir,' she began, improvising, the story and her lines unfinished even as she uttered them. 'I am running away from a marriage he wishes to force upon me. From a marriage I do not want.'

Chapter Three

If Samuel's prayers for company had been answered, he could not decide if it was God or the Devil who'd granted his wish. As he made himself comfortable in a small armchair which he'd pulled nearer to her bedside and began to listen to Miss Swynford's sorry tale, he realised that last night in the woods he'd found trouble. Quite literally, it seemed, since by all accounts this uncle Miss Swynford described was a deeply unpleasant character. Hellbent on carving up her inheritance between himself and an acquaintance, he'd concocted a plan to kidnap her and take her to Scotland, where he would force her to marry the co-conspirator, thus transferring her wealth to her new husband, who would then give the uncle his share. It seemed they'd travelled first to Lowhaven, to meet this awful acquaintance off a boat from the Isle of Man, before continuing northwards for the wedding. With her parents both deceased, the poor lady had been powerless in the face of his machinations, until some commotion at an inn had afforded her an opportunity to run away and board a mail coach.

'The coach was bound for Lowhaven, where we had just come from—not that I cared where it was going,' she continued, grimacing as she shifted in the bed. 'I just knew that it was fast, and it would get me away from them both.'

'Did your uncle or this other man see you board the mail coach? Did they try to pursue you?' he asked, trying to ascertain whether she remained in immediate danger.

She bit her lip. 'Unfortunately, I think they did. Two men were fighting in the courtyard, and one landed a blow on my uncle. This distracted them long enough for me to get away from them, but not without them seeing how I'd made my escape.'

She shifted again, clearly uncomfortable. Without thinking, Samuel leapt to his feet, plumping and adjusting the pillows behind her back. This prompted her to let out a nervous laugh, and he realised then just how close he was to her. Just how cream-coloured her bare arms were in that white shift. Just how deep the brown colour of her hair was, how it spilled over her shoulders in thick, wild tendrils.

Truly, he thought, he had found trouble, and not only because of the tale she was telling. He'd realised he'd found it the moment he'd walked into this bedchamber and observed those emerald eyes staring up at him. Something had stirred within his sore, lonely heart then. Something unwise. Something which he could only blame on the long weeks he'd spent in solitude. Something he felt certain this poor lady could do without, given her recent ordeal. He could do without it too, he reminded himself, given his own recent failed romantic endeavours.

'So what did you do, once you got back to Lowhaven?' Samuel asked, retreating to his armchair and forcing himself to focus on their conversation.

'I did not make it as far as that. I'd scrambled atop the coach as it was about to depart, and handed over the only two shillings I had. It turns out that two shillings doesn't get you very far. I've been trying to make my way on foot across the countryside ever since.'

'And where were you hoping to go?'

'London.'

'You were going to walk to London?' Samuel asked, incredulous.

Miss Swynford gave him a sad smile. 'In the circumstances, I had little choice. Anyway, I got thoroughly lost and utterly exhausted, before falling and hurting myself in the woods near to wherever this is. The rest you know.'

'Hayton,' Samuel informed her. 'You're in Hayton, and this house is Hayton Hall. So then, why London?' he continued. 'Is that where you're from?'

She seemed to hesitate. 'No, not really,' she replied evasively. 'But I have a good friend there. A married friend. I was going to go to her and her husband for help, and for protection.'

Samuel nodded, sensing for the first time that there was something she wasn't telling him, but deciding not to press her further. She barely knew him, after all, and could hardly be expected to trust him with every detail of her life, especially in the circumstances. Indeed, given all that she'd endured, she'd be entirely justified in never trusting anyone again.

Samuel rose from his seat, offering her a polite bow. 'You have my promise, Miss Swynford, that you will be well protected here. Once your injuries have healed and you are well enough to travel, I will accompany you and see to it that you reach your friend in London safely.'

He watched as those bright green eyes widened at him, unsure if it was mere surprise or sheer horror he saw in her gaze. 'You do not have to do that, sir,' she protested. 'Please, do not inconvenience yourself on my account.'

'It is no inconvenience. I have thought often about how some time away from Cumberland and a little society would do me the world of good,' Samuel replied, giving her a broad smile. How true that statement was, after so many long, lonely weeks. 'We will travel together, in my carriage. If anyone asks, I will say that you are my sister.'

Miss Swynford pressed her lips together, appearing to accept his plan even if her serious expression told him that she remained unhappy about it. Again, he reminded himself, she was hardly likely to jump for joy at the prospect of travelling with a man she'd only just met. A man who, for all she knew, could prove to be just as much of a rogue as those she'd recently fled from. A man who she had no reason to put any faith in. He made a silent promise then that he would work hard to earn her trust. That by the time they set off in his carriage she would have no reason to harbour any more reservations about Samuel Liddell.

'Do you have a sister, sir?' Her question, softly spoken though it was, pierced the silence which had hung between them.

He shook his head. 'No. We'll have to invent one, I'm afraid.'

She chewed her bottom lip, considering his answer. He found himself staring at her, drawn to the pretty features of her heart-shaped face—her slim pink lips, her small button-like nose and those big emerald eyes which had so taken him aback when he'd first walked into the room. She was, without doubt, uncommonly beautiful. And he was, without doubt, uncommonly ridiculous for entertaining such thoughts about a lady whose only concern was evading her fortune-seeking uncle and finding sanctuary in London.

'What about a brother?' She continued her line of questioning, thankfully oblivious to the inappropriate turn his thoughts had taken. 'Or a wife?'

He chuckled wryly at that. 'I am as yet unwed,' he replied, trying to sound nonchalant. 'I do have a brother, but he is not here at present,' he added vaguely, finding that for some reason he did not wish to talk about Isaac.

'So you live here alone?' She stared at him, incredulous. 'All by yourself?'

'Not entirely alone,' he countered, feeling suddenly defensive. 'My brother will return and…well, there are servants here, of course. Indeed,' he continued, moving away from her bedside and towards the door, 'I think it is past time that I arranged for a maid to attend to you.'

He placed his hand on the door knob, ready to leave, his inner voice giving him a stern talking-to. Why had he not just explained the situation? Why had he not simply told her that his solitary life was only temporary while he cared for his ancestral home and estate in his brother's absence? That the real master of Hayton Hall would return soon and resume his duties, liberating his inconsequential younger sibling to do as he pleased once more.

'Yes, thank you, and please forgive me, sir,' she called after him. 'I did not mean to offend you. I was merely curious.' She glanced around the bedchamber. 'This is a lovely room. I'm sure the rest of Hayton Hall is very fine. Hopefully, when my ankle is strong enough, you will be able to show me.'

He smiled proudly. 'It is indeed a fine country house. A little old-fashioned, perhaps, for modern tastes, but I believe it will stand the test of time. It was built around two hundred years ago, by the first baronet.'

He realised as soon as he said that word that he'd given her the wrong impression. That she'd made an assumption about him, an assumption which he ought to immediately correct. Along with the other assumption he'd undoubtedly led her to—that Hayton Hall belonged to him, that he was the master of a grand house and a vast estate.

And yet, as he looked up and met her lovely green gaze, he found himself unable to say the right words. To tell her that it was Isaac who was the baronet, and Isaac to whom the estate belonged.

'I promise you will be safe here, Miss Swynford,' he said instead, opening the door. 'Safe and well cared for. I'll ask for a tray to be sent up from the kitchen too. You must be famished.'

What in God's name had got into him?

Samuel paced up and down in the library, this same question circling around in his mind. He'd always regarded himself as a very straightforward, decent sort of fellow. He'd travelled all over Europe and mingled with all sorts of people, from country squires to wealthy merchants, to the sons and daughters of earls and dukes, and he'd never once felt any temptation to present himself as anything other than what he was. He was Samuel Liddell, a Cumberland gentleman, a younger son, a man sufficient in both means and good sense to enjoy a very comfortable life. A man who was glad not to have the responsibilities which came with an estate and a title. And yet there he'd stood in that bedchamber, allowing that lady to believe that everything here was his. That he was the master of Hayton Hall, and that he was the baronet. It was unfathomable.

Samuel slumped down into an armchair, sighing heavily and tugging uncomfortably at his collar. Outside, the day had grown dull and blustery, the loss of the earlier sunlight combining with the wind to usher in an autumnal chill. By contrast, however, the library felt stifling, the warm air heavy with the scent of leather-bound books and old wooden shelves. Samuel had no idea why he'd fled in here; this room was Isaac's domain, with everything about it pronouncing the real baronet's taste and temperament—from the dark green leather of its chairs to the decanter of brandy with a single glass and a newspaper placed neatly by its side. It was a quiet, brooding space, and one which had never suited the irrepressible cheer and sociability of the younger brother. Until recently, anyway. Bound by duty to the estate and disinclined towards society, thanks to the whiff of scandal Isaac had left in his wake, it was clear to Samuel that he'd been emulating many of his brother's habits during these past weeks. That glass and that newspaper, after all, were for him.

'None of which makes it all right to let Miss Swynford believe you're the baronet, you foolish man,' he muttered to himself. 'The question is, what are you going to do about it now?'

He had to tell her the truth, of course, before matters went any further. After all, he had not lied to her, exactly. But he had unwittingly misled her, and upon realising he had done so, he had failed to clarify who he in fact was. It was this clarification that he had to now offer, as soon as possible. It would be embarrassing, but by dealing with this swiftly, a simple apology for not explaining the situation to her immediately would suffice. He would not need to offer any further explanation about his reasons for initially misleading her.

What were his reasons, exactly? Why had he not been able to bring himself to utter a handful of simple words, explaining that neither Hayton Hall nor the baronetcy were his? Had these past weeks of effective isolation sent him quite mad? Was he so in want of company that one short conversation with an emerald-eyed young lady was enough to make him lose all reason? It would seem so.

Samuel put his head in his hands, letting out a heavy sigh. Allowing himself to attribute his behaviour to loneliness, no matter how convenient an explanation it was, would not do. There was little point in lying to himself, in failing to acknowledge that the thought of contradicting the lovely Miss Swynford's assumption about him had brought back those painful feelings of the summer. How it had reminded him that he was not quite good enough, that he'd been assessed on society's marriage mart and had been found lacking.

How it had reminded him of the way a certain flame-haired beauty had looked down her nose at him as he confessed his growing affection for her for the first time. The way her words had cut him down and put him firmly in his place—a place which was far below every titled man in England.

'Mama says I must have a London season, for that is where the very best gentlemen are found. I dread to think what she would say if she knew what you have asked of me today...'

Samuel shook his head, trying to push the humiliating, hurtful memory from his mind. The fact that he still ruminated upon it was bad enough, but allowing it to cloud his judgement when it came to being honest about himself was ridiculous. Quite apart from anything else, he'd no intentions towards Miss Swynford, or indeed towards any lady. This summer he'd thrown himself wholeheartedly into the turbulent waters of courtship and where had that left him? Washed up, rejected and deserted—quite literally. It was not an experience he was in any hurry to repeat.

He groaned, dragging his hands down his face. He had to put the recent past firmly behind him. And he had to be honest with Miss Swynford—as soon as possible.

His resolve suitably strengthened, Samuel rang for the butler. A moment later the older man arrived, one wiry grey eyebrow raised as he waited expectantly for his orders.

'Smithson, Miss Swynford will remain with us while she recovers from her injuries. Please see to it that she is kept comfortable and please ensure that no one outside of this house learns that she is here. It seems that the poor lady has fled from the clutches of a nefarious uncle who was seeking to force her into a marriage.'

'Poor Miss Swynford,' the butler remarked. 'Of course, sir, I will make sure the staff treat the lady's presence here with the utmost secrecy.'

Samuel inclined his head gratefully. 'As soon as she is well enough, Miss Swynford plans to travel to London,' he continued. 'I have promised to escort her; my absence won't be prolonged, and I'm sure that between you and the steward, the estate will be well cared for,' he added, offering the man an appeasing smile.

'Indeed, sir. Unless Sir Isaac has returned by then, of course.'

The mention of his brother caused Samuel to wince. 'Ah—

yes,' he began. 'You see, Smithson, Miss Swynford seems to have formed the opinion that I am the master here...that, um, well, I am Sir Samuel, I suppose.'

That wiry eyebrow shot up again. 'Miss Swynford has formed this opinion?' the butler repeated. 'Can such things be considered opinions, sir?'

'Perhaps it is more of an impression then,' Samuel replied, grimacing.

Smithson nodded slowly. 'I see. And to be clear, sir, this impression was formed by the lady herself, rather than given to her by someone else?'

Samuel groaned. 'The lady formed the impression and someone else—namely me—failed to clarify matters.' He gave the butler an earnest look. 'I do intend to give that clarification when the appropriate moment arises. However, the lady is vulnerable and her health is clearly delicate, so it is important that the clarification comes from me, rather than a servant, wouldn't you agree?'

He watched as his brother's loyal servant pressed his lips together, his brow furrowing deeply for a moment as he considered his words. 'Just to be clear, sir—you want the household to pretend that you are the baronet?'

Samuel felt his face grow warm. 'I'm not asking anyone to lie, Smithson. I'm simply asking them not to say anything until I can...'

'Until you can clarify matters?'

Samuel nodded. 'Exactly.'

Smithson gave Samuel another tight-lipped look. 'I will ensure everyone in this household does as you wish,' he replied after a long moment. 'I would only caution you, sir, that often what begins as a small deception tends to have a way of getting out of hand. It would be best to be honest, sooner rather than later.'

'I fully intend to be, Smithson.'

The butler nodded, apparently satisfied. 'I dare say you'll need to have clarified matters before your friends arrive, in any case.'

Samuel frowned. 'My friends?'

'The ones due to visit from Lancashire, sir,' Smithson reminded him. 'Mr Gordon and his sister. Are they not arriving next week?'

At this Samuel groaned, dragging his hands down his face once more. In the midst of everything that had happened since last night, he'd quite forgotten about Charles and Miss Gordon's visit. They couldn't possibly come now, not while there was a lady hiding in his home. A lady whom he'd sworn to protect. A lady whose whereabouts he'd promised to keep secret.

'I'll write to Charles and ask him to postpone. I'll tell him I'm unwell,' Samuel replied. 'I cannot possibly entertain guests while Miss Swynford is convalescing in secret. I gave her my word that no one else would know she was here.'

Smithson nodded politely. 'Very good, sir,' he replied. 'Hopefully, the letter will reach Mr Gordon in time.'

Indeed, thought Samuel, it had better. As much as he'd been looking forward to seeing Charles, and meeting his sister, keeping Miss Swynford safe and hidden, and keeping his promise to her, was more important. He might not be a baronet or a landowner, but he was still a gentleman. A foolish, heartsore gentleman, but a man of honour nonetheless.

Chapter Four

The next few days passed in a blur of sleep and soup—the latter served eagerly by a maid named Maddie, who'd been charged with Hope's care. For the first time in her life, Hope discovered what it was like to be waited upon hand and foot, to recuperate in a house which was warm and comfortable, and where no one wanted for anything. As a child, the spectre of illness had frequently cast its shadow over their humble farmer's cottage, taking all of her siblings before they were old enough to help in the fields. Even the merest hint of sickness or injury had spelled danger in a home which was always damp and where there was never quite enough to eat.

If she was being generous to him, she could understand why, in the face of such hardship, her father had turned to more illicit ways of earning a living. What she could not understand, however, was how he'd allowed it to corrupt him so utterly. How he'd allowed it to drag her mother down, her spirit so broken by his cruelty that she'd sought solace in her deadly tinctures.

How he'd been able to face remaining in that cramped cottage near Lillybeck once everyone else had gone. Hope shuddered, her thoughts briefly returning to the night she'd been dragged back there, how it had struck her that nothing about the cottage or him had changed during her five-year absence. The place was still bitterly cold, and so was he—icy and filled with contempt for the daughter who'd disobeyed him and dared to have a life of her own.

Shuffling beneath her sheets, she brushed the memory aside. She could not dwell upon Hope Sloane's difficulties, not when she was meant to be Hope Swynford. After all, the runaway heiress she'd invented had enough problems of her own.

'Can I fetch you anything, miss?' Maddie asked, noticing Hope's discomfort. She was an attentive woman, perhaps ten years Hope's senior, her dark eyes framed by thick brown brows which were drawn together with concern for her charge. Hope tried not to dwell on what Maddie would think if she knew who the woman she waited upon really was.

Hope shook her head, offering Maddie a reassuring smile. 'No, thank you,' she replied. 'Honestly, you have cared for me far better than I have ever cared for myself.'

That much was true. In many ways, life in the theatre had been just as unforgiving as the precarious existence of a farmer turned free trader's daughter. The hours spent rehearsing and performing were long and relentless, while life off-stage presented endless dangers for her to avoid, from gin and opium to men who regarded actresses as little more than harlots. There had been no respite, and little opportunity to either eat or sleep well.

Maddie beamed at her. 'Oh, thank you, miss,' she replied, the colour rising in her cheeks at the compliment. 'I must say, you are looking much better already.'

Hope was inclined to disagree with that. With Maddie's

help she'd managed to wash earlier, and had caught sight of herself and her wounds in the mirror. She was indeed purple and blue, just as the physician had said. Thankfully, her face was unscathed, but her pallor was horribly grey, and her lower back bore a particularly nasty, swollen bruise. In short, she looked anything but better. She had to admit that she was beginning to feel better, though; the pain in her head had largely abated, and while her ankle remained swollen, it was not as sore as it had been. After washing, Maddie had given her a clean shift to wear, which had helped to lift her spirits further.

'It's one of mine,' the woman had remarked. 'It's a bit big for you, miss, since you are so slender, but it'll do until we can sort out some proper clothes of your own.'

Hope had nodded, wondering what Maddie had meant by that. Lending her a shift to wear in bed was one thing, but poor Maddie couldn't be expected to give items of clothing to her indefinitely. In the end, however, she'd decided not to question her further. Since becoming Hope Swynford and pouring out her deceitful tale, Hope had decided that remaining silent and compliant was the best approach. Saying too much, and asking too many questions, risked those around her growing suspicious. Lies had a way of tying you in knots if you weren't careful, and Hope had already told enough of them in the cause of concealing her true identity.

An identity which, thus far, she had successfully hidden. It seemed to be a stroke of incredible luck that she'd not encountered any familiar faces at Hayton Hall. There did not appear to be anyone here who knew who she really was. Perhaps the master of this fine house was completely unacquainted with her father and his unscrupulous dealings. She had no way of knowing; despite being situated mere miles from Lillybeck, she knew nothing of Hayton or its foremost family.

Before running away and joining the theatre, her world had been small, revolving around that damp cottage, household chores and keeping watch over her father's stills, tucked away in nearby caves. A world which only expanded when she was required to accompany her father into Lowhaven, or forced to assist with one of his night-time runs to the coast to shift contraband under the cover of darkness. Hardly a reprieve. Still, she thought, perhaps Hayton was far enough away to offer her sanctuary. Perhaps she had been very unlucky, after all, to have been recognised in Lowhaven.

Hope remained relieved and somewhat surprised too that her hurriedly invented tale had been accepted so readily by Sir Samuel, as she assumed she ought to call him now. When he'd questioned her, she knew she'd been vague and foolish with her answers. Goodness knew why she'd said she was going to London, of all places! Her careless words had not gone unpunished, with Sir Samuel's insistence upon escorting her on her journey south, meaning that she would now have to go there and work out how to survive in a city about which she knew nothing and where she was acquainted with no one. A city which was many miles south of Richmond, of her theatre company. Of her real life.

Her lies, indeed, would tie her in knots. She would have to be careful not to become trapped in a tangled mess of her own making.

A knock at the door broke the silence which had descended in the bedchamber. Maddie gave Hope a knowing look. 'The master again, no doubt.'

Hope smiled, smoothing the bedsheets down in front of

her. It was true that Sir Samuel was a frequent visitor, coming in periodically to see how she fared, or to ask whether she needed anything—which, of course, thanks to Maddie, she never did. Sometimes he'd simply sit by her side for a few moments, talking about nothing much beyond the weather or where he'd been on the estate that day, before apologising for tiring her and taking his leave. She supposed he wished to reassure himself that she was recovering well, that he saw this as his duty, since she was in his home and therefore in his care. Yet she also sensed there was more to his visits, that he did in fact desire her company. She recalled the remark she'd made during their first conversation, about him being at Hayton Hall all by himself, and how that had seemed to offend him. She wondered if, despite his protestations to the contrary, Sir Samuel was in fact lonely.

'Come in!' Hope called.

She raised a brief smile as Sir Samuel entered, although her expression quickly dissolved into one of consternation when she saw the pile of clothing he carried in his arms. She watched as he placed them down gently on the end of the bed, then stood with his hands on his hips, surveying them with a pleased look on his face. He had the most genuine, open smile, one which made gentle creases gather around his grey-blue eyes. The sort of smile which could illuminate a room. The sort of smile which, she reminded herself, she had no business paying quite so much attention to.

'These are for you,' he began. 'I thought you would need something more suitable to wear, once you're well enough to come downstairs.'

Hope glanced down at the clothes, a feeling of panic rising in her chest as she noted the fine lace and muslin on display. 'That is kind of you, sir,' she replied. 'But really, you should not have gone to so much trouble on my account. I cannot repay you at present…'

'Repay me?' Sir Samuel raised his eyebrows in surprise. 'Oh! Heavens, no! I did not purchase these, Miss Swynford. No, in fact, we…er…that is to say, they were already in the house. They belong to my cousin, you see. She stayed here a few years ago, with my aunt as well, of course, until she married. For whatever reason, she neglected to take these items with her, in her trousseau.' He gave a nonchalant shrug. 'So now they are yours—for the time being, at least. I do hope they fit as my…er…cousin is perhaps a bit taller than you, if I recall.'

His awkward acknowledgement of her small stature made Hope laugh. 'I find that most ladies are taller than me, sir,' she replied.

He grinned, apparently too much of a gentleman to comment further. 'Indeed, well, I'm sure Madeleine is more than capable of making any alterations that might be required,' he replied, nodding briefly towards the maid, who gave him a distinctly displeased look. Perhaps, Hope reasoned, she wasn't quite so adept with a needle and thread as her employer believed.

Sir Samuel, meanwhile, had paced over to the window, surveying the view outside with his hands clasped behind his back. Hope found her eyes roaming approvingly over his trim physique, his broad shoulders and slender waist on perfect display in a deep green tailcoat, whilst his fitted fawn pantaloons showed off the strong legs of a man who spent much of his life on horseback. Every impeccably tailored inch of the man announced his wealth and his power, his status as a gentleman, a landowner and a member of Cumberland's elite. A status which was far beyond her own.

Hope swallowed hard, barely daring to contemplate what this man would say if he knew that he'd come to the assistance not of a genteel heiress, but an actress and the daughter of an outlaw.

'Do you think you might feel strong enough to come downstairs today?' Sir Samuel asked, turning back to face her. 'I thought I might show you a little of the rest of the house.'

His question surprised her. 'Perhaps for a little while, although I cannot walk very well, sir.'

He narrowed his eyes, looking thoughtful. 'I may have something which will assist you in that regard, although I will need to go and look for it.' His eyes shifted briefly to Maddie, who hovered beside the pile of clothes. 'Madeleine will help you find something suitable amongst all that, and can let me know once you are ready so I can escort you downstairs. If you are sure you are well enough, that is.'

Hope nodded. 'I am sure, sir.'

Sir Samuel gave her another of his broad smiles, then with a brief bow he took his leave.

Hope watched as Maddie held up each gown one by one, apparently assessing their size and suitability with a keen eye and careful hands. There were more dresses in that pile than Hope had ever owned in her entire life. Most of what she'd worn over the past few years had been costumes; her clothing had belonged to the characters she'd played, not to her. But then, she supposed, so did that pile of dresses. They'd been given to Hope Swynford out of kindness, and to allow her to present herself in a way which befitted her position in society. Gowns like those were not meant for the likes of Hope Sloane.

'It was very kind of your master to fetch those himself,'

Hope remarked, feeling discomfited by the stony silence which had settled in the room. 'I would have thought he'd be too busy.'

'Yes, well, he's very…organised,' Maddie replied. 'Likes to take charge of matters.'

'I suppose that is a good trait to have in a gentleman with an estate to run,' Hope pondered.

Maddie appeared to flinch before answering. 'Suppose so.'

'You don't agree?' Hope asked, her curiosity defeating her resolution not to ask too many questions. 'I did notice that you looked a little displeased with him. Is he not a good master to work for?'

The maid eyed her carefully. 'He's fine, miss, honestly. Except when he calls me Madeleine. I have said that he can call me Maddie, like everyone else does. That's just his way, I suppose—very proper. Very exact. Not a hair out of place, so to speak. He's not at all like…' Maddie paused, pressing her lips together as she made a show of examining a pretty blue dress.

'Not like whom?' Hope prompted. It was clear the maid had said more than she ought to.

Maddie ran a gentle hand down the fabric, brushing away imaginary creases. 'His brother,' she said flatly, avoiding Hope's gaze.

'What about his brother?'

It was clear, however, that the maid was not going to elaborate further. 'I think this one will do very well,' she continued, holding up the dress. 'And I don't think it requires altering, which is a relief.'

Hope nodded, giving the maid a wry smile. The woman really did not like sewing, that much was obvious, but to describe it as a relief seemed a little dramatic. Hope shuffled forward, wincing as she pulled herself out from beneath the bedsheets. Sir Samuel's invitation to come downstairs had intrigued her, and she was keen to see something beyond these same four walls. Nonetheless, she would have to take care not to exert herself too much.

'Let's try it then,' she said to Maddie. 'But without my stays. I'm not sure my bruises could withstand them.'

With a brisk nod, Maddie set about assisting her, and no more talk passed between them—not about brothers, or dress alterations, or anything else. It seemed the maid had decided to hold her tongue, and despite her vow to remain quiet and indifferent, Hope could not help but wonder what it was that the woman was unwilling, or unable, to say.

Chapter Five

Samuel waited at the top of Hayton Hall's stone staircase, clutching his father's old walking cane in his hand. He'd asked Smithson to retrieve it for him, and requested that some tea be brought shortly to the small parlour, as Miss Swynford would be coming downstairs for a little while today. Smithson had given a brief nod of assent, but Samuel had not been able to overlook how the man had pressed his lips together, as though to prevent himself from saying what was on his mind. Not that he needed to: over the past few days, Hayton's butler had left Samuel in no doubt about just how much he disapproved of the situation unfolding in the house.

'The servants are very unhappy about keeping up the pretence that you are the baronet, sir,' Smithson had told him in no uncertain terms. 'Especially Maddie. The poor maid is terrified that she's going to slip up and accidentally say the wrong thing to Miss Swynford.'

'Madeleine's only job is to ensure Miss Swynford is kept comfortable and that all her needs are met while she recovers, Smithson. She hardly needs to discuss my family's history with her and, in any case, I doubt the lady would be interested,' Samuel had replied, conscious of how hollow his protestations sounded. He was, without doubt, making life difficult for his servants. 'I fully intend to explain everything to Miss Swynford,' he'd added. 'When the opportunity arises.'

Smithson had been unmoved, reminding his master of the perils of deception, that even the most banal lies had a habit of getting out of hand. Now, as he waited to escort Miss Swynford downstairs, Samuel found himself reflecting upon just how true this was. Not only had he compelled his servants to join him in deceiving Miss Swynford, but today he'd told her an outright lie, this time about the clothing he'd brought to her. In truth, there had been no cousin who had left her gowns behind; those items he'd gathered up and taken into Miss Swynford's bedchamber had belonged to his brother's beloved and sadly deceased first wife, Rosalind. Since her death two years earlier, they'd remained tucked away in Hayton Hall's old drawers and clothes presses, and Isaac had thus far neglected to do anything with them.

Samuel had agonised over giving Miss Swynford some of Rosalind's old clothes, but ultimately he'd concluded it was the most sensible solution. After all, the lady needed something suitable to wear, and given that she was in hiding from her wicked uncle, he could hardly take her to a dressmaker in Lowhaven. Telling her that the gowns had belonged to the deceased Lady Liddell had, of course, been out of the question—he might be a fool and a scoundrel for allowing Miss Swynford to believe he was the master of Hayton Hall, but pretending that his brother's loss had been his own was a step too far, and so he'd concocted the tale about his imaginary cousin instead. He'd barely been able to meet Madeleine's horrified gaze as he'd laid out the fine garments once worn by her mistress and dared to suggest they might need to be altered. He did not even wish to consider what Isaac would say if he knew. He'd damn him to hell, at the very least.

Feeling increasingly agitated, Samuel began to pace back and forth down the hallway. He'd insisted to Smithson, and to himself, that he'd be honest with Miss Swynford as soon as possible, and yet so far he'd failed utterly to find the right moment. Every time he'd knocked on the door to her bedchamber, and every time he'd sat beside her bed and made polite conversation, he'd resolved to tell her the truth. Then he'd looked at her smiling, welcoming face, at those green eyes regarding him in earnest, and the words had died in his throat. He'd procrastinated, telling himself that she was still weak from her injuries, that the awkward truth ought to wait until she was feeling stronger.

However, if he was honest with himself, he knew it was more than that. There was something about Miss Hope Swynford which had captivated him. Perhaps it was the soft, articulate sound of her voice, or the feeling of her petite form as he'd carried her in his arms, or the way she managed to make a maid's old shift look becoming, but something about her made him want to impress her. He knew that the moment he corrected her assumptions about him, the moment he confessed to being little more than Hayton's caretaker, he would be put back firmly in his unimpressive place.

'I do not mean to be unkind, Mr Liddell. You are very witty, and very charming. Perhaps if you had been born into your brother's position, things might have been different...'

Samuel shuddered as a certain red-headed young lady's words haunted him once more. Like it or not, memories of how it had felt to be rejected not for who he was but for what he was not had thus far rendered him hopelessly silent. That bitter experience had taught him that as soon as Miss Swynford knew the truth she would likely be very disappointed indeed.

Not that he was planning to court her! Of course not. His only role was to protect her, to ensure she recovered from her injuries before seeing her safely to London.

The sound of Madeleine calling to him from down the hallway startled Samuel from his thoughts, and he walked back towards Miss Swynford's bedchamber, twirling the walking cane in his hand with renewed determination. If Miss Swynford was indeed well enough to join him downstairs, then he would delay his embarrassing confession no longer. He would apologise for not clarifying sooner and he would renew his commitment to protect her. He would seek to put the lady at her ease, to make the best out of the situation in which they'd found themselves. To hopefully find enjoyment in each other's company during the short time that circumstances had conspired to bring them together.

When he reached her doorway, however, he felt himself freeze, the cane growing suddenly still in his hand as his gaze came to rest on his houseguest. Gone was the maid's hand-me-down shift, replaced by an elegant cream gown and matching shawl. Her dark hair, meanwhile, no longer hung loose about her shoulders but had been pinned up, except for one or two curls which framed her heart-shaped face. Standing there in the doorway, she looked every inch the refined, genteel young lady he knew her to be. She greeted him with a cautious smile and he found himself swallowing hard before he could return it. She was, without doubt, a thoroughly striking beauty.

Miss Swynford shuffled forward, leaning heavily against Madeleine, and a wave of protectiveness washed over him as he was reminded of what had happened to her. Of why she was here, and what he had pledged to protect her from.

'I want you to have this,' he said, holding out the walking cane. 'It belonged to my father. I thought it might help while your ankle heals.'

She gave him a grateful nod. 'Thank you, sir,' she said, accepting the cane and limping towards him, her steps tentative and unsteady after so many days of being confined to her bed.

Samuel offered her his arm, walking slowly at her side as they made their way towards the stairs. Her hand, like the rest of her petite form, was small and delicate, and he tried not to dwell on how pleasant it felt resting in the crook of his elbow.

'You must tell me if you feel at all fatigued, Miss Swynford,' Samuel insisted. 'I will return you immediately to Madeleine's care. I just thought that you may enjoy some respite from staring at the same four walls.'

'Thank you.' She inclined her head again. 'I will be sure to tell you, sir. I believe the walking cane will make moving around easier. It is fortunate that you still had it.'

He chuckled at that, gesturing around him with his free hand. 'Old family houses like this tend to collect people and their things, storing them within its walls like memories. At least instead of collecting dust, that old cane has come in useful. Alas, I am sure I do not need to tell you that, Miss Swynford,' he added. 'I'm sure you've enough dusty ancestry of your own somewhere.'

He watched as she nodded, her expression suddenly guarded and unreadable. 'Oh, indeed,' was all she said in reply.

Miss Swynford managed the short walk along the hallway well enough, but when they reached the stairs he saw her hesitate, glancing down with trepidation before turning to look at him. 'I'm not sure I can…' she began, shaking her head with regret. 'My ankle is not strong. I am worried I may fall, sir.'

'Of course,' Samuel began. 'Forgive me, it was silly of me to bring you out of your bedchamber so soon. I will return you to Madeleine.'

'No, sir, I am sorry,' she said. 'I admit, I was rather looking forward to seeing some of the house.'

The look of genuine disappointment in those large green eyes did strange things to his insides, and before he could give it due consideration, an idea had come into his mind.

'Then, if you will permit me…' he began, giving her a bashful smile as he scooped her up into his arms. 'I carried you up these stairs days ago. I believe I can carry you back down again.'

The sound of her laughter echoed around him. 'I have only a vague recollection of that, but I do distinctly remember you lifting me back on to my bed after I was unwise enough to try to get out of it and leave Hayton in naught but my bedclothes.'

That memory alone would have been enough to bring the colour to his cheeks, but coupled with the feeling of her wrapping her arms around his neck and clinging to him as he carried her, he was certain he must be glowing scarlet. Samuel tried to focus on taking one step at a time, to pay no heed to the way her alluring form had settled so perfectly into his arms. It was ridiculous to entertain such thoughts, he reminded himself. The lady was only in his home because of the unhappiest of circumstances; his duty was to protect her, not to admire her. Not to allow his recent loneliness to put ideas in his head which he had no business entertaining. Ideas which he most definitely did not want to have, after his recent brush with rejection.

'So where are we going, sir?' she asked softly, thankfully oblivious to the inappropriate turn his thoughts had taken.

'To my favourite room in the house—the small parlour,' he replied. 'For tea and cake—in my opinion, two of the very best things in life.'

Tea, cake, and confessions, he reminded himself silently.

'That sounds lovely,' she replied. 'I feel very safe here, with you. I do find myself wondering whether, should my uncle learn that I was here, the risk of offending an important local gentleman such as yourself might dissuade him from seeking me out.' She paused for a moment, her eyes wide as they searched his. 'After all, a gentleman in your position must be closely acquainted with those charged with upholding the law. That ought to make him think twice about doing anything...untoward,' she added quietly.

Her words were tentative, laced with fear, and Samuel felt his blood heat as the need to protect her gripped him. 'I can assure you that the Liddells have always been known to do what is right, Miss Swynford, and have always maintained a good relationship with the local magistrate. Please do not worry,' he added as he reached the bottom of the staircase and released her from his arms. 'You are indeed safe in this house.'

She smiled at him, those emerald eyes brightening with relief. 'I do believe that I was fortunate indeed to stumble into the home of a baronet.'

Samuel forced a smile in return, his heart lurching and descending rapidly into the pit of his stomach. The hopeful look in Miss Swynford's eyes, and all that it implied, was unmistakable. She believed that his position as the master of Hayton Hall, as a landowner and a baronet, meant that he could protect her better, that he had a standing in society which no wicked uncle could overcome. That his title and his estate could shield her. And in many ways she was right—except neither of those things were truly his!

But how could he tell her that now? How could he tell her that she did not enjoy the protection of a titled gentleman but a mere younger son, playing the master in his brother's absence? How could he, in all good conscience, dash her hopes of receiving the very best protection? How could he knowingly allow her to feel anything less than completely safe with him?

He knew the answer to all of that—he simply couldn't. As they made their way slowly towards the parlour, he almost groaned aloud. Lord help him, but he was going to have to be the baronet for a while longer yet.

Hope sipped her tea tentatively and took a moment to observe the neat little parlour into which Sir Samuel had brought her. She could immediately see why he liked this room, with its compact size and good number of windows making it both warm and bright. Her gaze fell briefly upon the fireplace around which the sofa and chairs were arranged, and she found herself imagining how cosy it must feel to sit in front of the fire on a cold winter's day.

She doubted she'd ever experienced such comfort in all of her life; even with the hearth lit, her childhood home had always felt so cold and damp, whilst the wages of an actress had only ever afforded her the most meagre accommodation, invariably shared with other women who made their living on the stage. She pushed the thought from her mind, reminding herself who she was now. Or at least, who she was pretending to be. Hope Sloane might sit in awe of a simple parlour, but Hope Swynford never would.

'Do you have everything you need, Miss Swynford?' Sir Samuel asked.

The master of Hayton Hall had sat down opposite her, leaning forward slightly as though anxious to ensure she was well before he would relax. Upon bringing her into the room he'd placed her gently upon the sofa, then set about fetching cushions for her back and a footstool upon which to rest her injured ankle. Truly, his attentiveness was rather endearing, and she found herself struck by how pleasant it was to be treated thus by a gentleman. She found herself thinking too about those few moments she'd spent in his arms as he'd carried her down the stairs. How she'd found the courage to broach the subject of his acquaintance with local men of the law, looking for even the merest hint of crookedness or, God forbid, of dealings with her father. How Sir Samuel had not hesitated to tell her what she'd already begun to suspect—that the Liddell baronets were decent, upstanding men.

How reassured she had felt, in that moment. How relieved to be in his home, to enjoy his protection. And how safe she had genuinely felt as she'd wrapped her arms around him and clung to him for dear life.

It was a disconcerting idea, and one which she pushed swiftly from her mind. No doubt she was simply in awe of this gentleman, of his grand home and his impeccable kindness to her. The gentlemen she'd encountered in theatres were usually very different—at best, drunk and unintelligible by the final act, and at worst, downright lewd and trying to procure the sorts of services she absolutely did not offer. She felt herself begin to blush at the thought of it. She was quite sure Hope Swynford would never have to put up with such humiliation.

'Miss Swynford?' he prompted her, and Hope realised she had not answered.

'Yes, thank you, sir,' she replied, offering a smile which she hoped would be reassuring. She glanced out of the window, spying the view to the front of the house. Neat gardens, stone walls and fields as far as the eye could see. From this aspect, Hayton Hall felt remote. But was it remote enough to keep her hidden? She had to hope so.

'So what is Hayton like?' she asked him. If they were going to drink tea and converse, she reasoned that she might as well learn a little more about exactly where she was.

'It's a small village, just a short walk away,' Sir Samuel replied. 'It has an old church, and a single inn. It is a quiet place. Not a great deal happens in these far-flung corners of England, Miss Swynford,' he added with a grin.

'It sounds lovely,' she remarked, thinking how like Lillybeck it sounded. Thinking too how small places so often appeared sleepy and innocent on the surface. Peel back the layers, though, and there was always some darkness to be found.

'And what about…wherever it is that you are from?' Sir Samuel asked.

Hope hesitated. She had not yet managed to invent a satisfactory explanation of where exactly she'd come from. In truth, her knowledge of England was piecemeal, confined largely to Lillybeck, Lowhaven, and the handful of northern towns she'd visited whilst travelling with her theatre company. She could not risk claiming to be from any of them; if Sir Samuel happened to know any of the prominent families from those areas, her story would quickly come unstuck. The south, meanwhile, was unknown to her; she could not convincingly claim to be from any part of it. Perhaps, she reasoned, it was best if she did not explain at all.

'If you will forgive me, Sir Samuel, I would prefer not to speak of home,' she said quietly, her heart beginning to thud in her chest. She avoided his gaze, hoping he would not press her further. Hoping he would not somehow sense the truth among the lies, that the last thing she ever wanted to tell him about was Hope Sloane's life in Lillybeck with a free-trading father and an opium-eating mother.

He held up his hands. 'Of course, of course. It was thoughtless of me to ask, after all you've endured of late,' he replied. 'Although if you'd said you were from Lancaster, I'd have definitely grown suspicious about your connections.'

Hope frowned, her stomach lurching as a wave of anxiety gripped her. 'What do you mean, sir?'

Sir Samuel grinned at her. 'I was referring to Katherine Swynford,' he replied. 'I am sorry, it was a terrible joke. An inaccurate one too, since the lady was likely from Hainault.'

Hope shook her head, still not understanding. 'Forgive me, I…'

'John of Gaunt's third wife,' he reminded her. 'I was referring to a remark I made when you first told me your name. You share the same name as the third wife of John of Gaunt, who was the Duke of Lancaster. As I said, a terrible joke.'

'Oh, yes,' she replied, recollecting now. Recollecting too the play from which she knew the name. 'John of Gaunt, from the play by Shakespeare *The Life and Death of King Richard the Second*,' she added, allowing herself a brief indulgence in her memories. Her company had performed that play during her first year in Richmond. She'd had only a small part as one of the Queen's ladies, but it had not mattered. Newly liberated from her father's clutches, everything about her life then had seemed so fresh and new. So full of possibility.

Sir Samuel nodded enthusiastically. 'Indeed, from Shakespeare and from history, of course. John was a younger son of Edward III. The story goes that John fell in love with Katherine, but he was already wed and so took her as his mistress. Together they had several children, and after the death of his second wife, he married her.' He regarded her carefully. 'Forgive me, I am perhaps telling you something you already know.'

Hope pressed her lips together, unsure if this was something which a genteel lady like Hope Swynford ought to know. Hope Sloane did not, but then what Hope Sloane knew had been learned from books and plays, from observation and conversation. It was knowledge grasped during a colourful and chaotic life, not the result of orderly tutoring or instruction.

'It is quite the love story, is it not?' she observed after a moment, choosing words which would neither suggest knowledge nor convey ignorance.

Sir Samuel chuckled. 'I suppose it is. Alas, neither of them lived many years after their marriage. And, of course, their offspring's descendants, the Beauforts, went on to be thoroughly embroiled in the quarrel between the roses, as Mr Hume called it.'

'Of course,' Hope replied, feeling thoroughly lost now. 'A love story with unintended consequences, then,' she added thoughtfully.

'Ah—yes, very good,' Sir Samuel agreed. He paused, finishing his tea. When he met her gaze again, she saw his blue-grey eyes seemed to have darkened. 'I don't know about you, Miss Swynford, but it seems to me that there are always consequences when it comes to matters of the heart.'

His words, though smoothly delivered, seemed raw, and Hope found herself wondering at the cause of such an observation. During the short time she'd known him, Sir Samuel had seemed to her to be a kind and gentle sort of man. The sort of man who would be generous with his affections, and perhaps the sort of man whose own feelings were easily wounded.

By contrast, she had always guarded her emotions closely; grim experience had taught her that she had to be the master of them, that feeling anything too deeply was unwise in a life dominated for so long by crime and cruelty. And as for love—that was something others traded, whether it was her father making her his part of a bargain with a fellow outlaw or the actresses she'd known, selling their affections for little more than trinkets and the whispers of gentlemen who made empty promises of a better life. No, she thought, love had played no role in her life thus far.

'Alas, sir,' she answered at length, 'I must confess I have little enough experience of these matters, beyond facing the prospect of a forced marriage, but that had nothing to do with love.'

As the words fell from her lips, Hope was pained to acknowledge that this was the most honest sentiment she'd expressed to Sir Samuel since they'd met. Pained too to note the look of earnest sympathy he gave her as she reminded him of her misfortune. An unexpected, unfathomable feeling rose within her, one which made her yearn to tell him more about herself. To tell him truths she'd never uttered to another person. Perhaps even to tell him the truth.

Hope swallowed down the rest of her tea, as though the hot liquid might bring her back to her senses. As benevolent as her rescuer appeared to be, he could not know the truth about her. No one here could. Her entire future likely depended upon it.

Chapter Six

After that first afternoon they spent together in the parlour, something of a routine was quickly established at Hayton Hall. Sir Samuel would spend the morning attending to his duties on the estate, leaving Hope to rest in her bedchamber. Around noon, Maddie would serve her luncheon in her room and then help her to dress before Sir Samuel arrived to collect her and carry her down to the parlour for tea.

If Hope was honest with herself, she'd already begun to look forward to their meetings, perhaps more than she should. After all, every conversation they had carried a risk—a risk that she might accidentally reveal some detail about her real self, or a risk that she might say something to provoke Sir Samuel's suspicions about the authenticity of the story she had told him.

Despite these risks, Hope did her best to immerse herself in the role she had created, allowing herself to enjoy the fine dresses she wore, the comfortable sofa she sat upon and the quality tea she sipped while getting to know her host better. Sir Samuel seemed to understand that she did not wish to talk much about herself. Since she'd politely refused to answer his enquiry about where she was from, he had not asked her anything specific about her life at all.

Instead, he engaged her on less contentious topics, everything from the minutiae of the day to discussions about favourite pursuits. Hope learned that he'd travelled widely, that his knowledge of the Continent, of its different countries and cultures, was second to none. She found his descriptions of all that he'd seen fascinating; from lakes flanked by towering mountains in Switzerland to crowds of boats on the Venetian lagoon, it was as though he was revealing new worlds to her through words alone.

'You are fortunate to have seen so much of the world,' she'd mused one afternoon as he concluded one of his tales. 'Especially with an estate to manage.'

'Well, of course, all of this took place before I had such responsibilities,' he'd replied, giving her an odd, strained look.

Realising he must have been referring to the time when his father still lived, she'd glanced at the walking cane she'd placed beside her, suddenly struck by all that had passed from father to eldest son. 'It must be a strange thing to inherit all of this,' she'd remarked, waving a hand delicately about her. 'For all the security it surely brings, it must also place limitations upon a gentleman. You cannot freely do as you please when you have duties to your family, your land and your tenants.'

Sir Samuel had given her a tight smile. 'I hardly think any gentleman born into comfort and wealth has any right to complain about his lot, however much he might wish to.'

His reticence had made Hope grin. 'Surely everyone has the right to complain sometimes,' she'd replied. 'It strikes me, sir, that running an estate well is very hard work.'

'Indeed it is,' he'd agreed, 'and not only for gentlemen, as you may discover, should you one day marry and find yourself the mistress of some grand house with many acres attached to it.'

Her smile had faded quickly at that. 'That seems unlikely,' she'd replied, grappling for the right answer, the one which Hope Swynford would surely give. 'My uncle all but dragged me to the border to wed a stranger,' she'd reminded him. 'He might not have succeeded, but I hardly think that detail will matter. I am doubtless ruined in the eyes of society.'

She'd half expected Sir Samuel to argue, but instead he had agreed. 'Polite society is apt to condemn, and apt to make ill-founded judgements upon others,' he'd remarked with such resignation that Hope could not help but wonder if his words had been provoked by more than her retort.

'Oh, I almost forgot,' he'd said, swiftly changing the subject as he lifted a pile of books off the nearby table. 'All that talk about John of Gaunt and Katherine Swynford the other day prompted me to remember these books. Mr Hume's *A History of England.* I thought they might help you to pass the time while you convalesce. That is, if you have not already read them.'

Hope had shaken her head, accepting the six volumes as Sir Samuel handed them to her. 'No, I confess I have not read them,' she'd replied as casually as she could manage. Again, she'd no idea if a woman like Hope Swynford would be expected to have read such books or not.

To her relief, Sir Samuel had seemed not at all perturbed by her admission, which was just as well because Hope had felt unsettled enough for the two of them. As much as she enjoyed Sir Samuel's company and conversation, it was moments like that which reminded her of all she was pretending to be, and all that she was really not. Sir Samuel was a learned gentleman, well-tutored and well-travelled. By contrast, Hope was fortunate that she could read at all; as a girl, she'd been taught her letters by her mother, but they had not owned books like the ones Sir Samuel had given to her. As a woman, she read broadsides and chapbooks, and perhaps the occasional well-thumbed novel which had been passed between the actresses.

Life had taught Hope most of the lessons she knew, and latterly, the theatre had been her schoolroom. Indeed, the theatre was the one area in which she could perhaps match Sir Samuel's knowledge, albeit whilst implying that she'd become acquainted with Shakespeare's plays from a seat in a box at Covent Garden or Drury Lane, and not because she'd spoken his words on stage at Richmond's Theatre Royal.

Unfortunately, it seemed to Hope that fate had more discomfiting moments in store for her. Today, as they rose to leave the parlour, Sir Samuel suggested that they dine together in the evening for the first time. Hope was reluctant; until now she'd eaten her evening meal in her bedchamber, under Maddie's watchful eye but with no expectation of displaying the proper manners or refinement. She knew enough about the habits of the wealthy to know that dining formally with Sir Samuel would be an entirely different matter, and one which she was not confident she would manage. Indeed, the thought of sitting at his fine table, completely lost in the face of all those dishes and all that cutlery, made her feel quite sick.

'I'm afraid my appetite is not as it should be,' she explained, trying her best to thwart him as gently as she could. 'I do not think I could manage it.'

'I do not propose we get through a pile of game and a

mountain of jelly by ourselves,' he replied. 'Indeed, most evenings I sit down to a bowl of soup followed by a small plate of fish and vegetables.'

That admission caught her by surprise. 'That is what I am served most nights, in my room.'

'That's right, because that is what my cook has made for us both,' Sir Samuel answered with an amused smile. 'You look startled, Miss Swynford.'

She shook her head. 'I do not know why, I just had not imagined you were eating the same meal as me.'

He began to laugh. 'Oh, heavens! Now I'm concerned you must have imagined me dining downstairs upon fifteen courses while Madeleine served you meagre soup and fish. I'm a country gentleman, Miss Swynford, not the Prince Regent.'

Hope felt her cheeks begin to flush. 'I can assure you, sir, I did not think that. It is just that I have found my meals very restorative and I assumed they had been served to me for that reason.'

Sir Samuel nodded. 'Yes, and what is good for you is also good for me. I prefer simple, hearty fare. I am not a great enthusiast for rich sauces or heavy puddings.'

'Except cake,' she countered. 'One of the two best things in life, if I recall.'

He grinned at her. 'That's right. Now then, on the promise of a small, simple meal, will you dine with me this evening, Miss Swynford?'

Hope felt her hesitation melt in the face of his convivial persuasion. That was something else she'd observed about Sir Samuel—what he had in learning was easily matched in charm and good humour. She found herself reflecting momentarily upon his qualities, his affability and aptitude for conversation, and contrasted that with what she knew of his life at Hayton Hall, alone and unwed. She wondered why that was, wondered too if it had anything to do with the remark he'd made just days ago about matters of the heart and their consequences. Then she pushed the thought aside, deciding it was none of her business.

Instead, she returned his smile, knowing that whatever misgivings she still had, there was only one answer to his invitation that she could possibly give. 'That sounds lovely, Sir Samuel.'

Samuel took a mouthful of his evening meal, believing it to be the best mackerel he'd ever tasted. Weeks of dining alone had led him to become largely disinterested in what was on his plate, the business of eating having become a mere necessity rather than a pleasure. This evening he was reminded just how much he enjoyed dining in company. He'd been delighted when Miss Swynford had agreed to join him, although acknowledging this delight had made him feel instantly guilty as he was forced to remember that he was enjoying her company under false pretences. That he was allowing this lovely young lady to believe she was dining with Hayton's baronet. Swiftly he had buried the thought, reminding himself of the reason for his ongoing deception. It made Miss Swynford feel safe and protected. That alone made the lie a worthy one, didn't it?

He'd wrestled with that question, and his conscience, ever since that moment at the bottom of the staircase when he'd made the decision to hold his tongue. He'd wrestled too with the uncomfortable knowledge that as honourable as his intentions were in keeping the truth from her, maintaining the deception had also saved him from seeing her evident disappointment when she learned who he truly was. He had to admit to himself that whilst his desire to make her feel secure with him was paramount, he was still allowing his wounded pride to rule his head, at least in part.

Across the table, Miss Swynford caught his eye and he offered her a smile. Like him, she'd dressed for dinner, the cream day dress she'd worn earlier now replaced by a very becoming periwinkle blue gown. Several times his gaze had been drawn to how the colour contrasted so sharply with her dark hair, how the silk fabric flattered her slender form, before he reminded himself that he had no business admiring her. Especially not when it was another of Rosalind's dresses that she wore.

Miss Swynford returned his smile shyly, before taking a tentative sip of the fine claret he'd had Smithson fetch from Hayton's cellars. She seemed on edge tonight, surveying the food and drink before her with wide eyes, consuming them slowly and deliberately, as though she was unsure of herself. As though she was unsure of him.

Samuel felt his smile fade, gripped now by the worrying thought that he might be responsible for her apparent discomfort, that perhaps dining together like this had been a step too far. However compelling the reasons were for her to remain in his home at present, she was nonetheless an unchaperoned, unmarried woman, convalescing in close confinement with an unmarried man. Perhaps she'd been able to countenance tea and cake in the afternoon light of a parlour, but the presence of claret and candles as day faded to night felt too intimate. He had not considered it like that before but, now that he did, he could see how dining like this could be construed in that way. How it might give rise to concerns about his intentions, and just how dishonourable he might in fact be. He reminded himself again of all that she'd endured of late. Certainly, her wicked uncle and his equally dreadful conspirator had given her no reason to trust a gentleman.

'I hope you will forgive me for asking you to join me this evening, Miss Swynford,' Samuel began, possessed now by the urge to say something, to explain himself.

She looked up from her plate, fork poised. 'Forgive you?'

'Indeed, it was very selfish of me. I occupied you for much of the afternoon in the parlour, and ought to have left you to rest this evening.'

She wrinkled her brow at him. 'Do I look tired, sir?'

'Well, no, of course not…'

She gave him another of those small smiles. 'Then all is well. I will be sure to say, if I wish to retire.'

'Yes, of course, very good.' He paused, momentarily unsure how much more he wished to say, before swallowing his pride and adding, 'I would just like to assure you that I have only the most honourable and gentlemanly intentions in inviting you to dine with me. I merely felt it would be nice for us both to have some company during dinner, that is all.'

Miss Swynford sipped her wine again, lingering somewhat over it, and he could tell that she was considering his words. Inexplicably, his stomach started to churn, and he began to regret eating that mackerel quite so enthusiastically. He would have to ask Smithson to have the cook prepare for him some of that sweet ginger drink she always swore aided digestion.

'I am relieved to hear it, Sir Samuel,' she replied at length. 'I cannot tell you all the wild thoughts I had been entertaining since we sat down to our soup.'

Samuel felt his heart skip a beat. 'Really?'

The horror on his face must have been comical, because Miss Swynford began to laugh. 'No, of course not,' she said between chuckles, clearly trying to retain a modicum of self-control. 'I cannot think why you would even feel the need to clarify your intentions, sir. I know we have only known one another for a matter of days, but you have given me no reason to think of you as anything other than the very best of gentlemen.'

He raised a smile at her compliment, even as it made him feel utterly wretched. Would she still think that if she knew he was not really Hayton's baronet? 'I only wished to put you at your ease,' he said after a moment. 'I am sorry to observe it, but you looked uncomfortable from almost the moment you sat down to dine.'

In the dim light offered by the candles and the coming dusk outside, Samuel was sure he saw her expression darken. 'I am not used to dining in this manner,' she replied quietly, 'with such fine food and drink, such civilised company.'

He frowned. 'What do you mean?' he asked, a furious heat growing in his chest as his mind raced to contemplate all that her words might imply. 'What happened to you, Miss Swynford? In what manner was this uncle of yours keeping you?'

She shook her head gently, declining to answer. When she looked up, her expression had brightened once more. She reached for her glass again. 'The wine really is very good, sir,' she remarked, taking a sip and, he suspected, collecting herself. Something was amiss, but he was damned if he could fathom what it was.

He nodded, lifting his glass in agreement. 'A Bordeaux wine, and one of my particular favourites, although I only indulge when in company. Drinking such fine wine alone always seems rather a waste,' he added.

'I must confess to wondering why you are alone here, Sir Samuel,' Miss Swynford replied, meeting his eye. 'Forgive me, but you must surely be one of Cumberland's most eligible gentlemen.'

Her directness took him aback. 'I'm not sure about that…' he began, before realising that he had no idea what to say. How could he possibly explain himself? He did not want to let yet more falsehoods fall from his tongue, to portray himself as some sort of humourless baronet, so committed to managing his estate that he had not yet troubled himself to find a wife. Yet he could not bring himself to tell her the truth either, that he was a lesser prospect, a younger brother, a recent reject on Cumberland's marriage mart because he had not quite passed muster. That final fact, in particular, was too humiliating an admission to contemplate.

It was clear from the expression on her face that Miss Swynford had seen his discomfort. 'I am sorry,' she said softly, before he could settle upon an explanation. 'It is none of my business. In any case, I dare say it will not be long before I hear of your marriage to some well-connected society beauty with a large fortune.'

Samuel gave a wry chuckle. 'She sounds…intimidating.' His smile faded. 'To be frank, I think I'd prefer genuine companionship, Miss Swynford. Wealth and connections might matter a great deal to some people, but not to me. If I marry, I would rather it was for love than status.'

Miss Swynford's eyes seemed to search his, as though she was surprised by this admission, as though she was trying to determine if he was in earnest. Truly, she must have only ever been acquainted with the most dreadful gentlemen if she could be so astonished by his heartfelt confession. Then again, hearing those words fall from his own lips had come as something of a surprise to him too. He'd heard the sharp edge in his own voice as he'd spoken about other people's considerations, and the frankness when he'd confessed his own.

He had not meant to be quite so blunt, to speak of marriage and love—two things he'd sworn off for now, and for very good reasons. Truly, what had come over him lately? Clearly, those smouldering embers of the hurt and humiliation he'd experienced had been given cause to reignite. Or perhaps, he considered, they'd never quite ceased to burn in the first place.

Samuel shook his head at himself. 'Forgive me…'

The sound of the door opening caused them both to startle and Samuel turned to see Smithson burst into the dining room, somewhat breathless, his cheeks flushed.

'Sir, I am sorry to disturb you at dinner,' the butler began. 'But I need to speak with you urgently.'

Samuel pushed back his chair impatiently, nodding an apology to Miss Swynford before turning to regard the older man. 'What on earth is amiss?' he asked as he strode towards him. 'Has there been some accident? Is it one of the servants?'

'No, sir.' Smithson spoke in a hushed tone, giving Miss Swynford a worried glance. 'No accident. But I must tell you that there is a carriage coming up the drive. A carriage I do not recognise. Someone is coming to call at Hayton Hall, sir. Tonight.'

Chapter Seven

Samuel hurried towards Hayton Hall's grand entrance, his heart hammering in his chest. Usually, he left the business of answering the call of visitors to the butler, but he'd instructed Smithson to escort Miss Swynford and find somewhere for her to hide. Besides, he reasoned, he was damned if he was going to put any of his servants in harm's way. In his brother's absence, he was the master of the house; dealing with unwelcome visitors was ultimately his responsibility. If, indeed, that was who awaited him in the carriage outside. It was possible that both he and the butler were jumping to the wrong conclusion, that this unexpected evening call had nothing to do with Miss Swynford's presence here, that her whereabouts had not somehow been discovered by those who sought her. That it was not the uncle coming to claim his niece, or the would-be groom coming to claim his unwilling bride.

But if it was not them, then who else could it be?

At the door, Samuel paused, pressing his eyes shut momentarily as he collected himself. As he prepared himself for the worst. Since Isaac's elopement and Samuel's retreat from society, Hayton Hall had received no visitors for weeks and, in any case, there was not a single person of his acquaintance who would consider calling uninvited at this late hour. Suppressing a groan, Samuel turned the doorknob and opened the door with trepidation. The chances of whoever waited outside being here to pay him a friendly call seemed vanishingly small.

Outside, the light was fading fast, and Samuel found himself peering at the carriage which had drawn to a halt before Hayton Hall's front steps. A driver had dismounted, opening the door for the person or people sitting within, and Samuel felt his breath catch in his throat as he watched a man step out. An imposing man, very tall and thickset, wearing a greatcoat and a conical hat.

A man, he realised immediately, who he did in fact know. A man whom he'd invited to visit before circumstances in the form of Miss Swynford had prevailed upon him. A man to whom he'd written and asked not to come at present, but who had apparently come nonetheless. Samuel felt his mouth fall open, his stomach lurching as his relief at seeing a familiar face came into conflict with his awareness of the other difficulties this unexpected arrival presented.

'Charles?' Samuel called out, hurrying down the steps to greet him.

'Hello, Sammy,' Charles replied with a hearty chuckle. 'I am sorry we are so late. The roads rather wreaked havoc with this dear old thing. Father let us take the family coach—I suppose it is well suited to long journeys but I do so prefer the landau.'

'Oh, I see, yes, very good,' Samuel stuttered, still collecting himself.

Charles reached back into the carriage and Samuel watched as a gloved hand accepted his. A young lady stepped out, immaculately dressed in a deep blue bonnet and matching pelisse. Samuel watched as she brushed a swift hand down her long coat, keeping her eyes fixed on the ground as she stood dutifully beside Charles and awaited the necessary introduction.

'Sammy, this is my sister, Miss Henrietta Gordon. Sister, this is Mr Samuel Liddell.'

Finally regaining his composure, Samuel inclined his head politely at Miss Gordon, who mirrored his gesture but did not lift her eyes to meet his. She was uncommonly tall, much like her brother, but, unlike him, she was extremely slender, a fact which leant her stature a willowy, almost fragile air. Samuel found himself rather unwittingly contrasting her with the diminutive Miss Hope Swynford, a thought which prompted him to remember that poor Miss Swynford was still hiding somewhere in the house, fearing her imminent discovery. A thought which also reminded him that he was now going to have to find a way to explain that young lady's presence in his home to his unexpected guests.

A young lady who still believed he was the master of Hayton Hall. At that moment, Samuel could have groaned aloud. What on earth was he going to do?

Charles regarded Samuel with a half-amused, half-puzzled expression on his face. 'You look rather astonished to see us. Had you forgotten our little visit this week?'

Samuel shook his head. 'Of course not. Only…only I had written to you, to ask if we could perhaps postpone for a few weeks. I presume you did not receive my letter.'

At this, Charles laughed, patting Samuel playfully on the back. 'Doubtless your letter arrived at Shawdale, but Henrietta and I have not been there for almost three weeks, have we, sister?'

Miss Gordon shook her head, still not meeting Samuel's eye. 'We have been in Buxton, taking the waters.'

'Why did you wish to postpone?' Charles asked, glancing up at Hayton Hall. 'Is something amiss? Are you unwell? You do not look unwell.'

'I am fine,' Samuel replied, bristling as he recalled that it was illness which he'd used as an excuse to postpone in his letter. 'It is just that…well, I have a guest already. She arrived rather unexpectedly several days ago and…'

'She?' Charles interrupted him. Samuel watched as his friend's gaze shifted briefly to his sister. 'Is this conversation suitable for a lady's ears, Sammy?'

'Of course it is—it is nothing untoward. The lady was injured…she needed somewhere to stay, to recover, and… listen, I will explain everything when there is more time. Poor Miss Swynford is inside; I need to go and tell her that all is well, that she can come out of hiding.'

Charles frowned. 'And who exactly is Miss Swynford? Why is she hiding? What the devil is going on?'

'I will explain everything in good time,' Samuel said again, wringing his hands in front of him.

He was anxious to return to Miss Swynford now, but that was not the only reason he felt so on edge. Determining what to tell Charles about how Miss Swynford had come to be in his home was difficult enough, but the thought of owning his deception of her caused panic to rise in his chest. Smithson's words of caution rang in his ears. Lies did indeed have a way of getting out of hand. Certainly, this one was entirely out of his hands now; Samuel had no choice but to place it into the keeping of his friend, and hope that he would understand or, at the very least, that he would keep the knowledge of it to himself. In that regard, he was cautiously optimistic—for all that Charles was loud and enjoyed a good piece of gossip, Samuel knew that he could be relied upon when it mattered most.

Besides, what choice did he have? The alternative was to risk Charles bursting into his home and unwittingly revealing Samuel's deceit to Miss Swynford. The notion of her learning the truth from someone else was unthinkable. No—it had to come from him. If he could ever find the right moment, the right words to explain…

The right words to reassure her that she would always be safe with him, whether he had a title or not.

Samuel stood in front of his guests, his back momentarily turned to Hayton Hall. 'I need to ask for your co-operation in one matter, though,' he began, lowering his voice.

The furrow in Charles's brow deepened. 'Sammy?' he prompted.

'If Miss Swynford refers to me as Sir Samuel, please do not contradict her,' Samuel blurted, detesting the words as they fell from his lips.

A mischievous smile spread across Charles Gordon's face and he glanced up at the grand house once more. 'The lady thinks all this is yours, does she, Sammy?' he asked. 'Good grief. Just what sort of trouble have you gone and got yourself into?'

Hope shuffled on her chair, grimacing at her ankle as it throbbed in protest at the evening's exertions. The imminent arrival of that carriage had thrown Hayton Hall into a panic, and Smithson had worked quickly to find her a suitable hiding place. She'd followed him down into the servants' quarters at a pace which had been far from comfortable, leaning heavily on the walking cane as the butler swiftly placed a chair inside a pantry and instructed her to wait inside. There she'd sat ever since, feeling sore and restless in equal measure as her mind reeled with a myriad of discomforting thoughts.

Guilt possessed her first of all—guilt at acknowledging that, unlike Sir Samuel and his butler, she did not fear that those arriving in that carriage were looking for her. Guilt at realising how her deception had made her host fearful of an uncle and a co-conspirator who did not exist, whilst keeping him in the dark about the menacing spectre of men who definitely did.

If her father or indeed the man she'd been meant to marry were seeking to find her, they would not come in a carriage. They would not call at the front door and announce themselves. Men who lived as they did, who were involved in the sorts of things they were involved in, were never so conspicuous. Men like them worked under the cover of moonless stormy skies or in the deep black of Cumberland's caves; they drew their power from the places where shadows and chaos reigned. If they ever came for her then, without doubt, they would have her in their possession before Sir Samuel even knew anything about it.

Hope suppressed a groan, dragging her hands down her face in despair as the evening's events forced her to consider just what a tangled web she'd woven with her deceit. Moments before that carriage's arrival she'd been sitting at that fine dining table, sipping wine, allowing its potency to blur the lines between the real and the imagined, between who she really was and who she was pretending to be. She'd let her mask slip too many times; she'd allowed the veil of ladylike refinement she'd worked hard to draw across herself grow too thin. Hope reddened to recall her response to Sir Samuel's efforts to reassure her about his good intentions, how she'd teased him quite wickedly about wild thoughts, and, worse still, how she'd met his observation of her discomfort with something alarmingly approaching the truth. Why had she not simply said she was tired, or out of sorts? Whatever had possessed her to all but admit that she'd never dined like that before? Why did she seem so intent upon allowing glimpses of Hope Sloane to be seen?

Because she did not like lying to him, that was why. Because since the moment she'd arrived at Hayton Hall he'd been unfailingly kind and candid, and the knowledge that she'd repaid him with nothing but deceit gnawed at her. Worse still, the guilt she felt seemed only to grow with every passing day and every conversation. With every new thing she learned about him. With every growing doubt that the master here would be the sort of man to have any acquaintance with her father or his business dealings. She had not known what to do with herself tonight when he'd spoken so honestly about his desire for genuine companionship over more worldly considerations.

'If I marry, I would rather it was for love than status...'

Hope straightened herself and forced her mind to cease lingering upon those words. Indeed, she'd had no right to draw them from him in the first place, to ask him such searching questions about his life. She definitely had no right to be impressed by them, no matter how heartfelt or genuine they had seemed. Not when she was deceiving him. Not when those words had been intended for Hope Swynford, and not for the ears of Hope Sloane.

The door to the pantry swung open, causing Hope to startle. Her alarm, however, quickly dissolved into relief when she saw that it was Sir Samuel who had come, presumably to collect her and take her back upstairs. Drawing a deep breath, she reached for the walking cane and got to her feet, resolving to set aside all that she'd spent these past interminable minutes mulling over. There was little point in dwelling upon her guilt or fretting over what she'd said or done. There was nothing she could do about that—there were only the consequences of choices she had already made. Those choices, she reminded herself, had left her with a role to play.

'Is all well?' she asked him. 'Was it my…my uncle? Did you send him away?'

Sir Samuel sighed. 'Not quite.'

Hope watched with growing confusion as he glanced over his shoulder before stepping into the pantry to join her and closing the door behind him. She became aware, quite suddenly, of the confined space around them, of the shelves crowded with jams and grains. Of his close proximity to her, of the soft rhythm of his breathing, of the lemon scent of his cologne.

'The good news, it was not your uncle,' he began. 'The bad news, a friend of mine has arrived, along with his sister. Their visit was arranged prior to your arrival here, after which I wrote to Charles and asked to postpone. It seems he did not receive my letter.' Sir Samuel shook his head. 'Suffice to say, I cannot simply send them away now.'

'No, of course not,' Hope replied quietly. 'I am only sorry that you felt you had to cancel their visit on my account. If I had known how my presence here would inconvenience you…'

Sir Samuel reached out, placing his hand on her arm. 'You have not inconvenienced me,' he insisted, his grey-blue gaze holding hers. 'Please, do not think that.'

Hope nodded her assent, conscious of the warm reassurance of his fingers against her bare skin. 'Then what are we to do?' she asked. 'I suppose I could pretend to be a servant here.'

'No.' He retracted his hand, leaving her feeling oddly bereft. 'Regrettably, we cannot do that, Miss Swynford.'

She frowned. 'Why not?'

'Because I am an utter blockhead,' he replied with a heavy sigh. 'Charles turning up like that had me in such a panic and I...well, I may have told him that I already have a guest staying with me.'

Hope felt her heart begin to race. 'I see. Does he know anything else about who your guest is?'

'Only your name, and that you arrived unexpectedly and are staying here while you recover from some injuries.'

Her eyes widened at him. 'You promised you would not tell a single soul about me...' she began. 'You may as well put up posters in the nearby village telling everyone my whereabouts and have done with it, sir.'

Sir Samuel met her eye, and she watched as he pressed his lips together as though he was trying to collect himself. It was an odd change on a face which was usually either serene or cheerful, and it irked her to observe that he wore a grave expression just as well as he wore a happy one.

'You must know that I would never deliberately put you in harm's way, Miss Swynford,' he said. 'My words to Charles were careless but he is a good man and, besides, he does not know the whole story. I am sure we can come up with something. Indeed, we must tell him something...'

Hope shook her head, feeling the heat of tears prick in the corners of her eyes. Not more stories. Not more lies piled upon lies. She could not countenance it. She huffed a breath then moved to step past Sir Samuel, suddenly possessed of an urge to leave that cramped little room, to retire to her bedchamber and put some distance between herself and this man. To envelop herself in dark silence and try to reconcile the conflict currently raging in her weary mind between her angry disappointment at Sir Samuel's momentary indiscretion and the guilt-ridden knowledge that he'd done little more than repeat a small portion of her tall tale. And she would have done all of that, had it not been for the walking cane she leaned on. Instead, the perfidious thing seemed to catch against the uneven stone floor. She jolted, losing her footing as her weakened ankle failed to bear her weight, and fell forward.

Straight into Sir Samuel's arms.

He caught her—of course he did—raising her slowly back to her feet, his gaze intent upon her own. She felt her breath hitch, felt her hands pressed against his chest, apparently powerless to move. Felt the furious beat of his heart through his white shirt, felt his hands remain gently upon her waist just a moment longer than was necessary. Felt the closeness, the sheer heat of him. She'd never stood like that with a man before. It was strange, intoxicating, and not at all unpleasant.

Then Sir Samuel cleared his throat and took a step back. 'Forgive me.'

'No...yes, of course,' Hope said, giving him a tight smile and doing her best to compose herself. She moved to step past him again, this time successfully. 'Excuse me. I think I shall retire for the night.'

'Indeed, you must be exhausted,' he replied with a brittle nod. 'I will need to go and attend to my guests. We can save formal introductions for tomorrow but, in the meantime, what would you like me to tell them about you? I'm afraid Charles is surely going to ask.'

Hope pushed the pantry door open, letting out a resigned sigh. 'Tell him the rest of the story,' she said, her head still spinning with the odd intensity of what had momentarily passed between them. 'I dare say that there's little else to be done about it now.'

Chapter Eight

'Well, Sammy, that's a fine mess you've made for yourself.'

Charles Gordon sat back in his chair and sipped his brandy as Samuel nodded glumly, finding it hard to disagree with his friend's assessment. Miss Swynford had retired some time ago, without so much as casting another word or glance in his direction, leaving him to entertain his new guests. After a hasty supper of whatever the cook could cobble together at such short notice, they had retired to Hayton Hall's largest and finest room to converse. Predictably, Charles had pursued the matter of Miss Swynford, and Samuel had rather uncomfortably answered his questions, acutely aware of just how much having her story told would displease his other guest. Although, of course, there was little for him to tell, since he knew only the barest details; she'd refused to tell him where she came from, and he knew neither the uncle nor the other man's names. Clearly, the lack of meat on the bones of the story dissatisfied Charles, and before long he'd returned to marvelling at his friend's pretence of being Hayton Hall's baronet.

'I simply cannot fathom it—Samuel Liddell, lying to a lady,' Charles continued, shaking his head slowly. 'I would never have thought you capable of it.'

'Unlike you, brother,' Miss Gordon interjected. 'As I witnessed for myself in Buxton.'

Samuel raised an eyebrow in surprise. Charles's sister had had little to say for herself during supper, and since sitting down in the drawing room she'd apparently preferred to sip her tea and stare rather vacantly at the fire which roared in the grate. The nights were growing colder, and in the larger, infrequently inhabited rooms of Hayton Hall the chill was particularly notable. He watched as Miss Gordon adjusted her shawl across her thin frame, tearing her eyes finally from the fireplace to meet the discomfited gaze of her sibling.

'Please, do tell, Miss Gordon,' Samuel prompted her, relieved at the opportunity to turn the conversation away from his own shortcomings.

Miss Gordon raised a tight smile. 'We attended several balls at the Assembly Rooms during our stay. I cannot say if it was the strength of the punch or the sheer quantity of eligible young ladies which made my brother dizzy, but something possessed him to tell some really rather tall tales about himself. By the end of our stay, several had been led to believe that Charles had been closely acquainted with the late Duke of Devonshire himself.'

'It is not so unbelievable, is it?' Charles replied, an unbecoming shade of scarlet creeping up from beneath his cravat. 'The duke has only been deceased for a handful of years and, as everyone knows, he took a keen interest in Buxton and its improvement. It is entirely possible that I might have known him or…or met him, at the very least.'

Samuel chuckled, shaking his head at his friend. 'I thought you would have learned your lesson during our travels, Charles. As I recall, you came unstuck on more than one occasion when a young lady discovered you were not the son of an earl or a duke as you had claimed to be.'

Miss Gordon's eyes widened and she leaned forward before saying, 'Did he, indeed?'

Samuel nodded. 'They were all most disappointed to learn that Viscount Faux-Title here had no aristocratic connections at all.'

Charles let out a heavy sigh. 'Alas, where some men shall inherit castles, I shall inherit calico printworks.'

Samuel let out another amused chuckle. 'To listen to you, anyone would think you were not from one of the wealthiest families in Lancashire. Perhaps if you spent more time telling young ladies about that and not pretending to be someone you are not, you would have more success.'

He watched as both his guests stared at him, mouths identically agape as the irony of what he had just said sunk in. He suppressed a groan as wearily he rubbed his brow, his mind wandering to the lady sleeping upstairs, the one who did not have the faintest idea who he really was. The one whose company he had been enjoying once again just hours ago, as they'd dined together, as they'd talked. The one who'd fallen into his arms in the pantry, and whom he'd relished catching more than he cared to admit.

Samuel gulped down the last of his brandy, flexing his free hand against the arm of the chair, still feeling the ghost of her waist against his fingers. After the abject misery of confessing his deceit to Charles, he'd gone down to the pantry, resolved to tell Miss Swynford the truth there and then. However, his resolve had wavered in the face of how panicked she'd been at the thought of his guests knowing even the barest facts about her, and how rightly upset she'd been with him over his poor judgement and loose tongue. He was reminded at once that she already had enough to worry about, that she was in very real danger. A danger which she believed that he, and the title and status she believed him to have, could shield her from. His duty, first and foremost, was to protect her, not to burden her with any further worries.

A duty which certainly did not involve letting his thoughts linger on the feeling of holding her in his arms, he reminded himself. No matter how pleasant such thoughts were.

'I realise I have no business lecturing you, Charles,' he said after a long moment. 'Please, forgive me.'

Charles shrugged. 'There's nothing to forgive, Sammy. I can be a complete cork-brain and I know it. But you, my dear fellow, are not. What I do not understand is why you told Miss Swynford that you were a baronet in the first place.'

Samuel hesitated. 'I did not tell her exactly...she assumed, and, to my great shame, I did not correct her. I've been torturing myself with exactly why that was ever since—foolish pride, I suppose. I've been either a younger son or my brother's heir all of my life and, God willing, now that he's wed again, I will not be his heir for much longer. When Miss Swynford presumed I was more than that, I suppose I just got a little carried away.' He paused, deciding that was all he was prepared to say. Charles was his friend but, even so, he was not about to confess to him just how much of a wounding his pride had suffered of late. Or indeed how much of a role his humiliating rejection in the summer might have played in his willingness to be the baronet.

Charles grinned. 'So it is not because you want to court her, then?'

'Hardly.' Samuel bristled at the suggestion, alarmed to

note the image of her looking up at him, her hands pressed against his chest, returning to him once more.

'In that case, why don't you simply tell her the truth?'

'I was on the cusp of doing so,' he replied miserably, 'but then Miss Swynford told me how safe she feels here, how protected. It's clear she attributes this protection in no small part to my title and standing in Cumberland—or at least the title and standing she believes me to have. How could I undermine that when she is in my home, alone and vulnerable? How could I knowingly allow her to feel unsafe? And what if I confessed all and she felt so unsafe that she left Hayton Hall before she had properly recovered and ended up back in harm's way with her uncle?'

'The Sammy doth protest too much, methinks,' Charles replied, chuckling.

'Shakespeare—yes, very good,' Samuel grumbled. He slumped back in his chair. 'Perhaps I should just tell Miss Swynford the truth, whatever the consequences.'

'No, I think you're right.' Miss Gordon spoke up, nursing her tea thoughtfully. 'Miss Swynford is here in your care, and as you've no intentions towards her beyond offering her comfort and shelter while she convalesces, then I'd leave the situation as it is rather than risk her fleeing and coming to harm.'

Samuel inclined his head at Miss Gordon's interjection. She was an odd lady, carrying herself with such an air of disengagement, of disinterest, and yet it was clear she was listening to everything that was said, weighing it up and drawing conclusions. There was a cold clarity, a steeliness about her which her loud, affable brother had never possessed. How different two siblings could be, but then,

Samuel already knew that. He'd grown up with a far more sombre, far more reserved older brother, after all.

Samuel found himself wondering about Miss Swynford's family then, about who had been there for her before her uncle had her in his clutches. Her parents were dead, he knew that, but had there ever been any brothers, any sisters? He reflected on that strange remark she'd made at dinner, about how unused she was to enjoying good food and drink, and civilised company. How long had it been since anyone had truly cared for her? A heavy feeling settled in his stomach as he found himself contemplating the possibility that no one had, that apart from her wicked uncle she was all alone.

'Well, if Henrietta agrees, then who am I to argue?' Charles said, placing his glass upon the table and rising from his seat. 'I will go along with it, Sammy.' He grinned. 'Or, should I say, Sir Faux-Title?'

Hope sat up in bed, the first volume of Mr Hume's *History of England* perched upon her lap. She'd awoken some time ago but, oddly, Maddie had not yet come to attend to her, and Hope suspected this had much to do with the arrival of the other guests. Proper guests, she thought, feeling her heart sink. The sort who were accustomed to maids and butlers, to grand houses, large dining rooms and lavish meals.

An uncomfortable feeling settled over her then, as she recognised that the familiar routine she'd hitherto enjoyed at Hayton had come to an end. There would be no more mornings spent with Maddie fussing over her; the maid simply would not have the time for that. There would be no more parlour meetings with Sir Samuel either, no more afternoons of cake and conversation. That particular thought bothered her most and she fidgeted, trying to cast it from her mind.

'You're just out of sorts, Hope, that's what's the matter with you,' she muttered. 'You just don't want to go and meet these new guests.'

That was true, certainly. Playing the role of Hope Swynford was challenging enough in front of Sir Samuel and a handful of servants; adding two further scrutinising pairs of eyes to the audience of people she had to convince was the very last thing she wanted. She looked down at her book again, forcing herself to concentrate on its lofty prose about a queen called Boadicea and her battles with the Romans, and trying not to think about last night. The way she'd allowed candlelight and fine wine to loosen her tongue at dinner. The way she'd reacted when she'd learned that Sir Samuel had told his visitors about her presence there. The way she'd fallen into Sir Samuel's arms in the pantry.

Hope felt the colour rise in her cheeks as she recalled how her senses had seemed to heighten, at once acutely aware of the muscular solidity of his chest beneath her hands, of the warmth of his arms as they circled her waist, of how his blue-grey eyes had searched hers, as though trying to discern the answer to a question which had not been put into words, as though…

As though he might kiss her.

Hope sat bolt upright in bed, pushing the book to one side in growing irritation at herself. What a fanciful notion to entertain! Of course a gentleman like Sir Samuel had not been about to kiss her, and nor had she wanted him to. Nor could she want him to—not when she was a guest in his home, enjoying his faultlessly kind and considerate hospitality under false pretences. Her ankle throbbed, giving her a timely reminder of the consequence of her clumsiness, and of the reason she was here at all. Hayton Hall was a place of refuge and its master had been a Good Samaritan to her, but there was nothing more to it than that. Indeed, she reminded herself, if he knew who she really was, and if he knew just how fundamentally she'd lied to him, he might not be so hospitable.

A knock at the door startled Hope from her thoughts. 'Come in,' she called, smoothing the sheets down in front of her and placing the book back in her lap. It was almost certainly Maddie, come at last to ask her what she would like for breakfast, and to help her dress. The poor maid must have been run ragged by the other female guest in the house if she had been detained until now.

'I am in no hurry, Maddie, so please…'

Hope's words died in her throat as Sir Samuel walked in and closed the door behind him. Immediately, thoughts of their close encounter in the pantry ran unbidden through her mind and she felt the heat rise inexplicably in her cheeks.

Stop it, Hope, she told herself. *Stop thinking about it. You're being ridiculous.*

She watched as Sir Samuel took a couple of steps into the room, then seemed to freeze. He stared at her, his eyes wide, his lips parted in surprise.

'Oh, you're not…' he began, waving a flustered hand in her direction. 'Erm, where is Madeleine?'

'Waiting upon your friend's sister, I expect,' Hope replied.

Sir Samuel gave a slow nod. 'I see. Perhaps I should go, then. We can speak once Maddie has been to help you dress.'

Hope frowned. 'Why? You sat by my bedside and talked

to me when I was most unwell.' She pulled irritably at her shift. 'This is nothing you have not seen before.'

Sir Samuel coughed. 'No, indeed, but…there are others in the house now. Others who may think thoughts which ought not to be thought if they…' He faltered, the expression on his face one of excruciating embarrassment.

'If they observe you slipping into my bedchamber in the morning before I am dressed. Or, I suppose, if they observe you coming in here at all,' Hope said, perhaps more bluntly than she should. After all, she doubted Hope Swynford would speak so plainly about such matters. In Hope Sloane's world, however, gentlemen being caught alone with actresses was of very little consequence. Certainly not something that anyone would bother to tiptoe around.

'Indeed,' Sir Samuel replied. 'I should not be here.'

Hope inclined her head in polite acknowledgement, before making a point of turning her attention back to the book on her lap. She could not explain why, but all that talk about the need to behave properly in front of the other guests troubled her. Almost as much as the realisation that Sir Samuel had probably sat them down last night and told them all about the poor runaway heiress sleeping upstairs. The thought of them all chewing over her concocted tale made her feel quite sick.

'Miss Swynford?'

Hope looked up from the pages, surprised to see he had not yet moved. 'Yes?'

'I came only to ask if you wish to come downstairs today. I realise that yesterday must have been quite a trial for you, so if you do not feel well enough then I understand.' He took a step closer, peering at her book. 'Is that Mr Hume's book you are reading?'

She nodded. 'It is. I have just reached the part where the Romans are leaving Britain. I have not managed to read very much of it yet.'

He smiled meekly. 'Of course, and gentlemen bursting into your bedchamber will hardly be helping.'

'Not gentlemen,' she replied. 'Only you.'

Sir Samuel laughed. 'I'm not sure whether I should feel complimented or affronted by that remark.'

'I'll leave that up to you to decide, Sir Samuel,' Hope quipped, trying and failing to suppress a smirk.

To her surprise, however, Sir Samuel's smile faded. 'Call me Samuel,' he said, his voice low and sincere.

Across the room, their eyes met and Hope found her thoughts straying to that odd moment they'd shared in the pantry once again. 'As you wish,' she answered him, trying her best to sound nonchalant. 'And I suppose you should call me Hope, rather than Miss Swynford.'

He inclined his head politely. 'I would like that very much, Hope.'

The way he said her name made the most disconcerting heat grow deep within her stomach. Hope looked down at her book once more. He needed to leave now, and not only because they risked the scandalous remarks of the other guests with each passing moment.

To her relief, Sir Samuel—or, rather, just Samuel now—moved back towards the door. 'I'll ask Madeleine to attend to you,' he said. 'You have waited long enough.'

'It is fine,' Hope replied, waving her hand. 'I am not in a hurry and, besides, it must be a lot of additional work, having all these people in the house who are not usually here.'

Samuel raised his eyebrows as though this was the first time that the extra burden having guests placed upon his servants had crossed his mind. 'Yes, you're right about that,' he conceded after a moment. 'You're right too to be cross with me for telling them about your presence here. I should have spoken to you first, to agree the best approach.'

'What's done is done,' she replied with a small shrug. 'I suppose they know all about me now, do they?'

'I have explained how you came to be here,' Samuel replied. 'I have also stressed how important it is that your presence at Hayton Hall remains a closely guarded secret.'

'Thank you. What did you say their names are? And where are they from? I'm afraid I cannot recall.'

'Charles and Henrietta Gordon, from Lancashire,' Samuel replied. 'I believe their home is called Shawdale, on the edge of a town called Blackburn, where their father does very well in trade.'

'Trade?' That all too familiar word made Hope look up in consternation. 'What sort of trade?'

'Calico printing, I believe.'

Inwardly, Hope breathed a sigh of relief. A proper sort of trade, and perfectly legal—of course it was. She was too quick to think the worst, to jump to the wrong conclusion when, realistically, she probably had nothing to fear. She'd never known her father to have dealings with anyone in Lancashire, much less those involved in calico printing. It did not seem likely that Mr Gordon or his sister would know who she really was.

Samuel's expression darkened. 'Why? Is that a problem?'

'No, of…of course not,' she stammered. 'Why would it be a problem?'

'Because, to some, the idea of associating with anyone who comes to wealth and prominence through means other than inheriting land and a title is offensive,' he said pointedly.

'Oh,' Hope replied, feeling as though Hope Swynford would probably have known that. 'Well, I assure you that I only asked out of curiosity.'

Samuel inclined his head, apparently appeased. 'So, you will come down to meet them today?' he asked hopefully.

Given the offence her questions had almost caused, Hope knew she had little choice. She knew too that meeting them was inevitable; she could hardly avoid them for the duration of their stay. The Gordons' visit was not ideal, but they were here now and that was that. This was the hand she'd been dealt, and she'd simply have to play it, and her role, very well indeed.

'Of course,' she replied, painting on a smile.

Chapter Nine

Samuel sat back in his favourite chair, trying his best to relax. He'd arranged to have tea with all of his guests in the small parlour, and hoped that the cosy familiarity of the room would put Hope at ease when meeting Charles and Miss Gordon. She'd seemed anxious when he'd met her in the hallway to escort her down, and for the first time since arriving at Hayton she'd refused to let him assist her on the stairs.

'I dread to think what your guests would say if they saw you carrying me,' she'd pointed out in a hushed tone. 'Besides, I am feeling much stronger. I managed to go upstairs by myself last night, and I am sure I can manage to walk down them today if I use the walking cane.'

Samuel had acquiesced, but nonetheless he'd remained close by her side as she'd made her way, somewhat unsteadily, down each step. Several times he'd observed her grimace in discomfort, and he suspected her ankle was not as healed as she'd suggested. But she was right; he could no longer be permitted to lift her into his arms, not when there were others in the house. An unexpected wave of regret had gripped Samuel then. Regret that his visitors had turned up as planned, that his letter had not reached them. Regret that his time alone with his unexpected guest had passed. Immediately he'd chastised himself for it. Hope was living in his home under his protection, not so that he might, quite literally, sweep her off her feet. That was something he had absolutely no intention of doing, especially not when he was being so untruthful.

The introductions over, their group had settled into some pleasant, if a little stilted, conversation. To Samuel's surprise and relief, Charles appeared to have decided to be on his best behaviour, engaging Hope in only the gentlest of enquiries about her convalescence and whether she was enjoying her time at Hayton Hall, notwithstanding the circumstances.

'This is the first time I have visited Sammy's home,' he said, looking all about him. 'And I must say that I have never laid my eyes upon a finer country house than this.'

'It is very lovely,' Hope agreed demurely.

Samuel, however, rolled his eyes. 'I am sure I recall you saying the same about almost every house we visited on the Continent,' he replied. 'And I am equally certain that Shawdale can compete with them all.'

Charles made a face. 'Shawdale is very grand, but it is not a country house. It is on the edge of a town and is barely ten years old. It does not have the depth that Hayton has, or indeed that any old family seat has when it has stood long enough to store the centuries within its walls.'

'You must forgive Mr Gordon,' Samuel said, turning to Hope. 'He has an unhealthy preoccupation with having an ancient noble lineage and a castle to keep it all in. You'll have to marry a duke's daughter, Charles,' he added, addressing his friend once more. 'Then you can ask your father-in-law if you can borrow one of his.'

Samuel was amused to see Hope splutter on her tea at that. She seemed to have relaxed a little now, and her laughter had made the colour rise in her cheeks, giving her a healthier glow. He found his gaze lingering upon her as he considered how well she looked in her cream day dress, her dark curls framing her face, her emerald eyes sparkling with merriment. Perhaps, he considered, their little group of four would not be such a bad thing, after all.

'He mocks me, Miss Swynford, but I am going to build my own castle,' Charles continued.

Hope's eyebrows shot up. 'Oh, like the Prince Regent? He builds castles for himself, does he not?'

Charles shook his head. 'The Prince Regent builds mansions and palaces. I shall build a castle which William the Conqueror himself would be proud to live in.'

Samuel chuckled in disbelief. 'You're going to build yourself a Norman castle?'

'Another of my brother's wild schemes,' Miss Gordon interjected drily. Until now she'd sat quietly, so much so that Samuel had quite forgotten she was there. 'When he inherits our father's fortune, he plans to knock down Shawdale and erect his monstrosity in its place.'

Samuel regarded his friend, aghast. 'And what does your father say about that?'

'He does not know.' Charles shrugged. 'Nor shall he.'

'You speak of legacies, Charles, yet you'd readily demolish what your father has built?' Samuel shook his head, unable to fathom it. 'And what about your mother? Or your sister?' he added, inclining his head towards Miss Gordon.

'Oh, I care not,' Miss Gordon said. 'When our father is gone, Charles can do as he likes, and so shall I.' She gave a self-satisfied smile then turned to Hope. 'I presume you had parents at one time, Miss Swynford?' she asked.

Samuel watched as Hope met his eye cautiously before answering, 'Yes, of course.'

'And have you committed yourself entirely to guarding their legacy?'

Hope sipped her tea, and Samuel saw that she was considering her answer. In truth, he was intrigued as to what it might be. In their time together, she'd said so little about herself, about her history. He knew nothing about where she'd come from, in terms of either location or heritage. He wondered now if Miss Gordon's rather abrupt questioning might yield more information than he'd thus far managed to gather.

At length, Hope shook her head. 'I confess I'm not sure I've ever thought much about it.'

'Well, what did they bequeath to you?' Miss Gordon put up her hand. 'And, before you think me impudent, I am not speaking of money. What I mean to say is, do you have happy memories of them to treasure, or would you too be happy to tear down the ancestral home?'

'Sister...'

Charles spoke gently, but the warning contained within his voice was all too clear. Samuel found himself wondering what on earth was going on, how a convivial conversation about Norman castles could have taken such a dark turn. Still, though, he was curious as to how Hope would answer. If she would answer.

He watched as Hope looked up, meeting Miss Gordon's gaze squarely. 'I dare say that, like many people, I can confess to cherishing some memories, while wishing to cast away others like stones.'

'And the ancestral home?' Miss Gordon pressed.

Hope gave a grim smile. 'It can remain standing, but I shall never set foot in it again.'

'I am sorry to hear that,' Samuel interjected quietly, glancing around him. 'I feel fortunate that I can look upon my family's home with such fondness.'

'Ah, and that is why Hayton is such a haven,' Miss Gordon answered, her tone lighter now. 'The perfect place to convalesce, I am sure. Well, except for Buxton. Its waters always do me the world of good, don't they, Charles?'

Charles might have answered but, in truth, Samuel was no longer listening. Instead, he found himself mulling over what Hope had said, trying to discern its meaning. He'd wished to know more about her, but what Miss Gordon's enquiries had revealed had only provoked more questions in his mind. What were the memories she wished to cast away? Why would she never return to her ancestral home? Did any of this have anything to do with the uncle from whom she was currently hiding?

Miss Gordon had spoken of guarding legacies. Well, Samuel thought, Hope was guarding something about her past, he felt sure of it. Something, he suspected, that was painful. Something she'd much rather forget.

Hope wasn't sure if she felt better or worse after her first meeting with the Gordons. Mr Gordon had seemed pleasant and good-natured enough, and she'd enjoyed the affectionate teasing which was clearly central to his and Samuel's friendship. Miss Gordon, however, was a different matter entirely. Frankly, the lady unnerved her, bestowing those dark eyes upon her as though she was peering into her soul, and asking questions in a way which seemed to suck the life out of the room.

Her behaviour had already caused consternation among the servants too. When Maddie had finally arrived in Hope's bedchamber that morning, she'd been flustered, explaining that it had taken several of the female servants to rouse Miss Gordon, such was the depth of her slumber.

'When, finally, she awoke, I thought she was unwell,' Maddie went on. 'She seemed weak and listless, and her eyes kept rolling back as though she was struggling to remain awake. I was ready to send for the physician, but she insisted nothing was amiss and ordered me to help her dress. Rather curtly, I might add.'

Hope had thought little of it at the time, reasoning that Miss Gordon was likely exhausted after her long journey to Hayton. Now, having met her, and having noted the sharp edge to her questions and the brittle way she spoke of family and legacies, Hope realised she would need to be on her guard. There'd been some pain and turmoil in that near-black stare, she felt sure of it. There'd been a story, barely concealed and threatening to spill forth, driving a tendency to want to unravel the stories of others. Hope knew her sort; the theatre had been packed with just such haunted individuals, taking to the stage to escape themselves. Hope wondered now what Miss Gordon's escape was, and whether it had anything to do with her difficulty in waking that morning. That was something she'd witnessed before too.

After tea, they took a walk in the beautiful gardens which sprawled to the rear of Hayton Hall. To begin with, Hope had hesitated about joining the group on their afternoon promenade. The walls of Hayton Hall, she realised, had become a fortress for her. Inside, she felt hidden away, protected from those who might be roaming the countryside, looking for her. The garden, by contrast, felt dangerous and exposed. Instinctively, Samuel had seemed to understand this.

'I can ask Madeleine to fetch your book and some more tea to the parlour, if you'd prefer to stay here,' he'd suggested. 'Although the gardens are very secluded, and we will not venture far from the house.'

Hope had felt the eyes of the other two guests upon her as she'd considered her options. Her gaze had wandered towards the window where, outside, a bright autumn day awaited. She did so long to feel the warmth of the sun on her face again. Surely, she reasoned, the risk of briefly venturing into private gardens, tucked between a large house and sprawling woodland, was not so great.

'I will come,' she'd said in the end. 'The fresh air will do me good. Although I'm afraid that my ankle means that my pace will be painfully slow.'

'There is nothing painful about a gentle promenade,' Samuel had replied, offering her a reassuring smile. 'I find it allows plenty of time for quiet reflection or, if in company, some delightful conversation.'

Equipped with the walking cane and a wide-brimmed bonnet sufficient to shield her face, Hope limped along the orderly paths which wove their way through beds thick with plants and bushes. She clutched Samuel's arm tightly, partly for support and partly, she realised, for reassurance. He had not left her side since they'd walked out of Hayton's rear door, nor had he spoken much, apparently preferring companionable silence to conversation.

Hope told herself that she ought to be relieved; she was still reeling from Miss Gordon's questions in the parlour.

Though her answers had been suitably vague, they had also contained much truth about herself—her real self. In light of that, the chance to keep her own counsel for once should have been welcome, yet instead Hope found herself wishing that Samuel would engage her on some topic, however ordinary. Wishing too to rekindle something of those short few days they'd spent together, prior to the Gordons' arrival.

'Is everything all right?' she ventured to ask in the end, finding herself unable to tolerate the silence any longer.

He gave her a bemused look. 'Of course, why would it not be?'

'You seem unusually quiet, that is all. I thought perhaps something was amiss.'

'I was just thinking about the last time I walked in these gardens.' He smiled at her. 'About hearing a scream coming from the woods. About finding you.'

She nodded. 'I am glad you did. Who knows what would have become of me?'

'I am glad that I did too.' He regarded her thoughtfully. 'You have made a remarkable recovery in…how long has it been? A little over a week?'

Hope drew a deep breath. 'It's odd—it feels as though I have been at Hayton Hall much longer than that. I agree, though, I am feeling much better. I have you to thank for that, sir.'

'Just Samuel,' he reminded her.

'I have you to thank, Just Samuel,' she retorted with a grin.

He chuckled at that. 'I dare say it's actually Madeleine you should thank. She has cared for you, after all.'

Hope inclined her head in agreement. 'It's Maddie,' she corrected him. 'She prefers to be called Maddie.'

He glanced at her again, a frown gathering between his eyes. 'Er…yes, you're right, I do recall her once suggesting that I call her Maddie.'

'Then why do you insist upon calling her Madeleine?'

'I do not know… I suppose because that is her proper name.'

'Well, it vexes her, Samuel. For whatever reason, she does not care for her proper name. Just as you do not care for being called Sammy by your friend,' she observed.

He gave her a quizzical look. 'How do you know that?'

'Because you flinch every time Mr Gordon says it,' she replied. 'However, Mr Gordon is your friend and your equal; if you really wanted to, you could insist that he call you Samuel. But Maddie is your servant—she can hardly challenge you over what you call her.'

Samuel cleared his throat, his countenance shifting into something less jovial, less comfortable. Hope saw that her words had struck a chord. 'Yes, quite,' he replied. 'I did not realise that it bothered her. But you are right, of course.'

She raised her eyebrows at him. 'Yes, I am right. Perhaps I shall begin to call you Sammy too. Perhaps I will do so until you start calling her Maddie.'

'All right, all right,' he said, a smile breaking on his face as he glanced at her. 'You are very direct—do you know that? Very plain-speaking.'

Hope felt her heart begin to thrum faster at his observation, conscious that she'd allowed her true self to be glimpsed once again. 'Miss Gordon seems to speak her mind too,' she retorted, nodding her head towards the siblings, who were now some distance away.

'Miss Gordon speaks in riddles,' Samuel replied, shaking his head. 'Quite what her conversation in the parlour was about, I cannot fathom. She even had Charles looking uncomfortable, and nothing usually ruffles his feathers.'

'I dare say all is not well at Shawdale,' Hope observed. 'Perhaps that is what lies beneath their stay in Buxton, and their visit to you.'

'I think you may be right about that.' Samuel regarded her carefully, his grey-blue eyes holding her own. 'It occurs to me now that when we were on the Continent, Charles never seemed inclined to return home, and he never said much about his family. Indeed, until he wrote to me to accept my invitation to visit, I did not even know he had a sister.'

'That is odd,' Hope mused. 'Although I suppose people have their reasons for not wishing to discuss their families.'

'Like you, you mean.'

Hope realised they'd stopped walking, standing instead in the middle of the path. When had that happened? She felt suddenly and acutely aware of her arm still resting in his, of his proximity, of his eyes fixed on hers. Of the weight of meaning in his observation. Of all that separated them, of the chasm wrought by his wealth and status. Of everything he did not know about her, and everything he could never know.

'Yes, like me,' she said quietly, looking away.

If she had expected an inquisition, it did not come. Instead, Samuel reached over, placing his free hand over hers, which remained in the crook of his elbow.

'Whenever you wish to talk about it, I am ready to listen,' he said.

The gesture was so tender that she could not bring herself to meet his eye. Instead, she simply nodded, not quite trusting herself to answer. Not quite trusting herself not to blurt out her story, and lay the unpalatable facts of her life at his feet.

Chapter Ten

'I am heartily sick of this interminable rain.'

Samuel looked up from his newspaper, suppressing his irritation at Charles's complaints, which were as endless as the biblical torrents falling outside. In the days since the Gordons' arrival the weather had indeed taken a turn for the worse, a fact which Charles seemed to have taken as a personal insult. Samuel had lost count of the number of times Charles had wandered over to the window, only to sigh heavily at the sight which greeted him. He knew from past experience that his friend was like a caged bear when confined to the house; a particularly wet few weeks spent in a villa by Lake Geneva had taught him that. Charles was a man who needed to feel the sun on his face and sense the world at his feet. It was a wonder, Samuel reflected now, that he'd ever returned to the damp confines of north-west England at all.

'There is nothing to be done about the weather, Charles,' Samuel said, chuckling. 'You'd be best to find yourself an occupation—the rest of us have. The ladies both look very content to sit with their books.'

He noticed Hope raise a brief smile at his remark, before returning her attention to the page in front of her once more. They'd retired to the library a little over an hour ago, after Miss Gordon had declared rather brusquely that she had nothing to divert her and Samuel had felt obliged to offer the opportunity to find some reading material. Hope had almost immediately taken the seat nearest to the fire, which burned brightly in the grate and kept the autumnal chill at bay.

His heart had warmed to observe that she'd brought one of Mr Hume's volumes with her and although there was plenty within his newspaper to occupy him he'd found his gaze wandering towards her more than once. He'd watched with some amusement as her upright, ladylike posture had dissolved into something more relaxed, sitting back, her chin resting on her hand, the book balancing on the arm of the chair. Once or twice he'd even seen her move to tuck her feet up beneath her, before remembering either the constraints imposed by her healing ankle or the requirement for decorum—he wasn't sure which. Whatever the reason, he found watching her forget then remember herself rather endearing. The distraction of a good book, it seemed, could make Hope Swynford almost drop her guard. In the end, he forced himself to avert his gaze. His eyes, and his thoughts, lingered upon her far more than they should.

'What do you do for enjoyment in this wet little corner of Cumberland, then?' Charles continued, still complaining. 'Are there no assembly rooms, no theatres?'

Samuel noticed Hope's eyes flick up briefly at Charles's question. 'We have both in Lowhaven,' he answered.

'And where the devil is Lowhaven?' Charles asked.

'A few miles away, on the coast,' Samuel replied. 'It is a busy port town, and has everything we need.'

'Then let us take the carriage there,' Charles suggested.

'We can enjoy a drive around the town. It will pass the time and we may discover what is on at the assembly rooms or the theatre.'

Hope's eyes flicked up again, for longer this time. Samuel met her gaze, saw what looked like panic rising within it.

'You forget that Miss Swynford cannot leave Hayton Hall,' Samuel reminded his friend. 'She is still convalescing and, besides, we cannot run the risk of encountering her uncle.'

'Oh, of course. Well…perhaps Miss Swynford could remain within the carriage?' Charles asked. 'Surely the chances of her being spied through a carriage window are vanishingly small and, anyway, I dare say this uncle has given up searching for her by now. It's been, what, more than a week since she fled from his clutches?'

'Nearly two weeks,' Samuel replied. 'Nonetheless, Charles, we cannot be certain, and I will not take any risks when it comes to Miss Swynford's safety. Take the carriage into Lowhaven if you wish but, regrettably, we cannot join you.'

'Neither of you have bothered to ask Miss Swynford what she wishes.'

Miss Gordon's interjection startled both men. Samuel turned to regard her, observing that she had made her remark without so much as troubling herself to tear her eyes from the pages of her book. She'd selected Walpole's *The Castle of Otranto* from the library's shelves, and clearly the dark and supernatural novel held her interest. How unsurprising, Samuel thought wryly.

'Miss Gordon is right,' Samuel said, returning his mind to the matter at hand. 'Forgive me, Miss Swynford,' he continued, addressing Hope now. 'I dare say you've had quite enough of gentlemen making decisions for you of late—decisions which they've absolutely no right to make. What do you want to do?'

Given the earlier look of panic he believed he'd glimpsed, he expected Hope to decline outright. Instead, however, she appeared to be giving the outing some consideration, chewing her bottom lip thoughtfully as she apparently weighed up her options.

'You have not asked Miss Gordon what she'd like to do either,' Hope replied after a moment, glancing at the other woman.

'Oh, I care not,' Miss Gordon replied airily. 'I find that it is best to remain indifferent, Miss Swynford, when your desires will not be taken into account in any case.'

Samuel saw Charles flinch at his sister's cutting remark. 'Then it is up to you, Miss Swynford,' he said, smoothing over whatever was amiss between the Gordon siblings. Frankly, he could not care less about that right now. 'If you would prefer to remain here, then I will stay with you.'

He watched as she looked towards the window, the rain still running like tears down its old panes. She bit that lovely pink lip once again, and he found himself wondering what she was thinking, if she was as taken with the idea of remaining at Hayton as he suddenly was. If it had occurred to her, as it now had to him, that they could sit together in the parlour and enjoy tea and cake, just as they had before the Gordons had arrived. That they could talk—really talk. That she might bring herself to confide in him, that she might answer some of the questions which had been whirling around his mind about her family, about where her home was and why she would not, or could not, return to it. About exactly what had happened to her to leave her at the mercy of such a wicked relative, and why it appeared she had no one except an unnamed friend in London to turn to.

Not that he had any right to expect such confidences, he reminded himself. Not when he was still deceiving her about who he really was.

At length, when Hope delivered her answer it came as quite a surprise. 'I will come,' she said plainly. 'But I will remain out of sight within the carriage, as Mr Gordon suggests.'

Charles clapped his hands with delight as Samuel mustered an obliging nod in Hope's direction. She met his eye but her expression gave nothing away. Nothing about what had informed her choice to venture out when she'd thus far been so cautious. Nothing about whether cake and conversation with him had even occurred to her and, if it had, why she had rejected it in favour of a rainy carriage ride with the restless Charles and his prickly sister.

'As you wish, Miss Swynford,' Samuel replied, forcing a smile.

Hope shrank back into her seat, her heart beating hard in her chest as the carriage rattled along Lowhaven's bustling streets. She kept her head bowed, allowing the wide-brimmed bonnet she wore to keep her fully in shadow. She'd barely dared to look out of the window, convinced that the moment she did she'd be immediately recognised by some keen-eyed, wicked associate of her father and dragged back to Lillybeck. That had happened to her once before, after all.

She suppressed a shudder at the memory of being hauled away from the back door of the theatre, a coarse hand clapped over her mouth, stifling her screams. Of how powerless she'd felt as they'd dragged her along a lonely alleyway before binding her hands and feet and bundling her into a cart.

These past weeks at Hayton, she'd found sanctuary, and not only from the very real dangers she faced. She'd found sanctuary from her thoughts too, and from her memories. By inhabiting the role of Hope Swynford, she'd put some distance between herself and Hope Sloane's troubles. Now, in the midst of this busy port town, it all returned to her, running unabated through her mind. The confusion. The fear. The desperation.

In her lap, she squeezed her gloved hands together. Why had she come here? Why had she not simply said she'd prefer to remain at Hayton Hall?

Because Samuel would have remained with her, that was why. They would have been left alone, and that was something Hope feared she could no longer countenance. Ever since that tender moment they'd shared in the garden, Hope had come to believe that she could no longer trust herself around him. The way she'd reacted when he'd touched her hand and spoken to her so earnestly…the temptation she'd felt to surrender to the truth, to admit everything—it would not do.

It was bad enough that she was clearly in awe of his good looks, his fine house and his gentlemanly manners. It was bad enough that she'd allowed her thoughts to linger too often on how it'd felt to be in his arms as he carried her down the stairs or broke her fall in the pantry. It was bad enough that she'd entertained ludicrous ideas about him kissing her. Now, was she seriously contemplating placing her trust in him and telling him the truth? What good did she think could possibly come of that?

No good—that was what.

Sir Samuel Liddell was hardly likely to greet the news that she'd lied to him, that she was no heiress or gentlewoman but an actress and the offspring of an outlaw, with anything other than horror and disdain. For all that he'd shown himself to be kind and decent, such qualities had limits, and a gentleman in his position could surely not countenance allowing a woman like her to remain under his roof. She was the lowest of the low—a common criminal's daughter who'd only managed to escape her father's grasp by taking a profession which, in the eyes of many, made her little better than a harlot. And she had lied about it—she'd dined at Samuel's table, slept in his guest bedchamber and socialised with his friends under false pretences. That, she realised now, was perhaps the most unforgivable part of all.

She had to hold her tongue, she reminded herself, and if that meant avoiding being alone with Samuel and using the Gordons as a shield, then so be it. As soon as they left, she would make plans to leave too. She would allow Samuel to escort her to London as agreed and she would begin her life anew from there, even if that meant making her home in the Rookeries and acting on the makeshift stages of the city's many penny gaffs. This time, she vowed, she would put as many miles between herself and her father as possible. She tried not to consider that the same distance would then exist between herself and Samuel. There was, after all, no point in dwelling upon that.

Hope was so lost in her thoughts that it took her several moments to realise that the carriage had drawn to a halt. She looked up to see Mr Gordon hurry out of the door, before reaching back in to assist his sister as she too disembarked.

'We shan't be long, Sammy,' Mr Gordon called, his tone so cheerful that Hope was sure he'd almost sung the words.

Behind them the carriage door clicked shut, concealing Hope from the outside world once more, and leaving her with the master of Hayton Hall once again. So much for avoiding being alone in his company, she thought wryly. Clearly, fate had other ideas. Across from her, Samuel attempted what looked like a reassuring smile, but it quickly dissolved into an exasperated sigh.

'Goodness knows if either of them will find anything at the assembly rooms or the theatre which will please them,' he said, shaking his head. 'I fear Buxton has spoiled them both. Lowhaven's meagre entertainments and lack of pump rooms can hardly be expected to compete. Do you know, Hope, that we have only seawater here? Appalling.'

Hope smiled at his witty remark. 'I dare say Buxton's plays differ little from Lowhaven's. They're all put on by touring provincial theatre companies, after all.'

'Very true,' Samuel replied, raising his eyebrows at her observation. 'You are quite the theatre enthusiast, I think.'

Hope shrugged, trying to ignore the way her stomach lurched. Once again, she'd forgotten herself. Forgotten who she was meant to be. 'I do enjoy a play from time to time,' she replied, doing her best to sound nonchalant. 'Although, of course, I will not be able to join you and the Gordons at the Lowhaven theatre, should they find a play they wish to see one evening.'

She watched as Samuel knitted his brow. 'No, of course, but as you cannot go, I shall not join them either.'

'But you must,' she protested. 'They are your guests…'

'They know the situation,' he insisted. 'They will understand. I promised that you would remain under my care until I escort you to London. I would be remiss in my duty to you if I left you alone and went to Lowhaven for the evening.'

'I would not be alone. I would have Maddie, Smithson and all the other servants there with me…'

'And what if that blackguard of an uncle were to come for you under the cover of darkness?' He held her gaze, his blue-grey eyes seeming to darken. 'What would my poor old butler or my maid be able to do about it then? I can see that you are fearful of your uncle, Hope. You have looked terrified all the way here, even though Charles is correct—there is little chance of him spying you in a carriage with us, if he even remains in Cumberland at all.'

'Trust me,' she replied, lowering her gaze. 'He will still be close by. He will not give in until he has found me.'

Samuel frowned. 'If that is the case, what difference will going to London make? Does he know you have a friend in the city and, if he does, isn't it possible he will find you there? Can this woman and her husband protect you, or are you simply going to be running for ever?'

'I do not know.'

Beneath her lashes, Hope felt a tear slip out. That was the truth, of sorts: Hope Sloane had as little a notion of what the future held for her as Hope Swynford apparently did. Beyond that, Hope was at a loss for what to say. Her story was quickly coming apart under Samuel's growing scrutiny; the tangled web of deceit she'd hurriedly woven together was disintegrating, and she could not even bring herself to attempt to repair it, to tell yet more lies.

'Forgive me, I have upset you.' Samuel leaned forward, placing his hand over hers, which remained folded in her lap. 'Tell me how to help you, Hope. Tell me what more I can do.'

'You have done enough already, Samuel,' she replied, attempting a watery smile.

'Clearly that is not the case, if I am to deliver you to London so that you may spend the rest of your life living in fear. And what sort of a life will you have there? Can you support yourself? Can you access your inheritance?'

'Please, do not concern yourself…'

'But I am concerned,' he insisted. 'I am very concerned about exactly what this nasty and ruthless individual has done to you. I am very concerned that you do not appear to have any family except him, that there is no one to care about your welfare…'

'You are right—I have no one,' Hope conceded, her tears continuing to fall. 'You have been very kind to me, Samuel, and I thank you for it, but you are not my father or my brother, or my…'

Husband.

She stopped herself, just before she could say the word.

Hope sniffled, trying to regain her composure. 'As I said,' she concluded quietly, 'it is none of your concern.'

At that moment the door to the carriage swung open once more, causing them both to flinch. Swiftly, Samuel withdrew the hand which had been resting over hers and, despite herself and all that had occurred in those past moments, Hope could not help but feel bereft at the loss of his touch. She watched as Miss Gordon climbed back in, followed in quick order by her brother who, judging by his broad grin, was very satisfied with his findings indeed. The air which blew in behind them was crisp and laced with salt, and Hope found herself wishing she could go outside and take a swift, restorative lungful of it. Right then, she needed something—anything—which might help to get her thoughts in order.

'Well, that was very enlightening,' Mr Gordon began. 'There is a ball each month at the assembly rooms, and the place has a card room, which suits me very well. And the theatre has a performance of *As You Like It* every evening, although it is finishing its run very soon so we must be quick to catch that one.'

'But that is not the most interesting thing we learned,' Miss Gordon interjected. 'Brother, tell them what we heard about the previous play.'

Hope felt her heart begin to beat faster as Mr Gordon leaned forward conspiratorially.

'Oh, yes,' he said. '*The School for Scandal*—one of my favourites. Apparently, an actress went missing on its penultimate night in town. Disappeared right after the show, it seems. No one's seen or heard anything from her since.'

'Really?' Samuel asked, furrowing his brow. 'The poor woman. I do hope she's not come to any harm.'

'I dare say that actresses absconding from the stage is not all that uncommon,' Mr Gordon scoffed. 'Such is the sort of life that many of them lead—or so I hear. Courtesans at best and harlots at worst, in many cases.'

'All right, Charles,' Samuel replied, making a face. 'I do not think that is a suitable topic of conversation with ladies present.'

By now Hope's heartbeat had grown so fast and so loud that it was a wonder the whole carriage could not hear it. Her cheeks burned as she looked down at her lap once more, wringing her hands together and praying that no one would spot her sheer mortification. Of course these people thought that—didn't everyone? Of course Samuel thought that. Whilst he had not said the words himself, he had not contradicted his friend either. Further confirmation, if it was needed, of exactly why he could never know who and what she really was. Confirmation too of exactly why he could never know just how profoundly true her words had been when she'd told him that she was none of his concern.

Gentlemen like Sir Samuel Liddell concerned themselves with high-born heiresses, not lowly actresses with criminal connections. As the carriage set off for Hayton once more, Hope decided that she would do well to remember that the next time she was tempted to be truthful with him. The truth, she realised, would only injure them both.

Chapter Eleven

Samuel cantered along the coastline on his horse, a salt-laced mist dampening his face to match his mood. He'd gone out a little while earlier with Charles, sensing his friend's characteristic restlessness might be best served by some fresh air. He'd been reluctant to leave Hope, but she had insisted that she would be fine sitting in the small parlour with Miss Gordon, who had no more wished to ride than it appeared she wished to do anything at all. Samuel had thought about protesting, about reminding her of his promise to protect her from the threat she faced, but something about the adamant look in her eye dissuaded him.

'I shall not be gone long, and we shall not venture far,' he'd sworn instead.

Hope joining them, of course, had been out of the question; even if she could countenance straying so far from Hayton Hall, her ankle was not yet strong enough to either ride or walk such a distance.

As he'd headed to the clifftops, Samuel had increasingly found himself wishing that she was there; indeed, that they could ride together, alone. That he could show her the wild and rugged parts of his county, and the sheer remote beauty of places where it was possible to ride for miles without seeing a single soul. He had quickly instructed himself to stop being ridiculous; the lady was convalescing in his home, not visiting for pleasure. His duty was to care for her, not to seek to impress her. Not to seek time alone with her.

Not to interrogate her.

He winced, thinking of their conversation in the carriage, how tense it had become. He'd been wrong to press her about her family, and to call into question the plans she had made. She was right; it was none of his concern what she did, or who she sought help from once she was in London. It was none of his business what had happened in her past, or what her terrible uncle had done to her. His questions had damaged the trust which had been building between them—a delicate trust, he reminded himself, which already rested upon the creaky foundations wrought by his lie about who he was.

Since their drive into Lowhaven, Hope had seemed to withdraw from him, burying her nose in her book every time he so much as glanced at her, and staying firmly by the side of Miss Gordon, whose conversation suddenly seemed to hold a great deal of her interest. Samuel understood her need to keep her distance, and had acted accordingly by keeping his. He knew that he'd crossed a line with his intrusive questions, and that he'd upset her. He'd taken too much of an interest and he was not, as she'd pointed out, her father or her brother, or…

Her husband.

She'd been about to say that, hadn't she?

Samuel stared vacantly out to sea, listening to the waves crashing below and wondering why that word felt so odd to him as it rattled around in his mind. Wondering too exactly why he had grown so interested in what the mysterious

Hope Swynford's tale truly was, and why he felt the heat of anger rise within him at his increasing suspicion that she was all alone in the world, left to face some malevolence which she could not bring herself to name. Anger was not an emotion which came readily to Samuel Liddell, and yet that was how he felt. He could feel it in his racing heart, in his blood as it boiled and coursed through his veins.

He tried not to consider that there might be other feelings at play, other reasons for this visceral physical response. Reasons connected to the sight of her emerald gaze, to the sight of her sitting abed in her shift, her dark hair tumbling in waves over her shoulders. To the feeling of her slight frame nestled in his arms, and the feeling of her slender waist beneath his hands. If she was so adamant that his concerns for her welfare were unwanted, he did not wish to contemplate her horror if she knew how often his mind lingered on thoughts such as those.

'I never had you pegged as the brooding type, Sammy.'

Charles brought his horse to trot alongside Samuel's and gave his friend a mischievous grin. Samuel braced himself for an onslaught of Charles's customary teasing.

'I'm not,' Samuel retorted. 'I believe that the reputation for brooding belongs to my older brother, not me.'

'Well, since you've borrowed his title, I dare say you can borrow his character traits too.'

Inwardly, Samuel groaned at the reminder. His continued deception of Hope was something else which increasingly preyed upon his mind. He would remind himself of why he kept up the pretence, of the need to make Hope feel safe, but that did not stop the lie looming like a spectre over every moment he spent in her company, and over every day that she remained within the sanctuary of Hayton Hall. He'd had the audacity to seek and enjoy her company, to express concern for her and to ask questions about her story, when he was not even being honest with her about who he was. The guilt of it was becoming intolerable.

'Do you know what I think?' Charles continued, undeterred by his friend's silence. 'I think you're a little bit smitten with Miss Hope Swynford. That's why you're pretending to be a baronet, and that's why you won't just admit your folly to her.'

'Nonsense!' Samuel declared, shaking his head.

Charles eyed him suspiciously. 'Is it? She's a pretty young chit, as I'm sure you have not failed to notice. And if the uncle's reckless actions in kidnapping her are anything to go by, I'd say she's wealthy too.'

Samuel bristled at his friend's observation. 'You know that such considerations are no inducement to me, Charles.'

'Which part—her uncommon good looks or her large fortune?' Charles teased.

'Both,' Samuel replied. 'Miss Swynford is in my home under my protection, Charles, not so that I can take advantage of her. That is not my way—you know me well enough to know that.'

Charles nodded. 'You were always a finer gentleman than me. I would be thoroughly dishonourable, if only I was better at it,' he added with a roguish grin.

'Just as long as you are not minded to be dishonourable towards Miss Swynford. The poor lady has been through quite enough,' Samuel lectured him.

'First brooding over the chit, now defensive of the chit—are you quite sure you're not pining for her?' Charles asked.

'Absolutely certain,' Samuel snapped back, although even he could hear his words lacked conviction. Her fortune—

large or otherwise—was of no particular interest to him. Her striking beauty, however…

'We should return to Hayton Hall,' Samuel continued, turning his back to the sea. 'We've neglected Miss Swynford and your sister for quite long enough.'

'I doubt Henrietta will mind,' Charles replied. 'She seems to quite enjoy Miss Swynford's company.' He shook his head in mock disbelief. 'Rich, beautiful, and capable of lifting my sister's sullen spirits. The Sammy I knew on the Continent would have been the first gentleman in the room to try to woo a woman like that.'

Samuel grimaced at his friend's words. The 'Sammy' Charles knew would not have allowed such a woman to believe he was someone he was not. But then, that Samuel had not yet had his pride dented by rejection. That painful experience, he acknowledged yet again, was part of what had driven his deceit. What prevented him from ending it was altogether more complex, and was just as attributable to the potent mix of protectiveness and affection he felt whenever he looked at her as it was to his residual feelings of shame and humiliation whenever he so much as contemplated explaining his lie. But he had to contemplate it, he knew that, even if it risked losing her respect. Even if it meant an end to the way she seemed to regard him, as though he was a knight who had come to her rescue. That was nothing less than he deserved.

If only he could find a way to tell her which would not cause her distress. If only he could be certain that the knowledge that she was not living under the protection of Hayton's baronet wouldn't cause Hope to panic, or to flee back into harm's way. The thought that it might was unbearable, and was another reason why he continued to wrestle with his conscience. And another reason, no doubt, why his blood heated with that overwhelming desire to protect her, to envelop her in his arms and not let go…

Where in damnation had that thought come from?

'I am not wooing anyone,' Samuel replied after a moment. 'And certainly not Miss Swynford. That is a ridiculous idea, given the circumstances.'

Impatiently, he cracked his whip, unable to stomach the sound of his own hollow protests any longer. Unable to abide the maelstrom of whirring thoughts as his honour, his conscience and his pride warred with each other in his mind. Instead, he raced back towards the home of which he was not truly master, to the life and title which were not truly his, and to the woman who, to his great shame, believed him to be in possession of all of it.

'Courtesans...and harlots...'

Hope sat alone in the small parlour, forcing her mind to focus on the book which rested on her lap, to absorb the information contained within Mr Hume's dense prose. Her mind, however, had other ideas, returning continuously to those injurious words which Mr Gordon had uttered. Words which Samuel had not refuted as accurate descriptions of actresses. Words which Hope had been smarting over ever since.

'Courtesans at best and harlots at worst.'

The irony of the insult was not lost on her since she was, without doubt, thoroughly unqualified to be called either. During her time in the theatre she had steadfastly refused to succumb to the easy virtues expected of those in her profession, rebuking many a man for his unwanted advances. Indeed, the only experiences she'd ever had of the opposite sex were in the form of those who'd tried to kiss or to touch her without invitation. She'd never experienced any welcome intimacy; she'd never been embraced by a man who made her heart race or kissed by one who stirred the heat of passion within her. These were feelings which she knew existed—she'd heard enough of the coarse chatter of other actresses, after all—but they were not experiences she'd had for herself.

Indeed, she realised, the closest she'd ever been to a man was when she'd unwittingly fallen into Samuel's arms in the pantry, or when she'd allowed him to carry her down the stairs. Encounters which she found herself replaying in her mind, picking over their details, reliving the feelings such closeness had evoked in her. She'd felt comforted, reassured, safe, but something else too. The heat of something which she could not find words for, but was there nonetheless, rising within her as her eyes met his, as his arms held her momentarily, tantalisingly close. Another irony, she reminded herself, forcing her mind to cease from lingering over those memories once more. Regardless of the feelings Samuel's proximity might provoke in her, in every respect that mattered—in status and in wealth—she could not be further apart from him.

Hope sighed heavily, putting the book to one side as finally she admitted defeat. Having grown weary of the Anglo-Saxons and the Normans, she'd jumped ahead, seeking diversion in the story of John of Gaunt and Katherine Swynford, which Samuel had briefly yet so tantalisingly recounted. In this, however, she was ultimately disappointed, finding only the smallest reference to their union, and even then it was to discuss how it was believed to have injured the dignity of the Duke of Lancaster's family. As a learned gentleman, no doubt Mr Hume had little time for mistresses who become wives, Hope had thought wryly. Just as baronets could not be expected to have any regard for actresses.

She fidgeted, kicking off the ill-fitting slippers she wore—another item borrowed from Samuel's cousin—and carefully stretching her legs out across the sumptuous fabric of the sofa. At least this unexpected time alone had afforded her some respite from playing her role of the society heiress. Samuel and Mr Gordon were still out riding, and Miss Gordon had retired to her room some time ago, claiming she was in the grip of yet another headache. She had seemed to suffer from a great many of those of late, excusing herself at least once daily on the insistence that she needed to rest awhile. Several times, Hope had observed her brother's brow furrow as his gaze followed her out of the room. It was a look which spoke of his concern, but it was knowing too.

Hope had spent more time with Miss Gordon these past days, feebly shielding herself from the possibility of further questioning by Samuel. Thankfully, the lady had largely desisted from asking Hope any more leading questions about ancestral homes and the like. Nonetheless, between her frequent headaches, clipped conversation and general aloof air, Hope found the unease she'd experienced when first meeting the lady to be fully vindicated. When it came to Miss Henrietta Gordon, it was clear that there was more going on than met the eye.

Then again, Hope thought, Miss Gordon was not the only one at whom such a charge could be levelled. She might be under no illusion as to exactly what Samuel would think of her if he knew who and what she truly was, but that did not stop her guilt at her deception of him continuing to gnaw at her. Moreover, after the way he'd questioned her as they'd sat together in his carriage in Lowhaven, Hope felt that the risk of him unravelling her story for himself was becoming very real.

If he continued to pick over the vague information she'd offered, if he continued to press her for more detail than she was willing to give, then a gentleman as learned as he was could not fail to grow suspicious, and then what would she do? Tell more lies and hope to assuage his desire for knowledge? Tell him the truth and watch the anger and disappointment cloud his usually cheerful countenance? Neither option held any appeal. She regarded him too highly to deepen the deceit, yet she feared the consequences of honesty—she feared losing his good opinion and she feared hurting him. She cared too much to do that.

She cared too much about him, didn't she? And that was the problem. That was the root of her current predicament. Because, as it turned out, deceiving someone so kind, so open and likeable as Samuel caused her pain, far worse perhaps than any of the injuries she'd sustained mere weeks ago. It made her heart sore, and her stomach ache.

Tentatively, Hope glanced at her ankle as it rested on the sofa. The acute discomfort was gone now, as were the bandages. Indeed, the only evidence of injury which remained was the bruising, which had gradually turned from an angry purple to a deep greyish brown. It was not strong enough to walk far yet and it still hurt if she spent too long on her feet but, to all intents and purposes, it had healed. She had healed. Perhaps, she reasoned now, the answer to her growing set of problems was not to choose between honesty and deceit, but to escape. Hayton Hall was only a temporary sanctuary, after all, offered to her while she convalesced. Well, she had recovered, at least well enough to travel. Perhaps it was time to make arrangements to leave.

The sound of horses cantering up the drive caused her to startle, and out of the window she saw Samuel and Mr Gordon approach. Quickly, she sat up straight, sliding her feet back into the slippers as she composed herself and resumed her role. It would only be for a little while longer, she told herself now. She would speak to Samuel about making arrangements for her journey south as soon as possible. He would remain ignorant of her deception and they would part on good terms. In time, his acquaintance with the enigmatic heiress would become nothing more than a strange, brief interlude in his life. Surely her swift departure was necessary. Surely it was for the best.

Hope picked up her book once more, determined to appear absorbed as, out in the hallway, the rhythm of approaching footsteps rang out. Determined too upon her chosen course and determined above all not to dwell on how the prospect of leaving had made her heart ache even more.

Chapter Twelve

'Is everything all right? Where are the Gordons?'

Hope limped into the dining room, feeling the absence of her walking cane with every tentative step. She'd left it upstairs after dressing for dinner, determined to demonstrate that she was fit enough to walk without it and prove she was well enough to leave Hayton Hall. She had not managed to speak to Samuel about that yet; indeed, she'd barely spoken to him since he'd returned from his ride with Mr Gordon yesterday. He'd seemed unusually subdued last night at dinner and had retired early, and today he'd spent much of his time locked away in his library, ostensibly dealing with estate matters. No doubt he was—as a landowner and a gentleman he would have business which required his attention and could not be expected to entertain guests all the time.

The Gordons, however, had not seemed quite so understanding and, after enduring quite enough of Mr Gordon's fidgeting and Miss Gordon's sullen temperament, Hope had excused herself and spent the remainder of the afternoon resting in her bedchamber. Now she'd returned downstairs at the appointed dining hour to find the house quiet, the table bare, and Samuel hovering beside it, leaning on the back of a chair.

'I thought we could take supper in the library this evening,' he said, offering her a small smile. 'I don't know about you, but I've rather wearied of formal dining of late. Too many courses, too much fuss.'

Hope gave a brisk nod. 'As you wish. Will Mr Gordon and his sister be joining us?'

'Afraid not,' Samuel replied, shaking his head. 'They've decided to go to the theatre. Apparently, it's the very last night for *As You Like It* in Lowhaven and Charles cannot countenance missing it. Miss Gordon seemed less enthused, but has done her duty and accompanied her brother,' he added with a wry smile.

'Did you not wish to go with them?' Hope asked.

'My duty is to remain here, with you,' he replied firmly, giving her a look which reminded her at once of his words in his carriage that day, when he'd spoken of his promise to protect her. When he'd acknowledged the look of fear he'd seen in her eyes.

'There will be other opportunities to go to the theatre,' he continued. 'Now, aren't you going to ask me why we're taking supper in the library and not the parlour?'

The mischievous grin he gave her piqued her interest, and she pushed all thoughts of invented nefarious uncles and all too real and threatening fathers to one side.

'All right,' she replied, raising a smile to match his. 'Why?'

'I thought, since we cannot go to the theatre, we would bring the theatre to us.'

Hope frowned. 'What do you mean by that?'

Samuel chuckled as he walked towards her, taking her by the hand. 'You'll see. Come on.'

The feeling of his gentle fingers holding hers made her thoughts scatter, and willingly she allowed him to lead her out of the dining room and down the hallway to the library. Once inside, she saw that a table had been laid with bread, cold meats and a healthy decanter of red wine set between two glasses. Nearby she spied another, smaller occasional table, bearing several leather-bound books. She turned to Samuel then, raising an expectant eyebrow as she awaited an explanation.

'I know it is a little unorthodox,' he said, relinquishing her hand. 'I can assure you, I don't make a habit of dining in the library, but it seemed like the most suitable place.'

'The most suitable place for what?' she pressed him.

'To read some Shakespeare. And to show you something rather precious, which I think you will appreciate, given your enthusiasm for the theatre.'

Samuel beckoned her over to the smaller table, where carefully he lifted up a very thick and apparently very old brown book. 'Shakespeare's Comedies, Histories and Tragedies,' he said as he passed it to her. 'A collection of his plays, printed in 1623.'

Hope gasped, gently opening the book to see the title page, where the Bard's famous image gazed back at her. 'It's almost two hundred years old,' she marvelled.

Samuel nodded. 'It's also very rare. I believe only seven hundred or so copies were ever printed. And we are fortunate enough to have one of them here, at Hayton.'

'Fortunate indeed,' she mused, still staring in disbelief at the treasure she held in her hands. 'I have never seen anything like it. The only scripts I have seen have been…'

Hope pressed her lips together, remembering herself just in time. Her heart raced at the knowledge of what she had almost unwittingly revealed. She'd felt herself—her real self—bubbling to the surface once more. This was becoming too difficult—to hide in plain sight, to suppress her true identity beneath polite speech, fine clothes and a character with the vaguest of histories. To keep lying to Samuel, to repay his unfailing kindness and generosity with deceit. This, she reminded herself, was exactly why she needed to leave. Perhaps she ought to speak to him about that this evening, if she could find the right moment, the right words…

'Oh, I am sure you must have one or two priceless heirlooms tucked away in a dusty family library somewhere,' Samuel remarked, apparently oblivious to her inner turmoil. 'Perhaps in that ancestral home which you've vowed never to set foot in again,' he added pointedly.

Despite herself, Hope found her mind drifting the several miles across the countryside to Lillybeck, to that damp stone cottage tucked on the hillside. She doubted her father kept so much as a broadside in that barren, cold place.

'Perhaps,' she replied, regretting now that piece of information which Miss Gordon had managed to draw from her at their first meeting. At the time she'd thought it an evasive enough answer; now she suspected Samuel had caught the scent of truth emanating from it. 'Here,' she continued, passing his book back to him and hoping to swiftly change the subject. 'You'd better take this and put it somewhere safe.'

Samuel accepted the book, placing it back on the table as he shook his head in disbelief. 'You are really not going to tell me anything, are you, Hope? About your past, about your life before you stumbled into that woodland that day.'

Unable to bear his consternation, she dropped her gaze, momentarily lost for words. Deep down, she'd known to expect this conversation, ever since that carriage ride. This was why she'd avoided being alone with him, why she'd stuck closely by Miss Gordon's prickly side. But sensing what Samuel wanted to say and knowing how to answer him were two different matters. What could she say that would not cause yet more harm? Lies were damaging, but the truth was damning.

Instead, she lifted her eyes to meet his, trying not to dwell upon how their grey-blue depths seemed to swirl with concern, with sadness. 'I thought we'd come to the library to read Shakespeare, not to talk about me,' she replied obstinately, folding her hands in front of her to stop them from trembling. She glanced over at the larger table, still laden with food. 'Perhaps first we should have some of that bread and meat, before it spoils.'

Samuel walked over to the table, lifting the decanter and pouring two glasses of wine. The only thing which was being spoiled, he thought to himself, was their evening together, and the fault for that was entirely his. He'd set out to make the most of their unexpected time alone, to indulge in something which he believed would interest her, to recapture some of the easy companionship they'd enjoyed before Charles and his sister had arrived. And, most importantly, to grasp the right moment to tell her the truth about himself, to offer his heartfelt apology and hope that she would accept it. To reassure her that whilst she might not have the protection of a baronet, she would always have the protection of Samuel Liddell.

Instead, he'd fallen right back into the same trap and had overstepped the mark with his questions, just as he had that afternoon in the carriage. Her life really was none of his business, he reminded himself, especially when he was still not being honest about his own. The problem was, not knowing the details of her story made his mind run wild, imagining the worst possible scenarios until his need to protect her felt quite overwhelming. He'd never been gripped by feelings like this before—burning, unpredictable emotions which made him feel quite out of kilter.

'Forgive me,' he said, handing her a glass of wine and forcing a smile. 'You are right, of course. We should read some Shakespeare, as I originally proposed. Although not from the 1623 book—I don't think future generations of Liddells would forgive me for that. There is a newer, smaller volume of his works on the table.'

He watched as Hope walked back towards the books he'd fetched out earlier.

'Do you have a particular play in mind?' she asked. 'A favourite, perhaps?'

He shook his head. 'To be honest, I like them all. Why don't we let fate decide? Open the book and see which play finds us.'

Hope did as he suggested, putting her wine glass down before picking up the book and opening it at random. He watched as those emerald eyes briefly scanned the page. 'Oh, goodness,' she said with a wry chuckle. '*Romeo and Juliet.*'

Fate, Samuel thought, was clearly laughing at them. Or at least it was laughing at him, given some of the thoughts about Miss Hope Swynford which his errant mind had entertained of late.

'Goodness indeed,' he replied, his throat growing unfathomably dry. 'The star-crossed lovers in fair Verona—which he never visited, or so I believe.'

'*"Two houses, both alike in dignity, in fair Verona where we lay our scene,"*' Hope recited, apparently from memory, since she was not reading from the book. '*"From ancient grudge break to new mutiny, where civil blood makes civil hands unclean."'*

Samuel grinned at her. 'Very well remembered. A favourite of yours, perhaps?'

She shrugged, closing the book before retrieving her wine glass and taking a considered sip. 'Not particularly—I have watched it a few times is all. If anything, I find it very disheartening.'

'You find a play about love disheartening?'

'Is it really about love?' she countered. 'Surely it's about the thwarting of love—first by the hatred between two families, and then by death. If anything, Shakespeare is telling us that sometimes love is impossible. Circumstances make it so. Fate makes it so. No matter how much two people want to be together, sometimes there are just too many obstacles. There is too much to keep them apart.'

'All right,' Samuel conceded, relishing the opportunity to debate. 'Although you must surely admit that there is beauty in the play too. The love between Romeo and Juliet is genuine, pure and heartfelt, is it not?'

'Of course it is, but therein lies the tragedy because ultimately it is not enough. It does not even serve to end their families' feuding—it takes them both dying to do that. As I said, disheartening.'

Samuel nodded. Her argument was persuasive and her knowledge impressive. She was more than a theatre enthusiast, he decided. It was very apparent that she was acquainted with at least some of Shakespeare's work inside and out.

'You would have enjoyed some of the dinner parties I attended on the Continent,' he remarked. 'Packed with scholars and intellectuals, brimming with opinions on the best and worst that English literature has to offer.'

He watched as her brow furrowed. 'You're teasing me.'

'Not at all—I am in earnest. Some of the best evenings I had while travelling were spent in the company of such people. Poets, writers, artists, philosophers, or simply avid readers. I think you would have liked talking to them too, and I think a great many of them would have liked talking to you.' He reached out, taking her hand in his. 'This evening with you has reminded me of some very happy times, Hope, and I must thank you for that.'

She nodded obligingly, her expression softening. 'That is kind of you to say,' she replied. 'Alas, I am unlikely to ever find myself moving in such circles, never mind on the Continent.'

'You could travel, Hope, it is not impossible. Now that you are free of your uncle, and as long as you can access the means…'

'Believe me, it is impossible,' she interrupted, refusing to meet his eye. 'My life has been very different to yours, Samuel. You do not understand. You cannot understand.'

'Then explain it to me.' Instinctively, he stepped towards her, still clutching her hand with his. Her fingers felt so small and delicate beneath his touch. 'You can tell me about it, Hope,' he said quietly. 'You can trust me, please believe that.'

'I cannot…' She was shaking her head vehemently now. 'I need to leave. I need to…'

'What do you mean, you need to leave?'

She did not answer, and the fear he saw swirling in her eyes was too much to bear. Before he could think about what he was doing, Samuel stepped forward, pulling her towards him and enveloping her in his arms. Instinct overcame thought as he held her and, to his surprise, she allowed him, her head coming to rest against his chest as her arms looped tentatively around him. The feeling of her warm hands against his back made his blood heat and, before he could stop them, his own hands had reached for the near-black curls of her hair, his fingers running unbidden through them, teasing them from their pins, then diving under them to find the soft skin at the nape of her neck…

Against him she sighed, before looking up at him, her green gaze no longer filled with anguish but something else, something he could not name.

'What is it, Hope?' he whispered. 'Please, tell me.'

She shook her head again but did not break eye contact, nor did she recoil from his embrace. Every sinew of his body was alive with awareness of her petite, alluring form pressed against him, rendering rational, gentlemanly thought impossible. Instinct continued to rule him as he leaned down, his lips gently touching hers. His heart sang as she welcomed his kiss—indeed, she kissed him back hungrily, pulling herself ever closer to him, sending shivers down his spine as she ran her fingers over his broad shoulders then through his hair. She kissed like she spoke about Shakespeare—passionately and with conviction. With her encouragement his own passion grew, sending his lips on a quest to find the soft flesh of her ear, then her neck, then the swell of her breasts which hinted at the neckline of her gown…

Good God, what was he doing? He was meant to be confessing to her, not kissing her!

'I am so sorry,' he blurted, pulling away. 'Forgive me.' He swallowed hard, shaking his head at himself in disbelief. 'I should not have done that. Not when there is so much

I need to say. Hope, I must tell you that I am not who you think I am. I am not…'

His words died in his mouth as the door to Hayton's library burst open. He heard Hope gasp as, like him, her eyes flew to see who had intruded so unexpectedly. He was stunned to see Smithson standing in the doorway, looking uncommonly rumpled, a serious expression etched on his heavily lined face.

'I am sorry to disturb you, sir,' the butler began, sounding a little breathless. Samuel watched as the wily old man's gaze flitted between the two of them, no doubt noting Hope's mussed hair and burning cheeks. 'Really—very sorry.'

'Well, what is it, man?' he demanded, his customarily gentle tongue abandoned. Now really was not the time. Not when he'd just kissed Hope. Not when Hope had just said she was going to leave.

Not when he'd been on the cusp of telling her the truth.

'It's Miss Gordon, sir,' Smithson continued, still regarding them both carefully. 'I'm afraid Mr and Miss Gordon have had to return from the theatre early. Miss Gordon has been taken ill.'

At that moment Samuel could have groaned aloud with frustration. The news about Miss Gordon's health was concerning, but the thought of leaving the unspoken truth hanging between himself and Hope was unbearable. However, there was nothing he could do. Duty called—his duty as Charles's friend, and his duty as Hayton's caretaker master.

'I'm sorry,' he said, turning back to Hope. 'I promise that we will talk soon.'

'Of course,' she agreed, regarding him just long enough for him to see the concern and confusion swirling in her green gaze. Then she turned away from him, striding purposefully towards the door. 'I think we should go and assist Miss Gordon, shouldn't we?'

Chapter Thirteen

'What on earth has happened, Charles?'

Samuel followed Smithson into the small parlour, where the broad frame of his friend loomed large, wringing his hands and pacing tirelessly. His sister, meanwhile, had been laid out on the sofa, her eyes closed as Maddie sat beside her, dabbing her forehead with a cool cloth. Hope, who'd followed behind him, immediately joined Maddie at Miss Gordon's side, tucking the loose tendrils of her dark hair behind her ears as she bent down to examine the patient. Realising he was staring at her, Samuel tore his gaze away and focused again on Charles, trying to force himself to focus on the matter at hand. Trying not to dwell on the memory of her lips pressed against his, of the feeling of her in his arms. Of how those heady, intoxicating moments had brought his guilt rushing to the fore. He'd been so close to telling her, so close to explaining everything…

'The physician has been sent for, sir,' Smithson informed him, answering when it was clear, after a long moment, that Charles would not.

Samuel nodded. 'Thank you, Smithson. Charles,' he said gently, trying again. 'Do you know what happened? Do you know what ails her?'

Charles shook his head, his face growing paler by the moment. 'She was fine until after the interval,' he replied. 'Then she began to behave in the most odd manner, calling out the strangest things, then laughing so much that she did not seem able to stop. People were staring at her like she was mad.' His friend paused, clearly collecting himself. 'I decided we ought to leave and got her back into the carriage. She fell asleep on the ride home and I have not been able to rouse her since. I do not know what the matter is with her, Sammy.'

Samuel glanced down at Miss Gordon. 'Is she feverish?' he asked Maddie.

'No, sir,' the maid answered.

'And she was absolutely fine all day, before you went out?' he asked Charles.

His friend nodded. 'She was her usual self, Sammy, warts and all.'

Samuel shook his head. 'Then I am at a loss. We will have to hope that the physician can offer further insight.'

'If he comes tonight,' Charles replied fretfully, glancing towards the window, which had been shuttered against the darkness outside. 'It is rather late, after all. What can we do in the meantime?'

'Keep her comfortable,' Samuel replied, staring glumly at Miss Gordon, who remained unresponsive. 'And keep watch over her, in case there is any change in her condition.'

His eyes shifted once again from the patient to Hope, who seemed to be observing Miss Gordon closely. He watched as she leaned forward, as though listening for something. Then, to his surprise, she reached over, lifting Miss Gordon's eyelids to open her eyes one at a time, frowning at whatever it was she saw.

'What is it, Miss Swynford?' Samuel asked, stepping towards her.

Gingerly, Hope stood up, turning to face him. Her expression, he noted, remained grave. 'I believe I might know what is wrong with Miss Gordon,' she replied, flashing Charles a wary look. 'If I may speak plainly, Sir Samuel.'

Samuel winced at her use of that blasted title. How he wished he could banish it for good! How he wished he could tell her the truth, here and now. But of course he could not—not in front of Charles and his servants. Not when Miss Gordon was plainly so unwell…

He nodded briskly, pushing his swirling thoughts aside. 'Of course. You may always speak plainly to me, Hope,' he replied, venturing now to use her first name in company and hoping she would do the same. In truth, right now, he was not sure how many more 'Sir Samuels' he could stomach.

'I believe Miss Gordon is suffering the effects of having taken laudanum,' Hope replied quietly. Those emerald eyes of hers met his again for the briefest moment before she turned to address Charles. 'Mr Gordon, I wonder if you can confirm whether your sister has been taking this, perhaps on the advice of your family's physician?'

Something about Hope's tone told Samuel that she suspected Charles was well aware of what was going on.

'No, well, indeed, she may have taken a tincture once or twice…' Charles prevaricated.

'This is important, Charles,' Samuel urged him. 'We cannot help your sister if we do not know what is amiss.'

Charles's eyes seemed to widen like saucers. 'For headaches,' he said after a moment. 'Yes—I remember now. She took laudanum on our doctor's orders, for headaches.'

'Took?' Hope repeated. 'Forgive me, sir, but it seems to

me that your sister continues to take laudanum, presumably for the headaches which, as I'm sure you've also observed, she continues to suffer.' Samuel watched as carefully Hope sat down at Miss Gordon's side once more. 'Her pupils are like pin pricks,' she explained, briefly opening one of the lady's eyes again. 'Her breathing is shallow. And the behaviour you described at the theatre sounds very much like the sort of delirium which laudanum is known to induce. In short, sir, if you check your sister's reticule I believe you will find a bottle of what has poisoned her within it.'

'Poison?' Charles said, aghast.

'Yes—poison,' Hope replied emphatically. 'Laudanum relieves suffering but if she has taken too much then… surely, sir, I don't have to explain to you how dangerous that may be.'

Samuel's mouth fell open at the bluntness of her warning. 'What can be done for her, Hope?' he asked.

'She must be watched over, as you suggested,' Hope replied. 'In my experience, we need to keep her propped up, as she is right now on the sofa. It is better for her breathing and better if…well, if she expels anything. And we should try to rouse her, if we can. Beyond that, we can only await the physician's advice.'

Samuel nodded dumbly, her words still sinking in. Knowing, confident words spoken, as she'd just admitted, from experience. Despite the severity of the situation, Samuel found himself wondering about the nature of those experiences, about what Hope might have faced in her past which had taught her how to handle something as dire and life-threatening as this. He wondered too if it was this very sort of experience that caused Hope to guard the story of her past so closely.

Now, however, was not the time to ask her questions such as that. Giving himself a mental shake, Samuel sprang once again into action.

'You heard Hope,' he said, addressing the room. 'Let us pray that the physician's journey here is swift and without delay. In the meantime, Miss Gordon shall not be left alone for a moment.'

Groggily, Hope opened her eyes, grimacing at the aching she felt in her neck and limbs after being curled up on a chair for goodness knew how long. She looked towards the window, relieved to see daylight hinting at the edges of the shutters, which were still closed to the world outside. It had been an endless night. The physician, it had transpired, had not been at home, having been summoned to an emergency elsewhere, leaving Hope and the others to care for Miss Gordon alone and without guidance.

Having checked his sister's reticule and found a small bottle of laudanum tucked within it, Mr Gordon had at last resigned himself to Hope's diagnosis and placed himself at Miss Gordon's side, insisting that he would watch over her first. They had each taken a turn while the others slept, and now, as she pulled herself upright, she saw Samuel was still at his post, his gaze intent upon the patient. For a moment she simply looked at him, taking in every detail from his dishevelled sand-coloured hair to his rumpled white shirt, long bereft of either a coat or cravat.

Memories of those heated moments in the library came rushing to the fore, her fingers tingling with awareness as though her skin itself could recall the feeling of the fine fabric of his clothes, of the outline of the muscles which hinted at their presence beneath them, of the warm softness of his hair. She felt her face grow hot as her mind lingered on how she had responded to his embrace, how she had kissed him back with reckless abandon. It had been an entirely new, entirely terrifying and entirely thrilling experience—to be held like that, to be touched like that. To be kissed like that.

The abruptness with which he'd ended the embrace had astonished her, but not as much as the tortured, guilt-ridden look on his face as he'd begun to speak of things he ought to say, of not being what she thought he was.

What on earth had he meant by that? That question, and all its possible answers, had circled around her mind throughout the long night. She'd replayed his words over and over, picking through them, searching for clues. He'd told her that he shouldn't have kissed her—why was that? Was he, in fact, a married man? Or was he betrothed, with a fiancée tucked away somewhere? Her face heated again as she recalled the enthusiasm she'd shown for his advances—an enthusiasm which was as mortifying as it was curious, especially if the kiss, for him, had been a grave transgression. An act of infidelity, and something to be regretted.

Of course, she reminded herself, if he had kissed her under false pretences, then he wasn't the only one. Last night the master of Hayton Hall had believed himself to be kissing a runaway heiress, not the penniless daughter of an outlaw.

Samuel had promised that they would talk soon, and certainly they both had much to say. Before that kiss had sent her thoughts and her wits scattering, she'd blurted out her intention to leave—an intention which now seemed more vital than ever. After last night, it was abundantly clear that her feelings for the master of Hayton Hall had grown beyond even her wildest imaginings, and it seemed from his actions that there was some attraction on his part too. An attraction, she reminded herself, which he felt towards Hope Swynford and not Hope Sloane. Extricating herself from this situation, and removing herself and her deceit from his life, was now essential. In that respect, whatever he'd been on the cusp of confessing to her last night surely could not matter.

But, God help her, she ached to know what it was…

'Good morning.'

Hope blinked, her whirring thoughts interrupted as she realised Samuel was looking at her.

'Did you sleep all right?' he asked, offering her a weary smile.

'Not too badly, considering.'

'In hindsight, it perhaps would have been best if you'd retired upstairs,' he mused. 'You are still recovering. It cannot have been good for your ankle, curling up like a cat in that chair.'

'I'm fine,' she assured him, resisting the urge to rub her throbbing foot. 'How is Miss Gordon?' She looked around. 'And where is Mr Gordon?'

'Charles is outside, smoking his pipe—as he does whenever he is vexed.' He glanced back at the patient. 'And Miss Gordon seems to be improving. Her breathing is steadier and she has stirred several times in the past hour. Maddie has just taken away the water and cloths as we agreed they're no longer needed.'

Hope smiled. 'You called her Maddie, not Madeleine,' she observed.

Samuel let out a small chuckle. 'I did. A perceptive and considerate lady once suggested to me that I ought to pay better attention to my servants' wishes, especially when they're in no position to challenge me.'

Hope inclined her head, acknowledging the compliment. 'Poor Maddie must get some rest too,' she reminded him. 'If she has been attending to Miss Gordon all night.'

Samuel nodded. 'I've told Smithson to give her the day off. I've also asked Smithson to arrange for some breakfast to be brought. I thought that if we can wake Miss Gordon, we may be able to get her to eat or drink something. And I do not know about you, but I am famished.'

Hope's stomach growled in agreement, and she remembered that they had never eaten the bread and meat which had been laid out in the library. Events, and passionate embraces, had intervened.

'Has there been any further word from the physician?' she asked, ignoring the heat which had crept into her cheeks once more.

'A message was left for him last night,' Samuel replied. 'I expect he will come today.'

'Good. Hopefully, he will confirm that Miss Gordon will recover well.'

'Hmm.' Samuel's gaze drifted back to the patient and gently he shook his head. 'It's a terrible business,' he said in a hushed voice. 'She could have died last night.'

'Laudanum is a terrible business,' Hope responded grimly.

'You sound as though you speak from experience.'

Those grey-blue eyes held hers once again. Hope could hear the tentative note in his voice, as though he had not been sure if he should broach the subject. But after last night, after seeing how she'd recognised what was wrong with Miss Gordon and taken charge of the situation, she knew he could hardly avoid talking to her about it. She knew too that she could not lie to him; she had offered too vivid a glimpse of the real Hope's life to do that. Only the truth, or at least a version of it, would do now.

'My mother,' she said at last, as evenly as she could manage. 'She began taking it for an ailment, to help with the pain. In doing so, she found that it could take away not just her physical pain but every other pain she felt too, and I think she rather liked the oblivion it offered her. But the rub with laudanum is that the more you take it, the more you need to take to achieve the desired effect. And the higher the dose, the greater the risk. My mother found this out to her great cost. She died a number of years ago, alone on her bed, an empty bottle of her beloved poison by her side.'

'I am so sorry, Hope. That must have been very hard to bear.'

Hope pressed her lips together, hoping Samuel could not sense how hard she was fighting to hold back her tears. 'I spent many nights watching over her, just as we had to do with Miss Gordon. And many days pleading with her to stop taking it. But that need she had to obliterate everything was just too strong.'

'Was there no one who could help? What about your father?'

'My father was the reason for much of her pain,' she replied bitterly, the words slipping out before she could prevent them. She should not have told him that. The last person she should be speaking to Samuel about was her father.

Samuel frowned, and she could see he was trying to make sense of her words. 'You do not have to tell me anything more, Hope,' he said in the end. 'Not if you do not wish to.'

But that was exactly the problem, Hope thought. She

did want to tell him. She wanted to break down and weep and tell him everything—about her mother, her father, her true self. About the childhood spent on that bleak hillside in Lillybeck, about her escape from a forced marriage and a life of crime. About her time on the stage, about those colourful years which had exposed her to so much culture and creativity on the one hand, and wickedness and debauchery on the other. About how her freedom had been snatched from her a second time, and how fate and fortune had conspired to send her into those woods, running for her life. Running, as it had turned out, into Sir Samuel Liddell's life, and into his warm, caring embrace.

An embrace, and a life, which she now had to detach herself from—to protect his feelings and to protect her own. Confiding in him was utterly out of the question; the hole she'd dug herself into with her deceit was now far too deep for that.

'I think that is quite enough misery for one morning,' she replied, forcing a smile as she rose carefully from her seat, ignoring how her sore limbs groaned in protest. 'If you will excuse me, I think I'd like to freshen up before breakfast.'

'Of course.'

Samuel too got to his feet. Hope could feel the heat of his gaze upon her as she walked towards the parlour door. She glanced down, feeling suddenly conscious of the state she was in. Her hair was hanging untidily about her shoulders and her clothes clung to her like a slickened second skin. She needed to wash, to breathe. To put some space between herself and Samuel and all that had been said and done. Perhaps then, she thought, her mind might not linger on the memory of his mouth pressed against hers quite so much.

'Hope? Can we speak again later? After last night…

well, there are some matters we need to discuss.' His voice sounded strained. 'Some things I need to explain.'

She glanced back at him, just briefly. 'Yes, of course.'

Hope hurried out of the room, reeling once more at the prospect of what it was he wanted to tell her, even while she told herself that whatever it was should make no difference to her now. The only thing that really mattered, she reminded herself, was leaving before any more harm could be done.

Chapter Fourteen

Samuel knew that he ought to have been exhausted, and yet he could not sleep. He'd spent the day dealing with the aftermath of the discovery of Miss Gordon's affliction, as Charles had rather euphemistically taken to calling it, in a daze brought on by his own lack of sleep. His turmoil over all that had occurred between him and Hope, and all that he had still to tell her, had conspired with his fatigue to leave him feeling thoroughly out of sorts. His stomach had churned almost incessantly, while every spare moment had been haunted by the confusion lingering in Hope's eyes as he'd uttered those most damning words.

'I must tell you that I am not who you think I am...'

More than once he'd given himself a stern talking-to, reminding himself that he had duties to perform, instructions to issue, and an unwell guest whose care required to be overseen. Miss Gordon had awoken properly by the middle of the morning, and the physician had turned up shortly afterwards. The good doctor had thankfully confirmed that Charles's sister was out of danger but had recommended bed rest and a lengthy abstinence from her tinctures.

Despite her weakened condition, Miss Gordon had protested at that. 'My headaches are severe,' she'd insisted. 'The laudanum is entirely necessary, to manage the pain.'

The physician, to his credit, was unmoved. Samuel had felt sure that Hope would have raised a knowing eyebrow at Miss Gordon's objection, had she been present. She'd gone to her bedchamber to rest after breakfast and he had not seen much of her since, although he knew from Charles's report that she'd spent some of the afternoon sitting with Miss Gordon while Samuel had been attending to estate matters at his desk in the library. She'd made only a brief appearance at dinnertime before retiring early, insisting she was still very tired. No doubt she was, but knowing that hadn't made Samuel crave her company any less. He still needed to speak to her, still needed to tell her the truth about himself. Kissing her had made his confession more vital than ever. And as for that kiss…

The memory of that had driven him to distraction more than once during his waking hours. Then there was her intention to leave and his promise to escort her to London—a promise he intended to keep, even if the thought of it made his heart sink and a lump grow in his throat. But he could hardly do anything else, could he? His duty was, and had always been, to protect her, and he would continue to do so, even after she learned he was merely Samuel Liddell. He would honour his promise, even if she despised him.

Even if he so desperately wanted her to stay.

In the ladies' absence, Samuel had spent the evening with Charles, although neither gentleman seemed to have much to offer by way of conversation. For his part, Charles seemed to be in shock over Miss Gordon's near-demise. He was clearly unwilling to discuss exactly what he knew about the extent of his sister's use of laudanum, although in his customarily clumsy way he did make some interesting admissions when referring to it.

'I suppose I ought to write to Mama and inform her of what has happened,' he'd said at one point. 'Although she will not be pleased. She'd put a lot of faith in Buxton's waters as a cure for my sister's many ills.'

'Many ills?' Samuel had repeated.

'I mean the headaches, of course,' Charles had blustered. 'My sister has for a long time been gravely afflicted. It affects her spirits too, as doubtless you have noticed.'

Samuel had nodded, deciding not to press his friend further but finding himself wondering if Miss Gordon, like Hope's mother, had pains beyond headaches which made the lure of oblivion too great to resist.

Once their brandy glasses were empty and their stilted conversation had all but evaporated, both gentlemen had retired. Since then, Samuel had tossed and turned in bed, unable to settle, and unable to quiet his thoughts. Everything he'd tried to push aside during the daylight hours had come racing to the fore, and now he found himself picking through the details relentlessly.

How delicate she'd felt in his arms, how warm her lips had been against his. How enthusiastically she'd kissed him back. How embracing her had felt so right, when in every sense it had been entirely wrong. Hope had sought sanctuary at Hayton, not seduction by its pretend baronet. How he could countenance kissing her when he was lying to her about the man he was… Well, he knew the answer to that. He couldn't. He could not countenance it at all.

Then there was the glimpse of Hope's past, which Miss Gordon's affliction had unexpectedly drawn from her. The thought of her losing her mother like that made his heart ache for her, even while he felt that now familiar protective urge burning within him at her veiled remark about her father and the pain he'd caused. Between her wicked uncle and the father she could not bring herself to discuss, it was clear that Hope had suffered at the hands of the men in her life. A fact which made Samuel's own deception of her even harder to swallow.

He had to tell her the truth, just as he'd begun to, in the library last night. He had to find a way to explain his actions, despite his fear that she would never be able to forgive him. That she would leave Hayton immediately and never look back.

Of course, leaving was exactly what she intended to do now, in any case! He pressed his fist into his pillow in frustration. It was clear that sleep would continue to elude him for some time yet, and his restlessness had left him hot and sweating beneath his sheets. Throwing off his bedcovers, he lit a candle, resolved to go downstairs and fetch some refreshment. Smithson could always be relied upon to keep the decanter of brandy in the library topped up for him; perhaps another small glass might see him on his way to slumber.

Stealthily, Samuel crept out of his room and along the wide, wood-panelled hallway. The house was silent, the servants having long since retired for the night. Just as well, Samuel thought, since he wore nothing but his drawers. For decency's sake he ought to have at least pulled a shirt on, but the cool air of the old house at night felt like a blessed relief against his bare skin.

Swiftly, he made his way into the library, closing the door so carefully that it barely made a sound. It was only once he was inside that he realised the room already had the dim illumination of a candle. Assuming that a maid had neglected to extinguish it before retiring, Samuel marched towards it furiously, muttering to himself about the risk of fire—in an ancient dwelling like Hayton Hall, filled with wood, the place would surely go up in flames in no time at all. It was only when he reached the table upon which it sat that he realised someone was there—someone who had curled up in one of the tall green wingback chairs which faced away from the door. Someone dressed in only a white linen shift and a shawl, with a book draped across her lap while she sat upright but fast asleep.

Hope.

Samuel swallowed hard, struggling to tear his eyes from the sight of her sleeping, her expression serene, her pink lips near-smiling, her dark hair loose and tumbling about her shoulders. Quietly, he stepped back, deciding to simply blow out the candle for safety's sake and leave her to rest. It was the proper and decent thing to do, especially given his own semi-naked state. Last night he'd all but seduced her in this very room; she did not need to spy him standing before her tonight, leaving little to the imagination in his undergarments.

Leaving was his plan, but fate—and Hayton's old floor—had other ideas. As he stepped away again, one of the wooden boards creaked loudly, betraying his presence, and waking Hope.

She jolted upright, blinking, then stared straight at him. 'Samuel?'

Sir Samuel Liddell in nothing but his drawers was a sight to behold. Even in her sleepy, confused state, Hope could not help but let her eyes rake over the details of him—from the broad shoulders and chest, sculpted by muscles usually buried beneath the finery of a gentleman's attire, to the trail of surprisingly dark hair which meandered down the lower part of his flat stomach and disappeared inside the white cotton.

Her fingers seemed to tingle with the urge to reach out and touch him; she fisted them, willing her mind, and her body, to behave. She had never seen a man looking like this before—at least, not a man she found so attractive. Like their kiss last night, this visceral, physical response was also a new experience for her. But that did not mean she should lose her head to the wanton and desirous thoughts currently racing through her mind.

'Samuel,' she repeated, almost choking on his name. Why was her mouth suddenly so dry? 'Is everything all right?'

He folded his arms across his chest in a manner which was endearingly self-conscious. 'You left a candle burning,' he said. 'I was just going to extinguish it, for safety's sake.'

His rebuke was gentle but clear enough.

'Forgive me,' she replied. 'I did not mean to doze off down here. I could not sleep so I decided to read awhile.' She forced a smile, trying to keep her eyes focused on his, and not the other, tempting parts of him, as she held up the book. 'You have a good selection of Mrs Radcliffe's novels. Have you read them?'

She watched as Samuel shook his head, those arms remaining stubbornly folded. 'Alas, no—gothic fiction is not really to my taste.' He continued to hover awkwardly for a moment, glancing down at himself. 'I should go. I only came down to fetch a brandy. I should not...well, should not be standing in front of you looking like this.'

Despite the fact that the way he looked was making her

heart continue to race, Hope found herself laughing. 'I've seen you now, Samuel, so I dare say the damage is done.'

'You may laugh, but what if Charles or Smithson walked in now and saw us together like this?'

Hope considered this for a moment, then carefully took off her shawl and passed it to him. 'Here,' she said. 'For your modesty. Now you can fetch your brandy.'

Samuel draped the shawl over his broad shoulders. In truth, its fine fabric offered little coverage, and Hope could still spy a great swathe of his bare chest and stomach beneath it. He looked ridiculous, and oddly more appealing than ever.

'Would you like one too?' he asked, holding up the decanter.

Hope nodded. Given her current state, a drop of something strong was perhaps not a bad idea. Although whether it was within brandy's capacity to dampen rampant desire, she had no idea.

'Have you finished reading Mr Hume then?' he asked as he poured two small glasses, handing one of them to her as he sat down in a chair opposite.

'No, but I was not in the mood for history tonight. Escaping into some fiction seemed much more appealing.'

'Too much on your mind?' he asked.

'Indeed,' she agreed, not daring to say more about the exact nature of the thoughts which troubled her. Thoughts about him, thoughts about leaving. Thoughts about all the lies she'd told.

Samuel held up his brandy glass. 'Same,' he replied. 'Hence the need for this.' He paused, taking a considered sip. 'Charles said you sat with Miss Gordon for a little while this afternoon. How was she?'

'In low spirits, if I'm honest. It's plain to see that she

fears the loss of her tinctures. I cannot say I blame her. Ceasing to take laudanum after the body has become accustomed to it can make you very unwell. My mother tried to give it up several times, but after days of fever and sickness she would always return to it.'

'Then we must keep a close eye on her, to ensure that does not happen. Tomorrow I will ask Smithson to ensure Maddie and one or two of the other maids take turns to remain with Miss Gordon throughout her recovery.'

Hope smiled. 'That is a good idea. I will assist them too.'

Samuel let out a long breath, clearly contemplating something. 'Charles seemed to suggest that Miss Gordon's headaches are responsible for her low spirits,' he said after a moment. 'However, I am unsure. He seems very evasive about the entire matter, which makes me suspicious that there's more to his sister's current woes than he's telling me. Has Miss Gordon said anything to you that might shed some light on what is going on?'

Hope shook her head.. 'No, but, like you, I think whatever ails her could be due to more than headaches. Between her sombre countenance and cutting remarks, it is not difficult to see that she is deeply unhappy.'

'I suppose it is none of our business,' Samuel mused, before draining his glass. 'I dare say once she's well enough to travel, both Charles and his sister will be on their way. I spent an awkward evening with him earlier—it is abundantly clear this whole sorry episode has left him feeling very uncomfortable. And if I know anything about Charles, it's that his usual response to such feelings is to flee.'

Hope took a gulp of her brandy, steeling herself. 'Perhaps I should go then too,' she said, her heart pounding so hard that the sound of it seemed to echo in her ears. She did her best to ignore it, to remind herself that this was something she had to discuss with him. She had to make plans to leave, no matter how hard, how painful it seemed. 'I am well enough to travel now. Perhaps, if Mr and Miss Gordon would oblige me, I could travel as far as Lancashire with them, and make my own way from there.'

She watched with bated breath as Samuel's brows drew together in concern.

'I promised you that I would escort you to London, Hope.'

'But that was before the Gordons arrived and…' She faltered momentarily, her thoughts scattering as she saw the consternation growing on his handsome face. 'You have done so much for me, Samuel—truly, I am indebted to you. But I do not wish to cause you any more inconvenience, not when there is another possible solution.'

'But once you reach Blackburn, you will still be hundreds of miles from London, and you will be on your own,' he replied, shaking his head. 'Surely that is no solution at all.'

Samuel leaned forward, the shawl slipping from his shoulders and unveiling that magnificent physique once again. Hope swallowed hard, dragging her gaze back up to meet his.

'I do not wish to tell you what to do. Indeed, I am not your father, your brother, or…' He pressed his lips together momentarily. 'Or your husband. Therefore, as you once reminded me, you are not my concern. And yet I am concerned. I'm concerned about you going to London, about this uncle of yours, about you wandering straight back into danger. I'm concerned that there is so much more to your story than I know…'

'Well, that makes two of us,' Hope countered, giving him

a pointed look and trying to ignore how her heart lurched at the thought of how little he did know. How dreadful the truth was. 'Last night you told me that you are not who I believe you to be. What did you mean?'

Even in the dim candlelight his grim expression was unmistakable.

'What I meant was…' He faltered, his blue-grey eyes seeming to darken. For a long moment he pressed his lips together, steeling himself. 'What I meant to tell you was that I have lied to you. Hayton Hall is not my house. Its lands are not my lands. And I am not a baronet.'

In the night-time quiet of the library, Hope heard someone gasp. She presumed it was her own voice she'd heard, but the sound seemed somehow separate, somehow distant, as a maelstrom of sudden spiralling thoughts gripped her. Of all the possible explanations for his words last night, this was the very last one she could have imagined. To learn that he was not Hayton's baronet at all had shocked her and yet, as she sat there, her mouth agape as she regarded him, she realised that was only the beginning of her concerns.

A deathly cold chill crept up her spine as the full ramifications of his deceit flooded through her mind. If he was not a baronet, and if Hayton Hall was not his, then the protection she'd felt and the sanctuary she'd enjoyed was surely no such thing at all. Her father was a ruthless, dangerous man—if Samuel was not the prominent, important gentleman she'd believed him to be, then her father would think nothing of snatching her away from him and, worse still, perhaps even harming Samuel in the process. No matter who Samuel really was, she could not bear the thought that she'd unwittingly endangered him. She shivered, feeling suddenly exposed, as the illusion of her safe hiding place crumbled in the face of Samuel's lies. What if her father was drawing near? What if he'd already found her and was just waiting for the right moment to take her away?

'I am so sorry, Hope,' Samuel continued, clearly grappling with her stunned silence, with the look of horror she doubtless wore upon her face. 'Please understand that I only want to protect you, that I care about you. When I kissed you last night, I…'

'No,' she interrupted him, unable to bear her own thoughts or his words any longer. Unable to countenance hearing that he cared about her when her mere presence in this house might yet lead him into danger. 'That kiss was a mistake—a moment of madness.' She rose from her seat, hurrying now towards the door. 'I must leave Hayton as soon as possible. I must speak to Mr Gordon tomorrow.'

Hope hurried out of the library before Samuel could spy the tears which had begun to gather in her eyes. Tears of shock, tears of terror—tears which acknowledged that the safe haven she'd put so much faith in lay in ruins, and the protection she'd believed Samuel had given her had turned to dust.

Chapter Fifteen

'*A moment of madness.*'

Samuel replayed those words over and over in his mind as he sat at his desk, trying and hopelessly failing to concentrate on working through the pile of papers in front of him. He'd been like this for a couple of days now, attempting to bury himself in the business of running the Liddell estate, to avoid everything and everyone as much as he reasonably could. Mostly, all he'd managed to do, however, was revisit that night-time encounter with Hope again and again, picking over its details while he licked his wounds.

The sight of her sitting in the library, ashen-faced, eyes wide with horror as he confessed the truth seemed to have etched itself indelibly on his brain. He'd expected her to be shocked, angry even, but the fact that she'd appeared so appalled, so offended by the idea that he was neither a landowner nor a baronet, had devastated him. And then there were those words she'd uttered as she'd retreated from him, rejecting his affection for her so emphatically that he felt as though his heart had been trampled on all over again.

That kiss was a mistake—a moment of madness.

All he'd said was that he cared for her, and yet now that

she knew who he truly was she could not even countenance that.

Samuel groaned, burying his head in his hands. How could he have got it so wrong, how could he have so gravely misunderstood a woman's feelings for a second time? In the summer he'd wrongly interpreted Charlotte's flirtatiousness as genuine interest in him, and now he'd allowed himself to imagine that the way Hope had kissed him back might have been an expression of her affection for him. Perhaps it had—but it was an affection which had been easily extinguished as soon as she'd discovered that it held no promise of becoming Lady Liddell.

Of course, she would have known there was no prospect of that if he'd been truthful with her from the beginning. In that respect, Samuel knew he only had himself to blame for her evident disappointment in who and what he really was. He deserved every bit of her dismay, her ire, her swift retreat from his affections. He deserved to feel humiliated.

If only he had explained who he was straight away. If only he hadn't kissed her. If only holding her in his arms like that hadn't felt so perfect. If only he hadn't lost his head in that moment of madness in the library, then he wouldn't be on the cusp of losing his heart now too. Because he was, wasn't he? That was why Hope's rejection of him hurt so much.

And now she was going to leave him. She was going to step into Charles Gordon's carriage and never look back. It was the prospect of that, Samuel realised, which hurt most of all.

Despite being preoccupied by his sister's woes, Charles had not failed to notice that something was amiss between Samuel and Hope.

'Trouble in paradise, Sammy?' he'd asked after knocking on the library door yesterday and trying to coax Samuel out for some tea.

Miserably, Samuel had informed his friend that Hope now knew that he was not Hayton's baronet, and that she had not taken the news well. He had not been able to bring himself to talk about that kiss, or the way she'd rejected him—the wound that had inflicted was still too raw to be confided to anyone. But he had told Charles that Hope now intended to leave, and that she wished to enlist his help to do so—if she hadn't already.

'She'd talked of leaving before now, and no doubt learning the truth about me has made her more desperate to do so,' he'd finished with a heavy sigh. 'I've made a terrible mess of this, Charles. I have only myself to blame.'

His friend had sat down at the other side of his desk, an uncharacteristically serious expression on his face. 'Miss Swynford hasn't said anything to me about leaving,' he replied. 'Perhaps she's had a change of heart?'

'Somehow, I doubt that.'

'Well, even if she hasn't, do you not think you should talk to her about it, rather than skulking around in here? I'm not blind, Sammy. I've seen the way you look at her. You cannot possibly want her to leave. Why don't you just tell her how you feel?'

Samuel had winced at the thought of it. He'd tried to speak to her about his feelings once, he'd told her that he cared for her, and look where that had got him.

'So, I am correct then?' Charles had continued, taking his friend's silence as acquiescence. 'You are smitten with the chit?'

'I care very much about her,' Samuel had begun, his

voice sounding odd and strangled, even to himself. 'I want to protect her. I want to help…'

'Then I would suggest that you talk to her,' Charles had concluded as he rose from his seat. 'You've told her the truth about yourself, Sammy, but perhaps it's time for a bit more honesty. All cards on the table, so to speak.'

Charles's words rattled around Samuel's head as he tried once again to apply himself to his work. In the end he pushed his papers aside, frustrated. Samuel was more accustomed to being on the receiving end of Charles's teasing than he was to being the recipient of his advice. But for all that he was boisterous and more than a little ungovernable at times, his friend's heart was usually in the right place. Perhaps, Samuel considered, his advice was worth heeding. Perhaps he should try to talk to Hope, to explain himself properly. Certainly, it would be better than sitting at his desk feeling sorry for himself.

Surely it couldn't do any more harm. Could it?

Resolved to act rather than dwell any further on it, Samuel leapt out of his seat and hurried out of the room in search of Hope. He strode along the hallway, contemplating where she might be. Often she spent the afternoons sitting with Miss Gordon; if that were the case, he could hardly go bursting in. Perhaps he ought to find Maddie first, and request that she ask Hope to join him in the small parlour…

The sound of soft laughter coming from that very room reached his ears just as he placed his first footstep upon the stairs. Followed by two voices—a woman's and a man's—deep in conversation. Furrowing his brow, Samuel drew closer to the door, then turned the doorknob and walked in.

Hope's wide-eyed expression was what struck him first, as though his sudden intrusion had alarmed her. He watched as her lips parted in surprise, her teacup suspended in mid-air. Across from her sat Charles, that usual broad smile of his illuminating his face as he rose from the comfort of the sofa.

'Ah! Finally dragged yourself away from all that work, have you, Sammy?' Charles greeted him. 'Come and join us for some tea.'

Despite his friend's beckoning, Samuel found that he could not move. Instead, he seemed frozen to the spot, his gaze flitting between the pair of them, taking in the cosy scene. The teapot on the table, the small plate of neatly arranged slices of cake at its side. The way their conversation, and Hope's laughter, had ceased the moment he'd walked in…

'Sammy?' Charles prompted, frowning now.

But still Samuel could not answer. He could only look at the scene before him and think how it reminded him of the events of the summer, when another woman had decided he was not good enough for her and had sought out his older, titled brother instead. Charles might not be titled, but he was the heir to a tradesman's fortune—a better and wealthier prospect, to be sure. As he met Hope's eyes once more, holding her astonished gaze, his blood heated with an intolerable jealousy as it dawned on him that she knew this. That, having learned the truth of who Samuel was, she'd found him lacking and had set her sights far higher.

Just like Charlotte had.

'I think that I will go and get some air.'

Hope watched, aghast, as Mr Gordon made his excuses and hurried out of the parlour. Little wonder, she thought. The tension in the room was so thick that she doubted a knife could cut through it. Near to the door stood Samuel, his expression severe, his usually merry blue-grey eyes uncharacteristically stormy. Something was amiss, but she was at a loss to understand exactly what.

Since that last meeting with Samuel in the library late at night, and since learning who he really was, she'd managed largely to avoid him. She'd spent her time grappling with the turmoil his deception had caused, placing it with that gnawing guilt of knowing that she continued to deceive him. She could not possibly have done anything to offend him. Indeed, if anyone ought to be angry right now, it was her, wasn't it?

'Well, are you going to sit down and join me?' she asked, gesturing towards the chair which Charles had recently vacated.

'I wasn't aware you and Charles took tea together in the afternoons,' he said, ignoring her question.

She frowned. 'We don't usually. However, I wanted to speak to him about travelling with him and Miss Gordon to Blackburn. I believe I told you I would do so, the last time we spoke properly.'

He seemed to bristle at her reference to that ill-fated conversation. 'I see,' he replied, giving her a brittle nod. 'And what did Charles say?'

'He assured me that once they'd made firm plans for their departure, I would be included in them,' she replied.

In truth, Mr Gordon had been a good deal more noncommittal than that, professing a lack of certainty over when his sister would be fit to travel. Certainly, he would not wish to name a date, or so he'd told her. Indeed, he'd confided to her that he'd made the grave mistake of mentioning their return to Shawdale to Miss Gordon and she'd reacted terribly. He would have to tread carefully from now on, he'd said, which meant that Hope would simply have to wait. He'd changed the subject then, trying his best to amuse her, to occupy her with lighter topics of conversation. In response she'd smiled and feigned laughter in all the right places, whilst quietly wondering what on earth she was going to do. The longer she remained at Hayton Hall, the longer she risked bringing danger to its door. Not that she even knew who that door, and this house, actually belonged to…

'You both certainly looked very at ease in each other's company,' Samuel observed, snapping her out of her thoughts. 'Given that you were merely discussing travel plans.'

Hope felt the heat of indignation rise in her chest at his insinuation. 'What are you suggesting, Samuel?' she asked, getting to her feet and marching towards him as she challenged him to spell it out.

'I'm suggesting that the two of you seem to be getting along very well. Perhaps that is why you are so keen to travel to Blackburn with him and his sister…'

'Oh, for heaven's sake!' Hope threw up her hands in despair. She stood merely a foot away from him now, her hands planted on her hips as she glared up at him. 'That is completely ridiculous. I've no romantic interest in your friend, Samuel. None whatsoever! I must leave Hayton because my injuries have healed and it is time to do so.'

And because he'd lied to her, she reminded herself quietly. Because she could no longer trust that he was able to protect her, or indeed himself, from the malevolent men who sought her. And because she continued to lie to him too.

Samuel stared at her, unmoved. 'Charles has much to recommend him,' he began again. 'He is extraordinarily wealthy, for a start, although he has no title, which I dare say is the paramount consideration…'

'Not to me!' Hope prodded an angry finger against his chest. Why was he being so insufferable? Where on earth had all this talk of her and Mr Gordon come from?

Touching him, it transpired, was to be her downfall. Almost as soon as she had tapped that finger against the fine fabric of his shirt, her hand seemed to develop a will of its own, her fingers splaying out across his chest, the gesture dissolving from one of fury into one of tenderness. She felt her breath catch in her throat as beneath her hand she sensed his heart beating faster. She looked up at him, her eyes locking with his as he raised his hand, capturing her chin beneath his delicate touch as their lips drew closer.

The kiss which followed was as explosive as it was brief. Hope wasn't sure who deepened it first, such was the speed with which instinct and desire overcame them both. She pressed herself against him, her hands roaming and revelling in the promise of that masculine, athletic physique, hinted at beneath his fine clothes. For his part, Samuel seemed to have absolutely lost control too, his lips firm and hungry against hers, his hands similarly seeking out the curve of her breasts, her waist, her bottom. Then, somewhere within the recesses of her mind, a voice emerged, the one reminding her of his deceit, and of her own. Of the danger of falling for a man she could not have, a man who would be utterly horrified to know who and what she really was. A man she had to leave behind.

'Enough,' she breathed, stepping away from him, breaking the spell.

She hurried out of the parlour, reeling at what had just occurred. One moment they'd been arguing, the next they'd been kissing—how had that happened? How could she lurch from being in the grip of guilt and anger one moment to melting into his arms the next? She made her way up the stairs as quickly as she could, frantically straightening her hair and her gown as she determined to put a safe distance between her and Samuel.

Perhaps she would go and sit with Miss Gordon for a while. She'd passed many an hour at her bedside of late, relieving either Maddie or one of the other maids of their duties for a while, and finding a sort of refuge in the woman's prolonged silences as she either slept or stared vacantly towards the window. Occasionally, Miss Gordon would reach over and tentatively pat her hand, or offer her an appreciative nod of acknowledgement. It was plain to see that the lady's low spirits persisted, although she had said nothing to Hope about the reasons for her continued malaise. For all her suspicions that at the root of the lady's ills lay something more than headaches, Hope had not attempted to press the matter. After all, she knew as well as anyone what it was like to have things about herself that she was unwilling or unable to discuss. She had a veritable list of them, growing day by day.

Topping that list was her hopeless attraction to a man who had lied to her about who he was. A man who'd just as good as accused her of pursuing his friend! A man who did not even know her real name.

Hope drew a deep breath, composing herself as she reached Miss Gordon's door and knocked gently. It would do no good to torture herself with such thoughts yet again.

'Maddie?' Hope called softly through the door, frowning that as yet the maid had not come to answer her knock. Usually, Maddie took her turn to care for Miss Gordon in the afternoon, and was always a committed presence at the lady's bedside, just as she had been while Hope had convalesced.

Hope listened for several moments, surprised that she could hear no sound coming from within. Maddie must have been called away, but what of Miss Gordon—was she sleeping? Or had she taken ill once more? Hope's mind returned to her conversation with Mr Gordon, to his words about his sister's reaction to the prospect of returning home. What if she'd had one of her little bottles hidden away and had sought oblivion from it the moment her brother's back was turned?

Gripped by a wave of panic, Hope pushed open Miss Gordon's door and rushed inside. Her eyes darted frantically about, her heart thudding ever harder as she spied the room's damning details one by one: the empty, unmade bed; the pile of clothes abandoned on the floor; the large chest, all of its drawers wide open, as though someone had been looking for something in a hurry.

Hope heard herself gasp.

As though someone had left in a hurry.

But how? When? And where had she gone?

Hope rushed out of the door, her recently healed ankle throbbing in protest as she began to run along the landing and back towards the stairs. 'Samuel! Mr Gordon!' she cried as loud as she could. 'I need your help. I think Miss Gordon is missing!'

Chapter Sixteen

Samuel stared out of the window of his carriage, watching as the wind swirled the fallen leaves into a frenzy of red, yellow and brown at the side of the road. At least the rain had ceased for now, making the search for Miss Gordon easier. A short interview with a very tearful Maddie had established that the maid had left her charge to attend to some clothing upon which Miss Gordon had spilled her soup, giving the lady ample time to make her escape.

'I am so sorry, sir,' the maid had wept. 'I should have returned right away, but Miss Gordon was very concerned about the stain. She said it was her favourite shawl and that it was so fine, no lye could be used upon it. She insisted that I supervise the laundry maid myself while she cleaned it.'

Samuel had tried to comfort poor Maddie, reassuring her that she was only doing what the lady had asked. It was clear that the prolonged dismissal of Maddie by Miss Gordon had been deliberate, to allow her to get away unseen. It was clear too that she had not been missing for very long, and therefore could not have gone very far. Samuel had proposed searching for her in Hayton village, since it was only a short distance away and if she'd followed the road she'd have likely ended up there. Since the quickest way to search was on horseback, he'd informed Charles that he would ask his groom to ready two of his fastest beasts.

Charles, however, had hesitated, his gaze shifting back and forth between Samuel and Hope. 'I think we need Miss Swynford to come with us,' he'd said. 'My sister seems to like you, Miss Swynford. If—when—we find her, we stand a better chance of her returning with us if Miss Swynford is there to speak with her. And besides, we must take a carriage in any case. We can hardly throw dear Henrietta across the back of one of our horses, can we?'

Samuel had been forced to concede that his friend's logic was sound. For her part, Hope had insisted that she wished to help rather than sit in the parlour waiting for news, and the determined expression on her face was such that Samuel had not dared contradict her. And so, with reluctance and a few cautionary words about Hope remaining inside the carriage and out of sight, Samuel had agreed. An agreement which had left him in exactly the position he found himself now, sitting across from Hope in his carriage as it rumbled along the road towards Lowhaven. Charles had also insisted that he should ride ahead, leaving Samuel and Hope to follow together. For all his evident concern about his sister's welfare, Samuel could not help but wonder if his friend had contrived to throw them both into close confines.

They'd gone to Hayton first, and in the sleepy village where not much went unnoticed they'd quickly learned that a young lady matching Miss Gordon's description had pleaded her way on to the back of a local harness-maker's cart bound for Lowhaven docks. Samuel had made the enquiries while Hope had remained quietly in the carriage.

Indeed, since leaving Hayton Hall she had not uttered a word, apparently preferring to gaze silently out of the window or at the floor—at anything apart from him. Not that he could blame her, he thought glumly. Given his behaviour of late—deceiving her, reacting jealously to the sight of her sitting with Charles, not to mention losing his head and kissing her again—he wouldn't want to speak to him either.

He knew he ought to say something, to offer a proper explanation for what he'd said and done, for why he'd lied to her. Yet now, sitting in her presence, he found himself struggling to formulate the words. His feelings, he realised, were like those swirling leaves outside the carriage window—utterly all over the place, and completely at the mercy of a stronger, higher force. He clasped his hands tightly together, as though praying for some divine intervention, some guidance out of the mess he'd created. Some way to assuage the myriad of feelings which continued to assail him—the hopeless attraction to Hope, the burning desire to protect her. The sorrow and guilt which his deception of her had provoked. The humiliation and hurt of knowing that the real Samuel was once again not good enough for a woman he'd begun to care for.

As the rugged countryside finally fell away and the humble cottages on the periphery of Lowhaven beckoned, his unspoken turmoil finally bubbled over.

'I am so sorry, Hope,' he began. 'I know this is a terrible time to talk about this, while Miss Gordon is missing, but I have to say something. I...'

His words faltered as she looked at him squarely, those emerald eyes steely and challenging. 'Which part are you sorry for, Samuel?' she asked him. 'The part where you let me believe you were a baronet, that I was living in your home, or the part where you accused me of dallying with your friend?'

He flinched at her caustic tone. 'I didn't say you were dallying with Charles. I…' He shook his head at himself as another wave of shame gripped him. Shame at allowing jealousy to get the better of him. Shame at how he'd allowed his wounded pride to rule him so often of late.

That stern stare of hers was unrelenting. 'But you did suggest that, how did you put it, we were getting along very well, and that Mr Gordon's extraordinary wealth might be of paramount interest to me.'

Samuel grimaced to hear his words repeated back to him. To hear how cold, how mercenary they sounded. To realise just how much he'd let his hurt and humiliation poison his thoughts.

'You were right—I was being ridiculous, suggesting that you and Charles had formed an attachment.' He drew a deep breath, trying to order his thoughts, to swallow his damnable pride. 'In truth, Hope, I am sorry for all of it. For everything. For what I said about you and Charles. For leading you to think that Hayton Hall, its lands and the title that goes with it, was all mine. It was wrong of me. Indeed, it was unforgivable.'

'How on earth did you manage to pretend to have a grand house and a title?'

Hope continued to hold his sorrowful gaze as she finally gave voice to a question which had been swirling around her mind. Once she'd managed to quell her initial panic at learning she was likely not as safe as she'd thought, questions about the practicalities of Samuel's deception had plagued her. It was unfathomable—all these weeks at Hayton Hall, cared for by the man she believed to be its master. Convalescing in one of his rooms, being attended to by his servants, dining with him, enjoying tea with him in his parlour. How could none of that have been real? How on earth did someone pretend to have a grand house, to have a title? How could they have guests and servants in that house who all believed that to be the truth?

'Who are you, Samuel?' she continued, her questions flowing freely now. 'What are you—are you Hayton's tenant?'

'Not quite.' His tone was unmistakably grim as he stared down towards his boots. 'Hayton Hall is my home—at least, it is my family home and it is where I have lived since returning from my travels on the Continent. However, I am my father's second son. My elder brother, Sir Isaac Liddell, is the master of Hayton Hall and its estate. He married recently—eloped, in fact—and is travelling in Scotland with his new bride. I am caring for the estate in his absence.'

Hope frowned, her thoughts still racing. 'But the servants all call you Sir Samuel…'

'They do—because I instructed them to.' He paused, grimacing. 'As you once reminded me when you rebuked me for calling my maid Madeleine, masters and servants are not equals. Please do not blame them for deceiving you; they had no choice in the matter.'

'And Mr and Miss Gordon—what do they know of this? Have you been deceiving them too?' This question had circled her mind earlier, while she'd enjoyed tea with Mr Gordon. She'd wondered what he knew, if he was being deceived too. If she ought to say something…

Samuel's expression grew increasingly pained. 'No—Charles and his sister know exactly who and what I am. When they arrived unexpectedly at Hayton Hall, I begged them to play along with the lie. They agreed, although it's clear Charles thinks I'm an utter blockhead and of course he's absolutely right.' He looked up then, his grey-blue eyes sorrowful and heavy with regret. 'Please do not blame them either. I am so sorry, Hope. The fault for this deceit is entirely mine.'

For several moments, Hope simply stared at him, stunned by the extent of his deceit, a thousand thoughts whirling around her mind. Samuel had lied to her about who he was, and he'd involved everyone else in his deception too. The thought of Smithson, Maddie, and the Gordons all being privy to the lie made her feel foolish, gullible even. But then, how could she possibly have known any different? She—the real Hope—knew nothing of gentlemen, titles and grand estates.

That was another thing, she reminded herself yet again. Samuel was not the only one of them who was lying about who he was. Like him, she was not what she had appeared to be. Hope searched Samuel's handsome face, her mind racing with memories of their weeks together. Memories of cosy afternoons in the parlour, of candlelit dinners, of their meeting of minds over Shakespeare's plays. Memories of his embrace, of his kisses. Throughout all of this time, had they come to know each other at all? Or were they each only familiar with the role that the other was playing?

And if she did not know the real him, then who had she been in danger of losing her heart to?

'Why?' she said quietly. 'Why did you lie to me?'

She watched as Samuel dragged his hands down his face. 'Please believe me when I say that I did not intend to lie to you,' he began. 'The day after I found you in the woods, when we spoke properly for the first time, it was clear you'd assumed I was the baronet, that the estate was mine and…

and I could not find the words to correct you. The way you looked at me, like I was someone important…' He paused, shaking his head at himself. 'To my eternal discredit, my foolish pride got the better of me. I vowed I would tell you the truth, but then you told me how safe and protected you felt with me, how fortunate you'd been to find yourself in the home of a baronet. I couldn't bear to take away that feeling from you, to allow you to feel anything less than completely safe. I know it was wrong, but I decided then that I would keep up the pretence.'

'So why tell me at all?' she asked. 'Why did you decide to tell me the truth, that night in the library?'

She watched as he appeared to wrestle with her question. 'As I said that night, I care about you and, besides, after I kissed you, I knew I had to say something.'

Hope felt her cheeks colour at the memory of that first kiss. That was one thing he had not apologised for, she noted. Not that she was sorry for it either. Nor could she find it within herself to regret the way their passions had spilled over in the parlour earlier…

Her thoughts were interrupted by the sharp sound of the carriage door clicking open. Cold air raced in, laced with a spicy sweetness as the scents of rum, cocoa and coffee all mingled. Hope jolted. Until that moment, she had not even realised that they'd stopped. Had not even noticed the bustle and noise of Lowhaven's docks as they sat in the midst of them. She looked up to see Mr Gordon peering in at them.

'If we're going to find Henrietta, we'd best make haste,' Mr Gordon said, his gaze flitting between them both.

Samuel nodded. Hope saw how he swallowed hard, as though collecting himself, before he turned back to address her. 'Will you be all right here?' he asked.

'Of course,' she replied in the most reassuring voice she could muster. 'Please, just find Miss Gordon and bring her to the carriage. Tell her not to worry, that I am waiting here for her.'

Briefly, Samuel seemed to hesitate, as though there was something else he wished to say. If there was, then he decided to keep his own counsel, instead offering her a brisk nod before disembarking. Involuntarily, Hope shuddered as the carriage door slammed shut behind him, feeling a final blast of that cool, pungent air before she was cut off from the outside world once more. She fiddled with the large bonnet she wore to shield her face, before peering tentatively out of the window. From this vantage point she could see Samuel and Mr Gordon begin their enquiries, doubtless describing Miss Gordon to dockworkers and passers-by in the hope that someone might have seen her.

Hope sighed heavily, collapsing back in her seat. She wished that she could be out searching too, rather than stuck inside with only her spiralling thoughts for company. However, that was utterly out of the question. Lowhaven docks might as well be a lion's den. As a centre of trade, they crawled with associates of her father—people who might recognise her even disguised in a fine dress and wide-brimmed bonnet. As she'd learned to her great cost that night at Lowhaven's theatre, her years of absence had not left her quite so unrecognisable as she'd hoped. As much as she wanted to help, she could not run the risk. So instead she sat there, feeling useless, as she stewed over Samuel's lie and his explanation. An explanation which she had still to fully digest.

An explanation which left her with absolutely no idea how she should feel.

On the one hand, she still felt the joint sting of betrayal and anger as potently as ever, and on the other hand, she was acutely aware of the irony of feeling upset at all. Samuel had lied about who he was, but so had she, albeit it for very different reasons. Hope had deceived Samuel to protect herself—in a weakened state, riddled with injuries, and in the home of an unknown gentleman, she had done what was necessary to conceal an identity which, for all she knew, would have meant her being handed straight back to her father.

Samuel had lied to her to…what, exactly? Impress her? Or at least to impress the woman he thought she was—wealthy and well-bred. The thought of that made her groan aloud. How mortified he would be if he knew that he'd dragged his servants and his friends into a complex web of deceit to impress a mere actress and outlaw's daughter.

What a terrible mess.

Then there was his confession that he'd kept up the pretence to make her feel safe. Her heart had ached when he'd spoken of how he couldn't bear the thought of her feeling unprotected. After all, it was undeniable, wasn't it? She had believed in the sanctuary that a titled man and his grand home could offer her. Yet no matter how good and pure his intentions had been, his actions had ultimately fallen far short of being honourable and that was enough to make her question her judgement of him.

Weeks ago, she'd put her faith in a gentleman who'd been unfailingly kind and gentle, who'd seemed so decent and honest. It was Samuel's good nature, and her growing closeness to him, which had made her own deception harder to maintain, which had tempted her to share the truth of her situation with him. Now she wondered if she'd been wrong in her assessment of him. If he could lie to her so effortlessly, perhaps he would cast her out just as easily if he knew who she really was. If he knew she was no genteel heiress at all.

Hope huffed a breath, looking out of the window once more. Both Samuel and Mr Gordon had slipped out of sight now. In vain, Hope searched for them, her eyes skimming frantically over a busy scene of cargo, men and masts. Then, amongst the chaos of the quayside, a figure caught Hope's eye. A tall woman wearing a deep red cape, the hood pulled up to conceal her face. She seemed agitated, darting around and approaching men at random, seemingly asking them something, because each in turn shook his head at her. Miss Gordon—it had to be.

Hope searched again, trying to see either Samuel or Mr Gordon, but neither gentleman appeared to be near. Desperation burned in her gut and her heart raced. Leaving the carriage was an enormous risk, but so was leaving a vulnerable woman wandering alone around a port.

She had to act now.

With a deep breath, Hope pushed open the door of the carriage, hurrying towards the red-caped woman and praying that she was indeed Henrietta Gordon. Praying too that no one on that quayside would recognise the face of Hope Sloane beneath all her borrowed finery, because if they did she would be in serious trouble.

Chapter Seventeen

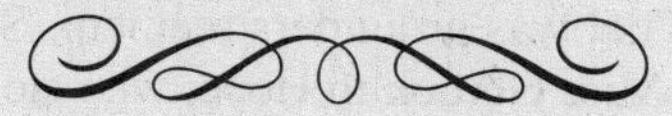

The scream Miss Gordon let out was like nothing Samuel had ever heard in his life. Even above the din of the port it rang out, a high-pitched yet feral, guttural sound. Part-banshee, part-bear. Across the quayside he saw her, a spectre of chaos in her dishevelled red cape, her arms flapping wildly, her hood falling down to reveal a veritable bird's nest of dark hair. Yet it was neither the sight of her nor the sound she made which horrified him the most. It was the smaller woman standing in front of her, clad in cream, her wide-brimmed bonnet insufficient to shield her face from all the attention which Miss Gordon's scene was drawing. Hope.

Samuel dashed towards her, his heart racing and his hackles slowly rising. What on earth was she thinking, leaving the carriage? After all these weeks in hiding, why would she put herself in such danger?

As he drew nearer, he saw Charles had joined them now, his gestures suggesting he was trying, and failing, to calm his sister down. If anything, the sight of her brother seemed to make Miss Gordon more hysterical. Samuel ran faster, his agitation growing at the woman's relentless cries. They needed to get her away from here. And, more to the point, he needed to get Hope back in that carriage and back to the safety of Hayton Hall.

'Oh, Sammy, thank goodness!' Charles called out as, finally, Samuel reached them. 'Is there a physician nearby? I think we're going to have to call upon the man and ask him to attend. Henrietta is unwell.'

Unwell? That was an understatement. Samuel's gaze shifted from Miss Gordon to Hope, who stood in front of her, speaking softly and calmly, trying her best to reassure her. It seemed to work as slowly the woman's wailing abated, replaced by quieter sobs. Around them he could sense the onlookers circling, their collective breath bated as they watched the scene unfold.

'We need to get you away from here, Hope,' Samuel said, not answering Charles. His thoughts were consumed now with only this—making sure Hope remained safe. 'Now.'

Hope glanced up at him, her green eyes challenging, her jaw set hard. 'I must help Miss Gordon,' she insisted. 'Besides, I dare say the damage has already been done.'

In breach of his usual calm temperament, Samuel felt his temper flare. How could she be so flippant about the threat she still faced? How could she be so obstinate when she was in such clear danger? For several moments he stared at her, her choice of words stinging him as though he'd been struck across his cheek. Words which could easily refer to more than her recognition, her discovery out here. The damage had indeed been done—by him, weeks ago, when he'd lied to her about who he was.

'Please, Hope,' he replied, swallowing down the fire which had risen in his throat. 'Please, go back to the carriage.'

'Not without Miss Gordon,' she replied, her voice quiet

but firm. 'I am not yours to command, Samuel. I am not your sister, or your wife.'

Samuel blinked at her, those words ringing in his ears and whirling around his mind.

'I am not...your wife.'

But what if she was—at least for now, in this moment? Would a new name and a husband be sufficient to throw any malevolent onlookers off the scent? Or, if she was recognised, would the news that she'd wed protect her, if it reached the ears of those who sought her?

No, he told himself, he could not countenance pretending that Hope was his wife, not under any circumstances. He'd quite finished with the business of telling lies, even for good and noble reasons. Even if he rather liked the idea of hearing the words *Mrs Liddell* fall from his lips...

Before he could say anything further, however, Hope turned away from him and back to Charles's sister, who stood trembling and sobbing quietly at her side. 'Come now, Miss Gordon,' she said softly as she took the lady tentatively by the arm. 'Let us return home. A little tea and cake, that's what you need. Then you will feel much better.'

It was hard to discern whether Hope's gentle words had the desired effect on Miss Gordon or whether she'd simply exhausted herself but, either way, Charles's sister submitted to Hope's coaxing without complaint. The audience which had gathered began to fall away as the four of them walked back towards the carriage, apparently losing interest now that it was clear that the scene Miss Gordon had made was over.

Inwardly, Samuel breathed a sigh of relief. Perhaps all would be well, after all. Perhaps no one there had known Hope for who she really was; perhaps word of her presence in the docks today would not reach her uncle's ears. Perhaps no damage had been done.

Except the damage he'd caused by lying to Hope, he thought glumly. He was not sure if that could ever be repaired.

Charles strode up beside Samuel, emitting a heavy sigh. 'Thank goodness that is over. I suppose I should be grateful that Henrietta's hysterics were witnessed here and not in Blackburn. The damage to her reputation there would have been irrevocable. At least here, no one is likely to know us.'

Samuel gave his friend a stern look. 'Frankly, Charles, I am more concerned about someone here recognising Hope, and about the danger that would place her in,' he replied, his voice hushed.

'Ah—of course. Indeed, Henrietta and I owe Miss Swynford an enormous debt for intercepting her like that, despite the risk to herself.' Charles gave Samuel a pointed look. 'Miss Swynford did not look delighted by your efforts to steer her away from danger, however,' he whispered. 'It's clear she's still angry with you. I presume you did not heed my advice about laying all your cards on the table.'

Samuel grimaced, watching Hope as she clambered into the carriage beside Miss Gordon a short distance away. This was a conversation he was not prepared to have—especially when Charles was partly correct. In the carriage, he'd begun to explain himself, but he'd not laid his cards on the table; he'd thrown them up in the air, leaving them to land wherever they might and leaving Hope to make of them what she would. And, of course, he kept one card hidden away—the one which told of the events of the summer, of his pain and humiliation. Of the hope he'd begun to harbour that, no matter who he really was, Hope might care for him too.

'As you said, Charles, you owe Hope a considerable debt for her actions today. I think you can begin by explaining exactly what is amiss with your sister, the moment we return to Hayton.'

'Ah...yes, of course,' Charles replied, looking suitably chastened.

Samuel strode towards his carriage, his heart sinking when he climbed in and saw how steadfastly Hope avoided his eye as she sat beside Miss Gordon. After all that had happened today, Samuel was not sure what tortured him more—the irrevocable damage that his lies had caused between Hope and him, or the uncomfortable, unexpected knowledge that he'd rather liked the idea he'd fleetingly entertained, of calling her his wife.

Throughout the journey home, it was this latter thought which his mind kept returning to. Along with another thought—that even if by some miracle a woman like her would have ever considered him, his deceit now meant that she would never trust him again, never mind consider marrying him.

Hope sat quietly opposite Samuel, sipping her tea and wishing she was a million miles away as they waited for Mr Gordon to join them. Samuel had asked her to come to the parlour almost the moment they'd arrived back at Hayton and put the ashen-faced Miss Gordon safely into Maddie's care.

'Charles is going to explain everything,' he'd said, leaning close and speaking in a hushed voice. 'After what you did for his sister today, he owes that explanation to you most of all.'

Hope had nodded obligingly, a flustered heat growing in her cheeks at her awareness of his proximity. 'Of course,' she'd replied, unable to bring herself to meet his eye.

In truth, she'd wanted to slip away into her room, to put some distance between herself and everything that had happened today. Between herself and Samuel, and that maelstrom of emotions she felt whenever she so much as glanced at him. Her confusion, her upset, and her anger. Her niggling worry that she should not trust him, even as she wished with every fibre of her being that she could. Nonetheless, she was still curious to hear what Mr Gordon had to say about his sister's behaviour. It was, it seemed, a day for honesty—from everyone else, at least.

What a strange day it had been. A strange and dangerous day. As Mr Gordon hurried in, looking flustered, Hope tried not to dwell on just how risky her actions at the docks had been. Neither did she allow herself to consider the sheer horror on Samuel's face at the sight of her standing with Miss Gordon in the midst of the gathering crowd. How tinged with fear his words had been as he'd pleaded with her to return to the carriage. How he'd once again sought to honour that solemn promise he'd made to her weeks ago, to keep her safe.

Samuel rose from his seat, interrupting her thoughts. 'Well, Charles?' he prompted. 'How is Miss Gordon?'

Mr Gordon gave a curt nod. 'She is resting.' His gaze flitted between Hope and Samuel, his agitation evident. 'I hope that you appreciate that what I am about to tell you must be treated with the utmost discretion...'

'Of course,' Samuel replied. 'I am not one to meddle in

the affairs of others, Charles. But this is my family's home and until my brother returns I am its master. I have a duty to know what goes on under Hayton's roof but, more importantly, as your friend I am concerned. Your sister's behaviour today was as alarming as it was reckless. It cannot be left unexplained.'

Mr Gordon gave his friend a pained look. 'I know,' he said in a tight, strangled voice. 'God, Sammy, if only you knew…' He paused, pressing his lips together in a clear effort to collect himself.

'Take your time, Mr Gordon,' Hope interjected, leaning forward and gesturing for him to sit. It was hard to see this usually jovial giant of a man so evidently perturbed. 'Did Miss Gordon go to the port today to try to procure more laudanum? I did see her talking to some of the men around the docks.'

Mr Gordon let out a bitter laugh as he slumped down in a chair. 'Worse than that, I'm afraid, Miss Swynford. It turns out that she was trying to buy herself passage on a ship.'

'A ship?' Samuel repeated. 'What ship? Going where?'

'Any ship, going anywhere,' Mr Gordon replied. 'Ireland, the Isle of Man, the Caribbean—it appears my sister cares not. Such is the strength of her desire not to return to Shawdale that she is willing to go anywhere in the world on any vessel which will take her.'

Hope's mouth fell open. The sea was a dangerous, often lawless place; she knew from bitter experience just what sort of rapscallions sailed its rough tides. A woman like Miss Gordon would have no idea if she was throwing herself upon the mercy of legitimate merchants or a crew engaged in far more nefarious activities. As desperate as Hope had been to escape her father's clutches—not once but twice now—she'd never even contemplated going to sea. Whatever had led Miss Gordon in that dark and potentially deadly direction must have been grave indeed.

'What happened to your sister, sir?' she asked.

Mr Gordon drew a deep, shuddering breath. 'She fell in love, Miss Swynford. A love which my parents forbade. That love is at the root of all that ails her.'

Hope listened as Mr Gordon finally told his sister's sorry tale. Several years earlier, he explained, his sister had become involved with a worker in one of their father's calico printworks. The young man had been about her age, and was known to be decent and hardworking. Miss Gordon, it seemed, had fallen head over heels in love with him, and by all accounts those feelings were reciprocated as the young man had proposed marriage. The pair had planned to run away and elope. However, before they could do so, word of their relationship and their plans reached Miss Gordon's father's ears. Mr Gordon senior had reacted furiously, effectively locking Miss Gordon away in Shawdale and dismissing the young man from his employment. Unable to find work because of the scandal, the young man had been forced to leave Blackburn, and Miss Gordon's heart had been broken. She'd not been the same since.

'I left for the Continent not long after the scandal broke. I hoped by the time I returned that Henrietta would have recovered from it. Unfortunately, she was worse than ever,' Mr Gordon concluded. 'She complained constantly of headaches, chest pains, stomach pains—pains of every sort. She was given laudanum by our physician but, as you know, that has only made matters worse. I've tried everything to help her, getting her away from Shawdale as much as I can. That was why I took her to Buxton to take the waters, and why I jumped at your invitation to come here. But I fear now that she is lost—if no longer to her tinctures, then to her despair.'

'Oh, dear, Charles,' Samuel said. 'You never breathed a word of any of this during our travels.'

'I confess, I was content to be far from my family's woes,' he replied glumly. 'I proved very capable of putting it all out of my mind.'

Hope, meanwhile, found herself overcome with sympathy for the lady who lay in bed upstairs. Little wonder that she was so prickly, so sombre, so prone to drowning her sorrows in the bottom of a laudanum bottle.

'Poor Miss Gordon,' she interjected, shaking her head sadly. 'To have been denied love like that… Really, could they not just have been allowed to marry?'

'What?' Mr Gordon just about leapt out of his seat. 'I am sorry for Henrietta's pain, Miss Swynford, but are you honestly proposing that my father should have consented to the match? With one of his workers?'

Hope felt her hackles begin to rise. 'I am proposing that Miss Gordon should have been permitted happiness, sir,' she replied, standing too. 'I am proposing that she should have been allowed to make her own choice.'

'Are you really?' he scoffed. 'Well, I suppose that having an uncle who tries to sell you off to anyone willing to split the proceeds would affect your judgement on these matters.'

'Come now, Charles,' Samuel intervened, getting to his feet now and standing close beside her. 'That isn't fair on Hope…'

'I'm merely pointing out that your mysterious heiress here might be as embittered by her experiences as my sister is. Not that any of us know much about what those experiences were. Indeed, Miss Swynford, it is odd that you have so much to say about my sister's story, and so little to say about your own.'

Hope's heart sank like a stone at Mr Gordon's pointed observation. The truth, as ever, bubbled not far from the surface.

'You are right,' she said, changing tack. 'I have said too much. It is not fair to discuss this when your sister is not present to talk about it herself. Indeed, with hindsight, I should have liked to have heard her story in her own words rather than yours, sir.'

Mr Gordon's nostrils flared. 'I suppose you think her wicked family has deprived her of those too,' he replied. 'Just as you clearly think we deprived her of the chance to marry so far beneath her.'

Hope sighed, wishing now that she'd held her tongue. It was clear that she'd provoked Mr Gordon and he was spoiling for a fight. She glanced at Samuel, noticing how he remained at her side, watching his friend carefully, every muscle in his body apparently tense. She knew she ought to back down, apologise meekly and extricate herself from this conversation. And yet, as she stood here, she felt the fire of indignation burning in her gut. Indignation for that young man and indignation for herself, her true self, and the way others looked down upon them when their rank in life was nothing more than an accident of birth. Who they were—who they truly were—was a matter of words and deeds, not wealth and titles.

'I just… I find it sad that people are considered above or beneath each other at all,' she said in the end. 'Surely, we love who we love and that should be all that matters. You said yourself that this young man was hardworking and decent, yet such traits meant nothing because he was not wealthy and therefore your sister marrying him would be viewed as an embarrassment or a scandal. Never mind that it might have made her happy.'

'Outrageous, revolutionary nonsense.' Mr Gordon's face grew a rather unbecoming shade of scarlet as he turned to address Samuel. 'Are you going to tolerate such talk under your roof, Sammy? Or are you going to tell us that you'd quite happily wed one of Hayton's servants?'

Hope watched as Samuel studied his friend, his expression unreadable. 'As a gentleman, I'd never presume to tell you your business, Charles. However, as your friend I sincerely hope that you and your family can find a way to ease Miss Gordon's suffering.' His blue-grey eyes shifted from Mr Gordon to Hope, growing serious as they locked with hers. 'If you are asking me my personal opinion, then I am sympathetic to Miss Swynford's view. I wish to marry for love, and nothing else. Frankly, I do not care if the lady in question is a maid or a marquess's daughter.'

'And yet, until recently you were pretending to be a baronet,' Mr Gordon countered.

Still Samuel held Hope's gaze, his eyes at once searching and sincere. She was in no doubt that his words, whatever they would be, were meant for her.

'I was,' he said after a moment, 'because even I, for all the many advantages life has bestowed upon me, know what it is like to be looked upon as less than someone else. To have the wind knocked so thoroughly from your sails that you wonder if your pride will ever recover. However, that is no excuse. I should never have deceived you, Hope, and I am deeply, sincerely sorry that I did.'

The hurt and the shame which clouded his expression

was palpable. Before she could stop herself, before she could remember that Mr Gordon was still in the room, Hope reached out and took Samuel's hand in hers. Surprise flickered across his handsome features in response to her touch, before melting into such an affectionate smile that it caught Hope thoroughly off-guard even while it seemed to warm every part of her. She wanted to place her trust in Samuel, and she wanted to understand the nature of what pained him. Of who or what had cut him down and caused him to feel so thoroughly diminished.

In spite of everything, she realised, she wanted his affection. She wanted Samuel to look at Hope Sloane the way he'd just looked at Hope Swynford. And above all she wanted to find the strength to tell him the truth.

Chapter Eighteen

Hope sat in front of the mirror, watching her reflection with a soft gaze as Maddie brushed her hair, teasing the tangles out of her curls with a look of pained apology. She had retired early, excusing herself not long after dinner and retreating to her bedchamber to wash and to change for bed. After the day's events, she doubted she would sleep easily, but at least the night-time hours alone would give her time to think. And goodness, did she need to think.

She understood now that Samuel's lie had been born of some painful, unspoken experience and not simply a desire to impress her or to make her feel safe. She wondered about the nature of that experience, about who would look at a gentleman who was so kind, so caring, so jovial, so undeniably handsome and draw the conclusion that he was not good enough. Whoever they were, they were wrong. If she could muster the courage, Hope would tell him so.

Courage. That was something she was going to need in abundance, if she was going to also admit the truth about herself. If she was going to find the words to explain why she'd deceived him, not only when she'd first arrived at Hayton but for all the weeks since. She had to hope that he would understand, that he could forgive her. At the same time, she had to acknowledge that telling the truth was the right thing to do, even if he could not. She owed him that much for his protection, for his generosity. For the affection he clearly had for her. She could not countenance allowing that affection to be directed towards a woman who did not exist for a moment longer. She cared about him too deeply to do that.

Nonetheless, the very real prospect of losing that affection, of watching it disappear along with the character of the enigmatic heiress which she'd inhabited for so many weeks was terrifying.

'I suppose it's all been a lot to take in,' Maddie said, meeting Hope's eye in the mirror and no doubt noting the pensive expression on her face. 'I do hope you're not too cross with Mr Liddell. He isn't a bad sort, I promise you.'

Hope acknowledged the remark with a tight smile. Hayton's servants had now been released from the obligation to keep up their caretaker master's pretence and, unsurprisingly, Maddie seemed relieved. Hope had rebuffed her attempts at an apology earlier, insisting that she had nothing to apologise for when all she'd been doing was following orders.

'I just wish I knew why he told you that he was the baronet,' Maddie continued to muse as she began to plait Hope's hair. 'It's not like he's ever appeared envious of his brother for inheriting all of this. No, I'd say he's always seemed quite content to be his own man, and his brother's heir, of course. Although I dare say he won't be the heir for much longer, now that Sir Isaac has wed again.'

'Again?' Hope asked, giving the maid a quizzical look. She knew that the true master of Hayton Hall was travelling with his bride, but she did not know that this recent elopement was not the baronet's first trip down the aisle.

Maddie nodded. 'That's right. Oh, my mistress, God rest her soul, was such a wonderful lady. So beautiful and so elegant. I remember the first time I saw her, I thought she looked like a princess. How I loved to help her dress! She had the best taste in gowns, although I don't need to tell you that, do I?' Maddie added, grinning at her.

'What do you mean by that?' Hope asked, furrowing her brow.

Hope watched as the maid's smile slipped from her face, her eyes widening in horror as realisation dawned.

'Forgive me,' she said quietly. 'I should not have said that. I just assumed that Mr Liddell had told you everything.'

Hope stared at Maddie's reflection, following her gaze as it slowly crept towards the mirror image behind them. When her eyes came to rest upon the bed, and the cream dress which lay discarded upon it, the penny finally dropped. The wardrobe he'd so easily produced for her—of course. He'd lied about that too.

'There was never a cousin, was there?' Hope asked quietly. 'There was never a trousseau, or a set of dresses left behind.'

Maddie shook her head sadly. 'I hope now you understand my reluctance to alter them for you,' she replied in little more than a whisper.

'Of course,' Hope replied grimly as she turned around and took her by the hand. 'You were being loyal to your mistress. You didn't decide to offer me her dresses—Mr Liddell did. And besides, for all your reluctance, you did take up a few of them for me.'

'Well, of course—you needed something proper to wear,' she said, blinking back her tears. 'And of course you should have worn them. But I think Mr Liddell ought to have told you who they'd belonged to.'

Hope bit her lip, the heat of her own tears stinging as they threatened to fall. What a fool she was! A gullible, thoroughly humiliated fool. To think she'd been sitting there, wanting to trust Samuel again, recognising that he'd been hurt and wanting to understand the painful experience which had led him to make such an error of judgement in deceiving her. To think she'd been agonising over going to him and confessing all, matching his honesty with her own, when all along he was still lying to her!

And why lie about the dresses? What possible reason could he have for spinning her a yarn about a cousin and letting her put on a dead woman's clothes without her knowledge? Was he laughing at her, or could he simply not help himself? Perhaps she really had misjudged him. Perhaps he was not the decent gentleman she'd believed him to be, after all.

Perhaps she was finally seeing the real Samuel Liddell. A serial liar.

Hope leapt out of her seat and hurried towards the door. 'Excuse me, Maddie,' she said. 'I think I need to have a word with Mr Liddell.'

'But…but he's retired for the night. And you're only wearing your shift!' Maddie called after her, aghast.

Hope, however, was not listening. She was already halfway along the hallway and hurrying towards a heavy oak door, beyond which lay the bedchamber of Hayton Hall's pretend baronet.

* * *

The sight of Hope standing in his doorway, feet bare, wearing only a shift, made Samuel sit bolt upright in bed. He blinked—once, then twice—convinced he must be dreaming. Convinced that he must have fallen asleep over the book he'd been trying his best to distract himself with after such an eventful, fraught day. A day in which they'd learned the truth about Miss Gordon, and he'd unfathomably allowed Hope to glimpse the hurtful, humiliating truth about him. A day in which Hope had taken hold of his hand and looked at him with such affection, such understanding. A look he hadn't deserved. A look which had occupied his mind ever since.

As Hope marched towards his bedside, however, her dainty feet stomping on the wooden floor, he realised that he was indeed awake. She really was here, in his room. And apparently, if the fierce expression on her face was anything to go by, she was very angry. Now there was a look he really did deserve to see from her.

'You lied to me!'

Samuel threw the bedsheets back, remembering just a moment too late that he wore naught but his drawers. Self-consciously, defensively, he folded his arms across his chest as he got to his feet and stood in front of her. She stared up at him, her green eyes wild and challenging, her plait half loosened in her fury, leaving several curls of dark hair to make their bid for freedom. He found himself overcome with a momentary urge to undo the rest of it, to run his hands through that lovely hair. Resisting temptation, he clamped his hand harder against his chest. Given her anger, any such move would be seriously unwise.

'You lied to me,' she said again, quieter this time.

'Yes—I know I did, and you've every right to be angry with me. I should never have told you that I was a baronet.'

'I'm not talking about that,' she replied pointedly. 'I'm talking about the dresses. The ones which belonged to your brother's dead wife. The ones I've been wearing.'

'Oh—yes. That.' Damn. His thoughts had been so pre-occupied with his enormous lie, he'd omitted to confess to the smaller one he'd also told. 'I'm sorry, Hope. I should have explained to you about the dresses.'

To his surprise, her face began to crumple, those earlier flashes of anger slowly replaced by the glint of tears as they formed in her eyes.

'Why would you lie about some dresses?' she asked, stepping back and turning away from him. 'Why would you lie about who they belonged to?'

He let out a heavy sigh, unfolding his arms and rubbing his brow wearily. 'If I'd told you the truth about poor Rosalind, then because I'd let you believe I was the baronet, I'd have had to pretend she'd been my wife. I couldn't do that—it was bad enough that I'd claimed my brother's title; I couldn't lay false claim to his wife and his grief as well.' He stepped tentatively towards her, though her back remained turned to him. 'Besides, you needed something to wear. I thought it was better for you to think that those clothes had come from a well-attired cousin who did not miss them rather than a lady who'd lived and died in this house. In my own foolish way, I was trying to make you feel at ease.'

'Surely that was my decision—whether to wear those dresses or not,' she countered, still not turning around.

'And if you had known, would you have worn them?' he asked.

'Yes. No. I don't know.'

He stepped closer again. 'I know I've acted badly, but it was never with mal-intent. Please believe that.'

He watched as her shoulders sagged. When, finally, she turned around, he was alarmed to see that tears streamed down her face. 'This is all such a mess,' she sobbed. 'So many lies. Do we even know each other at all?'

'Of course we do.'

The sudden urge to reassure her overtook him and, before he could stop himself, he pulled her into his arms. She didn't resist. Indeed, just as she had the last time they'd embraced like this, she tucked her head against his chest. Unlike the last time, however, she wore only a thin undergarment and he was naked from the waist up. The sheer intimacy of the moment meant that tender feelings quickly gave way to more carnal thoughts—thoughts he worked hard to suppress as he forced himself to focus on all that he still had to say.

'You do know me, Hope,' he said, softly running his hand over her hair. 'The man you've seen, the man you've taken tea with, the man you've discussed books and theatre with—that man is me. Calling myself a baronet and all the lies which sprang from that—it was all just costuming. All just foolish window-dressing by a man who, when you wandered into his life that evening in the woods, was feeling more than a little lonely and sorry for himself.'

'You said earlier that you knew what it was like to be looked upon as less than someone else,' she murmured. 'What did you mean by that?'

Samuel felt his breath catch in his throat. He'd been expecting that question ever since his remark in the parlour earlier, but that didn't make the events of the summer any easier to speak about. For a moment he pressed his lips together, composing himself. Resolving finally to be entirely truthful, and to hell with the consequences.

'There was a lady in whose company I spent some time this summer,' he began. 'Her name was Charlotte Pearson. We seemed to get on well, and I thought—hoped, really—that it would progress to a courtship. However, Miss Pearson was very clear with me that she did not wish to continue our connection, and it quickly became apparent that she favoured my brother over me, on account of his title and estate.'

She glanced up at him, aghast. 'This woman is now your sister-in-law?'

Despite himself, Samuel laughed. 'Thankfully, no—Charlotte was never likely to succeed with Isaac. He only had eyes for Miss Louisa Conrad, who is now Lady Liddell.'

Hope leaned her head against his chest once more. 'Did you…did you love Charlotte? Did she break your heart?'

He drew a deep breath. 'I didn't love her, though I was more than a little captivated by her, at the time. And whilst she didn't break my heart, she did hurt me, and she certainly wounded my pride. I'd never been made to feel that way before, as though I was so unworthy.' He shook his head, remembering Charlotte's words. 'She spoke as though my affection for her was offensive—she even told me that things might have been different if I had been my brother.'

'Oh, Samuel…'

'I don't deserve your sympathy, Hope,' he said, interrupting her. 'Not after I've lied to you. But the damnable fact of the matter is that when you looked at me and thought you saw a titled gentleman with a grand house, I couldn't bring myself to contradict you. I liked to impress you, and I liked the way you looked at me. I couldn't bear to see your disappointment when you learned what I really am. And when I realised that it was the house and the title which made you feel so protected, telling you the truth felt completely impossible.'

'But you did tell me, in the end.'

'I did, but not soon enough. I should have told you right away. Indeed, I should never have lied at all.'

'Painful experiences make us do all kinds of things to protect ourselves,' she said, her voice almost a whisper.

He sighed into her dark curls. 'They do, but that is no excuse. I am so sincerely sorry, Hope. I'm not a man who is accustomed to telling lies, please believe that. Please believe me also when I say that if you cannot forgive me, I understand. It is enough for me to know that you will leave Hayton knowing who I really am, because the truth is, Hope, I care for you. When I kissed you in the library that evening, it was not a moment of madness for me. It was an admission of my feelings for you—feelings I had no right to feel, given I was deceiving you, but feelings which had grown nonetheless. Feelings which made telling you the truth about myself even harder. A cruel irony, but no more than I deserve.'

Hope looked up at him then, her emerald eyes still watering as they searched his. He became aware once more of her hands resting against his bare chest, of the warmth of skin on skin, of the feeling of her alluring form pressed against him. Of the proximity of his bed behind them, and the less than gentlemanly thoughts laying siege to his mind.

His heartfelt words surrendered to lust-filled passion as he captured her lips with his own, lifting one of his hands to brush her cheek whilst the other remained steadfast on the curve of her waist. His heart sang as Hope responded in kind, her mouth greeting his while her hands left the confines of his chest to explore his stomach, his arms, his back. He shivered at her touch, fighting himself to maintain control. He would not allow this to go too far. He would not take her to his bed.

Not unless she became his wife first.

The sudden thought astonished him, but not as much as Hope's swift action in breaking their embrace.

'No,' she breathed, stepping back from him. 'We must stop.'

He nodded, swallowing hard as he struggled to regain his composure. 'Of course. I'm sorry. I promise I have no intention of ruining you.'

If he'd hoped his words would be reassuring, he was to be deeply disappointed. Instead, he watched as her face crumpled once more, tears spilling unabated down her cheeks.

'Oh, Samuel, this is all such a mess,' she said, pacing about the floor.

He frowned. That was the second time tonight that she'd uttered those words. His heart began to pound in his chest as it dawned on him that all the obvious affection and ardour he had for her might not be enough. She might never be able to forgive him, to overcome the lies he'd told…

'I know the damage my lies have caused between us, but…'

'You're not the only one of us who has lied about who they are,' she sobbed. 'You cannot care for me, Samuel, and you could not ruin me, even if you tried.'

'What on earth do you mean?'

Finally, she stopped pacing. When she spoke again it was in a voice which sounded quite altered and which was laced, he was astonished to note, with a distinctly local accent.

'I am not an heiress. I am not wealthy. I have no uncle

and no inheritance,' she said. 'My name is not Hope Swynford, it is Hope Sloane. I am an actress and the daughter of an outlaw. I am unruinable. I am the lowest of the low.'

Chapter Nineteen

Hope had never believed that telling Samuel the truth would be in any way cathartic but, even so, she was wholly unprepared for the depth of the shame which possessed her as she told the sordid story of her life. She watched the expressions of shock then horror cloud his handsome features as finally she unmasked herself, shedding Hope Swynford like a second skin and allowing Hope Sloane to walk free.

She told him about her childhood on that bleak Lillybeck hillside, about the lack of food and warmth, about how, one by one, her siblings had perished until she'd been the only one left. About how her father had sought to solve their problems through a life of crime, allowing life on the wrong side of the law to corrupt him so thoroughly, whilst her mother had tried to drown her sorrows in a bottle of laudanum. That part of Hope Swynford's story, she said grimly, had been true.

She told him about her mother's death, how it had left her at the mercy of her father's cruelty and callousness, and how he'd tried to force her into marrying one of his associates. Despite herself, and despite knowing how unsavoury Samuel would doubtless find it, she could not help but speak fondly of running away and joining a theatre company. Those few years of freedom, she told him, had been the making of her, and for all the danger and vice which lurked at the periphery of such work, she'd been happy for the first time in her life.

Her lighter tone dissipated when she reached the final chapter of her tale: the story of her return to Cumberland, of her kidnap and her father's second attempt at forcing a marriage on her. She barely managed to utter the words as she spoke of how depraved he'd become, how sinister, how hateful. How ready he had been to condemn her to a life with a man who, she knew, had the same blackened soul as him.

'I've spent my life living on my wits, and when fortune smiled upon me for long enough to allow me to escape a second time I took the chance and I fled. I had nothing but the costume I'd been wearing the night that my father and his men snatched me from the theatre in Lowhaven. Nothing but that and my sheer determination to live my life on my own terms, and not his.'

'And then you found Hayton, and me,' Samuel added sombrely, slumping down on his bed with a look of unmistakable disbelief. 'So you're the actress Charles mentioned that day in Lowhaven. The one who went missing on the penultimate night of…' He shook his head, apparently struggling to remember.

'*The School for Scandal*,' Hope confirmed with a grim nod. 'I was playing Lady Teazle. Hence the beautiful gown I was wearing the night you found me in the woods.' She regarded him carefully, trying to ignore the tears which pricked at the corners of her eyes. 'You have to understand, Samuel, that I did not know you—I did not know if you were good or bad, if you knew my father or not. My father supplies his wares to many of the big houses across Cumberland, and has more than a few landowners and magistrates in his back pocket. For all I knew, telling you my true identity and story would have led me straight back into his clutches. So when I realised that my clothes had led you to make certain assumptions about me, I decided to play along. I created Hope Swynford and her story to protect myself.'

'Well, you are a consummate actress.' His grey-blue eyes were wide with dismay. 'Never for a moment did I think you could be anything other than a gentleman's daughter with an enthusiasm for the theatre. You certainly had me fooled.'

'Just as you fooled me into believing you were a baronet.'

'Fair point.' He offered her a grim smile as he got to his feet again. 'You were right—this is a real mess.'

She felt her lip tremble at his observation. 'Like you, once I'd begun my deception I found it so hard to end it, even when I suspected that you would have no idea who Jeremiah Sloane is and, even if you did, I knew you were too good a man to give me up to him.' She shook her head at herself, tears still threatening to overwhelm her. 'You said before that you liked the way I looked at you. Well, I liked the way you looked at me too. In truth, I felt ashamed of who I really was. I thought you'd be horrified if you knew who you'd allowed into your home. Gentlemen like you have nothing to do with low-born actresses with wicked outlaw fathers. The only time a woman like me encounters gentlemen is in the theatre, and believe me when I say that they are often anything but gentlemanly then.'

She watched as he flinched at her implication, and she realised then that she'd said far more than she should. It was bad enough that she'd spoken so frankly about the poverty and criminality which ran through her past like a poison, but to then confront Samuel with the sheer seediness and, at times, outright depravity of what she'd been exposed to off-stage and after dark—that was beyond the pale. Worse still, Samuel might believe that she'd been a willing participant in such behaviour—that she was, as Mr Gordon had once said of actresses, little more than a harlot.

'What I mean to say is…' she began, now filled with the sudden urge to explain herself.

'No—I understand,' he interjected, shaking his head again. 'Believe me, I know exactly what some gentlemen are capable of. But surely you know me well enough to know that I would not…' He strode towards her, and her heart sank as she saw him reach out a hand to touch her before retracting it. Of course, he'd thought better of it. He always would now. He shook his head, as though he was trying and failing to find the right words. 'I cannot imagine what you've had to endure…'

The look of horror which was etched in those wide, blue-grey eyes made Hope feel sick as it dawned on her that he was, indeed, trying to imagine it.

'I'm not a harlot,' she said quietly. 'I was never any man's mistress either. I'd run away from my father because he'd tried to trade me like contraband, and I didn't escape his clutches just so that I could sell myself to the highest bidder. I was determined that my life would be my own.'

'But that didn't stop well-dressed drunken wastrels trying their luck,' Samuel pondered.

Hope smiled bleakly at his observation. 'Quite. And some not so well-dressed wastrels, at times.'

An awkward silence descended between them as Hope waited for Samuel to say something—anything—more. But his words, if he had any, did not come. Instead, he simply stood before her, blinking, his sheer mortification and consternation etched on his face. His entire demeanour, from his wooden posture to the distance he'd placed between them, telling her that everything had changed. That what she truly was had shocked and appalled him, such that he might never recover. Such that he would never care for her again. Indeed, that he likely regretted ever saying that he did.

'It is late,' she said in the end, stepping towards the door. 'I should go.'

Samuel stared at her from across the room, but made no move to follow her. 'Yes, of course,' he said after a moment.

He conceded defeat easily—perhaps, Hope considered, too easily. He crossed his arms over his bare chest, and Hope's fingers tingled with the memory of exploring that part of him a short time ago. A profound sense of loss gripped her as it dawned on her that she'd never touch that skin again, that there would be no more embraces. The chasm wrought between them by the truth was simply too great. Looking at his astonished expression, Hope could see that Samuel knew this too. He knew that he could never look at Hope the actress the way he'd looked at Hope the heiress. There had been too much deceit on both their parts. Too many lies. At least now they both knew that.

'Goodnight, Samuel.'

Then, before he could utter a word in reply, she hurried out of his room. It was only when she reached her own and saw that Maddie had left that she allowed herself to weep in earnest—for all that had happened, and for all that could never be.

They'd both been lying. As he tossed and turned in bed, unable to sleep, Samuel's mind kept returning to that thought.

They'd both told stories, and they'd both had their reasons for keeping the truth from one another—some better reasons than others, but reasons nonetheless.

Hope's reasons, he knew, had been a matter of survival. Had he been in her position in those woods weeks ago, had he been injured and vulnerable and taken into a stranger's home, he might well have invented a tale about himself too. Hearing her confess the dreadful details of her past had been hard enough, but realising that it was shame which had motivated her to keep up the pretence of being Hope Swynford had been unbearable.

His heart had broken for her as she'd stood there and told him that she was ashamed of who she was and, in turn, he'd felt ashamed of himself too. Ashamed of the way he'd allowed his own wounded pride and misguided sense of honour to get the better of him, to lead him to pretend to be more than he was. Little wonder she'd felt unable to tell him her real story—between the baronetcy and the big estate, he must have seemed utterly intimidating. The bitter irony of this was not lost on him. In keeping up the pretence, he'd sought to make her feel safe and protected. Instead, he'd unwittingly placed a barrier between them.

If only he had been honest from the outset, he might have seemed more approachable.

Perhaps.

On the other hand, as she'd told him, in her experience, gentlemen were not to be trusted. His stomach had lurched at her remark about the so-called gentlemen at the theatre, at her implication as to how they'd often behaved. He'd desperately wanted to show her that he was not like them, that his affection for her was heartfelt and genuine, and that it endured—whether she was a wealthy heiress or an actress without a penny to her name. He'd wanted to gather her into his arms and kiss all her feelings of shame away, and yet he had stopped himself. He had held back from her.

Why? Because, despite those familiar tender, protective feelings he had for her, he'd realised he had to tread carefully. The last thing he wanted her to conclude was that he was just another rich rapscallion, seeking to take advantage of her. So he'd kept his hands to himself, and when she'd wanted to, he'd let her go, even when so much remained unsaid.

Such as telling her that she was still the Hope he'd come to know and care for, whether her surname was Swynford or Sloane, and whether her father was a gentleman or a common criminal. Whether she spent her life in drawing rooms playing cards or on the stage playing roles. Such as reminding her that her pretend heiress, just like his pretend baronet, had been a mere costume, that it did not alter who either of them were underneath.

The Hope who'd been on the run from her invented nefarious uncle was the same Hope who'd escaped the clutches of a very real, very wicked father—a woman who loved to read, whose knowledge of Shakespeare was second to none. A woman who'd lost her mother, and whose own pain had made her alert to and empathetic towards the suffering of others. A brave woman, and one who, he now knew, had carved out a life for herself, escaping the clutches of those who'd sought to drag her down not once, but twice. If anything, her runaway heiress story—a story which, notwithstanding the wicked uncle, had implied a certain amount of wealth and status—had meant that he'd not been able to fully appreciate the sheer amount of hardship and wretchedness which she'd overcome.

He did now.

He did, and the strength of feeling that knowledge provoked in him was overwhelming. As he lay in bed, sleep still eluding him, he realised that he wanted to protect her from all of it. From her father's cruelty, from a forced marriage, from men leering at her in the theatre. From cold, damp cottages and poverty and hunger. Weeks ago, he'd offered her sanctuary in his family home; now, he knew, he wanted to offer her love and security, with him. Because he did love her—he understood that now, and knowing that truth had done nothing to diminish how he felt about her. If anything, he loved and admired her more than ever. To him, she was beautiful and she was perfect, and honestly, the way she spoke in that soft local tongue had the ability to drive him wild. He wanted to hear that voice to the end of his days.

He would tell her so, he decided, squeezing his eyes shut. In the morning.

The indigo light of the autumn dawn bathed Hayton's gardens as Hope stepped out of the door at the rear of the house. She breathed in deeply, allowing the cold air to refresh her as the wind teased the shrubbery and tangled the branches of the tall trees in the woods beyond, warning of an unsettled day ahead. How fitting, since it had been a restless night. Hope had not slept a wink, her room growing more stifling and her thoughts more relentless as the hours wore on. Eventually she had felt the need to escape, and so she'd slipped on a day dress and shawl—or rather, as she now knew, Rosalind's dress and shawl—then put on her boots and wandered outside for some air.

She walked slowly along the path, acutely aware of

how heavy her weary limbs felt, and how her swollen eyes pricked and throbbed after so many hours of crying. For the first time in her life, she found herself at a loss. No matter what life had thrown at her, she'd always been able to formulate a plan or, at the very least, to take what she'd been given and run with it—sometimes literally. Now, she realised, she'd simply no idea what to do. No idea where she was going. Not to London—now that she was no longer Hope Swynford, there was no need for that. Back to Richmond? Back to her life in the theatre? Was that even possible? She didn't know.

All she did know was that the truth had changed everything, that Samuel would never look at her in the same way again. Her time at Hayton, her time with him in this blissful, peaceful sanctuary, was coming to an end.

The sound of stones crunching underfoot was the first clue that she wasn't alone. It was a clue which came too late, since by the time she realised a hand had already been clapped over her mouth, stifling any attempt she might have made to scream. The hand was dirty, coarse and all too familiar, as was the cold sting of the knife which was pressed against her throat.

'Time to go home, my lady,' he said mockingly, hissing the words into her ear.

Finally, after all these weeks of searching, he'd found her.

Chapter Twenty

She'd left him.

Samuel pulled on the riding coat which Smithson had handed to him, that same handful of words circling around his mind over and over again. She'd left him. The shame, the pain and the guilt she'd so clearly felt about all that she'd confessed last night had been too much for her to bear. And he, to his eternal damnation, had been thoroughly inadequate in the face of it, failing to comfort her, to properly reassure her. To tell her that none of it changed what he felt for her. Instead, he'd simply stood by as she'd walked out of his bedchamber and now out of his life.

She'd left him, and now he might never see her again.

Now, because of his hesitation, she was wandering the countryside, alone and vulnerable. God forbid she should end up injured again or, worse, find herself a captive of her father once more. If some dreadful fate befell her, it would be all his fault.

She'd left him, and now he had to find her. He had to make amends.

'She could be anywhere by now. This will be like searching for a needle in a haystack.'

Next to him, Charles gave voice to Samuel's niggling

fears as he fiddled with his top hat. Outside, the grooms were readying two horses as fast as they could, after Samuel had all but press-ganged his friend into assisting him in his search for Hope. In the sheer panic he felt following Maddie's revelation that Hope was nowhere to be found, Samuel had appraised his maid, his butler and Charles of what Hope had revealed last night. All three had expressed their surprise. Like Samuel, they appeared to have harboured no suspicions that she'd been anything other than what she'd said she was.

'We have to try, Charles,' Samuel implored him. 'I cannot just sit here, knowing that Hope could be in danger. What if her father finds her?'

'But where should we even begin to look?' Charles countered. 'We don't know where she's going. Try not to fret, Sammy, I dare say she can look after herself. Women like her are…'

'What do you mean, women like her?' Samuel almost growled the question.

Charles held up a hand in protest. 'I mean no offence, of course. All I mean to say is that she's hardly lived a sheltered life. Surely she's proven just how resourceful she is, considering how well she's pulled the wool over your eyes for all these weeks.'

'And surely you can see that she had her reasons.' Samuel wished the grooms would hurry up, so that he could end this conversation. So that he could begin his search.

'I can see that given the chance and the talent required to pull it off, any base-born woman would pretend to be a princess if it meant ensnaring a wealthy gentleman.' Charles fiddled with his collar in front of the mirror, his reflection shooting Samuel a pointed look.

'That isn't why Hope deceived me,' Samuel replied, bristling. 'She lied to protect herself. If either one of us could be accused of lying to impress the other, then it is me. I know what you think of her, Charles, now that you know she's an actress without a penny to her name...'

'It doesn't matter what I think, Sammy,' Charles replied, turning around. 'I'm not the one who is besotted with Hope Swynford or Sloane or whoever she is.' He raised a knowing eyebrow. 'Or perhaps this is something more than infatuation?' he added searchingly.

Samuel shrugged, having neither the will to deny his feelings nor the desire to elaborate upon them. What he felt for Hope had gone beyond mere infatuation, but Charles did not need to know that. The only person in the world who needed to know the depth of what he felt was Hope herself. If he found her.

When he found her.

'Richmond,' he said after a moment, answering Charles's earlier question. 'Her theatre company came from Richmond. Perhaps that is where she is hoping to return to now. It would make sense, wouldn't it?'

'You want to go all the way to Richmond?' Charles stared at him, incredulous. 'That is several days of hard riding across the dales.'

Samuel put up a hand in protest. 'I'm saying that is the direction we should head in,' he said. 'It would appear that Hope is travelling on foot and, whilst she has recovered from her injuries, her ankle in particular will still be delicate. She will not be moving quickly. On horseback we stand a good chance of catching up with her.'

'If we can correctly guess the route she has taken,' Charles pointed out.

'To find her way there, she will surely have to follow the roads,' Samuel replied with a confidence he did not feel. He glanced towards the door impatiently. Where in damnation were those grooms with their horses? The longer they delayed, the further Hope would have travelled from Hayton, and the harder it would be to find her…

'Excuse me, sir.'

The soft, wavering voice of Maddie interrupted Samuel's spiralling thoughts. He spun around to see the maid standing in the middle of the hallway, tears spilling down her cheeks, clutching a delicate swathe of cream fabric in her hands. She held it up towards him, revealing that it was in fact a shawl. His heart lurched in recognition—it had belonged to Rosalind, and had been one of the items he'd given Hope to wear.

'I found this in the garden,' she explained, her bottom lip trembling. 'I was attending to Miss Gordon when she spotted it out of the window, stuck to one of the shrubs.'

'So she has fled via the woods then, and lost this on her way,' Charles interjected.

Maddie shook her head. 'I'm not sure about that, sir. You see, when I went outside to retrieve it, I noticed that the stones covering the path have been disturbed as though…as though there may have been a struggle. As though someone has been dragged along.' She turned her gaze to Samuel, looking at him imploringly. 'Oh, sir, what if her father has taken her? What if he's found her after all these weeks?'

Samuel's heart seemed to sink like a stone into the pit of his stomach. He'd been so wrapped up in the events of last night, so consumed by his own shortcomings in the face of her revelations, that he'd neglected to remember the danger Hope was in. The danger she'd always been in.

She had not run away from him at all. She'd been taken.

'I fear this is all my fault.' A faint voice crept into the brief silence which had descended in the hall, and Samuel glanced up to see a pale and frail Miss Gordon making her way gingerly down the stairs. Immediately, Maddie stepped forward to help her, but the lady waved the maid away.

'I don't quite see how any of this is your responsibility, Henrietta,' Charles said.

Samuel watched as a small frown gathered between Miss Gordon's dark eyes. 'That day at the docks in Lowhaven, when I…when Miss Sloane, as Maddie tells me she is in fact called…when Miss Sloane left the carriage to intercept me, she must have been recognised. If I had not gone there that day, then this might not have happened.'

'Miss Sloane's father is a common criminal, sister,' Charles replied. 'I dare say he would have gone to any lengths to locate her. I am quite certain this is not your doing.'

Miss Gordon put up her hand. 'From what I hear, her father is a smuggler, amongst other things. The notion that she was not recognised by someone at that port is therefore laughable. No, brother, I must take responsibility for the consequences of my actions.' She turned to Samuel. 'I implore you, Mr Liddell, please find her and bring her safely back to Hayton. Whoever she is matters not a jot. She has been good and kind to me, even when I have not deserved it.'

Samuel gave her a solemn nod. 'You have my word,' he replied. 'At least now we know where we need to look for her, and it is much closer to home than Richmond.'

'Where?' Charles asked, frowning.

'An isolated hamlet called Lillybeck, a few miles north of here,' Samuel said, stepping along the hallway towards the library, the semblance of a plan starting to form in his mind. 'But first I'm going to fetch a couple of pistols. If we're going to get Hope away from that villain of a man once and for all, then I dare say we ought to be armed.'

Hope's eyes flickered open, and for several moments she struggled to fathom where she was. Her head was pounding, and she felt sick and dizzy as she tried to focus on her surroundings. Before she'd awoken she'd been dreaming—she could recall that much. She'd been in Samuel's bedchamber, just as she had been when she'd confessed to who she truly was, except that in her dream, Samuel had not appeared frozen in horror, and she had not left. Instead, he'd told her that he loved her, he'd taken her in his arms and embraced her, before taking her to his bed, where she'd spent many hours wrapped up in his crisp white sheets. Wrapped up in him.

It had been a wanton, desirous dream, and one which ought to have brought a blush to her cheeks at the remembrance of it. Instead, as her blurry vision and sleep-addled mind finally gave way to clear and grim reality, she felt the colour drain from her face. Having relished her dream, she'd now awoken to a nightmare.

'Welcome back, my lady. Sorry about the sore head. You weren't for co-operating so I'd no choice but to knock you out cold.'

Hope blinked, trying to force her eyes to focus. 'How did I get…'

'Here?' Jeremiah Sloane finished her question for her. 'In a cart, lass. Roddy's cart. You remember Roddy, don't you?'

Hope grimaced at the memory of her father's long-standing accomplice. His had been one of the few faces she'd recognised that fateful night outside the theatre in Lowhaven, all those weeks ago. Now she thought about it, it had been his cart in which she'd been conveyed, bound and gagged, to her father's cottage that time too.

Jeremiah Sloane sat across the table from her, his customary mug of his strong brew clutched in his hand. Around them the cottage was dim and damp, the light of a single tallow candle doing little to ward off either the shadows or the creeping chill.

Gripped by panic, Hope tried to move, only to realise that she'd been tied to the chair upon which she sat, her hands and feet tightly bound.

'Oh, aye, I wasn't taking any chances this time,' he said, his eyes narrowed at her even as he chuckled. He took a long drink from his mug before wiping his mouth with the back of his filthy hand. 'Hayton Hall then, eh? You did well for yourself there, lass. And, judging by the look of you, you've not been working as a scullery maid neither. Aye, quite the lady. George will love that. He likes nothing better than to spoil fine things.'

'Still intent upon marrying me to one of your disgusting associates, then?' she asked, trying to ignore the bile which rose in her throat.

Her father simply shrugged. 'Marry you, not marry you—George can do as he sees fit. It's naught to me what happens to you, not after all the trouble you've caused.'

Hope stared at him. 'What on earth are you talking about? I've done nothing to you, Pa. Nothing at all.'

She tried her best not to flinch as Jeremiah Sloane launched himself towards her. 'Done nothing, have you?' he repeated, his face mere inches from hers. 'You cost me dearly is what you've done.' He slumped back down in his chair, reaching immediately for his mug and taking another large gulp of its potent contents. 'If only you'd wed five years ago when I arranged it, then all this unpleasantness could have been avoided. Instead, you ran away, and I had to pick up the pieces. Malky was not happy, you know. He'd taken quite a shine to you, so much so that he'd agreed to write off my debt to him as soon as you'd wed. Instead… well, as I said, you cost me dearly.'

'Malky?' Hope repeated, grimacing as her head continued to pound. Five years ago, her father had kept her in the dark about exactly who she was to wed, and she had fled before she'd had chance to find out. She did not recall anyone called Malky, although apparently he'd known her. 'Who is he?'

'Was,' her father corrected her, before draining the contents of his mug. 'He lived on the Isle of Man, traded from there. Died a couple of years back—drowned at sea during a storm. Always a risk-taker was Malky. He wasn't the worst sort, though. A better man than George, to be sure. The man's a beast.'

'A beast you're forcing me to wed,' she goaded him.

Jeremiah Sloane slammed his mug on the table. 'And for that you have only yourself to blame! Unpaid debts don't go away, my lass. They grow and grow. Things started to get desperate, and I had to pay Malky somehow so…'

'So you borrowed from Peter to pay Paul,' Hope said, the penny finally dropping. 'And kept on borrowing, from the sounds of it.'

'Aye, except these men aren't the apostles. In George's case, more like the Devil himself.'

'And let me guess, when word reached you that I'd been

spotted in Lowhaven theatre, you saw a chance to settle your debts for good this time. You offered me up on a plate to this George and he was willing to take me instead of payment, just like that?'

Her father shook his head. 'No, George insisted on seeing you first. A man like that wants to know what he's getting. I knew he'd want you though, the moment he saw you on stage.' He smiled bitterly. 'You got your mother's good looks, after all.'

Hope shivered at the thought of that beastly man surveying her like a prize heifer at a market. 'I'm not goods to be bartered and traded,' she said quietly. 'How could you, Pa? Your own daughter?'

'Sold yourself, though, didn't you?' he retorted, not answering her question. He filled his mug again, then took a self-satisfied sip. 'I wonder what fine clothes like that cost you, Hope? What price the master of Hayton Hall put on dressing you up and letting you parade around his grand house and gardens like a duchess? He must have thought all his Christmases had come at once. An actress? No better than a bawd.'

Hope felt the heat of indignation rise in her chest as she strained against the ropes which bound her. 'Samuel is not like that!' she snapped. 'He has been faultlessly kind to me and never asked for anything in return.'

An amused smile crept slowly over Jeremiah Sloane's face, showing off an incomplete set of brown teeth. 'Samuel is it, eh? You really did get your feet well under his plentiful table. He certainly kept you well hidden. A shame you got careless and went wandering about the port with your fancy gentleman.' He began to chuckle, although quickly it gave way to a terrible hacking cough.

Hope felt a solitary tear trickle down her face and wished with all her heart that she could swipe the evidence away. The last thing she wanted her cold and callous father to see was how much his words hurt her, or how much she cared for Samuel. She was all too aware how capable he was of using even the merest hint of emotion against her and turning it into a weakness to exploit. So she bit her tongue, forcing herself to remain silent rather than letting him know how wrong his sordid view of her relationship with Samuel was. Rather than telling him exactly what sort of gentleman she'd been living with, or just how blessed she felt to have spent time in his company.

Because truly, she thought now, Samuel had been a blessing, and not just when he'd come to her rescue that night in the woods. He'd been a blessing every day since, treating her with a kindness and gentleness she'd never before known. He'd welcomed her into his life and whilst he had lied about having a title, in every respect that mattered he'd shown her who he was. He was a considerate, thoughtful man who was interested in the world, and interested in her, listening to her and talking to her as an equal.

But of course, she reminded herself, she had been pretending to be his equal. The truth of her lowly birth had brought an end to that and, with it, an end to his affection for her. Perhaps, she reasoned, that was what had really brought tears to her eyes, and not her father's insults.

Perhaps she was crying for the loss of a future she'd almost fooled herself into thinking she could have. A future with Samuel. A future where he loved her and she loved him.

Because if she was honest with herself, that was what she felt. She did love him. But that love was as futile as it was unwanted. Samuel could never love her—that much had been plain in his horrified gaze and his distant demeanour last night. No doubt her disappearance from Hayton would come as something of a relief, marking the end of an embarrassing episode in his life when he'd been fooled into caring for an actress and an outlaw's daughter.

'Pity you won't find life with George quite so comfortable,' Jeremiah Sloane continued to taunt her, his fit of coughing abating. 'I sent Roddy to tell him that you're here. Word is that he's in Lowhaven finishing a job, so I dare say it won't take him long to come for you. If you know what's good for you, you'll wipe that sour look off your face and try your damnedest not to provoke him. He's been in a foul temper since you ran away as it is.'

He began to cough again, uncontrollably this time, forcing him to rummage in the pocket of his breeches and fish out a filthy rag with which to stifle the rasping, barking sound. From her restrained position Hope could do nothing but watch and, as she did, she began to study the man, to really look at him as though she might be laying eyes on him for the first time. As a girl she'd been terrified of his ferocity, of his temper, of the power she believed his life of crime had granted him. Now, watching him, she saw an ageing man, his skin sallow, his dirty clothes hanging from his emaciated frame, his would-be handkerchief bloodstained and betraying the illness which gripped him. She saw a man who was no longer in control, whose fate rested in the hands of monsters like George. She saw what all the years of corruption and vice had wrought, saw how it had hollowed him from the inside out.

'You're afraid of George, aren't you?' Now it was her turn to goad him. 'I used to think you weren't afraid of anything—not even the gallows. But now I see there's a lot that frightens you.'

'There's a lot that should frighten you too,' he snapped, breathless, before draining his second mug as though his life depended upon it. As though the potent contents could cure whatever canker had taken hold in his lungs. 'You'd just better hope that George sees fit to make you his wife, because otherwise I dare say he'll take whatever innocence you have left then drown you in the Eden river.'

The stark threat was like a punch in the gut. Unable to bear the sight or sound of her father any longer, Hope looked away, her eyes drifting towards the little window and her thoughts wandering across the rugged countryside to Hayton Hall. To afternoons drinking tea in the parlour, and to gentle promenades in the gardens. To conversations about Hume and Shakespeare. To passionate kisses in the library, in the parlour, in his bedchamber. To the feeling of being safe and cared for. To the happiest weeks of her life.

And, above all, to the man she loved and who, she felt certain, she would never see again.

Chapter Twenty-One

'Should we not alert the local constable?'

Samuel shook his head at Charles's question as they made their way along the rough track which led to the cottage where Hope's father lived. Information about the precise whereabouts of Jeremiah Sloane's abode had been difficult to come by. No one living in the scattered collection of low stone dwellings which made up the hamlet of Lillybeck seemed particularly willing to acknowledge that they knew the man, much less part with the details of where he might be found.

The offer of a few coins, however, had sufficiently loosened tongues, leading Samuel and Charles to an isolated spot on the very fringes of an already remote community. Although Lillybeck lay only miles from Hayton, it was far enough beyond Liddell land for Samuel to feel quite unfamiliar with this corner of Cumberland. Quite simply, it was a place he'd never had reason to travel to—until now. His scant knowledge of the area made him feel decidedly uncomfortable, as did the warning he'd received from the frail old man who'd taken Samuel's bribe for information. A warning which now rang in his ears.

'Have a care, sir. From what I hear Sloane is sickening,

but I dare say he's still a dangerous man. Whatever your business is with him, if you know what's good for you, you'll keep one hand on your pistol.'

Samuel had thanked the man for his advice, before enquiring if he knew anything about Jeremiah Sloane's daughter. 'Perhaps you've seen her recently,' he'd probed. 'I heard that she'd returned to Lillybeck.'

'If she has then I pity the poor lass,' the man had replied, shaking his head sadly. 'She ran away from him years ago—no one knew where she went. If she's come back then I doubt it'll have been willingly.'

Samuel shuddered at everything those words implied before glancing at Charles, who looked at him expectantly. 'No constables,' he said, finally answering his friend's question. 'From what Hope said, her father supplies his wares to some of the so-called great and good around these parts. If he's got magistrates in his pocket, then he's likely got a few constables in there too. I think we have to proceed without the help of the law, for now at least.'

'I don't like the sound of that,' Charles replied.

'Neither do I. But needs must.'

'So, what is the plan, Sammy?'

Samuel let out a long breath as he drew his horse to a halt. They were near the cottage, although now that he'd laid his eyes on it, Samuel felt that calling it a cottage afforded it too grand a title. It was a crumbling, ramshackle place, barely fit to house livestock, never mind people. Around it the grass grew tall, its days as grazing pasture for sheep clearly a distant memory. Near the rough track on which they now stood, lay the detritus of what would have once been needed to run a small farm: the rotting wood of abandoned carts, the remnants of broken fences and pieces of scythes and other tools, long since forgotten. The whole place reeked of neglect and decay. Samuel swallowed hard as his gaze wandered towards the tiny windows of the cottage. He prayed to God that Hope was indeed inside, and that she was unharmed.

'We leave the horses here,' he said, dismounting and leading the creature to a nearby tree, before tethering him carefully to its thick trunk. 'We approach quietly on foot and try to get a look inside the cottage first. We need to assess exactly what we're dealing with.'

Charles nodded his agreement, and together they crept towards the decrepit building, using the tall grass to shield them. If the situation had not been so grave, Samuel would have found the sight of the pair of them laughable. Well clad in fine riding coats and Hessian boots and sneaking towards a place which was the rural equivalent of the slum houses found in larger towns and cities, they looked just about as out of place as it was possible to be. As he tiptoed along, it struck Samuel again just how acutely aware Hope must have been of the difference between their worlds. The poverty and hardship she had known stood in such sharp contrast to the sumptuous comfort of his life at Hayton Hall.

A fresh wave of guilt washed over him. His life, and by extension the life he'd offered her these past weeks, must have seemed utterly intimidating. She must have spent every day feeling like a fish out of water. Little wonder she'd struggled to bring herself to tell him about it. Little wonder she'd felt the need to pretend to be someone else.

Well, there would be no more pretending now, on either of their parts. When he reached a little window, he made a silent vow. He would find her and bring her safely back to

Hayton, and he would offer her a life, with him, for ever. A life they would share and build together.

He just had to find her first.

'I can't see her,' Charles whispered as he peered tentatively through the window. 'The place is deathly quiet. I don't like it.'

Samuel found himself bristling at his friend's poor choice of words, before taking a look for himself. Sure enough, Charles was right—even in the dim light of the single-room dwelling it was evident that Hope was not inside. He cast his eyes around, taking in the simple, sparse furnishings, the bare stone walls, the last remnants of a single tallow candle, left burning in the middle of a table. Someone had been there, and not so very long ago from the looks of it.

'If this place is anything to go by, I'd say crime doesn't always pay,' Charles whispered. 'I always thought smuggling was a lucrative trade, but it seems not.'

'It's a cut-throat enterprise,' Samuel replied. 'Some win and some lose. It looks like Jeremiah Sloane has been on the losing side for some time. Hope said he runs some illicit stills from nearby caves too. However, that old man told us that his health is failing. Perhaps his business has been failing at the same time.'

Out the corner of his eye, Samuel caught sight of something, like a flicker of movement on the ground. 'What's that?' he hissed. 'See there—behind the table? It looks like a boot.' He squinted, trying to peer through the gloom and murk to see more clearly. 'I think it's…it's moving. Someone is in there, lying on the ground.'

Instinctively, he darted away from the window, rounding the cottage and heading towards its single wooden door. If it was Hope and she was bound or, God forbid, injured, then there was no time to lose. He'd detected no other signs of life within. If she was alone, then he had to rescue her before her father returned. He had to get her away from this dreadful place—now.

'I think it is a boot,' Charles hissed, scurrying behind him. 'But Sammy, it might not be…'

Charles's words were cut short by the loud thump of Samuel's boot as it made contact with the door, followed by the brittle crack of the old wood as it gave way feebly to his force. Samuel hurried inside, Charles still following him, to be confronted by a scene which made them both gasp loudly. Beside the table, a man was lying on the floor, groaning softly, his limbs twitching and his eyes rolling as he seemed to drift in and out of consciousness.

Samuel bent down, his gaze immediately drawn to the large bloodstain which was growing across the man's filthy shirt. 'It looks as though he's been shot,' he called, looking over his shoulder at Charles, who lingered behind, looking distinctly pale about the face.

'Should I send for a physician?' Charles asked.

Samuel looked back at the man. He suspected there was no time for that—the man was in all likelihood mortally wounded and would be dead by the time a physician arrived. However, Samuel decided, they had to at least try.

'Yes,' he began. 'Perhaps ask that old man…'

'No…' The man's voice was raspy but insistent. 'I'm done for.'

'Are you Jeremiah Sloane?' Samuel asked, his shock at the scene he'd uncovered abating, and the urgency of finding Hope gripping him once more. 'Where is your daughter? You must tell me, man. Tell me now!'

A sliver of a smile appeared on the man's weathered face. 'You must be Samuel,' he croaked. 'She really must have been like a harlot between your sheets if you want her back.'

Samuel felt the heat of indignation rise in his chest at such a remark—uttered by her father, no less. The man really was the lowest of the low. It was a mystery to him how such a person could have sired such a lovely, brave and intelligent daughter.

'Where is she?' he repeated, through gritted teeth this time. Samuel was not a man to allow his temper to get the better of him but, even so, he could feel himself close to losing it.

Jeremiah Sloane coughed weakly, causing blood to bubble up and trickle down the side of his cheek. 'George has her,' he wheezed, his eyes rolling again. 'They've gone north.'

'North?' Samuel repeated, his heart lurching as all that those words implied became clear. 'You mean to Gretna? To wed her?' he asked. Hope had never named him, but he realised George must be the terrible forced fiancé she'd described.

'Doubt…he'll…do that.'

Jeremiah Sloane's breathing grew laboured now, and Samuel realised they were almost out of time. If Hope's father would not part with his knowledge before slipping away to meet his maker, then their chance of finding Hope might be lost. She might be lost to him, and that was a thought he truly could not bear.

'Then where?' he prompted, hearing the desperation in his own voice as he shook the man by his shoulders in an effort to rouse him one final time. 'Damn it, tell me!'

'Rockcliffe.'

The word was a whisper, barely audible. Jeremiah Sloane

choked again, then let out one more whistling, agonising breath. His bloodied body grew still and limp, his grey, leathery face freezing in a contorted expression, eyes wide, lips parted in an O shape, as though death had come as a shock. As though, perhaps, he'd glimpsed something on the other side that he had not wanted to see. A gruesome testament to a lifetime of wickedness, law-breaking and cruelty, indeed.

Samuel got to his feet, turning away from the grim scene at last. 'Let's fetch the horses,' he said to Charles, hurrying towards the door. 'You must find the local constable. It's clear Jeremiah Sloane has been murdered, and we have a duty to report it. Do that, then return to Hayton, to your sister.'

'I thought you said not to involve constables, that Sloane had the law in his pocket around these parts?' Charles asked, frowning.

'Then if that's the case, hopefully they will be motivated to bring the killer to justice,' Samuel quipped. He sighed heavily. 'Honestly, I don't know, Charles. I only know that we must report what we have found here, immediately. To do otherwise might bring the law's suspicions down upon us.'

Charles grimaced. 'All right, point taken. And what will you do?'

'I must ride for Rockcliffe at once.'

'But where the devil is Rockcliffe?' Charles asked him, following behind. 'And who is this George her father spoke of, anyway?'

'A monster, Charles,' Samuel replied, recalling again Hope's words about the man her father had tried to force her to marry. Shuddering, he glanced back into the gloom of the cottage. 'One monster is dead, and now Hope is in the clutches of another. I must follow the road north, find Rockcliffe and this George, then I will find her. There is no time to lose!'

Samuel ran along the uneven track and back towards his horse, the same silent prayer circling around in his mind.

Please God, let me find Hope, he prayed. *Let her be safe and well. Let her come home with me, so that these malevolent men might never try to harm her again.*

Hope winced as the cart jolted on the road, the sudden movement making her already pounding head ache all the more. Despite herself, she let out a sob, partly at the pain and partly at the shock of it all. Tears ran unabated down her cheeks as her mind replayed all that she'd witnessed once again.

The way George had waltzed into the cottage so casually, as if he owned the place. How he'd licked his lips when he'd looked at her, an unmistakably greedy look lingering in his dark eyes. The way her father had scurried over to him like a beggar asking for his supper, pleading for reassurances that his debt was now settled. How George had refused to answer him, laughing and shoving him out of the way as he'd marched over to claim his prize. The way her father had begun to wail and yell like a man overcome by the realisation that he could never win. How that screaming had caused something in George to snap. How George's cheeks had flushed with anger, a cloud gathering over the already foreboding features of his angular face before he swiftly drew his pistol, took his aim, and fired.

How Hope had watched as her father tumbled quietly to the ground, his desperate wailing replaced by the soft moans of a man whose life was ebbing away.

When they'd left the cottage, Jeremiah Sloane had still lived—just. As George had untied her from the chair, unbound her feet and hands and dragged her away, Hope had been gripped by the most overpowering urge to run to her father's side. To remain with him in his final moments. To not let him die alone. It was strange. After all he'd done to her, Jeremiah Sloane deserved neither her concern nor her care, and yet both feelings had plagued her. His cruelty and callousness were unforgivable, but in the end the brute he'd become had been subsumed by an even greater monster—a leviathan who'd enfeebled him, who'd preyed on his weaknesses as age, debt and misfortune consumed him bit by bit. She would not mourn her father but, inexplicably, she realised that she did pity him. Better that, she supposed, than pitying herself. She would not surrender to such feelings. At least, not yet.

'Stop weeping, or else I'll give you something to weep about.' The monster spoke without even looking at her, his eyes intent upon the road ahead. He sat close by her side on the bench at the front of the cart, his hands firm upon the reins of the single horse which pulled them along. He'd left her feet unbound but had tethered one of her wrists to the cart, subtly enough that it would not be noticed by anyone else on the road, but firmly enough to ensure she had no chance of getting away. Not that she had any intention of trying to leap on to the road and run—she'd already seen what a good shot he was, and any such attempt to flee would undoubtedly be answered by a bullet from his pistol.

Hope straightened herself, fighting back the last vestiges of her tears. He was right; she did need to stop weeping. The options for escape, she knew, were vanishingly small as it was, and would certainly be undetectable if she was too busy crying.

'You already did—you killed my father,' she retorted, mustering a feistiness she did not truly feel. Better that, she decided, than allowing him to sense her fear.

'Ha!' He glanced at her, baring his yellow teeth and grinning in amusement. 'I've done you a favour there, trust me.' He reached out, placing his hand upon her knee and giving it a firm squeeze. 'Do as you're told, and you'll have a better life with me than you ever did with him.'

Even through the fabric of her dress, the feeling of his fingers made her skin crawl. Hope shivered, partly at his unwanted touch and partly at the cold which seeped increasingly into her bones. She wore only the plain blue day dress which she'd been wearing when her father had snatched her from Hayton Hall, and although its sleeves were long, its fine fabric was insufficient against the autumn chill. She was sure she'd been wearing a shawl in Hayton's gardens too, but when she'd awoken at her father's cottage it had been nowhere to be seen. Obstinately, Hope stiffened—against the monster's touch, and against the cold. She would not allow this man to detect even a hint of her discomfort, lest he perceive it as a weakness to exploit.

'And what does this better life entail?' she asked him. She gave him a haughty look, once again masking her fear as her father's warning about being drowned in the river rang in her ears. 'Because I had a perfectly good one, without my father and without you.'

'Which life would that be?' Briefly, he took his eyes off the road, looking at her with a gaze so dark it appeared almost black under the gloom of the surrounding trees. 'The one you spent on stage, or the one you spent at Hayton Hall, playing the harlot for its master?'

Hope scowled at him—better that than allowing the fresh tears which pricked in the corners of her eyes to fall. When her father had made similar insinuations, she'd protested. Now, she decided, she would hold her tongue. Allowing this dangerous, evil man to know anything about Samuel, about how much she'd adored her short time with him or about how much she cared for him, could put him in danger, and she would not be able to live with herself if anything happened to him. Better to let George believe that she'd spent these past weeks being ill-used than letting him know she'd spent them falling in love. A love, she reminded herself, which was lost to her now, even though she would feel it deeply to the end of her days.

'My life in the theatre, of course,' she lied, meeting his eye. 'A life in which I did no man's bidding.'

'Aye, well, you'll do my bidding now,' George snarled at her.

'As what?' Hope challenged him, although she hardly dared to ask. 'Your wife, or your harlot?'

George returned his eyes to the road. 'I've not decided,' he said coldly. 'But, either way, you'll be running contraband and having my bairns, Hope. That's what I've got planned for you.'

Hope looked away, biting her lip so hard that she might draw blood. All the pity she'd fleetingly felt for her father simply disappeared as she faced up to the sort of life the man had condemned her to, and in its place her anger grew. She'd spent her formative years living with a man who used fear, threats and sometimes violence to get his own way, and she was damned if she was going to spend the remainder of her life with another such man. She was damned if she was going to be forced into committing crimes or going to bed with a man who repulsed her. Frankly, she decided, she'd rather he did just drown her in the river and have done with it.

But first, she vowed, she would defy him every step of the way. She would use every opportunity she got trying to regain her freedom. Starting right now. Hope wiggled her bound wrist, straining against the rope, carefully trying to tease it loose without him noticing. She would bide her time, she would play the hand she'd been dealt, and when the right moment came along she would seize it—just as she always did.

Chapter Twenty-Two

Hope grimaced as George directed the horse to slow down and turn into the courtyard of a coaching inn. She'd long since lost any sense of where they were or how long they had been travelling. She knew from the scant details George had offered that he was taking her north, and since he'd admitted he had not decided whether or not he planned to wed her, she presumed they were not going directly to Gretna—a small mercy which she was thankful for. She also knew that the farm from which George ran his nefarious operations was somewhere near the Scottish border, not far from the Solway Firth, where the rivers Esk and Eden meandered out to sea. She had to assume, therefore, that that was where they were headed.

Realising that, however, served only to make Hope begin to panic. Despite her best efforts, she'd had little success in loosening the rope which bound her to the cart, and with each passing mile she felt the weight of her fate bearing down upon her. If she could not escape now, while it was just the two of them on the road, what chance did she stand once she'd arrived at his farm, no doubt living under the watchful eye of his many criminal accomplices? She had other, more immediate concerns too, such as what George had planned once darkness fell. Surely, he could not hope to travel all the way to the border today; they would have to stop somewhere tonight. At this, Hope shuddered—the thought of spending the night anywhere with that monster, and all that such a night might entail, did not bear thinking about. Which was why, when he turned into the coaching inn, she felt her heart sink.

'Why are we stopping here?' she asked, trying her best to sound curious rather than fearful.

'Because I need a drink, and so does the horse.' He glanced at her, a knowing smirk spreading across his face. 'Sorry to disappoint you, Hope, but I don't plan to take a room here for the night. I know you've been used to living like a duchess as Hayton's harlot, but you'll have to make do with a straw bed tonight—unless we forgo that and sleep under the stars,' he added, giving her an unpleasant wink.

'And where is this bed of straw, exactly?' Hope asked. If she could draw some specific information from him, she might better understand where she was. Information which she needed, if the opportunity ever arrived for her to make a bid for freedom.

'A friend's cottage,' he snapped. 'That's all you need to know.'

Hope suppressed a sigh as the horse drew to a halt in the courtyard and George climbed down from the cart. He was never going to tell her anything useful; he was far too cunning for that. She glanced down at her wrist, which was red and raw-looking from all the wriggling she'd done in a vain effort to free herself. Sitting next to him, she had not dared use her free hand to try to remove the shackle; to do so would have surely drawn his attention. However, if he left her to fetch a drink…

'I'll remain on the cart,' she said quickly. 'I can keep an eye on the horse while the stable boys attend to him.'

George began to laugh, walking round to her as he shook his head. 'You must think I'm stupid.'

'No, I'm just not thirsty, that's all.' A lie, of course. She was thirsty, hungry, tired, terrified—all of it. She was running out of options, running out of opportunities. If she was honest with herself, she was beginning to despair.

'I don't care what you are,' he said through gritted teeth. 'You're not leaving my sight.'

He untied the rope, liberating her poor sore wrist—another small mercy, she supposed, although likely useless to her whilst ever she remained under his watchful eye. Unceremoniously, he hauled her down from the cart, all but dragging her along as he approached two wide-eyed stable boys and handed them some coins to attend to the horse. His thirst for beer clearly growing, he hurried her around towards a small kitchen at the rear of the inn, coins again crossing palms—this time those of the innkeeper, who looked at Hope with some concern when he observed George's rough handling of her. However, he said nothing, instead wordlessly pointing them both through a weather-beaten wooden door and into a humble room, where they found a table laden with bread and beer mugs and a handful of other travellers crowded around it. Several male faces glanced up briefly to see who had joined them, before returning to regard their fare once more.

'Here. Sit.'

George pushed her towards a wooden stool, forcing her to sit down. He remained close at her side, still standing as he grabbed a hunk of bread and a mug and ate and drank as though he'd had no sustenance for years. Hope tried hard to ignore her dry mouth and empty, groaning stomach;

she'd sworn she was not thirsty and, besides, she would take nothing that he'd paid for. As her father had learned to his cost, this was not the sort of man you wanted to owe a debt to. This was the sort of man who would always want something in return.

Unlike Samuel. Generous and decent Samuel, who had wanted nothing from her. Kind and loving Samuel, who had given her so much more than sanctuary. If only she really had been Hope Swynford. If only she really had been a gentleman's daughter and an heiress. Then, perhaps…

She did not realise that she was crying until one of the other travellers, an older, stocky man with a round, kindly face, remarked upon it.

'Now then, lass, I'm sure it's not so bad,' the man said, offering her a small smile. She watched as he glanced warily at George, who was still devouring his bread and beer. 'Do you want to eat something? There's plenty to be had.'

'She doesn't want anything,' George snapped, his mouth full.

Hope watched as the man's keen gaze continued to flit between them both, as though he was trying to work something out, and a seed of an idea began to grow in her mind. She raised her sore, rope-marked wrist above the table, giving it a rub so that he could clearly see the marks upon it.

'I'm afraid I'm not very keen on plain bread and beer,' she said softly, putting on her Hope Swynford voice as she eased back into character. 'I much prefer tea and cake, you see. Two of the very best things in life, I can assure you.'

Next to her, she sensed George cease chewing. One by one, each pair of eyes around the table seemed to settle upon her captor, and for several moments no one moved.

'I dare say they are, miss,' the older man said, although

he barely tore his gaze from George. 'But those are things you'll find in the parlour, not the back kitchen. Perhaps if you went in there, you'd find something more suited to your tastes.'

'Don't you dare move.'

George gripped her arm so tightly that it made her cry out, and stools scraped in unison against the stone floor as several of the men rose to their feet.

'What is this man to you, miss?' the older man asked, his kindly expression long gone as his eyes blazed thunderously at George. 'Are you in need of some assistance?'

At that moment Hope saw her chance, and she seized it with both hands. 'This man has kidnapped me!' she cried out, getting to her feet. 'He has stolen me away and means to marry me at Gretna against my will so that he can steal my inheritance. He is a villain and a scoundrel!'

Together, the men rounded on George. Apparently startled by what was unfolding, he took several steps back, his eyes wide with something which almost resembled fear. As the men drew nearer, Hope moved away, finally out of George's grasp. What happened next was as confusing as it was alarming—a frantic scramble of limbs as punches were thrown and angry, expletive-ridden words were exchanged between George and the men. At one point George launched forward, clattering into the table and sending bread and beer flying about the room. For several moments Hope simply stood there, frozen, until three simple words spoken by the kindly older man brought her back to her senses.

'Run, miss. Run!'

Of course—there was nothing else for it. Without another moment's hesitation, Hope hurried towards the door, and towards her freedom. Towards her life, towards the unknown. Towards whatever lay ahead of her. This was it, she realised—she would not get a better chance. Indeed, she would likely get no other chances at all.

Quickly, Hope turned the knob on the door, poised to flee.

Then a gunshot rang out.

Samuel was a good number of miles into his journey before he realised that he hadn't quite thought this through. Rockcliffe, he had managed to ascertain, lay to the northwest of Carlisle—reaching it within the day would be pushing the endurance of both himself and his horse, especially at the speed he'd so far travelled. He had indeed been riding hard; his best chance of finding Hope was to catch up with her and her abductor on the road, although how likely he was to manage this, he did not know. He'd no idea by what means this man was taking Hope away with him, and therefore how many miles they would manage to cover before darkness fell. He prayed it was by old horse and rickety cart—the more elderly and ramshackle, the better.

Unfortunately, despite covering a good number of miles of road and making brief enquiries at every inn on the way, so far there'd been no sign of either Hope or the dreadful George, and riding so fast was quickly wearying his horse. Stopping to rest was the last thing he wanted to do, but as he rode towards the latest coaching inn he realised it was a necessity. The poor animal needed water and sustenance at the very least, and if he was honest with himself, so did he. He'd barely eaten or drunk anything that day, such had been his complete preoccupation with finding Hope. With a heavy sigh, he turned his horse into the inn's courtyard, catching the eye of a young stable boy and giving him a beckoning nod. Perhaps, he reasoned, it would be best to change the poor creature while he was here.

Samuel climbed down from his saddle and the boy walked forward. He glanced around briefly, suddenly struck by how eerily quiet the inn was. It was not so much that there were no carriages or coaches—indeed, he could count several, sitting stationary at the far end of the courtyard. It was more that there were no people standing outside—no ladies or gentlemen hovering, waiting to depart, no carriages being readied, and no drivers checking their horses or the position of their passengers' luggage. It was, without doubt, very strange.

'Where is everyone?' Samuel asked the stable boy who, it struck him now, looked a deathly shade of white.

'Most are in the parlour, sir.' The boy's voice was barely a whisper. 'A few have gone behind the stables. They dare not come out.'

Samuel frowned. 'Why?'

'There was a sound like a gunshot. It came from the rear kitchen not so long ago.' The boy paused, swallowing hard. 'The master went to see what was afoot and…and there's a man in there, sir, waving his pistol about. Says anyone who comes in will get their brains blown out. The master's sent for the constable and says everyone's to stay hid—except us, on account of the horses we've to attend to, but everyone else.' The boy looked at the horse, reaching out to give him a gentle stroke. 'You could go, sir. He's tired but the next inn's only a few miles away. He could manage it at a trot.'

Samuel pressed his lips together, absorbing the details of the boy's story. Could this murderous and unpredictable man be the one he was looking for?

'This man you mentioned—do you know if there is a lady travelling with him?' he asked.

'Aye, sir, although if I had to guess, I'd say she's not come with him willingly. Poor lady was shackled to the cart when they got here. The master reckons he's taken her from a fine house somewhere. Says the man's trying to hide it, leaving her looking grubby and without a bonnet, but there's no mistaking that her dress is quality.'

'And the lady, what does she look like?' Samuel tried to remain focused on ascertaining the facts but, despite himself, he felt his fists curl. The thought of any woman being so mistreated made him angry, and the idea that it might be Hope was frankly unbearable.

The boy frowned, apparently recalling. 'Small. Dark hair, all matted and hanging loose like she's been in the wars. But very pretty—meaning no impertinence, of course, sir. Just an observation.'

Any lingering doubt in Samuel's mind was immediately blown away by the boy's description. It was Hope, he told himself, his heart beginning to race. She was here, and she was locked in a room with a madman wielding a pistol. A room, and a man, he had to now work to free her from.

Samuel gave the boy a nod and a tight smile before pressing a shilling into his palm. 'Be good to my horse,' he said. 'Hopefully, this won't take too long.'

'But sir, you can't surely…'

Samuel did not hear the rest of the boy's protest. He was too preoccupied, creeping towards the kitchen which sat at the back of the inn. As he reached the building he ducked down, tentatively edging towards the single small window which offered the only view into the room, and to understanding what was happening inside. Cautiously, he peeked in, surveying the scene swiftly from a low position and praying he would not be noticed.

Immediately he spied Hope, the sight of her making his heart fleetingly lift, before the gravity of the situation she was in made his pulse begin to race with trepidation. She was perched on a stool, her eyes cast down and shoulders slumped in an expression of utter defeat. Near to her was a man with sharp features, pacing to and fro, waving a pistol around menacingly. George—it had to be. On the other side of the room, furthest from the door, stood a handful of men, all looking glum, their hands raised in surrender. Samuel frowned. Clearly, something had happened to provoke this potentially deadly scene, but he was damned if he could discern exactly what.

No matter. All that counted now was rescuing Hope from George's grasp, and ensuring no one else was hurt in the process. Samuel reached into his pocket, placing a careful hand upon his pistol. On the one hand, he felt relieved at having the presence of mind to come armed; on the other, he felt alarmed at the prospect of having to use his weapon. No matter, he told himself. He could not afford to deliberate on this; even a moment's hesitation could prove costly. He would do whatever it took to rescue Hope. If that meant aiming his pistol at her captor and pulling the trigger, then so be it.

He continued to watch at the window as George's pacing slowed and he came to a halt with his back to the door. This was his chance, Samuel realised. He had to act—quickly and decisively. He had to take a leaf out of Hope's book and live on his wits.

It was this thought which spurred him on as he hurried towards the door, launching himself at it with such force as to render turning the doorknob entirely unnecessary. He was aware of a deep, guttural roar coming from the depths of his throat as the door gave way, a sound which was so ungentlemanly and so unlike him that it would have taken him by surprise, had he not been so thoroughly consumed by his mission. Out of the corner of his eye, he saw Hope leap to her feet.

'Samuel? Samuel!' she breathed, part-question and part-affirmation.

A shocked-looking George turned. As Samuel threw himself towards the man he saw him move to raise his pistol but, mercifully, he was not quite quick enough. Overwhelming him with the element of surprise combined with sheer brute force, Samuel wrestled George to the ground, holding him with his face and stomach pressed to the floor while he tried to get the pistol out of his grasp. But his adversary was not about to give up so easily. He flailed about, yelling obscenities as he tried to fight back with a considerable strength of his own.

Thankfully, around him, Samuel sensed the reinforcements begin to assemble. The cluster of men whom George had been holding at gunpoint now sprang into action, several of them joining Samuel in pinning George to the ground, while another, burly man managed at last to prise the pistol from George's firm grip.

Disarmed and overwhelmed, George finally seemed to concede defeat, his limbs growing still, his breathing rapid and exhausted. For several moments Samuel and a couple of his assistants continued to hold him down, apparently not quite daring to move. One of the other men ran outside, returning swiftly with a couple of lengths of rope and offering them to Samuel.

'The stable boys say that the constable is on his way,'

the man said. 'We can use this to restrain him until he gets here.'

'I'll do that.' The burly man grabbed hold of the rope. 'It'll be my pleasure to shackle him like he shackled that poor miss over there, judging by the state of her wrist. You go and attend to her, sir. She's had quite the ordeal.'

Samuel nodded obligingly before hauling himself to his feet. He heard George groan as the burly man took over, holding him down with his considerable weight while tightly binding his hands behind his back.

'You must have been very worried about her,' the man continued. 'Is she your sister, or…?'

But Samuel was not listening. Indeed, his attention was no longer on the burly man, or on Hope's abductor, at all. Instead, his gaze had wandered across the room, towards the woman who stood there, frozen with shock, her dress filthy, her long dark curls mussed, her face drained of all colour. She lifted those emerald eyes to meet his and his heart stirred, just as it had the first time she'd gazed up at him from the floor of her bedchamber, all those weeks ago. Perhaps it had been love even then—it was hard to say. All he knew for certain was that he loved her now.

Wordlessly, Samuel strode towards her, reaching out and enveloping her in his arms. She melted into his embrace, clinging to him tightly as though she too had feared that she might never see him again. For several moments he simply held her, running his fingers gently over the knotted tendrils of her hair. Then she stirred, lifting her chin to gaze up at him, meeting his eyes with a look which spoke of tenderness, of admiration, of affection. Of love. A look which told him everything. He leaned down, his lips capturing hers in affirmation as he poured his heart and soul into that kiss. Everything she felt, he sought to show her, he felt too.

Behind them, an amused voice intruded. 'Not your sister, then,' the burly man said.

Against Hope's lips, Samuel smiled. 'No,' he murmured, breaking the kiss to see that Hope was smiling too. 'Not my sister,' he said, caressing her cheek as he gazed intently into her eyes. 'But I hope, one day soon, she will be my wife.'

Chapter Twenty-Three

Hope collapsed on the bed, completely exhausted. Outside, the afternoon had given way to evening, the sky darkening rapidly as heavy drops of rain began to fall. Given the coming night, the change in the weather and their weariness, not to mention that of Samuel's poor horse, Samuel had suggested that they should remain at the inn overnight before travelling back to Hayton Hall the next day. Hope had nodded her agreement; indeed, in her shocked state, nodding was all she seemed able to do. Samuel appeared to sense this, and with a reassuring smile he'd taken charge, requesting everything from rooms and food to a bathtub and some clean clothes. Once the constable had arrived and George had been taken away, Samuel had escorted her upstairs before leaving her to wash and change with the assistance of a maid he'd managed to secure for her.

'It's all over now, Hope,' he'd said, cupping her cheek with his hand. 'You're perfectly safe. I will just be downstairs in the parlour and will check on you in a little while.'

Now, lying on the bed and listening to the soft crackle of a small fire burning in the hearth, Hope pressed her eyes shut, replaying his words in her mind. She was perfectly safe, and it was all thanks to him. Samuel Liddell had been her rescuer, not once but twice. Weeks ago, he'd saved her from probable death in the woodland near his home, and today he'd saved her from a fate worse than death—a life spent with George. He'd ridden across the country to find her, and put himself in harm's way to save her from George's awful clutches. Then he'd taken her in his arms and he'd kissed her—a kiss which had told her in no uncertain terms that he loved her, before speaking words which left her in no doubt that he meant to ask her to be his wife.

But how could he mean to marry her, when she'd lied to him about who she was? How could he, a wealthy gentleman, want to wed a low-born actress and the daughter of an outlaw?

A knock at the door caused her eyes to fly open and her heart to race. Her head might know that she was safe, but it was clear it would take some time before her fight-or-flight instincts realised that too. Hope forced herself to take a deep, calming breath. More than likely, it was the maid returning, having left a short while ago to take the bathtub away.

'Come in,' she called out, pulling herself upright. She glanced at the plate of food the maid had left for her, a veritable platter of cheese, cold meats and bread which she'd barely begun to pick at. Her stomach, it seemed, hadn't realised that she was safe either, if the way it continued to lurch was anything to go by.

To her surprise, however, it was not the maid's face she saw peering round the door, but Samuel's. He smiled at her somewhat sheepishly. 'Sorry—the maid said you were dressed,' he said. 'But I will go if you're resting.'

'No, it's all right. Please, Samuel, come in.' She offered a smile to mirror his. 'I doubt I will manage to sleep anyway.'

Samuel slipped inside the room, closing the door softly behind him. 'It doesn't look like you've managed to eat much either,' he observed, nodding towards the almost full plate. He pulled a chair up to the bedside before sitting down next to her. 'How are you feeling?'

'Like I've been hit over the head, kidnapped and shackled, so, all in all, I think I have had better days,' she replied.

'What? He hit you over the head?' Immediately, Samuel leapt to his feet, gently brushing her still-damp hair back from her forehead and looking for signs of injury.

The feeling of his fingers against her scalp did strange things to her insides. 'My father did,' she explained. 'Apparently I wasn't a very cooperative kidnap victim so it was all he could do to silence me.'

'You were unconscious? I will summon a physician at once.'

'Samuel—' gently, she captured his hand with her own, lowering it and bringing it to rest at her side '—I will live. I do feel somewhat better after bathing and putting on clean clothes.' She smoothed her other hand over the skirt of a grey dress which felt about two sizes too big for her.

Samuel raked his eyes over her attire. 'Ah—yes. I'm afraid it was all the innkeeper's wife had to offer.'

She grinned at him. 'It is fine. I have grown accustomed to borrowed clothes.'

Samuel shook his head in embarrassment. 'Please, do not remind me.' He squeezed her hand ever so gently. 'When we return to Hayton, Hope, we shall visit a dressmaker in Lowhaven and you shall have a complete wardrobe of your own—I promise you that. And, despite your protestations, I am going to have a physician attend to you before we travel. I cannot believe your father did that to his own daughter.'

She felt her smile fade. 'George shot him—my father. He shot him, just before he took me away. He will be dead by now.'

Samuel nodded gravely. 'I'm afraid he is,' he replied. 'I went with Charles to his cottage, to look for you. He was near death when we got there. He just about managed to tell us where George was taking you before he…before he passed.'

For a long moment Hope pressed her lips together, putting her feelings in order. Holding back her tears. She would not weep for that man—not after all that he had done.

'At least he told you that,' she said in the end. 'And at least he did not die alone.'

'Oh, Hope.' Samuel slid on to the bed beside her, wrapping his arm around her shoulder and drawing her near. 'You really are a remarkable woman, do you know that? Truly remarkable. The life you've lived…the things you must have seen…'

'My life has been no worse than the lives of many men and women across England, Samuel,' she countered softly. 'Most people's experience of life is closer to mine than it is to yours. Not everyone grows up with a free trader for a father, but most know something of hardship.'

He nodded. 'You're right. It reminds me that I am fortunate but also…well, very sheltered. I have not had to be brave like you.'

She chuckled. 'I wouldn't say that. Just hours ago you wrestled a pistol-wielding madman to the ground, or have you forgotten about that already?'

He pulled her closer, placing a kiss on the top of her head. 'Oh, I haven't forgotten. That was probably the bravest and the best thing I have ever done.'

'Probably the most reckless too. You could have been killed.'

'I confess I wasn't really thinking about that. When I saw you through that kitchen window, all I could think about was getting you away from that monster and back with me.'

She looked up at him then, meeting those lovely grey-blue eyes. 'I'm glad you did, Samuel. I'm glad you found me.'

'I almost didn't.' His expression grew serious. 'When I first realised you were gone, I thought you'd left of your own accord, that after our conversation the night before you'd decided to leave. I wouldn't have blamed you if you had. You poured out your story to me and, instead of comforting you, I held back. I hesitated. Then I let you leave without saying all that there was to say.' He shook his head at himself. 'It was unforgivable.'

'No, it's not. It must have come as a shock to learn that the person you'd welcomed into your house wasn't who she said she was at all.' She paused, swallowing hard. Preparing herself for complete honesty. Preparing herself to face up to what she'd seen in his eyes that night. 'It must have been disappointing too, to learn that I am so far beneath you in status. Indeed, you'd have every right to be angry with me.'

'I cannot deny that it came as a shock, but I'm not angry, and certainly not disappointed. You hid your true identity for very good reasons, Hope—reasons far better than the foolish ones I had for borrowing my brother's title. Indeed, you're the one who ought to be angry with me. As for disappointment, surely you know me well enough by now to understand that neither wealth nor connections are of much interest to me. It is companionship, it is the meeting of like minds, it is love—those are the things I want.

Besides, you do yourself a disservice to speak about yourself in such a way.'

'I'm an actress, Samuel,' she reminded him. 'No better than a courtesan or a harlot, as I recall your friend Mr Gordon once saying. And, even worse than that, I'm the daughter of a criminal. I doubt it's possible to have a more dubious background than that.'

He caressed her cheek, lifting her chin gently and placing a brief, soft kiss upon her lips—a kiss which, despite their heavy conversation, left her wanting more. 'You're a beautiful, intelligent, strong and resourceful woman,' he replied. 'You are admirable, Hope—truly. You have survived everything that life has thrown at you. Indeed, against all the odds, I'd say you've flourished. You are clever and you are cultured and you are brave. That is what I should have said to you when you told me your story.'

She raised her eyebrows at him, trying to ignore how her heart sang at his words. She would not get carried away, no matter how sincere his sentiments sounded to her ears. 'So why didn't you?' she asked.

He sighed. 'Partly because I felt ashamed of myself. If I hadn't been so busy pretending that I was a baronet with a big estate then perhaps you'd have found me more approachable. Perhaps you would have told me the truth sooner.'

She smiled sadly. 'I doubt that very much, Samuel, although I do wish I had.' She frowned, searching his gaze. 'You said that was part of the reason. What was the other part?'

Samuel breathed out an embarrassed chuckle. 'The other part was the fact that we were in my bedchamber, late at night and only half-clad. You'd made some remarks about how gentlemen had treated you in the past, about what they had expected, and…and I did not want you to think I was just another gentleman seeking to take advantage of you.'

'You would never have done that,' she replied. 'You've always been impeccably good and decent towards me.'

Samuel nodded. 'Nonetheless, Hope, I was still a man standing in his bedchamber with a beautiful woman. Believe me, it took all my self-restraint not to kiss you or take you into my bed.'

Such loaded words made her cheeks colour, as did the realisation that she wished he had. She tried to suppress the thought, reminding herself that there were a hundred other matters they ought to be discussing. How he couldn't possibly wish to marry a base-born actress being top of the list.

Before she could say another word, however, Samuel sat upright and released her from his embrace. 'I should probably leave you to rest. We can talk more tomorrow. You need to sleep if you're going to be fit for the ride back to Hayton.'

'Don't.' She touched him lightly on the arm. 'Stay awhile—please. I know I am safe here but I'd rather not be alone.'

For good measure she shuffled over, patting the sheets where they lay over the space she'd made. She watched Samuel hesitate, his gaze switching contemplatively between the bed and her. He was a gentleman to a fault—a true, proper gentleman. That was one of the things she loved about him. It was also one of the reasons why she knew that in the cold light of day, when the dust had settled on the chaos and terror of today, he would realise that he could not marry her. If, indeed, he had not realised that already. After all, he had not broached the subject again. Hope pushed the thought from her mind; there was little point in dwelling upon that now. Samuel was right—she needed to sleep and, whether it was wise or not, she wanted to have him by her side.

After several moments of deliberation, something apparently made up Samuel's mind. 'All right,' he said, sliding back on to the bed beside her and taking her into his arms once more. 'I will stay, just until you fall asleep.' He kissed the top of her head as she nestled under his chin. 'I love you, Hope.'

'I love you too, Samuel.'

Hope closed her eyes, overcome by the comfort and reassurance she found in this intimacy, as well as the myriad of other, less familiar feelings she felt stirring within her. But even as she relished his warm embrace, her doubts and her fears continued to niggle at her. He loved her and she loved him, and yet she feared that would not be enough. She would not be enough and, sooner or later, Samuel would come to his senses and see that whilst Hope Swynford could have been his wife, Hope Sloane never could.

Chapter Twenty-Four

The ride back to Hayton was torture, almost as much as the previous night had been. The feeling of Hope sitting on his horse, nestled against him, continually reminded Samuel of their night spent in the bed at that inn. Indeed, it had been a full night. Despite his insistence that he would leave once she fell asleep, he had fallen asleep too and had remained there, holding her in his arms, until the first hints of the sleepy autumn dawn slipped through the thin fabric of the curtains which hung at the small window.

Nothing improper had happened, of course—they had both been far too exhausted for that and, besides, he was a gentleman. But still, the experience of waking beside her, of feeling her warm, petite form pressed against him, of burying his nose in those dark curls while he kissed her good morning had been overpowering. It was more than lust—although God only knew he had felt plenty of that. It was a sense of rightness, of belonging. A sense that if he was fortunate to spend every morning waking like that, with Hope in his arms, then at the end of his life he would die a happy man.

It was love, but then he knew that. He'd known that for some time. Now, as he caught first sight of Hayton Hall's castle-like roofscape, he knew he needed to make things formal. To ask, in the proper way, the vital question. In the aftermath of Hope's rescue and George's apprehension, he'd blurted out his intentions in the heat of the moment, and yet he had not actually asked her.

Last night he'd gone to her room intent upon proposing, but one look at her pale, weary, worried face was all he'd needed to understand that it was not the right time. It had been clear to him that Hope needed to talk about what was on her mind—her ordeal and the death of her father, not to mention her clear and persistent worries about what Samuel thought of her, now that he knew the truth. What she'd needed from him, he'd quickly realised, was comfort and reassurance. Proposals, he'd decided, could wait.

Although, he realised now, not for much longer. He wanted her to know that his intentions were serious and sincere. And he desperately wanted to know whether she would accept him or whether, in the cold light of a dismal, damp autumn day, she would decide that she wanted to return to Richmond and to the stage. To that life she had so admirably carved for herself against all the odds.

His horse drew to a gentle halt outside the grand front entrance to Hayton Hall, prompting a flurry of activity from all directions. Samuel was vaguely aware of the simultaneous approach of his groom, his guests and two of his household servants as he climbed down, before reaching up to assist Hope. Gently, he lifted her down, once again overcome by the feeling of holding her in his arms, the heightened awareness combined with those more desirous emotions which were absolutely not appropriate with so many people nearby. As he drew her level with him, Hope's eyes met his and he gave her a smile—one which she returned with just as much affection as he hoped his would convey. A good sign, if ever he wished for one.

Composing himself, Samuel turned to greet the assembling welcome party. He would ask her soon, he told himself. He would find the right moment, and until then he would simply have to be patient.

'Well done, Sammy,' Charles declared, patting him on the back. 'You've brought her back. I do hope there was no harm done, Miss Swyn—Miss Sloane,' he corrected himself swiftly as he turned to Hope.

Samuel watched as Hope nodded, a look of uncertainty momentarily clouding those lovely green eyes as she regarded his friend. 'I am quite well, thank you, Mr Gordon, all things considered. Samuel tells me that you went with him as far as Lillybeck, to look for me. I am grateful to you. I know what you must think of me, now that you know who I really am…'

'Ah, yes. I'm afraid that in the past I have been far too adept at judging books by their covers, Miss Sloane,' Charles replied, a deep blush rising from beneath his collar. 'Such opining will cease henceforth. As a rather spirited young lady once informed me, I'd do well to pay more attention to the character of my acquaintances rather than other, more avaricious considerations.'

Samuel smiled at his friend's words which, for all his embarrassment, were clearly heartfelt. Beneath that boisterous personality and propensity for outright snobbery lurked a good heart. Hope, meanwhile, inclined her head politely, the ghost of a smile playing upon her lips. 'I am glad of it,' she replied. 'Especially if you intend to extend such generosity beyond your own acquaintances and consider, perhaps, those of your sister's acquaintance by the same standard?'

Charles's beetroot visage was all the confirmation that was needed that Hope's message had indeed hit the mark. Samuel could have kissed her out of sheer admiration for the way that, despite her own ordeal and exhaustion, she did not miss the opportunity to champion Miss Gordon's lovelorn cause. Instead, he reached for her hand, threading his fingers through hers and giving them a squeeze in solidarity.

Miss Gordon, meanwhile, hovered beside her brother, looking somewhere between relieved and chastened. 'I owe you an apology, Miss Sloane,' she began, her lip trembling. 'If I had not run away to the docks, you might never…'

Hope shook her head. 'It was my choice to join the search for you, and to get out of the carriage when I saw you,' she insisted, touching Miss Gordon delicately on the arm. 'You have nothing to reproach yourself for. My father was determined to find me—if he hadn't then, he would have eventually. At least it is all over now.'

The brave smile Hope gave Miss Gordon made Samuel's heart lurch for her, and he squeezed her hand again before releasing it as Hope hurried towards Maddie. He watched as the maid gathered Hope into her arms, letting out a few heartfelt sobs of relief as she whispered words that Samuel could not quite hear.

Next to them, Smithson hovered, endearingly trying and failing to remain composed as he clasped his hands behind his back and grinned from ear to ear. Samuel could not help but think about the wily old butler's warning to him all those weeks ago, about lies and the way they could all too easily get out of hand. How right the man had been, although Samuel suspected that even the ever-perceptive

Smithson could not have predicted where Samuel and Hope's deceptions would have led them. Nor could he have known, that evening when he'd lectured Samuel on being truthful, just how close to the surface the truth had always bubbled between them and how, despite the disguises they'd worn, they'd come to know and understand each other's true characters nonetheless.

He knew the essence of her, and she of him. Everything else, as he'd once told her, was simply window-dressing. He could only hope and pray that she would agree. That she would consent to becoming his wife. As Maddie released Hope from her embrace he stepped forward, offering Hope his arm. He could bear the wait no longer—he had to ask her. The right moment, such as it was, could be created as well as found.

'Hope, would you mind joining me in the gardens for a few moments?' he asked her. 'There is something I'd like to discuss with you, then we can freshen up and dine.'

Hope's eyes widened briefly, before she nodded her assent. 'Of course.'

Samuel walked with her to Hayton's sprawling rear gardens, his heart hammering in his chest. The right moment could indeed be created, he told himself and, despite his nerves, this felt right. Hope deserved to be asked for her hand properly; she deserved to know just how sincere and honourable his intentions were. She deserved to know just how much he loved her. There would be no more secrets between them, and certainly no more lies.

They drew to a halt on the footpath, the earthy, damp smell of the surrounding shrubbery heavy in the air. Samuel drew a deep breath, hurriedly collecting his thoughts as he settled upon what he would say. He'd never proposed marriage before—he had to do it correctly, had to find the right way to express himself…

Before Samuel could utter a word, however, Hope relinquished his arm and turned to face him. 'If this is about what I said to Mr Gordon, about his sister's acquaintances, I was only trying to…'

Samuel placed a gentle finger over her lips, smiling at her. 'I know what you were trying to do, and I think Charles understood too. But this is not about Charles, or his sister's romantic entanglements,' he replied quietly. 'This is about us.'

She furrowed her brow, then looked away. 'It's all right, Samuel,' she began. 'You don't have to explain yourself. I understand well enough that whatever this is between us cannot go on. You are a gentleman, whereas I am an actress and a…'

'You are the woman I love, Hope,' he replied, still smiling. 'And you love me—you told me so, only last night. Surely that is all there is to understand.'

She nodded. 'I do love you, Samuel, but what if love is not enough? What if the circumstances make it impossible? What if there are simply too many obstacles?'

He gave her a knowing look. 'Like Romeo and Juliet?' he asked, recalling her words in the library that night when they'd discussed Shakespeare. That night when they'd first kissed. That night when everything had changed.

'Yes—like Romeo and Juliet,' she replied.

'But, unlike Shakespeare's lovers, the only obstacles for us are ones we make ourselves. And for me, Hope, there are no obstacles. When I look at you, I see a woman I cannot fail to admire. You are not shameful, you are remarkable. Being an actress has not made you a scandal or a harlot—it has made you a talented woman with a passion for the theatre, not to mention a knowledge of the Bard which is second to none. I love you, Hope, and I believe with all my heart that love is enough.' He took hold of her hand. 'As a clever lady I know once told a friend of mine, we love who we love and that should be all that matters.'

He watched as she pressed her lips together momentarily, suppressing a smile at hearing her own words quoted back at her. She regarded him carefully. 'Are you sure that it isn't Hope Swynford you've fallen for? How can you be sure you're not in love with a character?'

'How can you be certain you don't love Sir Samuel the baronet and not Samuel Liddell, the title-less younger brother?' he countered.

'Because they are the same…' she began. He watched with delight as a wry smile crept on to her face. 'All right—point taken.'

He held those lovely emerald eyes with his own. 'The night that you told me your story, you said you'd allowed me to care for a woman who doesn't exist, but that simply isn't true. Hope Swynford might be a character, but she is also you. Calling yourself Hope Swynford rather than Hope Sloane and an heiress rather than an actress didn't change who you are, Hope, and even while you kept your true story from me and everyone else at Hayton, it was always there, wasn't it? Indeed, I would venture to suggest that a sheltered heiress would have been far less likely to astutely point out the unfairness of me not heeding my maid's wish to be called Maddie, or to recognise and empathise with Miss Gordon's difficulties. Only you, the real you, could have done those things. I'm not in love with a character. I'm in love with you. Marry me, Hope.'

Her eyes widened and she searched his gaze, clearly

disbelieving. 'When you spoke of marriage at the inn, I thought it was only because of the situation—that it was the stress and the relief talking. Never did I imagine that you could be serious.'

'I have never been more serious,' he replied. 'Do me the honour of becoming my wife, Hope, and make me the happiest man alive.'

Samuel held his breath for what felt like an eternity, watching her as she seemed to consider his proposal. Then, to his sheer relief and utter joy, she leapt forward, throwing her arms around his neck and pulling him close to her. He responded in kind, wrapping his arms around her waist and vowing in that moment to never let go. To make her the happiest woman that ever lived. To build a life together, one filled with laughter and adventure, with family and fun. With afternoons sipping tea and eating cake in the parlour, surrounded by all the children they would have, and evenings out at the theatre or spent cosily inside, savouring the finest bottle of Bordeaux and poring over a good book. With nights curled up together, and mornings waking to each other's embrace. A comfortable, contented life which consigned hardship and heartache to the past.

He buried his nose in the thick curls of her dark hair, breathing her in, imagining the years stretching before them, filled with promise. Then he realised that he had not yet heard her answer.

'So, is that a yes, then?' he ventured, whispering the words in her ear.

Hope gazed up at him, an irrepressible grin illuminating her face. The best and most wonderful smile he'd ever seen. The smile he wanted to see until the end of his days.

She reached up, placing the briefest, loveliest kiss upon

his lips. 'It's a yes,' she replied, her mouth still close to his, inviting him to kiss her back.

Which he did, of course—thoroughly, and with wild abandon.

Epilogue

February 1819

'If music be the food of love, play on...'

Hope settled into her seat as the curtain went up, the many candles which illuminated the stage casting their bright glow over the darkened theatre. From her position in the box at Lowhaven's Theatre Royal she could see Duke Orsino strutting around, musing about his unrequited love for Countess Olivia. Next to her, Samuel reached out and took hold of her hand, giving it a tender squeeze. The irony of them enjoying a performance of Shakespeare's *Twelfth Night* together was not lost on him either. Indeed, he'd flashed her one of his amused smiles when he'd told her that the play was coming to town just after Christmas, pulling her close to him as he'd informed her that he planned to reserve seats.

'People in disguise, falling in love,' he'd remarked, kissing the top of her head. 'The Bard could have written that one for us, couldn't he? We must go and see it.'

Hope had laughed at that, reminding him that they went to see virtually everything that Lowhaven's theatre had to offer, a habit which would doubtless become fixed now that they had settled into their own home on the edge of town. They'd moved at the beginning of the new year, after spending the Christmas season at Hayton Hall with Isaac and Louisa. Hayton's real baronet had returned from Scotland with his wife in November, their travels brought finally to an end by the worsening weather and Louisa's delicate health.

The brooding older brother had been stunned to discover that in his absence his younger sibling had not only fallen in love, but had wed. Hope had observed Isaac's astonished expression as Samuel recounted the extraordinary tale, from their first meeting to their marriage in a private ceremony by common licence in Hayton's ancient, humble church, witnessed only by the Gordons.

The return of Sir Isaac Liddell had thrown Hope into turmoil, and her old fears about her base-born status and dubious past had briefly resurfaced. As Samuel's older brother and the head of his family had regarded her carefully during their introduction, she'd found herself fretting, convinced that he'd be horrified about their union. As it turned out, she need not have worried. Despite his serious demeanour and brusque manner, Isaac was a kind soul who'd welcomed her into the family without hesitation. When he'd learned about her lowly origins and her life on stage, he had not even flinched. Instead, he'd seemed to perceive her discomfort and had done his utmost to assuage it.

'You're a veritable woman of the world, Hope,' he'd remarked kindly, regarding Samuel with affection in his keen blue eyes. 'And therefore perfect for my brother, since he has seen so much of it.'

Recalling the memory, Hope smiled. Isaac and Louisa had joined them at the theatre this evening, although they planned to return to Hayton in their carriage as soon as the final curtain fell. Another thing Hope had quickly come to understand was just how besotted Hayton's baronet was with his lovely wife, and just how protective—even more so since they'd discovered that the fatigue and sickness which had been troubling Louisa did in fact have an altogether happy cause.

Hope glanced at Louisa. Even in the dim light she could make out the serene expression on her face, one hand resting firmly on her swollen belly as she watched the play. The baby's arrival was expected in the early summer. God willing, Hayton Hall would have an heir, and the Liddell brothers would greet the next generation of their family.

Although, Hope increasingly suspected, the child would not be the sole member of that generation for very long—not if her own morning queasiness and absent courses were anything to go by. It was a suspicion she'd not yet shared with Samuel, but with each passing day she felt more sure of it, more excited, and more anxious. Tonight, she was bursting to tell him the happy news, especially since it had already been a day for it. Earlier that day she'd received a letter from Henrietta Gordon, telling her that she was no longer Miss Gordon at all. Last autumn Mr Gordon and his sister had departed from Hayton on a mission to reunite Miss Gordon with her lost love. It was a mission which had taken them to the burgeoning mills of Manchester to find the man in question, and a mission which had ultimately succeeded.

Moved by the depth of their daughter's misery and their desperation to cure her of it, the Gordon parents had finally accepted the match. A wedding had followed, and the newlyweds had now settled back in Blackburn, where the new

Mrs Smith was, in her own words, blissfully happy. Her husband, she wrote, had secured a job alongside her father, and although it was early days, he was proving himself extremely capable in all that he did.

Hope had studied the letter several times, shaking her head in disbelief at such an incredible tale, committed to paper in the hurried hand of a woman who was clearly delirious with joy at the surprising turn her life had taken. It was a feeling which Hope recognised immediately, since it was one she knew only too well.

'If this were played upon a stage now, I could condemn it as an improbable fiction...'

Hope smiled at the familiar famous line in the Bard's play, a line which could just as easily apply to her own life of late as it did to a story written more than two centuries ago. A year ago she'd been a travelling actress, on the run from a terrible past. Now, here she was, sitting in one of the best seats in the theatre, married to the most wonderful man and probably expecting his child. Improbable—indeed, it was improbable. So improbable that sometimes she had to pinch herself to be certain she was not dreaming.

Perhaps Samuel was right. *Twelfth Night* could have been written for them.

On stage, disguises were dispensed with as, at last, all was revealed. In the faint candlelight Samuel's gaze caught her own and held it, even as all around them the crowd grew noisier, chuckling and murmuring in excitable anticipation. They were, for a moment, in their own little world, one of mutual affection and shared understanding. One which, Hope considered, was worthy of one last revelation of her own. Gently, she lifted Samuel's hand, bringing it to rest upon her stomach, and nodded slowly. She watched as those blue-grey eyes of his widened, and his mouth fell open in surprise.

Then he leapt to his feet, pulled her into his arms and embraced her as the final curtain fell to rapturous applause.

* * * * *

Keep reading for an excerpt of a new title
from the Historical series,
HOW THE WALLFLOWER WINS A DUKE
by Lucy Morris

Chapter One

London—June 1816

'Two whole days with those smug Moorcrofts! No, I don't think I can bear it...' grumbled Marina's mother with a heavy sigh, followed shortly by slapping her hands together decisively. 'Colin, I think we should go home—say I am ill or something. I know it is an excellent opportunity. But honestly, it would be better for your practice if we did not go!'

Marina brightened at the prospect. 'I would not mind going home. I have a new melody I wish to practise.' Which was true, but there were other reasons, too—uncomfortable reasons.

Her father shook his head, and both women gave a miserable sigh. Most people would have been thrilled to receive a house party invitation from the Duchess of Framlingham. They would consider it a great honour to stay at the palatial mansion owned by such an illustrious hostess, who was loved and admired by the *ton*, but Marina could not think of anything worse and neither could her mother.

The Moorcrofts spoiled everything!

The rivalry between the two families had been going on for years. Although, until recently it had mainly been one-sided, as Marina's family had always tried their best to ignore it.

It had all begun when her father, the son of a common bricklayer, had dared to not only set up his own architectural practice, but had—more importantly—succeeded at it, winning many contracts that Mr Moorcroft had wrongly presumed were his by right, because, unlike Marina's father, Mr Moorcroft was the son and grandson of celebrated architects.

It wouldn't have been so bad, if it had been confined to their professional lives. But the whole family seemed to take delight in trying to wage a war of their own making.

Herbert and Priscilla Moorcroft were a similar age to Marina and her brother Frederick. They might have been friends, if the Moorcrofts hadn't been so determined to prove they were better than them in every way, sometimes deliberately humiliating or embarrassing them in public to prove their point.

Marina had not cared about it until her most recent humiliation. Still, she should pity poor Frederick more. He had always struggled socially, and was now stuck with *Horrible* Herbert at school.

'Oh, but, Colin, it is not as if they will accept us anyway. Not after the Moorcrofts have got their hooks into them. Which is a pity. But don't you think it is better to cut our losses and run? Rather than face two days of torment for no good reason?'

Her mother's lament was made somehow worse by the sudden jostle of the hackney carriage, which sent her plump mother sprawling into her father's lap. Marina had to grab her own seat and thrust her silk slippers against the opposite bench to stop herself from falling to the floor.

Colin Fletcher, with his usual calm and methodical manner, gently pushed her mother back into her seat, taking a moment to squeeze her hand lightly before releasing it.

'Kitty, my dear, do stop worrying, all will be well!' He gave Marina a sympathetic smile, and she tried her best to return it. 'We will meet with His Grace and the Duchess. *They* will be the ones to decide who will redesign their ancestral home—not I and certainly not the Moorcrofts.' Then he turned to thump the side of the carriage with his large fist and shouted in an authoritative voice that Marina had only ever heard on building sites, 'I will give you an extra shilling if you *slow* down!'

There was no response from their driver, but Marina noticed the carriage gentled to a less terrifying speed. The Duchess's grand home was situated in Twickenham and overlooked the Thames. It was on the north side of the river, so they hadn't had to cross at London Bridge, but it had still taken longer than expected to slip through the swathes of travellers coming in for their evening's entertainment. They must have seemed like a fish fighting against the current as they made their way towards the Duchess's fashionable hideaway on the outskirts of town.

The Duchess's end-of-Season ball was legendary among the *ton*. She was well known for her extravagant house parties, too, and only the most impressive and fashionable of London's high society were ever deemed worthy guests. So, for Marina's family to receive such an honour was incredible and solely due to her father's success.

The two-day event, according to the gold leaf invitation, would consist of a dinner with entertainments upon arrival. The following night there would be a ball, where the entire *ton* would hear of the Duke's exciting plans for his new home.

The Duchess had asked them to stay for two nights so that she could *'better know the families of such incredibly talented architects'*. It was obvious she intended to employ either Marina's father or his rival, Mr Moorcroft, and that this whole event was a competition, with the winner announced on the night of the ball.

All hope of them avoiding such a spectacle had been quickly snuffed out by her father's firm refusal. It was a competition between the two best architects in London and Colin was determined to face it head on—despite the awkward history between the two families.

Marina patted her hair self-consciously to check it was all still in place. It was fashioned in an elegant chignon upon her mother's insistence with curls framing her face. Marina sighed with relief when she realised none of the pins had fallen out after the sudden carriage jolt.

Kitty had not been so lucky. A thick ebony lock had fallen out of place on the side of her head and Marina took a moment to carefully pin it back into place. Her mother gave her a grateful smile when she was done. 'Thank you, darling.'

They both had mountains of thick black hair that was difficult to tame. Marina took after her mother in face and colouring, with her pale complexion, and bright blue eyes. Her mother was a little plumper than she was, but Kitty claimed that was due to having two healthy babies and a husband who could never refuse cake. Neither of them could be described by society as great beauties, but that did not seem to matter to Colin who clearly adored them both.

'It's all a bit tasteless in my opinion. Having you and Mr Moorcroft compete against one another in a social setting! If they want an architect for the remodelling of their ancestral home, then why not request plans like any normal person would? What does it matter if they *like* us or not?' complained Marina, avoiding her mother's eyes—she had spent many days trying to tell Marina the same thing.

'Who are we to question the aristocracy?' said her father pointedly.

Kitty pulled her shawl closer around her shoulders primly. '*We* shouldn't have to waste our time on the eccentric whims of others! Either they want you to work for them or they don't. I agree with Marina. This is *undignified*.'

Marina nodded thoughtfully. 'Still, it is a bit odd that there are so many of us invited to dinner.' She marked off the names of the guests with her fingers. 'The Moorcrofts, Lord Clifton and his sister, Miss Clifton… I suppose I can understand them, I believe they are close friends of the family. But the Redgraves, too? They aren't even architects!'

Her parents exchanged a knowing look, before her father said, 'I think the Duchess is hopeful to find a match for her son as well as an architect. There have already been a lot of engagements this Season—very few debutantes are left.'

'So, *we* are the entertainment.' Marina groaned, then began to speak as if she were reading from one of the scandal sheets. 'Which architect will they choose? Place your bets, ladies and gentlemen! Or, if that doesn't interest you, which young lady will win the hand of the Duke? It is well known that the Duke likes to gamble, but will he gamble with his heart? That is—'

'None of our business,' interrupted her father with a stern expression.

Marina gave a light shrug of acceptance. 'True. Thankfully, it will be the well-bred *ladies* in that race, not I or Miss Moorcroft, as we are not part of the landed gentry.'

'But Mrs Moorcroft is an architect, too—of her own social climbing!' quipped Kitty. 'Don't look at me like that, Colin! She was crowing to Mrs Banks about it at tea last week.' Her mother put on a simpering voice. '*My* Priscilla has already caught the attention of the Duchess of Framlingham and it is barely even the end of her first Season! At this rate, she will be wed before the Princess! After all, she is such a *fine* beauty!' She finished with an insidious laugh that sounded like a cat wheezing.

Marina and her father both chuckled at her oddly accurate impression, although her father quickly tried to appear firm. 'Come now, Kitty. You will get yourself into trouble one of these days!'

But they all knew he would forgive her anything—Kitty had supported and believed in him when no one else had. Part of his great success was due to his constant need to prove her faith in him right.

An outsider might have thought her mother's criticism of the Moorcrofts as harsh, but Marina knew her mother was only trying to make her feel better about facing Priscilla again.

'I promise I will be on my best behaviour, my darling husband,' Kitty replied, before winking at Marina. 'But I suspect she has high expectations for Priscilla and wants someone like Lord Clifton or even, perhaps, the Duke… Which is laughable—I doubt that man will ever settle down, unless it is to avoid bankruptcy!'

Marina squirmed in her seat, uncomfortable with the subject of marriage.

At the beginning of the Season, she had been hopeful, but after that terrible incident at the Haxbys' soirée, she feared marriage was not an option for her. At least not a happy one like her parents' marriage and she wanted nothing less than true love.

Marina had learned in the worst possible way that she wasn't the type to turn heads or make a man fall madly in love with her—no matter what they might say. Especially not when she was sitting next to women like Priscilla.

After much consideration—and tears—she had decided that the prospect of becoming a spinster no longer frightened her. Family would always come first in her mind. Love, or the lack of it, was only a passing disappointment at best.

Music would be the love of her life. There was no *need* for her to marry.

It was as if her father had read her mind, because he said kindly, 'Well, do not feel under pressure to like any man. I would rather keep you at home than hand you over to anyone less deserving of you.'

Marina gave her mother a sharp look, which Kitty pointedly ignored. She had always suspected her mother of telling him about the Haxby incident, even though she'd begged her not to. It certainly explained why he'd never questioned the way in which Mr John Richards had suddenly dropped all interest in courting her.

A cold shiver ran down her spine as she remembered him laughing with Priscilla.

'Oh, she is nothing in comparison to your beauty, Cousin! But a man needs money to live and don't worry—I will put a stop to that awful music once we're wed! Marina the Wallflower Maestro—she is truly ridiculous. If she weren't so wealthy, I would never have considered her!'

Her father's apologetic tone cut through the pain of the memory, as he said, 'I only mean—you have more sense than to set your sights on someone like the Spare Heir Duke.'

Marina flinched at the nickname. She had never met the man, but she thought it very unkind that all of society called him that after his elder brother's sudden death. After all, she knew what it was like to be mocked and ridiculed behind your back.

'Oh, that's so unkind,' said her mother and both women

gave him a reproachful look. 'It must have been hard for the Duke. I hear he lost his father quite young in a riding accident, and then to lose his much older stepbrother in a similar way… He must have felt as if he had lost two fathers! Such a terrible shame.'

'Yes, sorry. I only meant to say that he seems unprepared and unwilling to face the responsibility of his dukedom—and I have heard that he's been quite the cad since returning home from the army. He's always in gaming dens or other places of ill repute. I will be shocked if this new house ever goes ahead—he spends most of his days in White's.'

Marina replied, 'Still, it seems wrong to judge him so harshly on gossip and hearsay…'

Her father nodded thoughtfully. 'I suppose we will discover the truth for ourselves tonight at dinner.'

At that moment, the carriage came to a standstill outside the Duchess's mansion and they carefully stepped out on to the drive. The gas lamps illuminated only half of the imposing building, which was grand in the extreme and built in the Palladian style. The white stucco render gleamed like marble in the lamplight and the ornate columns surrounding its classically styled entrance towered above them on top of a large, stepped entrance. Everything in its design reflected the elegance and wealth of its illustrious owner within.

It was an intimidating sight and Marina glanced at her father to see what his professional eye would make of it. To her surprise, he was staring at Marina pleasantly. 'What do you think? Do you think I could build something better?'

Marina grinned. 'Certainly!'

'That's what I like to hear!' he said and with a grin he turned to help her mother from the carriage. Footmen poured down the steps and began carrying in their luggage silently.

After paying the driver, he nestled each of their arms into his before guiding them up the steps.

They were promptly welcomed and shown into an offensively large drawing room by the butler who was wearing burgundy and gold livery that would have put many of the landed gentry to shame with its elegance. Marina was glad she had worn her best evening gown and she tried to subtly smooth out any creases of her pale blue dress before entering the room.

They were the last of the guests to arrive. The Moorcrofts appeared well settled, as if they'd been there some time—*no doubt blown swiftly here by the winds of their own self-importance*, mused Marina drily.

As the formal introductions were made, Marina couldn't help but stare at the Duke. She had never seen any man quite like him: tall, dark, with pale skin and green eyes that reminded her of a predatory cat. He was handsome in a sharp, cold sort of way, the lines of his body dramatic with narrow hips that flared up to impossibly broad shoulders. She had heard he was at Waterloo and could very well imagine him leading the charge to victory, his imposing figure striking fear into the hearts of the enemy.

Cad did not seem a fitting description for him.

Oh, she could well imagine him ruining many girl's dreams and virtues. But *cad* implied the sort of dandies who lazed around gentlemen's clubs writing bad poetry, in the hopes of becoming another Byron. The type of men who only actually succeeded in indulging in too much brandy, cards and debauchery, their heads too muddled by laudanum and increasing debt to be of any use to anyone.

This man did not look muddled, he looked like a demon, the kind that tempted weaker souls into vice and wickedness.

'What took you so long, Fletcher? Everyone has been

here almost quarter of an hour already,' said Mr Moorcroft, a wide smile that did not reach his eyes spread across his broad face. She had met the others before in passing: the handsome Lord Clifton, his pretty sister Miss Clifton, Lord and Lady Redgrave, Miss Sophia Redgrave and of course the Moorcrofts—minus Horrible Herbert—whom poor Freddie was dealing with even now.

Kenneth Moorcroft was older than Marina's father by at least ten years, his hair fully grey and patchy in areas. He squinted as if his eyes were poor. His body was an average build for a man in his sixties, but he dressed as if he thought himself a fine figure of a man, no doubt trying to hide the fact that he was much older than his wife, who was more around her parents' age. He had children from his first marriage, but little was spoken of them. They had been removed from London to live at one of his estates in the country. Only his current children seemed to matter to him now, as if his dead wife and all that she had left behind had been buried without a trace. All so that he could begin again with a fresh family.

Marina disliked him immensely, even more so when she was in his presence.

Her father looked a little embarrassed, but gestured pointedly at the ornate gold clock on the mantel. 'We are still ten minutes early and I thought it best not to rush our driver.'

'Quite right,' said the Duchess. 'Some of the speeds they drive at are terrifying!' Marina's earlier criticism of the Duchess suddenly felt more than a little mean-spirited as the woman in front of her looked younger than she had expected and was light and friendly in manner. Her gown was elaborately embroidered and as bright as a ruby.

'Did you take a hackney carriage all the way here?' Mr Moorcroft laughed. 'You are an eccentric fellow, Fletcher, walking everywhere! I bought a new carriage last week. A lovely post-chaise, comfortable and convenient. They will even paint your coat of arms on the side and at a good price, too—'

Marina rolled her eyes and deliberately ignored the rest of what Mr Moorcroft had to say. It was heavily laboured with self-indulgent peacocking and she could tell her parents were gritting their teeth through every word.

Green eyes caught hers and she realised the Duke was watching her with interest. Usually no one noticed her, so her little gestures would always go unmarked, but not tonight, it seemed. The smallest tilt at one side of his mouth revealed that he knew what she was thinking and found it amusing. Heat swept up her cheeks and she looked away, praying that he would do the same.

'You can't put a price on comfort! Especially when you travel around the country as much as we do,' said Mrs Moorcroft with a sickly-sweet tone, looping her arm into his and gazing up at him with an adoring smile, as if he wasn't the most odious man on earth. It made Marina's stomach churn just to watch.

'Or health,' added Marina, unable to help herself. 'Father has always been a firm believer in the benefits of walking for one's health and happiness.'

The Duchess smiled warmly at Marina. 'I must agree. I love to walk and ride around our country estate. Anything to get the heart beating! It makes me feel alive!'

Marina nodded—she could well imagine the Moorcrofts boring the Duchess with their talk of connections and travels to all the large country estates, paying less attention to what they had seen and more on the *importance* of where they had been and how much it had cost them to get there.

'I have spent most of my life in London, but sometimes

we travel to the coast and I think there is nothing more beautiful than where the land meets the sea,' said Marina.

'Oh, then you must come to our country estate, Stonecroft Manor. It is the estate we are hoping to modernise,' said the Duchess, 'It is beautiful, but very old. I go to sea bathe there each summer. It is not as entertaining as places like Brighton, but it is just as good for the constitution.'

'What a wonderful idea!' exclaimed Mrs Moorcroft breathlessly, as if she had suddenly realised she was late to the race. 'I also love to sea bathe!'

Glancing back at the Duke, Marina saw his smirk had raised itself another quarter of an inch, but his eyes remained fixed on her and she could not look away, no matter how much she knew she should.

It wasn't so much what the Duchess said next that surprised Marina, but the way in which his mother's words affected him. 'Brook loves it there. The hunting is excellent. I should arrange another house party for this summer! In fact, I should probably have my end-of-Season ball there instead of here! That will make a nice change, won't it, Brook?'

The Duke's amusement dropped like a stone, and his gaze slid to his mother. 'If you wish, but I will not be there. You know my plans. Our business is almost settled and I will be leaving to travel the Continent shortly.'

'Oh, but you have only just left the army and it has been so long since we were at Stonecroft together,' she replied, with a painfully bright smile that seemed a little forced to Marina. 'Surely you can delay a little longer? Besides, I have heard the weather on the Continent has been unseasonably bad this year. Better to stay in England and enjoy the beauty of your own home with friends!'

'I have delayed once already.' There was a firmness to his tone that made his mother flinch and Marina couldn't help but pity her. It was obvious she wanted to spend more time with her son.

How could he be so cruel?

The Duchess's voice was low and quiet. 'Please, Brook…'

'Until the end of the Season,' he snapped, after a moment of hesitation.

When he turned away from his mother, his scowl was thunderous and full of accusation. To Marina's horror it was focused on her, his eyes narrowing as if he blamed *her* for his mother's plans, as if she *alone* had deliberately engineered this invitation—when she'd never intended it in the first place!

Now, she feared she had made an enemy of the Duke and how would that help her father's business? Apart from her music, her family's happiness was the only thing that mattered to her.

Something this Duke could never understand. Look how cruelly he had treated his grieving mother, who wanted nothing more than to spend time with him!

Marina had never met a more offensive or selfish man in her life and for once she was glad she was a wallflower. He would forget her soon enough—all she had to do was suffer a couple of days with him.